Maggie Alderson is the author of eight novels and four collections of her columns from *Good Weekend* magazine. Her children's book *Evangeline, the Wish Keeper's Helper* was shortlisted for the Prime Minister's Literary Award. Before becoming a full-time author she worked as a journalist and columnist in the UK and Australia, editing several magazines, including British *ELLE*. She writes 'The Rules' style column for the *Sunday Age* and a blog at maggiealdersor.com. She is married and has one daughter.

Praise for *Secret Keeping for Beginners*

'Alderson ... controls her material cleverly. She has a nifty ability to leave each vignette or chapter with a cliffhanger, and then keep you waiting as she proceeds to another character's personal drama'
Sydney Morning Herald

'Alderson injects her trademark sense of fun and fashion into this chic-lit tale about a family's secrets'
Newcastle Herald

'It is Alderson's real-life drama style that is so enjoyable – in so many cases you see a little bit of yourself in her characters' Toowoomba *Chronicle*

'Alderson lets her characters collide, events and life continue, the plot develops and then she swiftly gathers up her loose ends and brings them together for a successful finale to a most satisfying read'
Newtown Review of Books

'Reading a Maggie Alderson book, I swear, is like slipping into a bubble bath after a long day of bleurgh ... Just because she is writing about romance and domestic issues doesn't mean that her writing isn't still witty, well-structured and, essentially, entertaining'
Set In Motion blog

Maggie Alderson

Secret Keeping for Beginners

HarperCollins*Publishers*

HarperCollins*Publishers*

First published in Australia in 2015
This edition published in 2016
by HarperCollins*Publishers* Australia Pty Limited
ABN 36 009 913 517
harpercollins.com.au

HarperCollins*Publishers*
Level 13, 201 Elizabeth Street, Sydney, NSW 2000, Australia
Unit D1, 63 Apollo Drive, Rosedale, Auckland 0632, New Zealand
A 53, Sector 57, Noida, UP, India
1 London Bridge Street, London, SE1 9GF, United Kingdom
2 Bloor Street East, 20th floor, Toronto, Ontario M4W 1A8, Canada
195 Broadway, New York, NY 10007, USA

National Library of Australia Cataloguing-in-Publication data:

Alderson, Maggie, author.
  Secret keeping for beginners / Maggie Alderson.
  978 0 7322 9923 1 (pbk.)
  978 1 4607 0301 4 (ebook)
A823.3

Cover design and photography by HarperCollins Design Studio
Background texture by shutterstock.com
Author photograph by Adrian Peacock
Typeset in Sabon LT Std by Kirby Jones
Printed and bound in Australia by Griffin Press
The papers used by HarperCollins in the manufacture of this book are a natural,
recyclable product made from wood grown in sustainable plantation forests.
The fibre source and manufacturing processes meet recognised international
environmental standards, and carry certification.

For Sally Brampton

'If you want to keep a secret,
you must also hide it from yourself.'

George Orwell, *1984*

Sydney Street, Chelsea, London SW3

Rachel bounded up the stairs two at a time, then paused for a moment just outside her boss's office door to catch her breath. She knew she was going to be sweaty – she'd run all the way there from the South Kensington Tube station – she didn't want to be audibly panting as well.

'Hark,' said a man's voice from inside. 'Did I hear the sound of maidens' feet upon the stairs? Or was it a herd of elephants? Rachel – is that you?'

Quickly smoothing a hand over her hair, Rachel stepped around the door into the room.

'Yes, hi Simon, hi everyone,' she said to the man sitting behind a large shiny white desk and the four women in front of it, notebooks and phones on their laps.

'No, really, it's fine you're late,' said Simon. 'Again. I was just saying what bad luck it is that it's always your Tube line that has a problem when everyone else's gets them here in plenty of time.'

Rachel smiled at him as naturally as she could manage, pulling up another chair and sitting down. She was determined not to rise to his sarcasm. Or give him the pleasure of apologising for being late. She didn't want him threatening

...r with instant dismissal as he had twice already that week. Jokingly, she thought – or hoped – but with just enough edge in his voice to make her nervous.

She'd only been working at his PR firm, Rathbone & Associates, since February and was still in her six-month trial period, so it could happen. But if it was a joke, she didn't think much of Simon's sense of humour. There was nothing funny about the prospect of sudden unemployment for a single mother of two children under ten.

'Now, where were we?' said Simon. 'Oh yes, pulling together some additional ideas for our pitch on Wednesday to Arkwright Industries, the biggest manufacturers of garden furniture in the UK. Although it's all actually made in China now, of course. Which is why they need our help launching their new British-made elite brand, Lawn & Stone. Quite a good name, I think.'

He tapped his laptop and an image of an elegant sun lounger, with plump cushions upholstered in a bold floral pattern, was projected onto the white wall to the side of the desk.

'This is the merch,' he said, tapping again to start a slideshow of pictures of lavish garden furniture, all featuring tropical print fabrics. 'It's really classy stuff, or I wouldn't be talking to them. Their usual gear is the kind of thing you see people sitting on while having a picnic in a lay-by. Auntie's day out.'

All the other women tittered. Rachel didn't. What a snob. What a bunch of brown-nosers.

'As you know from my brief,' Simon continued, 'old man Arkwright has never seen the need for a PR company or any kind of marketing before, but he's ancient and his kids are running the show now and they're a little more with it. So we'll be appealing to them with our ideas, not the old codger, although he is insisting on coming to the pitch.'

'Are you sure about that?' said Rachel.

Every head in the room turned to look at her.

'Sure about what?' said Simon, eyes narrowed.

'About focusing the pitch towards the kids, rather than Arnold Arkwright.'

'Go on,' said Simon, leaning back in his chair and tilting his head to one side.

'Well, when you forwarded that email to us from his son – the one who's MD now – I noticed as I read down through the exchanges between the two of you that every time you asked him a question, he'd answer it, but then sign off saying he'd have to confirm his response after he'd spoken to his dad.'

She paused, letting it sink in. 'So,' she continued, 'I think we should be addressing our pitch directly to Arkwright Senior, because he's clearly still the boss, whatever it says on his son's business card.'

She saw Simon open his mouth to speak and got in first.

'And we need to make him think that hiring a PR company was his idea in the first place.'

To her surprise – and some relief – Simon smiled.

'You're absolutely right,' he said, nodding slowly. 'Now you mention it, I do remember those irritating "I'll just run it past Dad and get back to you ..." endings to those emails. The son's not running things at all. Well done, Rachel.'

Rachel smiled back at him. His response seemed genuine and that was the thing she still couldn't quite work out about Simon Rathbone. He could be such a snarky obnoxious git, yet he could also be funny and nice. If he was pleased with one of his staff he'd make sure they knew it. Her colleagues had told her about times they'd come in to find a bottle of champagne on their desk, with a handwritten note thanking them for something they'd done.

His eccentric management style left his staff in a permanent state of combined terror and devotion, but Rachel was prepared to put up with it for all his other qualities. He had exquisite taste, seemingly endless energy and a faultless instinct for where brands belonged in their market – and the client roster to show for it. He was widely acknowledged as the best in the business and she wanted to learn from him.

'So that's the new tactic,' he said. 'We'll aim it all at the old bloke, but does that mean we have to suggest a fifties-style campaign to go with it? "Delight your family with these charming picnic chairs ..." Who's got some ideas how we can persuade Arnie Arkwright that we're the perfect people to promote his swanky new range? Cecilia, you were about to tell us your thoughts before Rachel decided to join us – do go on.'

'Well,' said Cecilia, sitting up in her chair and seeming to wiggle slightly with excitement, 'as it's garden furniture, I think it should be launched in a garden ...'

Rachel saw a brief glimmer of amusement cross Simon's face.

'So, I thought,' continued Cecilia, 'who's got a garden? My father-in-law. Bingo. Don't you think?'

She looked around, beaming at them all. Her husband was the younger son of a marquess. The garden in question the park of a stately home. And pretty much Cecilia's default suggestion for any campaign. Which Simon clearly didn't mind – her address book was worth paying her salary for.

All the other women emitted little squeaks and coos of excitement at Cecilia's idea, and Rachel did her best to join in. Simon's chin had dropped down onto the top of his pristine white shirt collar, and Rachel couldn't help wondering if he was trying not to laugh.

'Well, Stronghough certainly has a beautiful garden,' he said, looking up again. 'The cascade rivals Chatsworth, but I don't think it's quite the right feel for this brand. We need to aim more at the sophisticated urban thinker. Even if it's for their country place, they're not *Country Life* people. They're cashed up, but more Babington, than Badminton. Anyone else got any thoughts?'

'How about Chelsea Physic Garden?' suggested another woman.

Rachel had to supress a groan.

'Not sure that would work with the timing,' said Simon. 'We'll be launching to the magazines in late September, aiming for their spring issues, and the weather's just not reliable enough in London then. Anyone else?'

Rachel saw that his eyes had automatically flicked over to her as he spoke. He was obviously hoping she would have another suggestion as good as her first one. She most certainly did, but she was going to make him wait for it, plus she didn't want to appear too much of a try-hard in front of her colleagues.

So she stayed quiet while the other women cast around various ideas of increasing banality, until it felt like the right moment to present her plan.

'I do agree with Cecilia,' she started, 'that it would be great to show the merchandise in a garden and, as you say, Simon, it will have to be somewhere sure to be warm in late September, so I think we have to take them abroad – but obviously we'll have to watch the budget. We can't expect a new client to stump up to take four editors to the Caribbean ...'

'So, all we need,' said Simon, 'is somewhere with guaranteed good weather and affordable yet ultra-stylish accommodation,

that's not too far for busy editors to travel for a few days ...
Where do you suggest? Shangri La? Atlantis? Middle Earth?'

'Tangier,' said Rachel, and before Simon could resume his
smart-arse tone, she added, 'One of my contacts has a hotel
there with an amazing garden. He's offered to give us the
accommodation free, in exchange for editorial mentions in
the magazines we bring over.'

She tapped her iPad and passed it to Simon, open at the
site of an expat American blogger she'd been cultivating for a
couple of years, knowing she might one day want to use the
historic *riad* he had converted into an exquisite boutique hotel
as a location.

Simon's eyebrows shot up as he scrolled down the blog.
'This is perfect,' he said, glancing up at Rachel and then
passing the tablet to Cecilia. 'How do you know this guy?'

'I've been following the blog for a couple of years,' said
Rachel, not wanting to go into any more detail that would give
her edge away to her colleagues. She'd worked hard to develop
close connections with all the key interiors style bloggers, well
before other PRs in their sector had realised how important
they would become.

'As well as promoting the hotel,' she continued, 'he's got
a book coming out, so he's thrilled at the idea of us bringing
over four of Britain's top interiors magazine editors. He's
offered to take them on a food and shopping tour of the city
too, which will add another positive angle to their experience
and make sure they leave feeling warm and fuzzy about Lawn
& Stone. And us, ha ha.'

'Very good,' said Simon, looking at her thoughtfully.

Rachel glanced over at her colleagues, who were making
their cooing noises over the blog now, but with noticeably less
enthusiasm than they'd had for Cecilia's father-in-law's garden.

'Do you have any more brilliant ideas, Rachel?' asked Simon.

'Yes,' she said. 'We'll repeat the press trip next spring with four of the best interiors bloggers. So their real-time coverage will be coming out on Instagram and Twitter and their blogs, at the same time as the magazines featuring the Lawn & Stone furniture hit the newsstands. Double whammy ...'

Simon smiled again.

'Superb,' he said. 'You've nailed it.'

He was leaning back in his chair, rolling a classic Bic Biro between his fingers as he spoke. Then he absently put the end of it in his mouth and began chewing on it like a schoolboy, before realising what he was doing and snatching it out again. Rachel had to make an effort not to laugh.

'I would like you to take over this pitch, Rachel,' he said, sitting up straight again. 'We'll have a final planning meeting tomorrow, so get prepared for that, but it seems like you've already got it covered. So, thanks everyone, you can go – but Rachel, can you stay behind for a minute?'

She could see from their expressions and the little glances they shared as they left the room that her colleagues were surprised, and a little miffed, that the new girl had been given such a big responsibility, but she couldn't think about that. She had a family to feed and a mortgage to pay. She didn't need friends at work; she needed this job to be confirmed. Money was tight enough, even with her fairly generous salary.

'That was very impressive, Rachel,' Simon said after the others had gone. 'I could employ a thousand girls more punctual and reliable than you, not to mention better groomed ...'

Rachel's hand flew up to the ponytail she'd hastily pulled her hair into that morning after a less than successful effort with dry shampoo. Was it that bad?

'But you do have remarkable vision,' he went on, 'so I'll continue to put up with you a little longer. At least until the end of your trial period.'

'Is it even legal for you to talk to me like that?' Rachel answered, not sure whether to feel flattered or furious, and deciding on the latter. 'And I'm not a girl. I'm a public relations professional of considerable experience and esteem.'

And a forty-three-year-old mother of two, she thought, but restrained herself from mentioning either of those details. Simon was hilariously coy about his own age and Rachel strongly suspected he found her responsibilities as a parent extremely inconvenient.

'All right,' he said, shooting the cuffs of his immaculate suit and leaning over the desk towards her, 'take a look at your shoes and then tell me how professional you are.'

Rachel felt like rolling her eyes. Just because he was Mr GQ Magazine, with his perfect grooming and polished shoes, he expected them all to dress like something out of Mad Men.

She did know wearing Birkenstocks to the office was pushing her luck, but she'd been delayed so disastrously that morning trying to get the girls to school in horrendous traffic, she'd ended up having to turn the car around and leave them at home with the au pair and hadn't had time to change her shoes.

Which was lucky considering she'd then had to run to the Tube station from home and then to the office at the other end and it was late May ... and then she glanced down at her feet and saw what he was talking about. One sandal was black, one was orange.

Simon burst out laughing.

'Did you really not notice until now?'

Rachel shook her head, mortified.

'I'll go out and buy a proper pair of shoes at lunchtime,' she said.

'Oh, don't bother,' he replied, 'make it a trend. Just make sure you have something decent to wear at the Lawn & Stone presentation on Wednesday.'

'I will,' said Rachel, as her phone pinged to let her know she had a text. It had been going all morning, but she hadn't had a moment to stop and see who they were from. She'd thought the earlier ones were probably from Simon, trying to find out where the hell she was.

'You can go now,' he said, turning his gaze to his computer, rude sod.

Rachel gathered up her belongings and headed for the door, embarrassed that her co-workers were going to see her mismatching shoes. They probably already hated her for showing off at the meeting; now they had a good reason to laugh at her too. As she reached the doorway, Simon spoke again.

'Rachel,' he said.

She turned to look at him.

'Bloody good work.'

She smiled at him and nodded, then headed up the stairs to her office, in a garret right at the top of the building. Seeing the orange sandal coming up past the black one on the first step, she decided she couldn't bear it – she took them off and stuffed them into her handbag. Her gym kit was under her desk; she'd rather wear her trainers than walk around like this all day.

She'd like to have nipped out to the shops right away to buy some more appropriate work shoes, whatever Simon had said, but all the way from Queen's Park to South Ken that morning she'd been doing sums on the back of an envelope, working out what essential outgoings she had for the rest of the month. The figure at the end of her calculations had made her feel slightly nauseous. Shopping for anything non-essential was out of the question. She'd just have to brazen it out in her trainers.

As she climbed the last flight of stairs up to her attic office, she checked her phone and saw that the texts she'd heard beeping earlier were from her sisters, each asking her to call them. That was a pleasant surprise – much better than the furious messages from Simon she'd feared – but her siblings would have to wait until later. She had way too much work to do on this brilliant opportunity she'd just landed. She was determined to make him see how indispensable she was.

Much as she loved her sisters, neither of them had to worry about supporting their kids the way she did, and they couldn't possibly understand how focused she needed to be that morning.

Her older sister, Tessa, had three boys, but with a very successful husband, she didn't have to work at all, lucky her. She just seemed to waft around their lovely big house all day obsessively painting murals. Practically every wall in the place was covered with her whimsical depictions of plants and wildlife.

At the other extreme, Natasha, the youngest, worked madly hard, constantly globe-trotting with supermodels and movie stars as a very high-end make-up artist. She'd made a mint for herself, but she didn't have kids or a husband – or even a boyfriend – to worry about, so she could dedicate her time entirely to her career. And herself.

Natasha's main worries, as far as Rachel could make out, were that she might have accidentally eaten some carbohydrate, how best to store all her free designer handbags, and deciding which celebrity friend's invitation to accept.

She adored both her sisters, but their ideas of 'stressed' and 'busy' did give Rachel the pip sometimes. So, she decided, she wouldn't call either of them just yet. She knew it would only irritate her to talk to them before she'd got some solid work in.

The most recent text, however, did demand an immediate reply. It was from her nine-year-old daughter, Daisy, sent from the au pair's phone.

'Please ring me Mummy,' it said, 'I'm desperate. Ariadne won't stop playing One Direction and it's affecting my mental development.'

Rachel laughed. Daisy. Never was a child more inappropriately named. Rachel hadn't been able to get anything past her since the moment she could speak. Just the week before she'd had to do a deal with her not to tell her six-year-old sister the truth about the Tooth Fairy. A pound coin under the older girl's pillow had secured her silence.

She was more of a Venus Fly Trap than a Daisy, thought Rachel, settling at her desk and turning on her computer. But then she hadn't had a say in it.

She'd still been recovering from a traumatic labour followed by an emergency C-section when her then husband, Michael, had chosen the name, registered it and sent out a group text announcing the birth of Daisy Elizabeth.

When Rachel eventually felt strong enough to protest, Michael had come over all hurt, saying he thought she'd be pleased he'd taken care of it for her so she wouldn't have to worry about anything while she recovered.

So typical of him, thought Rachel, skimming down her emails and marking the important ones with a priority alert. Simultaneously controlling and guilt-tripping. How glad she was she didn't have to be around that on a daily basis any

more, even if it did mean negotiating her current terrifying
financial tightrope walk.

But she'd chosen to marry him, she reminded herself,
nobody had forced her. She had loved him once – or thought
she did – and he'd given her two beautiful daughters, who
he was still a good father to in his own way. Two beautiful
daughters she was now going to treat herself to a quick chat
with.

Branko, her Serbian manny, or bro pair as she preferred to
call him, answered. How lucky that the disastrous school run
had happened on the one day a week he stayed at the house
doing the laundry and cleaning, rather than going out to the
various courses and other jobs he did.

Along with collecting the girls from school and looking
after them until she came home, that one day of domestic
chores was the full extent of his formal duties in return for
meals and a nice place to live. With no contract and no hourly
rate, the simple barter set-up had been his idea and it worked
brilliantly for both of them.

'Are you surviving?' Rachel asked him.

'Very nice time,' said Branko, in his strong accent. 'I much
prefer these girls than ironing.'

'Are you managing to keep them off the iPad and away
from the TV?'

'Yes. I hide pad and pull out plug.'

'Daisy texted me something about One Direction ...' said
Rachel.

'Yes, these pretty boys on all the time. I like it too, we tell
Daisy majority rule. She make earplugs out of kitchen roll. All
good.'

'What are they doing at the moment?' asked Rachel,
wanting to picture her darlings.

'Ariadne make castle out of pink marshmallows, she say is school project. She eat many marshmallow. Daisy ask me to teach her Cyrillic alphabet.'

'Really?' said Rachel. 'I didn't know she knew what that was.'

'She call it funny writing, same thing.'

'So are you teaching her Serbian?'

'No,' said Branko. 'Russian. She say more useful for job.'

Rachel laughed. Daisy had so clearly inherited her brain – and her attitude – from her grandfather, Rachel's late father, who'd been a minister in Harold Wilson's Labour government in the 1960s. Rachel had been very young when he died, so what she knew of him was mostly from old TV clips she'd found on YouTube, but Rachel's mum had also often commented how like her grandfather Daisy was. He'd been famous in the House of Commons for his smart comebacks.

'Can you put the future prime minister on?' said Rachel.

Cranbrook, Kent

The phone calls started before Tessa even had time to put the kettle on.

She saw it was the business number which was flashing and only answered it because she thought it might be the customer who had promised to call back first thing about a rare Regency chimneypiece. Normally she would have let it go to a message for the manager to deal with when he came in later, but it was a big price-tag item.

'Hunter Gatherer Reclamation,' she answered, using her best sing-song staff voice from when she used to answer all the business calls.

'Is Tim there?' asked a woman.

Late forties, Tessa guessed, her heart sinking. Could be younger. Lovely northern Irish accent, which at least added a touch of novelty. Her eyes flitted automatically to the piece of paper she'd stuck on the wall by the phone. Her script for these calls. To stop herself from just hanging up. Or bursting into tears.

'No, I'm afraid he isn't,' she chirped. 'Is there anything I can help you with?'

She'd had to put that in, on the off chance the caller might be a crazed fan who wanted to buy something, as opposed to just a crazed fan.

'Can you give me his mobile number?' asked the woman.

Tessa kept her eyes focused on her typed script.

'I'm afraid I'm not at liberty to disclose that. May I ask ...'

The woman interrupted her.

'Can you give him a message for me?'

'If it's a business enquiry,' Tessa continued, determinedly keeping her tone even, 'I'm probably the best person to help you at the moment, or you could ring back in a couple of hours and speak to the manager.'

Tessa paused for a moment, really hoping the woman might ring off. They often did at this point, but not this one.

'I just need to speak to him,' she was saying, a slightly desperate tone creeping into her voice.

OK, there was no choice, it would have to be the full cruel-to-be-kind flick-off. Tessa hated doing that, but it had to be better than giving someone false hope.

'Or if it's to do with Tim Chiminey,' she said, pasting a false smile on her face, to try to keep her voice sounding friendly, 'then the best thing would be to go to the program's page on the Channel 4 website and send an email with your enquiry to the address you'll find there.'

And if it is to do with Tim flipping Chiminey, Tessa pleaded in her head, can you please get a life and stop harassing me at home at such an ungodly hour on a Monday morning about my husband?

My husband *Tom*, who's been randomly turned into this Tim person, which has somehow made him the property of every lonely woman on earth with a tradesman fetish. And boy, were there a lot of them. Who knew?

The woman finally hung up, without saying thank you or goodbye. Bloody rude really, but Tessa couldn't feel angry with someone so pathetic they'd ring up a total stranger they'd only ever seen on television, yet really believed they had a special connection with. It made her feel like crying.

She closed her eyes for a moment, holding the phone in her hand, trying to put the sadness out of her mind, before she put the handset back on its wall mount. If she let it get to her she'd spend the whole day feeling that woman's loneliness trailing around with her.

But still, 'Tim' ... She shook her head at the thought of it, putting slices of bacon into a frying pan and turning on the burner. She would never get used to it. *Tom.* His name was Tom, he'd always been Tom, but all it had taken was one smart TV producer and a vowel in his name had suddenly changed – and their entire life with it.

The producer had spotted Tom when the architectural salvage company he and Tessa had started together over twenty years before was featured in a show about renovating old houses with leftover bits of other old houses.

Tom had been recommended as a vintage-fireplace expert when they were planning an episode that involved putting all the open fires back into a grand Georgian townhouse they'd been stripped out of in the 1970s, and he was definitely the right man for the job.

Not only had Tom supplied and fitted all the elegant and historically appropriate mantelpieces, grates, marble hearths etc., talking about them with great knowledge and enthusiasm as he went, he'd then climbed up on the roof with his sweep's brushes and liners and made sure all the chimneys were working safely. By the end of the filming there were glorious log fires blazing in four rooms – but even that wasn't the defining moment.

The producer had looked at the footage of Tom skimming down a vertiginous ladder at high speed, grinning, his face covered in soot, and that was it. From an unknown junk merchant called Tom Chenery, suddenly *Tim Chiminey* the television show – and Tim Chiminey the heart-throb – had been created.

Tessa had objected strongly to the awful name change but the producer was adamant, insisting *Tim Chiminey* was a brilliant name for a show about putting open fires back into old houses. And Tom had just gone along with it, laughing off Tessa's protests, seeing the whole thing as a bit of a lark and free publicity for their business.

The show was an instant hit, with its rather thrilling element of derring-do adding a new twist to the tired home renovation format, as Tom shimmied up and down his rickety ladders and skipped about on the endless roofs of stately homes. In one particularly memorable episode, he discovered three grisly mummified cats in the chimney of a former coaching inn.

Suddenly Tessa's junkyard husband was everybody's property. He'd even been on the cover of the *Radio Times*: 'Tim Chiminey – sweeping us off our feet' read the headline. It was framed in the downstairs loo and Tessa cringed every time she saw it. As she did at all the other cheesy publicity his agent, Barney, insisted he did, to boost his profile.

Turning the bacon in the pan, Tessa groaned inwardly at the thought of him. Why Tom had signed with such an old-school 'entertainment' manager she had never been able to understand. But Tom insisted Barney's decades of experience and contacts were exactly what he, a total TV novice, needed. Tessa called him Barney the Dinosaur and dreaded his phone calls almost as much as those from the fans.

The last time he'd rung was to ask her to take part in a reality show called *Real Housewives of TV Celebs*. He'd been amazed when she told him a flat no.

'But Tessie, sweetheart,' he'd said. 'They really want you, darling. They love your look, and you'd be famous too, if you did the show. Then you and Tim would be a golden couple, which would give you both much more traction. Think about it, the next stage could be *Strictly* ...'

Tessa shook her head at the memory, which pretty much summed up her very worst nightmare. She found it insulting that he would even think she'd consider doing something like that. She didn't need to be a television personality. Even apart from the salvage yard, she already had a profession she was proud of, as a highly regarded mural artist. There was a time when London's top decorators had fought over her.

She didn't make a living from it any more, but Tessa had never stopped painting. Now she used the talent that once embellished the drawing rooms of some of London's grandest houses on her own home. She was passionate about the murals that now covered practically every wall in the place, and it was pretty big, a detached Victorian house with seven bedrooms and a rambling ground floor.

It had been featured in *Interiors*, which must count for something. They'd used a shot of the staircase on the cover. Quite a few years ago, admittedly, but she still considered her mural painting to be work, even if her ambitious younger sisters made it clear they didn't.

Tessa had learned long ago never to refer to it as 'work' in front of them. She'd seen them exchange knowing looks, so better not to use the word, because she was aware that she was privileged to have the time to do it, without having to worry about finding money to pay bills and all that. And that was one upside of Tom's new life – and it had only been a little over two years since the crazy celebrity circus had begun – that she did have to acknowledge was good; they were much better off than before.

There was the money from the show and a lot more from the various guest appearances and deals Barney brokered. Plus, the salvage business turnover had nearly tripled since he'd been on the telly, as Tom always reminded her when the stalkers got her down, but she still couldn't quite get used to her new role as a celebrity's wife. And the occasional hate mail didn't help.

She'd had to come off Instagram for a while, after a nasty trolling on there by a jealous fan. That was when the TV production company had sent someone down to advise Tessa on how to cope with it all, because it didn't help living in a very small Kent town where the only other famous person was the crossword compiler for a broadsheet newspaper.

Staring out of the window over the cooker, she was transfixed by the effect of the late-spring morning light on the glazed terracotta vintage chimney pots they used as planters in their herb garden. She was about to grab her phone and take a quick shot of them, when the Radio 4 pips heralded the turn of the hour and here he was, the man himself – Tom, or Tim, depending on how long you'd known him – raking one hand through wet hair, the other reaching immediately to take the pan of bacon, which Tessa had entirely forgotten about, off the heat.

'Oh, sorry,' she said, stepping out of his way, 'the phone rang earlier – one of your adoring fans. It put me off ... I forgot about the bacon.'

'That's all right, my dippy darling,' he said, sliding an arm around her waist and kissing her full on the mouth, 'I like it crispy.'

Tessa smiled back at him, taking in with a wonder that had never lessened in nearly twenty-five years together, how he had flipped over all the half-incinerated rashers with one flick of his wrist, filled the kettle and was now putting water in the bottom of his old stove-top espresso maker, without letting go of her.

Tom – not bloody Tim, Tom – was just like that. The quintessential practical man. He could make things, mend things, do anything with utter confidence. No wonder women found him so attractive. He was good with his hands. And not just his hands, thought Tessa, smiling to herself.

Leaning against the kitchen counter, she watched him as he cut bread, poured boiling water into the teapot, laid the table and put the plates to warm, seemingly in one movement, and remembered the moment she'd first met him.

His dark hair was grey at the temples now, there were deep laugh lines around his eyes, but he was still as straight and slim as he'd been that day.

Just a year out of art school, she'd been painting a mural in the dining room of a house in Belgravia and had answered a knock on the front door to find a man about her age, maybe a little older, standing there, wearing blue overalls and a big open smile.

He was a good-looking chap, not film-star handsome, but well above average, with one detail that had made Tessa catch her breath – a smudge of black coal dust on his nose. It was irrationally attractive.

'I'm here to do the chimney,' he'd said, and Tessa couldn't help bursting out laughing.

'I can see that,' she'd replied, just stopping herself from asking him where Dick Van Dyke and the other chimney sweeps were.

'I've got coal dust on my face, haven't I?' he'd said, rubbing at his cheeks and making it worse.

'Yes,' said Tessa, 'and please don't wash it off until I've drawn you.'

She broke from her reverie as Tom touched her arm.

'Hey, dozy,' he said, 'can you go and shout at the boys, it's nearly eight.'

'Oh, sorry,' she said.

'You looked like you were a million miles away,' he said, 'I didn't want to disturb you. Thought you might be having one of your big ideas.'

'I was,' she said, pinching his bottom as she went past, 'I was thinking about you.'

She heard him laughing as she went out to the hall.

'Breakfast!' she yelled up the stairs. 'You've got two minutes to come down or we're going to eat it all and there's absolutely no other food in the house ... Not a scrap.'

She heard two bedroom doors open immediately, but the third one she knew might need a threat even more terrible than the thought of missing out on food to make the person inside get up.

'Finn!' she called out, going halfway up the stairs. 'Time to get up. You'll miss breakfast ...'

There was no response. Tessa knew she should just go in there and wrench the duvet off him, but she couldn't face it. She'd had to do that to her oldest son the day before. The reaction had not been enjoyable and she still felt a bit peeled from the fan phone call. It was Tom's turn. There were so many mornings these days when he wasn't there to do it.

Going back into the kitchen, she saw there was a big pile of bacon sandwiches already on a plate in the middle of the table and Tom was at the fridge door pulling out ketchup, mustard and other sauces at such high speed, he was practically juggling them.

He just seemed to move on a different setting from everyone else, she thought. Like a film that was running slightly fast, while the rest of the world lumbered along around him.

'Can you go and wake Finn up, Tom?' she asked, sitting at the table and reaching for the teapot. 'I did it yesterday and I'm not feeling strong enough for a nuclear war yet this morning.'

Tom was already walking out through the kitchen door before she had finished speaking, passing two sleepy-looking boys on the way in, the younger one scratching his tummy, his school shirt coming untucked in the process.

Tessa was on her feet without thinking about it, kissing his head as she tucked the shirt back in.

'Morning, Mr Scruff,' she said, 'would some hot chocolate wake you up?'

The boy nodded, nuzzling into her like a calf. He was nearly twelve, but still a child, just, the very last thread of it. Sometimes Tessa found it hard to let him out of her sight in case she missed the last moment

'I'll have some of that too, please, Mum,' said the older boy, now at the table with his mouth full of bacon.

'Two hot chocs, for two growing chaps,' said Tessa, ruffling the older boy's hair as she went over to the fridge. Archie had already made the transfer to the next stage, his voice now octaves lower than his younger brother's, but so far he'd stayed pretty nice. She reminded herself not to take it for granted.

A howl pierced the air from upstairs.

'What are you doing?' yelled an outraged voice, followed by Tom's laughter. 'I'm going to do you for child abuse. You can't just throw water on someone when they're asleep ... It's illegal.'

A thunder of feet on the stairs and Tom was back in the kitchen, a big grin on his face.

'Sorry about soaking the bed, Tess,' he said, squeezing the shoulder of each boy as he passed and sitting down at the head of the table. 'It was the only way I could think of to make it less attractive to him.'

'Was it that big jug of flowers on the landing dresser?' asked Tessa.

Tom nodded. She smiled back at him, shaking her head indulgently as she put mugs of hot chocolate in front of each of her younger sons, and then sat down.

'As long as he gets up, I don't mind if you set fire to it – but that doesn't mean you can eat his breakfast as well as your own, Archie,' she added, taking two bacon sandwiches back from the large pile on his plate and putting them on the clean one next to her.

'Always worth a try though, Arch,' said Tom in a confidential man-to-man tone.

Archie grinned back at him, exactly the same gap between his front teeth.

'Now,' said Tessa, after the two boys had emptied their plates like a plague of really hungry locusts, 'both of you go and clean your teeth. Heccie, you've got PE today, so make sure everything's in your bag and Arch, don't forget your music and flute, they're both on top of the piano.'

'Oh look,' said Tom, 'here comes Herman Munster ...'

Tessa glanced around to see her oldest son walking – or rather, skulking – into the kitchen. His hair hung over his face, his school shirt was completely unbuttoned, his tie slung around his neck inside the shirt collar, his trousers barely staying up.

He looked an utter mess, but Tessa couldn't help it, her heart fluttered a little. His limbs seemed to have grown out of proportion to the rest of his body, his facial expression could have soured milk, but he was still her baby. Her first born.

'Morning, Finn McChin,' she said brightly, ever hopeful that overnight he might have turned back into the boy who had once made a batch of biscuits for her all by himself spelling out the words 'SIMPLY THE BEST', iced in five different colours.

'Unngggh,' he replied, sliding into a chair and reaching for his plate of food, without even glancing at her.

Tom was frowning and looking a little puzzled. He had his right elbow over his head, his hand rubbing the back of his neck; one of his characteristic thinking postures. Tessa tapped his other arm to make him look at her and raised enquiring eyebrows.

Tom pointed at his own eyes and then at Finn, who was concentrating on getting as much bacon sandwich as possible into his mouth in one go. He had ketchup all over his chin. Amusement broke over Tom's face.

'Finn,' he said, 'look at me for a moment.'

Finn looked up, his mouth open, large amounts of semi-chewed food on display.

'Are you wearing eye make-up?' asked Tom.

'Wssanerghaffasnup,' said Finn, standing up and walking out of the room, still holding the sandwich, trailing ketchup down the front of his shirt as he went.

'He's wearing make-up,' said Tom to Tessa.

'He most certainly is,' said Tessa. 'I wondered where my favourite eye pencil had gone. Do you think it's freshly applied or left over from last night? I don't see how he would have had time this morning ... he's hardly got his clothes on.'

'I think it's definitely last night's,' said Tom, finishing his coffee, 'reminds me of you after a late one.'

'Shall I go and get my eye make-up remover?' asked Tessa, play punching her husband on the bicep and finding she was impressed how hard it was, although she knew he had started going to the gym at some poncy health club since he'd been doing that bloody TV show. Just one of the many small ways it had changed him. He used to get enough exercise hauling marble mantelpieces around.

'No,' said Tom, firmly. 'Let's leave the school to deal with it. I'll be interested to see if it's still there when he comes home. I'm sure his girlfriends will be queuing up to take it off for him.'

Only so they can meet you, thought Tessa. Or their mums can. Happy Birthday, Mummy!

Tom stood up, then leaned down to kiss her on the cheek, hardly pausing en route to the front door.

'I'm driving straight on to the shoot after dropping them off,' he called back over his shoulder. 'It's in Wiltshire. Not sure when I'll be back. They might want me to stay over, I've packed a bag. I'll call you later when I know.'

Tessa had her mouth open to reply, although she wasn't sure what she was going to say, but he was already gone. She leaned sideways so she could get a view of the front door, just in time to see Archie and Finn walking out of it. There was a pause, then Hector suddenly appeared back in the kitchen, blazer on, shirt untucked again, rucksack and PE bag over his shoulder, and wrapped his arms around her.

'Bye bye, beautiful Mummy,' he said, 'see you later.'

And then he ran out to catch up with his brothers and father.

Sudden silence. Tessa slumped back in her chair and was about to reach for the teapot again, when the phone rang. It was the business line again and still only 8.20 a.m., so none of the staff were in yet, but there was still the issue of the possible Regency chimneypiece sale. She had to answer it.

'I'd like to speak to Tim, please,' said a woman's voice. Another one.

At the same moment she heard Tom's familiar tones shouting from the front door.

'Tess, darling,' he was yelling, 'don't forget we've got that shoot for *You* magazine on Friday. Barney says they want to do some shots in the house but the main pics will be us in the garden. Can you ring your sister and remind her she was going to help you to get it ready? She said she might be able to lend us some of her client's stuff, remember? The garden furniture ... Barney said the magazine specifically wants some new product in the pics as well as our old gear.'

The door slammed shut. Tess put her hand up to her forehead. She'd completely forgotten about the shoot and she hadn't lost the five pounds she'd been going to shift before it. Shame about the bacon sandwich. Oops. And she hadn't had her roots done either.

She glanced in the mirror on the wall next to the phone. A harsh line of grey stood out along her parting. Oh Lord. The dashing Tim Chiminey and his ugly fat hag of a wife invite you into their family home. Great. The stalkers could use one of his grates to build a bonfire to burn her on. Which reminded her about the phone she was still holding.

A tiny voice was coming out of it. 'Hello? Are you there? I'm ringing for Tim Chiminey,' it was saying.

'I'm very sorry,' said Tessa, 'Mr Chiminey has left the building.'

Spring photographic studios, London NW5

Natasha was massaging the model's hands while Joe wound her hair around big pink rollers.

'Your hair is amazing, Gabriela,' Joe was saying, smiling at the young woman in the mirror, making as much eye contact with her as he could. 'It's so rare to find a natural blonde with your gorgeous honey skin tone.'

She stared back at him with big green eyes, looking more like a frightened rabbit than the next supermodel sensation she was tipped to become. Joe kept talking.

'I love your ringlet curls, Gabbie darling, but the stylist thinks they won't work with the simple lines of the clothes we're shooting today, so she wants me to do smooth volume. Very nineties Linda. Of course you'd look fabulous however I did it. How do you like London so far? Help me out here, Natasha ...' he added, not missing a beat, or turning to look at her.

'Have you had a chance to go shopping yet?' Joe continued. 'Go to Liberty, you'll love it, although at your age, still practically a foetus, all alone in a strange country, you'd probably prefer Topshop. That's where I buy all my jeans ... Mayday! Mayday! Natasha darling, this is Joe, can you read me? Over!'

Natasha looked up at him and then at Gabriela, plastering a cheery smile on her own face. This was a challenge, even for them. She and Joe had worked on shoots together for over twenty years, becoming one of the most sought-after hair and make-up teams for magazine editorials, fashion shows and luxury-brand ad campaigns. Along the way they'd managed every kind of diva strop and meltdown, but a total lack of a common language was a new one.

The young models from Russia and the rest of the Eastern bloc all knew a bit of English; some even arrived fluent. This poor little mite, from a remote part of Brazil, didn't seem to know a word and the interpreter booked to accompany her on the shoot hadn't turned up.

'I'm doing what I can, Joe, my darling,' said Natasha, giving Gabriela's hand a friendly squeeze. 'I rang Storm just now and they said the interpreter had accidentally gone to the wrong studio and is on her way here – but hold on, I've had an idea ...'

She grabbed her tote bag and pulled out a small speaker cube, which she set up on the work top, then she fiddled with her phone for a few moments until some Latin music, sung in a language Natasha was fairly sure was Brazilian Portuguese, started playing.

Gabriela's eyes widened in recognition.

'*Você gostou desta música?*' Natasha read from the translation app on her phone, trying to muster some attempt at the accent.

The girl's face broke into a smile, which Natasha could see was likely to adorn many future magazine covers.

'*Sim!*' she said. '*A minha avó adora esta canção.*'

'Any idea, Joe?' asked Natasha, nodding and smiling at Gabriela enthusiastically, as though she had understood every word and was delighted by them.

'Not a Fanny Adams,' he said, also smiling, 'but whatever she said, I think it's good. And you're a genius. I can't understand why you aren't more successful ...'

'Oh, shut up fish face,' said Natasha. She tapped her phone again. '*Você gostava de algum café ou água?*' she asked.

'*Sim, obrigada,*' said Gabriela, nodding keenly and looking much happier.

'I think that means "Yes to coffee or water", don't you?' said Natasha, beaming back at the reflection in the mirror. What a fresh new beauty.

'*Eu gostaria tanto, por favor,*' added Gabriela.

'The girl's got manners, whatever she's saying,' said Joe. 'I definitely heard a "please" in there. *Bueno, chiquita,*' he added, patting her shoulder. '*Sim ...*'

'I'll get both,' said Natasha, suddenly feeling the need for a strong shot of caffeine herself – she'd come straight from Heathrow off the JFK red-eye. '*Uno momento*, Gabriela. S'later, Joey boy.'

She patted Joe's shoulder as she headed out of the dressing room to find the catering team, but they were still setting up, so she ran down to the reception to ask if they could direct her to the nearest café.

The woman at the desk told her the closest one was in Kentish Town, a good fifteen-minute walk away, and offered to make her a 'cuppa' in the staff kitchen instead.

Natasha smiled at the word. She never heard it living in New York, and it reminded her so much of her English mum and her slight northern accent, which everyone had thought so quaint when Natasha had been growing up in Australia.

As soon as she was reminded of those days, other thoughts started crowding into Natasha's mind. Remembering how she and her two older sisters had been suddenly wrenched away from their happy life in Brisbane when her parents had split up, and shipped off with their mum to live in England, a strange, grey, damp place Natasha had never even visited before.

Until she'd decided to move back to Australia again to be with her dad, leaving her mum and sisters behind, deafening herself to their pleas to stay, to the point where she'd almost convinced herself she didn't care.

Anyway, that was all a long time ago, Natasha told herself, taking the tray of mugs and glasses from the receptionist and heading back upstairs to the studio.

No point going back over all that now. She'd been young – only fourteen – and very confused when she made that choice, as her shrink was always telling her. Besides, New York was a lot closer to Tunbridge Wells than Brisbane had been, and she always saw her mum when she came over to Europe for work, which was frequently with the ready-to-wear and couture shows twice a year each, as well as all the editorial and advertising jobs.

She was going to see her mum the day after next, in fact, and then they were both heading over to Tessa's to spend a lovely weekend with the rest of the family, before she went over to Paris for a big designer ad campaign. Time to leave that teenage guilt-trip behind and concentrate on her work.

Walking back into the dressing room to see the interpreter still hadn't arrived, she was going to need all her wits to get through it. After raising her eyebrows complicitly at Joe, she put the tray down on the table and held the milk and sugar up to Gabriela, with an enquiring look on her face.

Gabriela pointed at the sugar, nodding, then held up three fingers.

'Nice work, Tashie, baby ...' sang Joe, roughly in tune with the samba track now playing through the speaker, breaking off from his rollers to do a few steps, a spin and a shimmy. '*Olé!*' he shouted.

Gabriela laughed and Natasha turned up the volume a bit

then joined in the dancing. Tucking his comb behind his ear, Joe put his hand out, pulled Gabriela from her seat and then twirled her around in some fairly convincing Latino moves.

'*Dancing with the Stars*, are we?' said Natasha. 'Pig Latin section ...'

'Anything to get through the day,' said Joe, as he let Gabriela down in a dip. 'In the universal language of camp.'

'Just try not to drop her,' said Natasha as the song came to an end.

Joe bowed to Gabriela and gestured for her to go back to her seat. Natasha glanced at the young woman's face in the mirror as she settled herself. The frightened bunny had gone; she was looking relaxed and much more confident. Result. They were well on their way to getting this homesick little thing through the shoot feeling fantastic, so there would be beautiful pictures of her for *Vogue*, which was what they were all there for.

Now that Gabriela was more comfortable, Natasha felt she could get on with sorting out her kit, ready to start her part of the job. She normally had an assistant to do it for her, but she'd decided to travel alone on this trip. She had two local ones lined up in Paris for the big job the following week.

She quite enjoyed this ritual, on the rare occasions she had time to do it any more. It was a great opportunity to reconnect with all her products in some fundamental way. Sometimes she got great ideas just from handling it all.

Maybe she should give up having assistants altogether, she thought, as she checked over her foundations, stored in her case in strict tone order and subdivided by texture: matte, translucent, whisper light, full metal jacket.

She held up one of her sheerest bases next to Gabriela's cheek to judge the colour.

'Don't think you'll be needing the full kabuki for this face, do you?' said Joe, breaking into another dance move, simultaneously juggling three rollers, which made Gabriela giggle.

'She hardly needs any base,' said Natasha, scrutinising the immaculate golden skin with a scattering of freckles across her cheeks. 'With the very sculptural hair you're planning and the severe clothes, which will look quite oversized on her frame, I think a bare face could look really strong. Just let her eyes shine out like beacons. White liner inside the eye rims. Maybe a coloured mascara? Green ...'

Joe nodded. 'I am loving the sound of that,' he said. 'She's so beautiful, she's almost an alien.'

Natasha grinned at him. 'That's exactly what I was thinking,' she said.

They high-fived, then Joe turned to Gabriela and high-fived her as well, making her feel part of it all, even if she didn't understand a word they were saying. She laughed again, gazing at Joe with the expression of a little girl looking at her favourite naughty uncle.

He's done it again, thought Natasha. Well, they both had. There was no denying it, they were a great team and their presence on this shoot had probably saved it. And there could be ongoing benefits from that, because Gabriela might specifically request them for future shoots – as so many other supermodels and film stars already did.

Natasha had grasped right from the start of her career how crucial this aspect of her job was. Photographers, models, art directors and even stylists (but only the very best ones) could be tricky, but one of the make-up artist's and hairdresser's crucial roles on a shoot was to keep the talent happy and the mood upbeat, to make everyone's job easier.

Just as much as her original ideas and sure hand with a lip brush, Natasha knew a large part of her success was due to a natural disposition to be positive and cheery, no matter how she was feeling inside. She could smile and joke through a hangover, period pains and a broken heart. And she'd had plenty of recent experience with the last one. Two years of it.

She shook her head quickly to throw that thought off. She wasn't going to mar her day by allowing that misery in.

'How much longer do you think you're going to need?' she asked Joe, who was now taking the rollers out of Gabriela's hair.

'Well, in light of what you were just saying about the make-up, I think we need to make the hair even bigger and more structured. Like a kind of helmet, so I want to use my really giant rollers.'

Natasha nodded. 'That sounds great,' she said. 'So, ten minutes?'

'Fifteen,' said Joe.

As Natasha turned to leave the room, she saw a small, flustered-looking woman being brought over by one of the photographer's assistants.

'I think the cavalry's here,' Natasha said over her shoulder to Joe, as the woman practically ran into the room, speaking very fast and very loudly in what was definitely Portuguese, judging by Gabriela's enthusiastic replies.

She left them to it, wishing she could pop outside for a quick head-clearing walk, but knowing she couldn't leave her post. The stylist and photographer could appear at any moment to ask what she was planning to do. She was on duty until the very last picture was taken.

The squashy old sofa against the far wall looked very appealing, but she knew she would fall immediately asleep, so she found a hard chair and pulled it over to an open window. Fresh air, daylight on the pineal gland and plenty of coffee were the best things she could do for her jet lag until she could get some exercise.

She flicked through some magazines, then scrolled through the *New York Times*, the *Sydney Morning Herald* and the *Daily Mail* online. Feeling slightly grubby from how much she had enjoyed the latter, she was wondering what to do next, when the obvious struck her: ring her sisters.

Calls to Tessa's home phone and mobile went to voicemail, but Natasha didn't bother leaving any messages because she knew her dreamy eldest sister would never listen to them. She was probably curating an arrangement of birds' nests, rusty nails and gardening twine on top of a knackered old factory trolley in her sitting room, or adding another tiny bird to one of her endlessly developing murals.

Tessa was such a talented painter; Natasha just couldn't understand how she could be happy squandering her gift like that. She'd been doing so well, working for some of the biggest interior decorators in London, before she'd thrown it all in to be a full-time mum in the provinces. It just seemed a terrible waste.

Maybe having kids could do that to you, thought Natasha, although it didn't seem to have had the same effect on her other sister, Rachel. She had two and was as ambitious as ever.

In fact, since she'd separated from her husband, Rachel seemed to have the perfect set-up, thought Natasha. She had the fun and reward of the children, a lovely house in fairly central London, the satisfaction of a successful career – and the freedom of a single woman every other weekend, when the ex had her daughters. She was always asking Natasha for tips about cool hotels and restaurants for her kids-free weekend jaunts to interesting European cities. Rachel had always been an operator – maybe she was the proof you could have it all?

Natasha decided to send Tessa an email, reminding her of their catch-up that weekend at their mum's place (dates weren't one of Tessa's strong points), and adding that she was really looking forward to seeing her and the boys. Then she sent Rachel a text saying she was in town and asking her to call when she had a spare moment, thinking all the while how she couldn't wait to spend time with her, Daisy and Ariadne.

Oh, those gorgeous girls! Natasha felt a wiggle of excitement at the prospect and scrolled through photos of them on her iPad, taken the last time she'd been over. It was only a couple of months, but felt like ages ago, which gave her a sharp pang. After those two miserable years in Brisbane, separated from her sisters, it seemed a horrible repetition of her own emotional history that she now lived so far from her two adored nieces.

She felt such an intense closeness to them, when they were together. Getting down on the floor with them, playing with Barbies – she could almost pretend they were her daughters. Which was a great blessing, because they were the nearest things to kids of her own that she was ever likely to have.

Trying to remember what her therapist had told her to do every time that devastating realisation blind-sided her – take deep breaths and hold on to something solid – Natasha didn't hear her name being called, and Joe came out of the dressing room to find her staring into space, gripping her tablet to her chest.

'Oy, missus,' he said, 'wakey wakey. I've done my bit for now. It's your turn to make her look even more beautiful, if that's possible. *Por favor.*'

Natasha leapt to her feet and hurried over to the dressing room. It was time for her to shine – and she was not going to allow herself the luxury of one more negative thought.

Tunbridge Wells, Kent

Joy was standing in her hallway staring down at a letter she'd just picked up from her doormat.

Her practical left brain was telling her she should just open the bloody thing and find out what it was about, but her intuitive, creative right brain – always her dominant lobe – wasn't ready yet. She needed to calm it down so she could process the contents of this most unexpected delivery with rational detachment.

But it could be anything, she thought, panic rising, as wild possibilities stampeded into her mind.

She grasped the rose quartz crystal hanging around her neck with her left hand, closed her eyes and started to breathe in and out through her nose very slowly, carefully leaving the all-important pause after the very last bit of the out breath had left her body. After doing this for ten breaths, she felt her heart rate starting to slow.

Finally feeling steady enough to move, she carried the letter through to the conservatory and laid it carefully on the coffee table, as though she were handling a volatile explosive device.

'I think we'll have some tea before we open that, don't you, Muffin?' she said to the black-and-white cat who had followed her in and was sitting on the floor beside her.

He looked up at her with intense golden eyes and let out a single loud meow.

'Oh, I see,' said Joy, smiling down at him, 'you think if I'm having tea, you should have some biscuits, do you? Well, that's fair enough. Come on.'

She headed through the sitting room and down into the kitchen with Muffin at her side.

'What do you think that beastly letter might be, Muffie?' Joy asked him as he sat watching her filling the kettle and taking down a mug. 'You don't think it's anything nasty, do you?'

Muffin didn't reply. Not that Joy really expected him to, but she still felt they communicated at some non-verbal level. Either that or she really was just a cat-chatting nutter lady as her daughter Rachel liked to tease her.

'Ah, I think Relaxed Mind is what's called for,' said Joy, considering her large array of herbal teas.

She reached for her glasses, hanging on a cord around her neck, and after disentangling them from the various crystal pendants, read the back of the box. 'Lavender, nettle leaf, chrysanthemum ... yes, that should do it.'

Leaving Muffin to enjoy his biscuits, she carried her tea up to the conservatory and placed the mug on the table next to the letter. After concentrating on her exhalations again for a few breaths while the tea cooled, she took a careful sip, then picked the envelope up and held it in both hands, reading the name at the top of the address again and again.

'Mrs Elsie Lambton (nee Ainsworth)' it was addressed to, and that was what made the letter so alarming. The Lambton was OK, that had been her first husband's surname, which her older two daughters had, although Tessa had changed hers when she got married. Rachel, characteristically, had not. But the other two names made her shiver.

She hadn't seen 'Elsie Ainsworth' written down for about fifty years, although it had once been her name. She hadn't had contact with anyone who had known her by it since she left home in 1960. There was nobody in her life now who knew she'd been christened Elsie, rather than Joy. Certainly not her daughters.

She'd taken on her new first name, which she had felt was far more appropriate for her personality and the life she intended to have, when she'd moved to London, aged nineteen. No one had known her as anything but Joy since.

Well, Robert, her first husband, had known for the marriage certificate and all that, but he'd been happy to forget it. 'Elsie' didn't fit in with the image he wanted for his glamorous young Westminster wife, any more than it did for the woman herself and on his advice, she'd changed it legally, by deed poll.

Then, as her estranged parents had both died not long after and she'd long ago lost touch with any extended family, there were no complicating relatives to call her by the appalling Elsie, or remind her of the unhappy years she'd been forced to live with that name.

Elsie Ainsworth had died quietly in 1960 as far as Joy was concerned, along with every other aspect of her religiously repressed, penny-pinched, educationally inadequate, emotionally retarded childhood. Goodbye and *namaste*.

So it was Joy Younger – the new surname a very lucky addition from her second husband – who finally took a deep breath and slit the envelope open with a sword-shaped, silver-plated letter opener, which had been on her first husband's desk when he was an MP.

This seemed appropriate as soon as she saw the address at the top; the letter was from the firm of solicitors who had looked after his affairs all those years ago. Wilkins, Harald & Held wasn't a name you forgot. Especially as her dealings with them at the time had been so distressing.

It had been a terrible shock when Robert had died of a sudden catastrophic heart attack, aged just forty-seven, made even worse when she had found out, in the very offices this letter was from, that he had left her far less money than she would have expected. In fact, he was in quite serious debt. With two young children to care for, the whole experience had been very traumatic.

Had it not been for a Labour Party emergency fund for political widows in financial straits, Joy wondered what would have happened to them. Although, she reminded herself, leaning back against the sofa cushion, there are valuable lessons to learn from every difficulty.

It was the urgent need to feed her daughters well on very little money which had led to frequent visits to her local wholefood shop, because beans and lentils were the cheapest form of protein. She'd started working shifts there, then making pies and tarts to sell in it and from that had come her career as a vegetarian caterer, which had provided her with an income for many years.

It had also brought her the great love of her life. She'd met her second husband, Natasha's father, Tony Younger, doing the food for a party given by one of his artist friends. He'd complimented her on her baba ganoush and that had been the start of a very happy time, with her catering business transferring seamlessly over to her new life with him in Brisbane.

And, of course, she reflected, taking some more sips of her herbal tea, her interest in vegetarianism had only come about because she'd been so unhappy as a child. If her father hadn't been such an angry man, who resented his only child for being female, she wouldn't have spent so much time in the town library, where a kind librarian had noticed the eager girl who came in every Saturday for a new pile of books and positively encouraged the young Elsie to think of the place as her own.

Browsing in non-fiction one day she'd come across books about yoga and diet which had shaped her whole life, and been the cause of many more conflicts with her father, who thought such interests were scandalously irreligious.

She still had the copy of Indra Devi's *Forever Young, Forever Healthy*, which she'd bought with her first pay packet when she'd started her new life, as Joy, in London. Closing her eyes, she could clearly remember her excited shyness going into Foyles for the first time to find the book. She could hear the tap of her stiletto heels on the lino floor, smell the dusty atmosphere … when Muffin suddenly jumped up onto her lap and she was snapped back into the present moment, just saving her hot tea from spilling everywhere.

Her heart sank. The letter. The envelope was open and she knew who it was from but she just couldn't bring herself to read it. Why on earth were those lawyers contacting her now? It was decades since she'd last had any contact with them. She sat up straight with alarm as she realised that it was now exactly forty years since Robert had died – was the letter something to do with that?

For a moment she was terrified it was to take away the one useful thing he had left her, this house, which she'd had the good sense to hold on to and rent out when they'd moved to Australia. That money had given her the freedom to fly back to the UK when it had gone sadly wrong with Tony and she'd lived there ever since, with a lovely big kitchen for her catering and plenty of room for lodgers, when she needed extra money.

Once again her rational brain was telling her there was no way that could be what the letter was about, because she owned the house, it was in her name, end of story – but she just couldn't stop her imagination spinning out of control.

Just as clearly as she'd seen her young self, she could now picture a homeless old lady wheeling a shopping trolley festooned with bulging Waitrose carrier bags around Tunbridge Wells. Oh, that's Joy. She's harmless, poor old duck. Had a beautiful house once, such a sad story.

Even as she was imagining that, other possible reasons for the letter crowded into her mind. Things she really didn't want to think about. Take charge, Joy Younger, she told herself and visualised herself as a warrior woman, upper arms bulging with muscles, batting the thoughts away with her shield and sword. Thwack! Thwack!

Her mind cleared of unwanted concepts – she'd worked on that technique for years – Joy let her head drop back again, staring up at the blue sky through the glass conservatory roof, puffy white clouds moving swiftly across it. What to do? she asked the universe. What to do?

She knew the 'sensible' thing would be just to read the bloody letter and get it over with, but Joy didn't really do sensible, it was too bound up with the materialistic world of form. She liked to function at a higher energetic level, and she knew an object such as a letter from a solicitor from way back in her unhappy past couldn't possibly bring anything but negativity into her lovely simple and contented present life.

Anything to do with the law equalled aggravation. Her time as an MP's wife had taught her that. And a thorough reading of Dickens in that life-saving library.

Still gazing up, mesmerised by the moving sky, she could have nodded off, but Muffin nuzzled her arm with his head, snapping her back to attention.

'You're quite right, Muffie,' she said, 'I need to do something, don't I? Not just sit here, inert.'

So she put her glasses back on, pulled out the letter and looked at the letterhead again. Immediately an idea occurred to her.

'Perhaps it's some kind of practical joke,' she said out loud. Or a con trick – she'd heard about those letters from people in Nigeria telling you they needed your bank account details so you could be paid a huge lottery prize.

She still couldn't imagine who else, apart from these lawyers, knew Elsie Ainsworth had been her birth name, but it did make sense to check the letter was genuine.

After a moment's pause stroking one of Muffin's silky ears, as he purred in loud approval, she picked up the phone and rang directory enquiries asking for the number of Wilkins, Harald & Held, solicitors, London SW1.

The one they gave her was the same as the number on the letter, so after thanking the nice young man who'd given her the information, she rang it, her right hand finding her rose quartz again and holding on to it tightly.

The phone was answered immediately by a woman's voice, saying: 'Wilkins, Harald & Held, how can I help you?'

Joy quickly pressed the button to disconnect the call and let her hands fall into her lap, still holding the phone.

How unsettling on a sunny Monday morning when you'd been planning to go to yoga as usual, have a cuppa with one of the girls after, and then spend an afternoon in the garden. All the pots needed attention.

'I think I need some help with this, Mr Muff,' she said.

She stood up and went into the sitting room, blinking for a moment as her eyes adjusted to the dark after the brightness of the conservatory. She walked over to the bookcase on the wall opposite the fireplace and took three joss sticks out of a box on the shelf.

After lighting them and blowing out the flame, she placed them in a small holder in front of a large bronze statue of Buddha, the smoke curling up from the glowing embers at the tips.

She stepped back, then reached down to grab her right ankle, pulling up her leg and bracing it against the inner thigh of the other one. Then, after putting her hands into the prayer position against her heart, she closed her eyes and took a deep breath.

'Oooooohhhhmmmmmm ...' she chanted, as she breathed out and Muffin took his place next to her, sitting perfectly still, like a chubbier version of a cat statue in an Egyptian tomb.

As she hummed out the very last of her third om, she heard her home phone ring and then shortly after, her mobile tinkled its little tune, but with her brain gently sinking into theta waves she batted it all away as peripheral noise.

And when her mobile whistled to signal the arrival of a voice message and then buzzed for a text, she didn't even hear them.

Several minutes later, Joy opened her eyes, put her right foot back on the ground and took a moment to enjoy the sensation of her customary calm, balance fully restored. She bowed deeply to the Buddha, then turned and walked purposefully into the conservatory, where she picked up the letter and envelope from the table.

Then, with Muffin trotting along beside her, she went back through the house to the smaller room at the front, which she used as a study.

'What a mess,' she said to Muffin, taking in the dusty piles of paper that had built up on all the flat surfaces, as she bent down to flick the switch on a wall socket. 'I think we need to do a bit of space clearing in here, get rid of this negative energy that is trying to get in, don't you?'

And once the red light indicated the machine was on, she fed the letter and envelope through her shredder.

Thursday, 29 May

Cranbrook

The minute she heard the jaunty raps on Tessa's front door –
knock knock knocketty knock – Natasha ran to answer it.

'Rachie!' she cried, hugging her sister.

'Tashie!' said Rachel with equal enthusiasm. 'So great to
see you, loving the hair. Very Eton crop. Doesn't your neck get
cold?'

'Not in the New York summer, no.'

Rachel laughed. 'Good point. Where's Tessa?'

'Who knows where Tessa is in the space–time continuum?'
said Natasha. 'She was in the kitchen a few minutes ago, but
then she just drifted out.'

Natasha made wafty movements with her arms and
Rachel smiled and nodded in recognition, no need for further
explanation about their older sister's tendency to wander off,
irrespective of where she might be needed at any particular
moment.

How lovely it was to slip back into sister shorthand,
thought Rachel, but then the beeping sound of a reversing
lorry snapped her back into the moment.

'Well, I've got a van full of the garden furniture we're
lending Tessa for this shoot tomorrow, blocking the road out

there, so I'd better find her quick so she can tell me where she wants it.'

As Rachel walked into the hall, big enough to hold a small banquet in, the curved staircase sweeping up, Tessa's crazy murals covering the walls, a set of stag's antlers hanging over a splendid marble fireplace, she was hit by the house envy that struck whenever she visited Tessa Towers.

And the really stupid thing was that the sprawling old rectory with its lofty ceilings, endless space and cosy corners, was probably worth about the same as her cramped London terrace. Less even.

Then she reminded herself it was an hour and a half, or more, to the nearest Ottolenghi and got over it.

'Tess!' she shouted up the stairwell, only to hear an answer from completely the opposite direction.

'Hey, Rachie-roo,' said Tessa, coming up from behind and tapping her on the shoulder.

'Oh, there you are, vagabond,' said Natasha, smiling as her two older sisters hugged warmly, noting with a professional eye how good their two heads – basically the same hair, but one blonde, one brunette – looked side by side, at exactly the same height.

But also feeling a familiar tug of envy that they shared all the same DNA, while she was some kind of half-blood afterthought. You'd never even pick out they were related to her in a line-up. Thanks to her lanky Aussie dad, she stood a good head taller than both of them.

'Where on earth have you been, Tessa?' Natasha asked. 'We were sitting at the kitchen table, I turned around to get the milk and when I looked back you were gone.'

'Oh, I just had to see to something in the garden,' said Tessa, hiding her phone behind her back. She'd taken some lovely pictures of the waterlilies flowering in an old copper water tank, clouds reflected in the still water. She'd had about twenty Likes on Instagram already.

'Good,' said Rachel. 'I hope you were getting some space cleared for the garden furniture I've brought you. There's enough to furnish Kew.'

'Great ...' said Tessa, not sounding quite as excited as Rachel thought she should, 'can I have a look at it?'

'Of course,' said Rachel, 'and you can tell Bill the driver where to put it, because he has to get the truck back to his depot.'

Tessa had no idea where she wanted Bill the driver to put the furniture, because up until the moment Rachel had mentioned it she'd completely forgotten it was coming. The shoot was the next day, she really needed to get organised, but she felt exhausted at the thought of it.

It wasn't that she minded arranging things around the house. Far from it, Tessa could spend whole days tweaking little corners into magic moments of perfectly curated objects. A bunch of long grasses in an old lemonade bottle. A rusty watering can at the foot of a paint-splattered wooden ladder. A bowl of antique marbles.

She could create visual poetry with random stuff, the more knackered-looking the better; it was just the house as a whole that defeated her. It was pretty big and with the three boys constantly leaving things lying around – and Tom wasn't any tidier – it was impossible to keep the place in some kind of frozen state of perfection. And she didn't even like houses that looked like that.

Whenever it had been shot for magazines before Tom was famous, when it was actually about the house, rather than 'TV's Tim Chiminey and his fascinating family home', the art directors had totally got her thing. Her Rousseau-esque mural, featuring all British native flora and fauna, winding up the staircase, had been in the *Telegraph* mag, as well as on that *Interiors* cover.

Now it was expected to look like some kind of luxury hotel and she'd have to be in the bloody pictures too, a human ornament. She groaned inwardly at the thought, her hand flying up to those disastrous grey roots again. Rachel was so lucky to be blonde, her grey just blended in. Thank heavens Tasha was there to help.

An hour later, after Rachel had drafted the burly manager over from the salvage yard to do the heavy lifting, the furniture was finally arranged in various spots around the garden. Tessa regarded the scene thoughtfully, grateful that Rachel was distracted taking pictures of the set-up on her phone while Natasha snapped shots of her doing it with hers. While the two of them were absorbed in their tiny screens, she took the opportunity to head off to the big shed at the back of the yard.

Somewhere in there, there were several interesting bits of old agricultural equipment and a bundle of ex-army blankets, which she could usefully press into service to take the edge off the shiny newness of Rachel's luxury sun loungers and chairs.

It wasn't that she didn't like them. Tessa could see what good quality it all was, and she loved the bold floral prints, plus she was very happy to help her sister promote one of her clients, but there was still a broader issue to consider.

Hunter Gatherer was all about re-using and re-purposing old things, so she needed to make Rachel's brand spanking new furniture blend in more before the shoot. Showing that used and new worked beautifully together would be a good thing for all of them, but it had to look just right. She wasn't going to compromise on that.

Tom might be doing the interview to promote the TV show, but she was going to make sure Hunter Gatherer got a mention too. She was increasingly worried about how he was neglecting the company they had worked so hard together to build up, and one day would have to rely on again. He couldn't expect his moment of telly stardom to last forever.

It couldn't end soon enough for her.

Their pictures posted on Instagram, Twitter and Facebook, Rachel and Natasha gave up waiting for Tessa, who'd done another of her disappearing acts, made themselves some tea and took it back out into the garden.

Rachel stretched out in a hammock made of a tropical leaf–print canvas, which the bloke from the salvage yard had slung up between two trees, and Natasha climbed inside a huge egg-shaped chair constructed from stiff knotted rope.

'This chair's amazing,' she said, putting her head out of the front and looking over at Rachel. 'I feel like I'm in a nest, or a chrysalis, but I can still feel the sun on my skin. I love it.'

'Good, isn't it?' said Rachel, smiling over at her little sister. 'We only won this contract yesterday and being able to say I'd already placed it in a *You* magazine cover story, really helped clinch the deal.'

She allowed herself a moment of pleasure remembering how well the pitch for the Lawn & Stone business had gone the previous morning. She could still see the expression on Simon's face when Arnold Arkwright had stopped him before he could even start on his outline of Rathbone & Associates' many previous triumphs, after she'd finished her presentation.

'Don't waste your breath,' he'd said, in his broad Sheffield accent. 'The lass has convinced me, you're worth a try for this new posh gear we're doing. I'll give you six months and if you've made me more money than you've cost me, we'll sign for longer. If you haven't, you're out.'

She'd been a little disappointed Simon hadn't confirmed her job there and then, but it had to help. Big time.

'That's great, Rach,' said Natasha, 'good job. You always have been a demon pitcher.'

'Thanks,' said Rachel. 'It was super lucky for me that the magazine editor specifically wanted there to be some new stuff in the shots today, that readers could actually buy, as well as all the Hunter Gatherer salvage one-offs.'

'Yes, that's all a bit model's own, isn't it,' said Natasha. 'Belt, model's own. Necklace, model's own. Falling-to-bits deadly dangerous old rotting ladder, model's own.'

Rachel laughed.

'In my world the one-off stuff is more "Tessa found the vintage ladder in a bed of nettles in the South of France."'

'Tessa found the moulding old sofa in a donkey's shed in Turkey.'

'Tessa found the rotted-through unusable copper pots in a toxic-waste dump in Chernobyl.'

'Tessa started collecting old nuns' knickers as a teenager and has used them to create a festive room divider.'

They sat in silence a moment, sipping their tea and enjoying the closeness engendered by making fond fun of the older sister they both adored.

'Where is she now, do you think?' Rachel asked eventually.

'I think she's gone into that wardrobe again,' Natasha replied.

'The one with all the fur coats?' said Rachel. 'And snow on the other side?'

'That's the one,' said Natasha.

They smiled at each other, not needing to say any more. Of course they'd loved C.S. Lewis as kids, like everyone else, but those books were particularly important to them because they'd been among the very small collection they'd been able to take along when they'd spent a year driving around Australia in a VW camper van, with their mum and Natasha's dad, Tony.

He was an art photographer and the road trip had been for a big project he was putting together for an exhibition. There'd been an awful lot of driving across flat red landscape and Tessa and Rachel had made their mum read the books out loud until they had practically known them by heart. Then, when Natasha was old enough, they'd read them to her.

'So when are you going to Mum's?' asked Rachel, reminded of her by association.

'Well, I was going to head down there yesterday, but I got held up in town another day for some meetings, so when Tessa rang in distress about tomorrow's photo shoot I came here instead. Mum's coming over later and staying. Tessa's had this great idea Mum can rustle up one of her fabulous lunch spreads for the whole crew tomorrow.'

They sat quietly again, Rachel flat on her back in the hammock, holding her mug on her stomach, Natasha cross-legged inside the enclosing chair. Neither of them spoke, but they both knew what the other one was thinking. It hung in the air between them, like a giant bubble floating past ready to pop.

Rachel broke first.

'You don't say,' she said, 'Tessa thinking of a nice exhausting job for somebody else to do.'

Natasha was laughing the moment her sister started to speak, knowing exactly what the theme of it would be.

'I know,' she said, 'so out of character for her, getting someone else to do all the hard work.'

'It's hard work wafting at that level, Tash,' said Rachel in a pretend-serious voice.

'Yes, it takes years of study. She's a black belt in drifting about, you know.'

'Has an Olympic gold medal in gliding through.'

They were both yelping with laughter, the spice of complicit guilt making it much funnier than it really was. Throwing her head back too vigorously, Rachel spilled hot tea all over herself.

Realising she'd better get out of the hammock quickly in case the tea ran onto the very expensive fabric and stained it, which would not be a good start with the new client, she threw her legs over the side. But in her haste to leave it, the hammock lurched backwards and deposited her on the grass, before swinging back and hitting her on the back of the head.

Leaping out of the egg chair to help her, Natasha caught her back foot on the edge of it and went crashing to the ground as well, her mug of tea launching into orbit. They lay on the soft overgrown grass side by side laughing hysterically, kicking their legs like a pair of naughty children.

'Hey, Rach,' said Natasha. 'We're actually ROFL-ing.'

'We are too,' said Rachel. 'Race you to be first to put that on Twitter.'

'I thought it first, so I win,' said Natasha.

'You don't own it 'til you've shown it, baby,' said Rachel.

'Do.'

'Don't.'

'Do.'

'Don't don't don't.'

'Do do do, double yours every time ...'

'Ow!' said Rachel suddenly, groping behind her. 'I've landed on something spiky. Ouch, it just got me again. What the hell is that?'

Looking over her shoulder, she found a small branch of dried-up holly.

'Bloody hell,' she said, lifting it up gingerly by one leaf to show Natasha. 'This stuff is deadly. I don't know how people can live in the country, it's so dangerous.'

'Give me the safe and cosy inner city any day,' said Natasha, sitting up and leaning against the bottom of the chair.

Rachel sat up too, looking around in case there was any more holly waiting to ambush her and their eyes met. They started laughing again. Both of them had tea splattered down the front of their clothes. Rachel glanced back to see if the hammock had copped it, but it seemed to be OK. That was a relief.

'That'll teach us to be nasty about our big sister,' said Natasha.

'Karma,' said Rachel. 'But it's nothing we haven't said to her face.'

'In fact we've said a lot worse over the years,' said Natasha.

'How long being back together did it take for us to be reduced to the mental age of my daughters?' asked Rachel.

'Over an hour, which is quite good going for us and now that you've mentioned them tell me about your gorgeous girlies. When am I going to see the little poppets? Could your bro pair dude bring them down here after school tomorrow? Then you could stay tonight and Mum can have a cosy dinner with her three girls, which she would so adore, and we can all help on the shoot tomorrow – Tessa will love that – and then we can hang out here for the whole weekend. Daisy and

Ari would enjoy it here much more than they would being at Mum's because they'll see their big boy cousins too. It would be like a spring Christmas.'

Rachel looked at her younger sister's face, its strong bone structure emphasised by her new short haircut, as she chattered on, radiant with excitement. Her mind raced, separating out all the different things Natasha was saying and their associated problems.

Obviously, she was heading back to town later that afternoon, because she had to go into work in the morning. Now she'd won Rathbone & Associates this big new account, she had a lot to do on it – and she wanted to make sure Simon saw her doing it. She needed this job confirmed. With a raise. And ideally a four-day week.

And as for the weekend, she already had plans for that. Plans she didn't particularly want to go into with Tasha, or anyone else in the family for that matter.

'Well,' she said, cautiously, 'the thing is, it's Michael's weekend to have the girls. He picks them up from me when he finishes work on Friday and I don't have them again until after school on Monday night.'

Natasha's face fell so dramatically, Rachel thought she might be about to burst into tears.

'But I thought you were all coming down to Mum's this weekend. That was the plan.'

It was the first Rachel had heard of it. She'd known Natasha was in the UK from the text on Monday, but she'd heard nothing else since and had been too caught up with the Lawn & Stone pitch to follow it up herself.

'Was it?' she asked, in genuine confusion.

'Didn't Mum tell you?' said Natasha.

'No,' said Rachel. 'I didn't even know you were coming over until your text the other day and no one filled me in on any other plans. I was waiting to hear from you.'

'Great,' said Natasha. 'I took a job in London specially to come over to see you all before my Paris shoot next week, and Mum and Tessa couldn't even remember to tell you.'

She was silent for a moment, staring into space.

'I can't not see the girls, Rachel,' she burst out. 'It's such an opportunity for me to spend some extended time with them. I love it so much when they come in and wake me up in the morning.'

Rachel laughed.

'Oh, the gloss soon goes off that,' she started to say, but stopped abruptly, realising that 6.00 a.m. wake-up calls from excited little girls were a sweet problem her thirty-seven-year-old, very single younger sister might never have.

That thought gave her a pang. It would be very hard-hearted of her to deny Natasha some cuddly love from Ari and laughs with Daisy. But what about her needs? They mattered too. What to do? She opted to play for time.

'I'll text Michael, right now,' she said. 'He can be a pain about arrangement changes, because his life is so micro-planned, but the girls would hate to miss you too. In fact, they'd kill me. They were furious enough when they heard I was coming down here today, because I might see their adored boy cousins without them and when they find out you were here too, I'll really get it in the neck.'

Natasha was grinning. It meant so much that Daisy and Ariadne didn't forget her between their way too rare meetings. Her fridge in New York was covered with their drawings and she bought them funny little trinkets and souvenirs wherever she went for work.

She was particularly looking forward to giving Daisy the present she'd found her on her last location job in Rajasthan; a backpack made from a woven plastic fertiliser sack with a picture of a pig and the words 'Big Pig Brand' on it. For Ariadne, she had a doll in a pink sari.

Seeing the broad smile on her sister's face at the prospect of spending time with her nieces, Rachel knew, with a sinking feeling, that she'd have to do the right thing.

'There isn't a very good signal out here,' she said, glancing down at her phone. 'I'll go back to the house and call Michael now, get this sorted.'

The signal was actually fine in the garden, but she needed some space to get her head round this. She was fairly sure Michael would capitulate about arrangements, as his belief in the importance of 'family' was just about the only thing which would override his phobic distrust of spontaneity, but she'd have to listen to some irritating complaining first.

Rachel sighed as she scrolled down to his number, hoping he wouldn't use this situation to lay on one of his full guilt-trips and to air, yet again, his disbelief at her decision to break up their cosy little family unit the way she had, but if he did, she'd deal with it the way she always did: not listening.

She was more concerned about how she was going to tell the other person whose weekend arrangements were about to be wrecked by this change of plan. That would be quite another kind of phone call.

One that needed to be made in private.

Joy sent a prayer of thanks up to the Higher Power. To be sitting at this table drinking tea with all three of her precious daughters was the greatest blessing she could think of. She looked around at them, smiling and chatting, so at ease with each other, and relished their beautiful differences.

The oldest, Tessa, with her dark hair and green eyes. The Celtic colouring, which was about the one good thing she'd inherited from her own parents, and the fey Irish temperament to go with it, which she'd figured out came from her maternal great-grandmother.

She remembered hearing her aunt whispering to her mother about it once, when her father wasn't around. 'The sight ...' she'd said. 'Granny O'Reilly had the sight.'

Joy had tried to ask her mother about it later, but her mother had got angry and told her that she'd heard nothing of the kind. And if she ever mentioned it again, she'd tell her father and she knew what that would mean. Young Joy, or Elsie as she was then, knew only too well and had kept quiet.

It wasn't until years later, when she was introduced to tarot cards, pendulums and the I Ching by someone she'd met through the food co-op, that she'd finally allowed herself to explore such things, although she still never talked openly about it. The girls teased her about being 'woo woo' but that was as far as it went. Just Mum's funny little ways.

But she'd long suspected Tessa also had the gift – she even looked like the old picture of Granny O'Reilly she remembered on her mother's chest of drawers – but she'd never brought it up with her. The unseen was often better left unsaid.

Joy's gaze moved over to Rachel. Her bright and sharp-witted middle daughter. So like her late father with her blonde hair and merry eyes. Always at the centre of whatever was happening, always the one to get things done. Even as a child she'd bossed her big sister about. It was a shame Robert hadn't lived to see her grow up, so like him, with her quick brain and quicker tongue.

Then her baby, Natasha. So different looking from the other two with her father's height, straight dark hair and high cheekbones. Tony had always made Joy think of a Native American chief with his strong jawline and deep-set dark eyes. Natasha was the feminine version, with a swan neck and those long loose limbs, although with this new haircut, cropped at the back and sides like the men of Joy's youth, she looked rather boyish. Anima and animus. The two energies in one. Very powerful.

Joy tuned back into the conversation and picked up that Rachel was telling a story about getting to work and finding she had two different shoes on, which was making the other two roar with laughter.

So like Rachel, thought Joy. She had that brain like a Swiss clock, never forgot anything, but was pathologically late and always looked a bit untidy. She had a big brown stain on the front of her white shirt now, Joy noticed, smiling to herself. As a little girl she'd go off to school as neat as a pin and come back looking like a compost heap.

Tessa, on the other hand, had always returned looking as immaculate as when she'd set off and she still looked exquisite whatever she put on. So calm on the outside, but, unlike Rachel, she'd never been able to concentrate on more than one thing at a time. Not in a stupid way, she just thought about each thing very intensely, one after another, whereas Rachel could keep a multitude of ideas tumbling in her head at once like a juggler.

And Natasha? She was a bit of both. She had Tessa's ability to concentrate, mixed with Rachel's energy and flexible brain. She was always on time, perfectly turned out and full of bright ideas when she got there. It was a dynamic combination.

How interesting children were, thought Joy. And soon her grandsons would be home from school. She saw them a lot and so enjoyed noticing the minute daily progressions of their development, and she'd be seeing her granddaughters the next day too, what a bounty.

'Hey, Mumsie,' Rachel was saying. 'Ground Control to Planet Joy, can you read me? Over ...'

'Yes, darling,' said Joy, smiling at her, always so cheeky. 'I was just counting my blessings.'

'Well, this blessing has to go, my taxi's just arrived, but I'll be back tomorrow, and so will the girls.'

'I can't think of anything nicer than having all my family together, thank you so much for making it happen, Natasha darling.'

Natasha darling? thought Tessa. Really? All she'd had to do was get on a business-class flight over from New York and then swan down to the country. I'm the one providing beds and food for the five thousand, in between enduring an intrusive photographic shoot in my home. I think I'm doing my bit too.

If only you all knew what I was giving up to be here this weekend, thought Rachel.

If I hadn't chosen to live on the other side of the Atlantic Ocean we could all meet like this every weekend, thought Natasha. It's my fault this is such a big deal. Normal families see each other all the time.

Rachel got up from the table and everyone went out into the hall to see her off. She kissed them all, with a special hug for Natasha.

'I can't believe I'm going to see you again tomorrow, Tash,' she said. 'What a treat. I'll try to get off work early so I can bring the girls down straight after school. My boss owes me a favour.'

Tessa had just started towards the front door to let her out, when it opened and Tom walked in.

'Blimey,' he said, 'what a welcoming committee. A hall full of beautiful women. Hey, Natasha, I didn't know you were coming today.'

He gave her a warm hug and Natasha felt oddly shy. She always forgot how charismatic her brother-in-law was when she hadn't seen him for a while. No wonder he was so successful on TV.

He wasn't super good-looking – and she was used to being around stratospherically beautiful people, for heaven's sake – he just had something about him. Not flashy, or smooth, just an inner confidence that was very attractive. Tessa was a lucky woman.

'Well, I'm just off to the station, Timmy dear,' said Rachel, pecking Tom on the cheek, 'but you'll be lucky enough to see me again tomorrow night. Bye all.'

Rachel settled into the back of the taxi and fished out her phone. Who should she ring first? she wondered, as she tapped to check her Instagram. A hundred and five Likes on the hammock, not bad. Two hundred and thirty-seven on the egg chair – excellent – and some very useful feedback in the comments. So far the edgier pieces were getting a stronger reaction. Interesting. She'd write them up for Simon and the clients, a bit of free market research. Another little credit towards confirming her job.

So the phone calls ... Should it be the ecstatically happy one to the girls? They'd just be home from school about now. Or the other, really disappointing one?

Well, it would be disappointing for her. It would make it real that she wasn't going to see him tomorrow night. She shouldn't make assumptions that Link would feel the same way, but it was only fair to let him know as soon as possible, so he could make other plans for his weekend.

He answered immediately.

'Hey,' he said.

Rachel's stomach and all areas near it did a somersault. She felt slightly sick.

'Hey,' she said back.

'Wassup?' he asked.

She exhaled, a sort of sigh/harrumph combined noise she hoped conveyed her discontent. Words seemed too banal when she spoke to him. In fact talking to Link on the phone was torture, all she wanted to do was touch him.

'I can't see you this weekend,' she said, in a rush.

He was silent, she could just hear him breathing.

'OK,' he said eventually.

'It's such a bore ...' Rachel started, finding her voice, part of her wanting to explain, to give him all the gory details, but really more glad that she didn't have to. They had been going to get together, now they weren't. That was it.

'Another time, soon, eh?' said Link.

Rachel had an idea.

'What are you doing tonight?' she asked him.

There was another moment's silence from his end.

'When?' he asked.

'Eight?' said Rachel.

'I'll text you,' said Link.

'Great,' said Rachel, her heart beating fast. 'I've just got to check something as well, I'll text you, too. See you later, I hope.'

'Hmmm,' he said, and then he hung up.

Rachel checked her calendar. Thursday – was that the night Branko worked in the wine bar? Yes, dammit. She scrolled through B on her contacts, wondering which of her babysitters was still young enough to be available, but not in a big exam year so still allowed out on a school night.

She was just composing a text to the mother of a fourteen-year-old girl who lived a few doors down when a text came through from Link.

'Not good tonight. Let me know when you can do a weekend. And come by the shop and see me. L x'

Rachel read it with tears pricking her eyelids. He was right. It was a tacky idea, she wished she'd never suggested it, she'd just been so disappointed to miss out on the weekend and thought it would be better to see him briefly than not see him at all. But what was 'briefly'? A quick one?

She stared blankly out of the taxi window at the countryside, beautiful in the late afternoon sun, feeling dirty with self-disgust for a moment and then deciding to get over it.

Hearing his breathing down the phone had lit her inner pilot light and made her act rashly, that was all. She was a spontaneous person. She couldn't help that, and suspected it was one of the things Link liked about her. But maybe this was a hint that he wasn't actually much more spontaneous than Michael. Which was pretty funny, because if you put the two of them in the same room you wouldn't think they could possibly have anything in common.

But at least he'd saved her the cash for the babysitter. That would have been at least £40. What was she thinking even considering splashing out cash like that, when she could barely pay the mortgage?

There she went again, acting on impulse. Where did attractive spontaneity end and rash impetuousness begin? Maybe Michael was right and she was all too often at the wrong end of that range. Rachel closed her eyes tight to make the thought go away. If she let herself think about all that, she might start wondering if she'd been foolishly impulsive when she'd ended her marriage for no more reason than she'd come to find her children's father boring.

Even going on a date with Michael in the first place had been something of a dare, when a work colleague had told her about this eligible friend of her fiancé's: good-looking, sporty, doing well at a big insurance company and very single.

'But he'd be much too straight for you, Rachel,' Sara had said, adjusting the huge diamond engagement ring her boyfriend had recently given her, and holding out her hand to admire it. 'I know you only like arty men. Just such a shame they never have any money.'

Rachel had risen to the bait like a trout. She didn't like being pigeon-holed. She'd show her she could like a bloke with a proper job and a flashy car just as much as Sara did. But why did she have to show her all the way to the altar and then twice to the maternity unit at St Mary's?

Rachel sighed. Of course she couldn't unwish meeting and marrying Michael, she scolded herself, because that would be to unwish her darling girls and no man could have given her more gorgeous treasures than them.

Which reminded her, she still had that happy call to make. And Daisy's scream when she heard she was going to spend the weekend with her big boy cousins and her beloved Auntie Tashie banished all other thoughts.

Sydney Street

Simon Rathbone was sitting at his desk thinking about Rachel. He had a large unlit cigar in his mouth. It was a nice one, an Ecuadorian *habanos* he'd picked up in St James after lunch.

He took it out of his mouth and lifted it to his nose, inhaling the sweet aroma of the tobacco leaves. Mmmm, it was good. A little hint of chocolate in it.

He really wanted to light the thing, to help himself think. It was his bloody office, no one else was there, or scheduled to come in, he should be able to smoke if he wanted to. But it wasn't his building and no smoking was a condition of the lease, and he really didn't fancy losing the six months' deposit he'd had to pay to secure the space, or the nightmare of having to find somewhere new.

There was a high price to pay for the prestige of having Sydney Street on his company letterhead and rents were only going one way. Up. Terrifyingly up. A couple of businesses which had been there for years had moved out of the street already that month.

He gently pressed the cigar between his thumb and forefinger. The perfect combination of smoothness and firmness, with a very slight give. Like the inside of a beautiful woman's thigh. Uh-oh, Rathbone, don't go there. So don't.

Thinking along those lines really wasn't going to help him make a rational decision on what to do about Rachel. Too late, he was already imagining what it would feel like to run his fingers down her thighs. Or better, up them.

God she was attractive. So slender around the middle and then swelling out so pleasingly. That very feminine body shape which seemed to be becoming endangered. Sometimes it took all his willpower not to reach out and run his hand over her hip. Dangerous curves, indeed. But it wasn't just her figure that was giving him sleepless nights, it was her ... her Rachelness.

Most of his staff were terrified of him, or too stupid to realise they should be. Rachel was properly nervous – and with more good reason than she knew – that she wasn't going to make it past her six-month trial period, but it didn't make her frightened of him. She still said exactly what she thought. It was so refreshing.

Especially as it was always worth listening to. He was learning a lot from her about digital media and her brilliant idea for the two press trips and the ideal location for them, plus the final coup of the shoot in *You* magazine, had definitely won them the Lawn & Stone contract the day before. And it was exactly the kind of new business Rathbone & Associates needed.

It was all very well representing the elite end of the interiors market, but a lot of his clients were rather elite about paying their bloody bills. Gentlemen's agreements and all that cock. The upscale arm of a big cashed-up company with a proper accounts department would make such a welcome change – and Rachel had immediately grasped every aspect of what was needed to win the account.

Everything about her presentation had been spot on, right down to the way she'd directed it at the old duffer. Simon had caught him checking out her rear view as well, the dirty bugger.

Took one to know one, he reminded himself, running his hands back over his hair. Was it chance or judgement that had made her wear a wickedly fitted skirt for that meeting?

Every time she'd turned away to look at the PowerPoint display on the boardroom wall, Simon had to pinch his own leg under the table. When she'd dropped the light pointer and bent down to pick it up, he'd completely lost track of what they were talking about.

Thinking about Rachel bending over again was not helping him clear his head where she was concerned. He'd never felt this way before about one of his staff, which was a good thing, as they were mostly women.

He had always made a point of keeping his business and private lives completely separate, to the point where he knew there was conjecture among the ranks about whether he was gay. They'd never met a girlfriend, or heard him talk about one, so they made their own assumptions.

He didn't give a damn what they thought. In fact he rather enjoyed the sport of it. He made a point of greeting the campest stylists and decorators who came to the office with lavish warmth and then covertly watched his staff exchanging significant glances with each other. *Look, he is gay! I told you!*

Simon grinned to himself thinking about it, rolling the cigar between his fingers. He must get one of the more glamorous magazine editors to come in soon – there were one or two who fancied their chances with him – so he could make a big fuss of her, get them chattering about that.

He knew exactly what he'd say to his PA on the way out: 'Not sure if I'll be back after lunch, Sophie ...'

What a tasty morsel that would be for her to share with the rest of them, when he'd gone. He chuckled, then, remembering what he was supposed to be thinking about, dropped his head into his hands, elbows on the desk.

He really had to come to a realistic decision about whether he could control his lustful thoughts and increasingly tender feelings towards a staff member whose input he could see would make a serious contribution to the business going forward.

Rachel was across that social media stuff like no one else he knew in their section of the market and while he still didn't feel entirely confident with it, he did understand how important it was. And ever more so.

He'd set up a secret account on Instagram so he could see exactly what Rachel did on there that was so popular. Not in a stalkerish way, it was professional interest – *ELLE Decoration* had put her in their list of 'taste makers' after all – but he did slightly dread coming across a selfie on there of her snuggled up with some handsome dude. That wasn't professional and he knew it.

And if he couldn't control himself and did something inappropriate in a heated moment he could lose a lot more. Thank god it was months until the Christmas drinks. Simon 'The Iceberg' Rathbone as the subject of a sexual harassment suit would have the whole decorating world in delighted hysterics.

Mind you, he thought, if he did bid her a professional farewell after the six-month trial was up, at least then he could ask her out with impunity. For a moment he enjoyed the image of looking at Rachel over his favourite table at The Delaunay and then snorted at his own stupidity.

She'd hardly be thrilled to have dinner with the man who'd just taken the food from her children's mouths. And that was another thing that made this ridiculous teenage crush so out of character. Simon really couldn't be bothered with children. He was sure it was very nice if you had your own, but other people's were noisy, messy things who ruined restaurants and parks with their screaming and squawking, and put mucky hand prints all over the paintwork.

She'd brought her daughters into the office once on a 'go to work with Mummy' day she'd claimed the school had insisted on, although none of the other staff had brought their brats in. That had dampened his ardour for a while. No one had got anything done.

He'd found one of his account managers painting the toenails of the younger child bright yellow and the older one had entertained herself by photocopying her face on his Xerox machine about fifty times. And there were some other printouts he didn't think were of a face. He'd been tempted to ask Rachel to pay for the wasted paper.

But then she'd come in a couple of days later wearing a tightly belted navy blue dress, with buttons down the front – what did they call those things? a shirtdress? – and he'd had to avoid her all day, for fear of being revealed as the mooning swain she'd turned him into.

Agghhh, it was no good, every time he tried to approach the problem as a simple HR issue his brain was distracted by thoughts like that. He stood up suddenly, the cigar back between his teeth, and, after taking his keys, sunglasses and gold Dunhill lighter out of his desk drawer, he walked out of his office.

He needed some fresh air.

At five after five he was not surprised to see, as he popped his head around the door of the big shared office on the same floor as his, that all of his employees' desks were already deserted. He knew they'd have excuses if he called them on it in the morning – and he would dammit – but he knew where they were all off to. Collecting the kids, the hairdressers, some essential shopping in Peter Jones.

He hired his staff as much for their looks, breeding, contact books and perfect manners, as any particular talent, so he knew what he got in return. A very thin veneer of work ethic. They all arrived perfectly on time, the need to be punctual had been so drilled into them as children, but they seemed to think that meant it was fine for them to leave on the dot as well.

That's why Rachel was such a gem. She didn't have the aristocratic connections that appealed to the multitude of snobs in their business, but she certainly had the looks and the savoir-faire – and she had the hunger. That's what he recognised in her.

She was always late getting to work, arriving hot and bothered in a chaos of bags, take-away coffees and outraged explanations about the Tube, but once she was there, she gave it everything.

He wondered where that came from in her. He had a pretty good idea in his own case, but he'd love to know what had put the stone in her shoe. Sounded like she'd had rather a rackety upbringing from what he'd been able to gather, including a year rattling around Australia in one of those camper van things, but she was so smart those experiences had stretched her horizons and made her thinking more imaginative.

And one of her sisters was married to that chimneypiece chap who was on television now – hence the *You* mag story. He'd done some very good salvage work before all that had kicked off, Simon remembered. He'd seen a story about their house in a magazine years ago.

It had looked rather filthy in an arty way, as he recalled it, messed-up sofas with the wadding coming out, falling-to-bits fabrics and revolting old stuffed birds, but there was no denying there was a certain bohemian style in the family, and that roughed-up look was very hot right down the supply chain now, nearly into the high-street stores.

Simon was beginning to think that if he went into another restaurant with an exposed brick wall he might have to punch it.

Reaching to open the front door, he looked down at his right hand and flexed his boxing knuckles. He still gave the punching bag a good going over every week at his gym. Great way to get the tension out and keep the ageing bod in trim. Did the skipping too. Nothing like a good sweat to get the brain cleared and doing plenty of that made up for the occasional puff on a cigar.

He paused outside the building, at the top of the steps down to the pavement, and lit the cigar. Oh, the joy as that sweet smoke filled his mouth. He rolled it around in a moment of pure bliss before blowing it out again.

Standing there with his eyes closed savouring the aromas as the vapour left his mouth and drifted up past his nostrils, he hadn't realised someone had walked up to him.

'Having a golden moment?' said Rachel.

Simon's eyes popped open. He let out a stupid bark of a laugh, which sounded forced even to him.

'Been trapped in my office for hours gagging for this,' he said, settling it between his teeth and looking down on her from his vantage point on the top step. He was glad of the distance it afforded him.

Maybe it's true about him being gay, thought Rachel, looking at the cigar wagging in his mouth. He was right into that phallic symbol. She wondered if he knew the staff called him Arthur behind his back – or Martha when he'd done something they thought particularly camp.

'So what are you doing coming back here so late?' he asked, rolling the cigar around to the front of his mouth and taking it out, hoicking his forefinger round it and holding it against his sternum.

'It's barely even five yet,' said Rachel, knowing full well it was at least ten past.

'Most of your colleagues have already headed off,' said Simon.

'Really? My working day doesn't finish until six,' said Rachel, deciding to go for it, big time.

She'd come straight to the office after getting back up to town from Tessa's place, expressly in the hope that her boss would see her do so. She knew all the slackers would be halfway back to Fulham by now. Might as well lay it on a bit thicker.

'And I need to pick up some stuff I want to go through at home tonight.'

OK, that might be over-egging it, but she really wanted to leave the office a bit early the next day. If she couldn't see Link, she was going to make the absolute most of the family weekend. Ideally she'd like to pick the girls up from school and head straight down there.

A smile twitched at the corner of Simon's mouth. What does she want? he thought. This will be amusing.

'Remind me where you've been all day,' he said, coming down the steps so he was on the same level as her. He kept the cigar by his chest as a kind of shield to stop himself in case he had an overwhelming urge to lunge.

'Getting things prepped for the *You* magazine shoot,' she said, 'for Lawn & Stone.'

'Ah yes,' said Simon, who knew exactly where she'd been, 'at your sister's house.'

He emphasised the word 'sister' to needle her. They both knew the promise of the *You* magazine shoot had clinched the Lawn & Stone deal, but it was too good to resist.

'Yes, that's right,' replied Rachel, feeling like Serena Williams returning Roger Federer's 264 km/h serve. She was

tempted to do the grunt. 'That house you remembered from
Interiors ...'

'How did it go?' asked Simon, trying not to smile as broadly
as he wanted to.

'Well, the shoot's actually tomorrow,' said Rachel. 'I just
went down today to install the furniture. It looks great, but
I'd really like to go back in the morning, to make sure it all
goes well. If you wouldn't mind me being out of the office
again ...'

The idea had only occurred to her while she was talking;
that the ideal way to get the most out of the shoot for the
client and maximise the family weekend was for her to spend
the day there again. Branko could bring the girls down on
the train after school. Simon hadn't said no yet, so she kept
going.

'It would be so awful if the magazine came out and the
furniture wasn't featured and we'd have to explain to the
client why they'd paid to have it shipped down, and it would
be a good idea for me to be there anyway, to keep an eye on
things and make sure it doesn't get damaged.'

'Judging by what I've seen of their house, your sister and
brother-in-law would prefer the furniture if it looked as
though it had been through a small hurricane.'

Rachel couldn't help laughing.

'Yes, they do like things to have the "character" of use,
those two,' she said, 'but the magazine has issued strict
instructions that they want new things in the shoot, as well as
all the rusted iron and frayed canvas from the salvage yard, so
she and Tom will have to go along with it. They do rather take
patina to the next level.'

'Actual dirt?' said Simon.

Rachel laughed again.

'It might look a little grubby, but it does really work when you see it all together. You should come down sometime and have a look. There's some amazing things in the salvage yard. I've often thought we should persuade Tom that he needs a PR company for it, now he's so tied up with the telly thing.'

Simon's heart did a little dance. She was so like him in that way. Always seeing the angle.

'Why don't I come tomorrow?' said Simon, the words out of his mouth before he'd even known he'd thought them. What had he just said? 'I've got a breakfast thing, but we could go down mid-morning. We wouldn't need to be there for the whole thing, would we? Just long enough to make sure they use the Lawn & Stone stuff, and it would be good for me to meet the *You* people and, as you say, I could see the house – I can probably get them some location shoot gigs as well, that's very well paid – and we can do a pincer movement on Tom with your PR idea.'

Now he was just babbling, but he'd started this. He couldn't back down.

Rachel's head was racing at the same speed. How could she say no? She'd just sold it to him as a work trip rather than a crafty day off, so it would have to be one. And maybe if Simon saw how fabulous her sister's house was, and if her mum, Tom and Natasha were in full charisma flow, and if Tessa could just float around being beautiful among it all, then perhaps he would see what an amazing asset she was to his business and confirm her in the job.

She'd just have to make sure he left well before the girls arrived. She didn't want to remind him about Daisy photocopying her bottom that time.

'Yes,' she said, mustering fake enthusiasm, 'that would be great. I'll check the train times.'

'I'll drive us,' said Simon, mouth on autopilot again, brain already wondering how on earth he was going to get through a car journey with Rachel in close proximity.

But she was nodding in agreement.

He'd just have to cope.

Friday, 30 May

Queen's Park, London, 9.07 a.m.

The door was wide open but Link didn't seem to be in the shop when Rachel walked in.

'Anyone here?' she called out.

'Hey,' said a voice nearby and turning towards it, Rachel saw him kneeling on the floor next to an upturned bicycle.

He smiled up at her, a spanner in one hand. Something inside her fluttered and for a moment she just stood there gazing down at his lovely face.

But then he was up, wrapping his arms around her.

'Mmmm,' he said, nuzzling his head against hers and kissing her neck. 'Where have you been, pretty lady?'

Rachel couldn't answer. Her heart was beating too hard, her breath shortening. She pressed herself into his embrace, the side of her face against his chest, inhaling the glorious smell of him. Freshly washed T-shirt, slightly sweaty man inside it.

Link pulled away and bending down slightly, lifted her chin with his finger and looked right into her eyes.

'I miss you when I don't see you,' he said.

Then he kissed her. Really kissed her, until Rachel thought she might stagger and fall over. She put her hands on his shoulders and pulled back.

'This is the first chance I've had,' she said. 'And I've got to get off to work in a minute, but I wanted to come in and say hi.'

'You OK?' asked Link.

She nodded.

'I'm sorry about this weekend ...' Rachel started, but he shook his head, smiling gently.

'It's all right,' he said. 'Stuff happens. Let me know when you can make it. I'm not going anywhere.'

'Well, hopefully next week. I'll text you, as soon as I can, to confirm it.'

'Great,' said Link, reaching both his arms over his head and moving them from side to side.

His T-shirt – 'Supergrass 1999' it said across the front – stretched across his chest and lifted up from his jeans to reveal a slice of hard, flat belly and a line of hair going down from his navel. Rachel experienced a stab of pure lust. She was going to call Michael to double check he was having the girls next weekend the minute she left the shop.

'My shoulders are sore,' said Link, bringing his arms down and rotating each one in its socket. 'Rode it hard coming in this morning. Where's your bike?'

Rachel felt her cheeks growing a little pink.

'Oh, I'm getting the Tube today. I'm going straight on to my sister's in the country and I'd rather have the bike back at home ready for Monday morning.'

Which was a massive lie. She'd be getting the Tube on Monday like she always did. Bakerloo line to Paddington, Circle line to South Ken, job done. She had tried cycling to work. That's why she'd come into the shop and bought the bike in the first place – well, that and the handsome young dude she'd noticed in there and looked out for every time she passed, which was pretty often as her favourite neighbourhood café was right next door.

He'd smiled at her one morning – first when she'd walked past en route to the café and then again on her way back holding her coffee – and she'd gone in the following weekend and ordered the bike. Which had meant he'd needed her phone number to let her know when it was ready.

'Does your husband need a bike as well?' he'd asked, glancing up at her with a mock-innocent cheeky expression, as he wrote her details in the orders book.

'I don't have a husband at the moment,' Rachel had replied, smiling back at him.

'Good,' he'd said, closing the book with a snap. 'Then perhaps I can call you anyway … not just about the bike?'

'You certainly can,' Rachel had said, feeling quite brazen. She didn't think she'd ever been so blatantly picked up. And she loved it. Especially as he had called her – that very afternoon. They'd been seeing each other ever since.

It was a few months now. Months of simple, easy times together. No complications, no expectations, but not just a casual sex set-up. In its own way, her time with Link was probably the most romantic Rachel had ever spent with someone. He was so blissfully uncomplicated. He said exactly what he was thinking and feeling when he was thinking and feeling it, never playing games with her head.

She sometimes thought it might be the best relationship she'd ever had with a man, which was why she didn't want to change anything about it. Or tell anyone about him.

And why she hadn't been able to bring herself to tell him that the bike thing hadn't really worked out for her. The first time she'd hacked in to town from home on it, she'd arrived at the office in such a mess, her hair flat from the helmet, her skin stinking of exhaust fumes, her clothes a crumpled mess, that Simon had laughed out loud when he saw her.

She had friends who cycled everywhere, with their heels and fresh clothes in a bag on the back, but it was all Rachel could do to get herself dressed once in the morning. The one time she'd tried that changing lark, she'd got to work to find she had the trousers, shoes, jacket and belt in her bag – but no shirt. She'd had to spend the day in her sweaty T-shirt.

She still loved the idea of cycling – at weekends, in the summer and preferably in a flat park – but the two-wheeled commute just wasn't for her. So it was a matter of finding the right moment to explain that to Link, who still happily believed she was another convert to his mission to get the whole of London cycling for health and sustainability.

He even thought she was managing to service the bike herself, when in fact the only times she ever got on the thing was when she spent weekends at his place and they'd ride down to Richmond together. She would have to tell him the truth sometime, but when she was with him she never wanted to spoil the moment.

She glanced at her watch. 'I'd better head off,' she said, pulling him towards her for one last hug, so she could remember the feeling of his strong, hard body next to hers.

He pulled her closer, breathing into her ear. She could feel his hard-on pressing tight against her stomach. She groaned slightly.

'Oh, you're making it difficult for me to leave,' she said.

He chuckled and nibbled gently at the lobe of her ear.

'Just a reminder to sort that weekend out, OK?' he said.

'I'll sort it,' she said.

And then with a final quick kiss on the lips, she forced herself to walk out the door.

Cranbrook, 9.48 a.m.

'Tessa! Tessa! Where are you?'

Natasha had searched every corner of the house for her sister and was now looking in the garden. Tom had no idea where she was either. There was less than fifteen minutes until the crew from the magazine was due to arrive and Natasha really wanted to have Tessa's hair done before they showed up. The make-up could wait until they'd chosen clothes and locations, but with the state of Tessa's roots, she needed to get going on her head as soon as possible.

Irritation was setting in. Natasha was delighted to be able to help out doing her sister's hair and make-up for this shoot, but she didn't think it was fair that she should have to track her down first. Tessa was the one who was going to benefit from it, so she could at least make a small effort to cooperate.

It just went to show how detached from the realities of making a living Tessa had become, thought Natasha. Most people she knew would have been sitting in a chair ready ages ago. Rachel would have approached it like a military campaign, with a clipboard and a meticulously timed action plan.

With no sign of Tessa in the front or back garden, the greenhouse, the orchard, the vegetable patch, the garage or the potting shed, Natasha headed over to the salvage yard.

It was pretty amazing, the stuff they had there, she thought, picking her way through a maze of red and slate roof tiles all neatly lined up. She stopped for a moment to take it all in. There were ranks of old stone garden statues covered in lichen, doors of many vintages, copper tanks in various stages of verdigris, a regiment of old radiators. It would all go for a fortune in New York.

'Tess!' yelled Natasha, tripping over an old watering can and starting to feel properly grumpy. 'Where the heck are you?'

The burly young man who had helped with the furniture the day before came out of one of the sheds, a pile of long floorboards balanced on one shoulder.

'Are you looking for Mrs Chenery?' he asked.

'Oh, hi, Jack,' said Natasha. 'Yeah, I am. Have you seen her?'

He smiled, a rather insolent look in his eye suggesting he was used to the boss's wife wandering about the yard vaguely and found it amusing.

'The last time I saw her, she was heading towards the big barn at the back over there,' he said, gesturing with his head.

'Recently?' asked Natasha.

'About ten minutes ago. I reckon she's probably still there. Sometimes she's in there for hours.'

'Thanks,' said Natasha, walking in the direction he'd indicated, picking her way across the rough ground, skirting around a herd of claw-foot baths, and serried rows of pottery chimney pots. They made her think of the terracotta army.

It was dark in the barn after the bright morning light outside and Natasha stood just inside the entrance for a moment while her eyes adjusted, wondering what the varied dark shapes would turn out to be.

She couldn't see Tessa, but she could hear someone moving around on the far left-hand side.

'Tess? Is that you?' she called out.

'Oh, hi, Tash,' Tessa's voice answered. 'I'm just coming.'

Natasha headed towards the direction the reply had come from, past what she could now see were old mantelpieces. Further on it changed into ranks of cupboards, shelves and dressers and at the very back she found Tessa, crouching on the ground going through a pile of dirty-looking, chequered nylon storage bags.

'Hi,' she said nervously, looking up at Natasha, who burst out laughing. Tessa was such a mess she practically had bits of straw sticking out of her hair.

'Look at you!' said Natasha. 'Have you forgotten you're having your picture taken in ...' she glanced down at the chunky diver's watch on her left wrist, 'well, under five minutes, they're due to arrive. They might be here already. You look like you've been helping Tom sweep some chimneys. What are you doing down there?'

Tessa looked apprehensive, as if caught in the act, a frown line appearing between her eyebrows.

'I'm just looking for some hessian feed bags I know are in here somewhere. They've got really good typography on them and I'm going to put cushions in them and place them in the hammock and on the chairs. It just all looks too much like a John Lewis catalogue the way it is. I want to help Rachel out, but the way it looks at the moment, it's just not us. We don't do *new* here, Tash.'

'The way you look right now, darling, no one's going to doubt that. You've got to get tidied up, Tess, and fast. I need to get your hair done. I've been looking everywhere for you. Come on.'

She put her hand out and after one last regretful look at the bags, Tessa grasped her sister's fingers and rose to her feet.

When they got back near the house they could hear Tom welcoming the photographic crew at the front door.

'Quick,' hissed Natasha, hurrying Tessa through the rear courtyard outside the kitchen, 'get inside and upstairs before they see you. I'll go and tell Tom I've found you – he was beginning to freak out a bit – and I'll meet you in your bedroom in two minutes. And wash your face.'

They both dashed into the kitchen through the back door, Tessa making a left towards the back stairs and Natasha heading in the other direction to the hall to let Tom know she'd found his wife.

Joy watched them with amusement from her post at the kitchen sink, where she was rinsing chickpeas under the tap. She always soaked and cooked them herself, but Tessa had bought them tinned. They'd have to do.

What were those two up to now? she wondered. She'd always been happy to see how close Natasha and Tessa were, considering there was nine years between them. Rachel quickly got impatient with Tessa's vagueness, but there was still an element of lingering hero worship in Natasha's attitude to her big sister.

How different her three girls were, thought Joy, cutting a cauliflower into small florets. Tessa probably was the beauty of them, she didn't have to make any effort; with her tumbling dark hair and those dreamy eyes, she had always turned heads, while being completely oblivious to it.

Rachel was more conventionally pretty, with the blonde hair and blue eyes which appealed to more conventional men, like her former husband, Michael.

Joy had been rather amazed, at the time, that one of her daughters was hitching up with a man with a good job, his own house and even a pension plan.

It had been especially surprising that it was Rachel who'd

made such a sensible choice, as all the young men she'd run after in her youth had been artistic types: dishevelled art students, or in hopeless rock bands. Although they were the sort who were generally more attracted to romantic-looking women, like Tessa, so Rachel had endured a lot more disappointments than a girl with her looks might have expected to. Joy had always felt protective of her middle daughter over that.

But while he hadn't been madly exciting, she did still wonder why Rachel had ended her marriage to Michael quite so rashly. He wasn't dashing like Tom, but he was a good-looking man and, more importantly, a kind and reliable one, qualities never to be taken for granted. The split had been very hard on Daisy and Ariadne, and Rachel having lost her own father so young, Joy couldn't understand why she had put her own poppets through something similar.

Not to judge, not to judge, Joy reminded herself, bringing the hand holding the paring knife up to her heart chakra. She held it there and released her negative thought about her daughter. Her journey, her karma. Not to judge. And, of course, it's never easy to be the middle child, although with Rachel's quick wits she was more up to it than most. She'd find the right man one day. Either someone as strong as she was, or someone willing to be dominated by her – it was anything in between that was a disaster.

Then there was darling Natasha. She needed a good man too, her precious autumn crocus, born from Joy's later life passion. Such a gift to have met Tony at an age when she'd thought intense love – physical and emotional – like that was behind her forever. It didn't matter that it hadn't lasted, because it had been so wonderful while it did.

And how lovely that although she and Tony hadn't felt able to stay together as a couple, they were still on good terms.

She sent him birthday and Christmas cards every year and he sent her postcards from wherever he travelled. It was their way of acknowledging that there had once been a connection between them too special just to forget. No point in holding on to hurts, just remember what had been good.

Which made it seem even more of a shame that Natasha wasn't on better terms with him. They met up occasionally when his work took him to New York, or hers to Australia, but Joy kept trying to persuade her to go out there for a longer visit, to stay with him and patch things up properly after that terrible time, when his new partner had made Natasha so unwelcome and she'd blamed her dad for it.

Scraping the cauliflower into a bowl and putting it to one side, Joy paused for a moment before starting on the onions. Was that why Natasha was still single? she wondered. She was so striking looking, you'd think she'd be fighting them off, but whenever Joy asked her if she'd met anyone, she just dismissed it, saying she was too busy with work to bother with all that.

Joy had asked Rachel once what she thought the problem was and she'd said it was famously tough to find a decent man in New York, and it would take a very confident one not to be intimidated by Natasha. Her stellar career, her independence and even her height could daunt the best of them, Joy could see that, but did those unresolved issues with her father play a part too? Did she give off a vibe of not trusting men?

Blinking from the sting of the chopped onion, Joy remembered how her own heart had broken when Natasha had insisted on going back to Brisbane with Tony, after he'd come over to England to see her for her fourteenth birthday. It had all happened so suddenly. Natasha had been vehement that it was her natural right to spend some of her upbringing with each of her parents and Tony seemed keen, so Joy had felt she couldn't object.

If only Tony had been able to be more honest regarding his new partner's feelings about having a sulky fourteen-year-old move in with them. It had been a very unhappy time for them all and after a little under two years Natasha had come back. That had been wonderful for Joy, but Natasha's relationship with her father had been pretty strained ever since.

Joy grasped her crystals and sent up a prayer that Natasha would soon find a partner worthy of her. For the good of all. And so mote it be.

Tessa was sitting in front of her old French dressing table, looking at her reflection in amazement. Her terrible grey re-growth had completely gone and all those frizzy old-lady hairs that stood up around her head like antennae were smoothed down, but it wasn't clinging-to-her-head artificially straight, as hairdressers on these wretched shoots had done to her in the past. It was her hair, long, dark, wavy, a little wild, flowing down her shoulders the way it used to.

'What did you do, my darling sister?' she asked, squeezing Natasha's hand, which was resting on her shoulder, as she leaned in looking at Tessa's reflection.

'Just a little trick of the trade,' she said, holding up something that looked like an eye shadow compact. 'Make-up's not just for faces, you know.'

'Whatever that is, can you leave it behind?' asked Tessa.

Natasha laughed. 'I'll get them to send you a lifetime's supply. I'll just put a very light pre-shoot make-up on you for now and then we can go down and show off Tim Chiminey's beautiful wife.'

Five minutes later, they headed down the stairs to find a flurry of activity, with what seemed like hordes of people carrying photographic equipment in through the front door. Tom came out of the sitting room and was clearly very relieved to see Tessa making an appearance at last.

'Ah, great,' he said, trying not to sound as though he'd been ready to put out an APB on her. 'There you are, Tess, come and meet the crew – and you, Natasha.'

He went over to the stairs and as he put his arm around Tessa, to escort her over to meet the photographer, he reached over and gave a little tug to the sleeve of Natasha's T-shirt to get her attention, then spoke quickly and quietly behind Tessa's head, so they could both hear.

'They've brought a make-up artist with them. I'll do my best, but you'll have to smooth it out, Tash. Sorry.'

She nodded to let him know she'd got the message. Tricky. She had strong principles about never cutting in on another make-up artist's gig, but this was a special case. It was family and she was going to do her sister's make-up. Final.

Tom performed the introductions with his usual easy charm, so everyone was smiling and nodding and shaking hands.

'And this is my wife's sister,' said Tom. 'Natasha Younger. She just happens to be over from New York and the thing is, Tessa would like her to do the make-up, if that's OK … she's a make-up artist,' he added by way of explanation.

The photographer opened his mouth, clearly about to explain that they'd brought their own hair and make-up person, thank you very much, when a woman came out of the sitting room, her eyes open wide.

'Did you say Natasha Younger?' she asked.

Natasha laughed. She could tell with one look that this small and slight blonde woman was the make-up artist.

Civilians didn't have eyebrows like that. Strong and defined, but not overshaped. Just a little pencil for definition, possibly powder shadow. Nicely done. A good no-make-up make-up generally.

'That's me,' she said, doing jazz hands.

'Oh, wow, I'm so excited to meet you,' said the woman, in an Australian accent which made Natasha smile. 'I follow you on Instagram. I saw those great pictures you did in a garden yesterday and I've just realised it was here. It's so amazing to meet you. I love your work.'

Natasha went over and shook her hand. 'Well, it's great to meet you. What's your name?'

'Mattie Sturton,' said the woman, still looking a bit starstruck.

'Are you an Aussie?' asked Natasha.

Mattie nodded. 'I'm from Melbourne, I moved to London five years ago.'

'I'm from Brisbane,' said Natasha.

'You are?' said Mattie.

'Well, I was born there and spent quite a lot of my childhood there, on and off. My dad's Aussie, he still lives there.'

And I really should go and see him sometime soon, but I won't think about that right now.

'I had no idea you were Australian, that's so cool,' Mattie said. 'We should claim you more. My dad's English, which is how come I can live here.'

'So we're both mongrels,' said Natasha, relieved the make-up artist she was about to usurp was so nice. It was time to sort that situation out.

'The thing is, Mattie,' she said, moving closer towards her and steering her out of the photographer's earshot with a gentle pressure to her elbow, 'we didn't know you were coming

today and Tessa would really like me to do her make-up. She's
really not very comfortable with this whole photography thing
and she'll feel much more relaxed if I do her face, but I'm not
going to steal your job from you. I'll do it, but you get the
credit and of course the fee. Is that cool?'

'Can I assist you?' asked Mattie.

Natasha laughed. She was a smart cookie, this Mattie.
She was clearly well beyond the assistant stage if she was
booked for a shoot like this, but she'd seen an opportunity
and grabbed it.

'Sure you can,' said Natasha. 'I'd like that. And you can
put it on your resume.'

Mattie smiled at her and they shook hands on the deal.

Sydney Street, 10.33 a.m.

Sitting at her desk, waiting for Simon to bring his car round, Rachel sent Natasha a quick text to say she would be arriving earlier than she'd thought and her boss was coming too, because he wanted to check out the furniture, so please could she tell Mum there would be two more people for lunch?

She deliberately hadn't rung Tessa to tell her the night before, because she knew her older sister would be in a right old tizzy about the shoot and the thought of more people turning up might push her over the edge.

Then, after a moment's thought, Rachel quickly sent Natasha a second text explaining that Branko was bringing the girls down after school, so she wouldn't fret about that. She felt as though she needed one of those battle plans you saw in old war films, moving ships around on a table to keep track of it all, but she was fairly sure she had it covered. Then Simon rang to say he was waiting outside the building and she should come down.

When she stepped out of the front door, Rachel was glad she already knew he drove a ridiculous car. What a ludicrous vehicle, she thought, climbing into the enormous black four-wheel drive.

Talk about Arthur or Martha, even his bloody motor didn't know if it lived in Chelsea or Chipping Norton. It was the worst of both, she decided, putting on her sunglasses, in case they passed anyone she knew while they were still in slow central London traffic.

Simon had his shades on too. At least they weren't as flashy as the car. They were rather fabulous actually. Heavy black vintage-looking frames. But then he was Mr Taste, so she didn't know why she would be surprised. He'd just had some kind of a major lapse when it came to this object they were riding along in.

'So, when did you win the Lottery?' she asked him.

He glanced at her, looking puzzled, before turning his eyes back to the road.

'What are you talking about? My winning numbers in the lottery of life? Looks, brains, charm etc. ...?'

'No,' said Rachel, 'this New Money car of yours. It's very out of your taste character. If you were going to have poncy wheels I'd expect it to be a Bristol, or something recherché like that. Maybe one of those lovely vintage Jags, or a beaten-up old Land Rover, not this Chelsea Tractor.'

For a moment he was silent and she wondered if she'd gone too far. He was her boss after all, but it was such fun teasing him, she sometimes forgot. Then he laughed and she relaxed.

'God, you're rude,' he said. 'I love my car. I'm a boy and I love nice wheels. Plus, it's practical. I can throw a chest of drawers in the back if I need to, I can drive it in town or the country, and it impresses clients. The more precious decorator and designer factions might despise this car, as you do, but they still know it was bloody expensive, which commands a different kind of respect, one that's harder to bluff. And above all, it's blissfully comfortable and very sturdy and I do a lot of driving. All right?'

Something about the way he said it made Rachel decide not to pursue her point. She did know when to shut up sometimes.

Simon pulled up at the junction with the King's Road and turned to look at Rachel.

'We're heading down beyond Sevenoaks, is that right?' he said.

Rachel nodded.

'You do know that means going south of the river, don't you?' said Simon. 'I haven't had any vaccinations or anything ...'

'I think you'll live,' said Rachel. 'You shocking old snob.' She tapped him on his upper arm with her finger.

'There,' she said, 'I've inoculated you against Clapham yummy mummy fever, OK?'

He laughed, turning to look at her and saw that she was smiling in that cheeky way which made him feel so happy and muddled simultaneously.

'Let's do this thing, then,' he said, quickly switching his gaze back to the road, and concentrated on negotiating the busy traffic and crazy pedestrians of mid-morning Chelsea, until they were away from the King's Road and rolling smoothly along the Embankment. They sat in silence for a while, Simon focused on the driving, Rachel happy looking out at the gorgeous houses, until she began to feel a strange sensation in her nether regions. They were getting very hot.

She looked over at Simon and saw a small smile playing at the corners of his mouth, as though he were trying not to laugh.

'Simon,' she said, 'is this some kind of an ejector seat?'

He turned to look at her, as he pulled up at traffic lights, the smile now broad across his face.

'Bit warm are you?' he asked.

'You could say that,' said Rachel, beginning to find it quite uncomfortable and lifting each of her thighs up off the seat in turn. She was wearing a summer dress and her legs were sticking to the leather. 'Ouch! Make it stop. I'm getting all itchy.'

'Well, if you're going to insult my car, you've got to accept it's going to demand revenge ...'

Rachel ignored him and peered down at all the buttons, knobs, switches, dials and gizmos on the raised area between the two front seats, looking for the seat warmer controls. It was like Apollo 12 and the only thing she was sure of was the cigarette lighter. Not helpful.

'Don't worry, I'll call her off,' said Simon, reaching over and turning a small wheel on her side of the dashboard and registering, as he did so, relief that the raised console was there, creating a kind of Berlin Wall between him and Rachel.

Or more specifically between his hand and her legs. She'd been wriggling around in the hot seat and her dress had ridden up alarmingly.

'Thank you, Simon,' said Rachel. 'Roasting the staff, very funny. Not. I'm going to look very professional to our important press contacts arriving in a muck sweat.'

Simon chuckled to himself, clearly delighted with his joke. What an odd man he was, thought Rachel. So sophisticated in his dress, taste and habits, all big cigars, bespoke suits and vintage sunglasses, then this flashy car. He could be very sarcastic and quite harsh in the office and then he plays a practical joke like a schoolboy and sits giggling about it. And that was before you even got onto his private life, which was such a delightful source of secret entertainment among his staff.

There'd been a leaving drinks a few weeks before, which had turned into a bit of a booze-up and the minute he'd left, conjecture about Simon's sexuality had dominated the conversation. One woman said he'd been at school with her brother and they'd all been 'at it like knives' in the dorm, but then she'd added that her brother was married now with four kids, so who knew?

Another one had a GBF – Gay Best Friend, or Grievous Bodily Fun, ha ha ha, she'd shrieked – who was a decorator and he swore Simon was totally gay. His gaydar lit up like the Las Vegas strip whenever he saw him, he'd said. And no straight man could ever dress that well.

Then there was another faction who were convinced he was straight, but some kind of perve, which meant he never had a normal girlfriend, but met up with other kinky people to do group kinky things in kinky outfits.

And there was one romantic who was sure he'd had his heart broken terribly when he was young and could Never Love Again. They'd all screamed with laughter, pelted her with peanuts and told her she'd read too many Mills & Boons.

Still very new at the company then, Rachel had just listened and laughed at the appropriate moments, wondering if perhaps he was one of those people who just aren't very sexual. He seemed to put all his energy into his work and his image, so maybe that was enough for him. Not everyone sat around thinking about sex all the time.

She had quite a few girlfriends who certainly didn't since they'd had children, all interest in hanky panky completely gone. She might have been one herself if she'd stayed married to Michael – in fact that was one of the reasons she'd divorced him. She simply hadn't fancied him any more, however fit he was with all his squash playing, and he hadn't been very happy about it either.

No problem in that department now, she thought, settling back into the leather seat, which was gloriously comfortable now it wasn't griddling her butt, and smiling to herself as an image of Link popped into her head.

Link lying back on the pillows, bare chested, sheets tangled around his hips. Mmmmm …

Simon glanced over and saw the smile. Whatever she was thinking about, she liked it. It made him want to ask her that dopiest of questions – 'What are you thinking?' – but he restrained himself.

What kind of thing was that to say to an employee? Holding the steering wheel a little tighter, he cast around for a work topic to bring up. Preferably something very dull.

Rachel got in first. It didn't feel right sitting next to her boss having X-rated thoughts about Link, it was supposed to be a working day after all, so she made herself sit up straight and asked Simon what he thought of the re-design of one of the leading interiors magazines, which had come out just the day before.

Simon was so relieved to have the distraction he answered in great and pompous detail, aware he might be boring her to death, but not caring. After that they chatted easily about work for most of the journey and it was only once they started to see Cranbrook on the road signs that he began asking her more specific questions.

'So tell me, who is going to be down here today?'

'Well, my sister Tessa and her husband, Tom – or Tim Chiminey, to use his ludicrous TV name ... but he's really called Tom.'

'I'm glad you reminded me of that,' said Simon.

'Have you seen the show?' asked Rachel.

'Of course,' said Simon, 'I'll watch anything about houses. I never tire of a home makeover and I love that one with the hoarders and the OCD cleaners. I could probably be one of those cleaners actually. I love getting the bleach out ...'

Definitely gay, thought Rachel.

'... but the chimney thing your brother-in-law does is actually rather interesting because you get some proper historical stuff, too. Not just new curtains and scatter cushions, proper bricks and mortar, structural stuff, what it's all based on.'

Maybe not gay.

'That's great,' said Rachel, 'you two will get on famously then. Tom is mad about bricks. The salvage yard has acres of them. So he'll be there with my sister Tessa ...'

Simon thought for a moment. 'What's your brother-in-law's surname?' he asked. 'Not Chiminey, I presume.'

Rachel snorted. 'Chenery. They renamed him Tim Chiminey for the program ... You know, like the song from *Mary Poppins* ...'

She sang it. '*Tim Chiminey, Tim Chiminey* ...'

Simon laughed. 'That is a bit grim,' he said.

'You should hear my sister on the subject,' said Rachel.

'So your sister's name is Tessa Chenery,' said Simon. 'That's what I was wondering. Isn't she a muralist?'

'Yes,' said Rachel, quite surprised. 'Well, she used to be, she only does it around their house now.'

'The penny has only just dropped,' said Simon. 'I know her work. She did the most beautiful walls for the dining room of a friend of mine's house years ago. Views of old Hong Kong harbour, in a rather Regency style. I enjoy it every time I go round there. And I've seen her murals in *Interiors* as well, were they from this house? All up the stairs? She's really good. What a shame she doesn't do it professionally any more. Perhaps we should add that to our list of missions for today?'

Rachel was so surprised Simon knew Tessa's work she didn't know what to say. The only thing that came into her mind with a firmness that rather surprised her was: No.

No, because Tessa didn't need to work. She had a husband who did it all, being on the telly and overseeing the salvage business on the side, bringing in lots of lovely money, while Tessa had her nice little hobby painting wild flowers on the skirting boards.

The next thing she knew Simon would be expecting her to place a story about Tessa's muralling somewhere and she'd be organising another shoot for that. No, thanks.

'Oh, I don't think she wants the bother,' she said. 'She's happy just doing it at home. Every time I go down there she's covered another bit of wall. The house is starting to look rather like a tattooed lady, no surface undecorated.'

'Sounds extraordinary,' said Simon.

Whatever, thought Rachel. She preferred her own walls, the matte charcoal on anaglypta wallpaper. Moving right along ...

'So they'll be there,' she continued, getting back to Simon's original question, 'and, of course, the photographer and the art director from *You*. I don't know if they're sending a fashion stylist as well ... and my sister Natasha, she's doing the make-up. She's a make-up artist – rather a famous one actually.'

'Is she the one who lives in New York?'

'Yes,' said Rachel, surprised again.

'I heard some of the girls in the office talking about her,' said Simon quickly. He didn't want her to think he was keeping a dossier. Even if he slightly was. 'They were very impressed she's your sister ... it's a big deal is it, what she does?'

'Yes,' said Rachel, feeling fiercely proud of her little sister, 'very big. She does Paris fashion shows and the ad campaigns for some really major designers, as well as editorial for *Vogue* and all that – US *Vogue*.'

'Handy for your other sister that she's over here then.'

'Very – and my mum's there as well actually.' Rachel started giggling, she couldn't help it. 'Tessa's drafted her in to do the food. She's a wonderful cook. All vegetarian, but not the crocheted bran kind, more Middle Eastern and Indian, a big delicious mix … you'll see. She's made a living as a caterer since my dad died.'

Simon's head flicked towards her for a moment.

'I'm sorry to hear that,' he said, 'when did it happen?'

'I was only three,' said Rachel. 'I don't really remember him, but he was a Labour Cabinet Minister, so there's quite a lot of old telly footage. Better than nothing.'

'Gosh, what a rich tapestry your family is,' Simon said, hurriedly continuing on in case she felt compelled to ask him any returning questions about his. 'So how did the camper van in Australia thing fit in?'

'Oh yes, I told you about that, didn't I? When we were talking about shades of terracotta, I remember now, I got rather carried away about the raw earth of the Red Centre … Anyway, that was with my step-dad. He's Australian. Mum met him here and then we all moved to Brisbane with him and Natasha was born there. Tony's great. I wish they'd never split up, but with five of us in that van for so long, while he was trying to take serious art photographs of rock formations and gnarly old trees, it was a miracle they lasted as long as they did.'

'So, just to recap, down at the house today we have the photographic team, your brother-in-law, two sisters and your mum. Have we missed anyone? No other relatives or siblings going to stroll in? Second cousins? A great aunt?'

Rachel giggled again. 'Well, there are my three nephews, but we should be finished before they come home from school.'

And my darling daughters, she thought, but you'll be long gone before they arrive. She was going to make sure of that.

Cranbrook, 1.24 p.m.

Natasha had completely forgotten to tell her mum that Rachel's boss was coming down with her. She'd been so caught up with the shoot, keeping a sharp eye out for wayward strands of Tessa's hair becoming vertical, and chatting to Mattie – who'd given her some great gossip from the London fashion scene.

But when Rachel walked into the dining room accompanied by a man in a very well cut suit, Joy wasn't at all surprised. The moment she saw him she felt like she'd been expecting him.

'Hello, Rachel darling,' she said, getting up from her lunch, which she was having in peace, while the others were out taking pictures in the garden.

She went over to them, kissing her daughter and smiling at the man.

'Mum, this is Simon Rathbone, my, er, boss,' said Rachel, feeling oddly shy and formal. 'Simon, this is my mum, Joy Younger.'

'Hello, Mrs Younger,' said Simon, putting out his hand.

Joy took his hand, noticing first how strong it looked. He was dressed like a smoothie, but he had a strong core. A very firm handshake. Joy put her other hand on top of his and patted it, to prolong the connection.

'Lovely to meet you, Simon,' she said. 'Do call me Joy and come and have some lunch, there's so much and the rest of them aren't going to have theirs until later.'

While she was talking, her brain was somewhere else entirely. Simon's energy felt very tight. Positive and benign, but bound up, as though he could never relax.

She let go of his hand, smiling at him. She liked this Simon, but as he smiled back at her, saying something about how he'd come down to help Rachel with some furniture, Joy's face suddenly fell.

His aura had become visible to her. It happened very rarely, and she could never predict it or make it happen, but sometimes when she connected with someone, tuned into their particular frequency, a halo of coloured light appeared around them, following their outline. It was always a bit of a shock.

She blinked and it was still there, not a trick of the light. Simon's aura was a very good colour, rather a beautiful golden green, but then she saw there was a big dark hole on one side of it, like a nasty black-and-purple bruise.

It looked painful and made her want to hug him, to tell him everything was going to be all right. She restrained herself and tried to paste the smile back on her face, but it was hard. There was something so dark there, she closed her eyes for a moment to block it out.

Luckily, Rachel hadn't noticed Joy's expression, she was over at the table, putting out plates and cutlery. Joy knew she'd be furious if she'd known her mother had tuned into Simon like that. She and Natasha hated all that 'joojie moojie nonsense' as they called it.

Simon was looking at her closely, his head lowered towards hers. 'Are you all right, Joy?' he asked quietly.

'Yes, yes,' she said, recovering herself and feeling relieved when the aura snapped off as suddenly as it had appeared, as though someone had flicked a light switch. 'Just a little dizzy spell. I think I may have overdone it with all the cooking this morning. Not as young as I was, despite the name. I'm fine now. Do come and eat.'

'I'd love to,' he said, 'it looks amazing.'

He put his hand very gently under Joy's elbow and steered her over to a chair.

Rachel watched out of the corner of her eye, rather touched. Simon could be so arrogant, but he was being very sweet to Joy. Still, the sooner the shoot was over and he left, the better. It was just too weird having him there and it would only get more peculiar when she had to introduce him to everybody.

She ate a few mouthfuls, but, delicious though her mother's salads were, she didn't feel hungry, it was all too anxious-making, and she really did want to see what was happening with the pictures. Simon had cleared his plate and was going back for seconds, so she grabbed her opportunity.

'Excuse me a minute,' she said, getting up from the table and legging it with no further explanation.

Joy was glad to be left alone with Simon. The dissonance between the good vibe she'd had from his hand and that horrible wound – that was the only way she could think of it – in his aura was intriguing. She wanted to look at him a bit more.

'This food is fantastic,' he was saying. 'It's so healthy, without making you suffer for it. I can feel the goodness spreading into my bones.'

No wonder Rachel was so gorgeous, he thought, if she'd been brought up on this grub.

'What kind of food did you grow up on?' asked Joy.

Simon was nonplussed for a moment. Had he just said that out loud, what he'd been thinking about Rachel? Or was it simply an obvious thing for Joy to ask in the context? He really didn't know.

'Well, I went to boarding school and the food there was horrendous and there was never enough of it and we did so much sport, we were always hungry. We used to go into the town sometimes and shoplift food. I was lucky not to come out of that place with a criminal record to go with my A levels.'

'What about in the holidays?' asked Joy, putting a piece of cucumber into her mouth with her fingers and watching his face closely. 'Did you get better food at home?'

Simon laughed, but in a rather brittle way, his easy manner gone. 'Oh, yes,' he said, feeling himself tense, 'it was always a great relief to get back to some home cooking.'

Images were flashing into his head. Things he didn't want to think about. Three overexcited boys, so happy to be arriving home from school for the holidays. Always a lavish afternoon tea ready to greet them. Piles of egg and cress sandwiches, scones, a fruit cake. Fighting over the toasted almonds on the top …

He made his brain lock the memories away again and looked round. There was plenty to distract him. Rachel hadn't been kidding about the extent of the murals, every inch of the room was painted with trees, creepers, flowers and foliage spreading up the walls, over the ceiling and down onto the edges of the wooden floor. Normally he'd be horrified to see lovely old parquet besmirched like that, but the painting was so well done, it looked amazing.

'I take it this is Tessa's work,' he said to Joy, gesturing at the walls with his free hand, as he lifted a large forkful of roast beetroot, rocket and goat cheese salad up to his mouth.

Subject change, thought Joy.

'Yes,' she said, 'it's almost an addiction for Tessa now, I think. She just has to get the creative urge out. Rachel says if you stand still too long in this house, Tessa will paint some ivy up your leg.'

Simon smiled. That was such a Rachel comment.

'Well, it looks extraordinary,' said Simon. 'It's like sitting inside a magical forest. I've seen her work before. She did a friend's dining room about twenty years ago and I've so enjoyed it, all that time. I'm looking forward to meeting her.'

'I think it's a shame Tessa doesn't do it professionally any more,' said Joy.

'That's exactly what I said to Rachel earlier,' said Simon, 'but she didn't think Tessa would be interested.'

Really? thought Joy. How odd.

'I think Tessa is just too modest to suggest she'd like to,' she said.

'Well, there's a massive market for this kind of work in London right now,' said Simon. 'All those multi-million-pound houses that need lavish decorating, so I think I might suggest it anyway.'

Joy smiled at him and raised her glass of water in a toast. 'You do that, Simon,' she said.

Rachel found Natasha sitting at one of the Lawn & Stone garden tables on the terrace at the back of the house. She was locked in an animated whispered conversation with a woman Rachel didn't know.

A few yards away, Tessa was perched on the edge of the rope egg chair, with Tom standing next to her, one hand on the top of the chair. Five people were looking at them. Tessa's face had the expression of a trapped stoat.

'That's great,' the photographer was saying, 'just lift your head up a bit, Tessa. Not just your eyes, your chin as well. Look towards me. Good. Can you relax your shoulders a little?'

'Boo,' Rachel whispered into Natasha's ear.

'Rachie!' replied Natasha, 'I got your text, but then I forgot you were coming down early. Oops, I didn't tell Mum, sorry. Sit down. This is Mattie. I've been helping her with the make-up.'

'She means I've been assisting her,' said Mattie, smiling broadly.

'Well, the magazine had booked Mattie for the job, but she's been very understanding about Tessa wanting me to do it,' said Natasha.

Rachel smiled at them both and then glanced over at the knot of people around the egg chair. The photographer was now trying the shot with Tessa standing up and Tom sitting in the chair. She still looked like she was standing in front of a firing squad.

'Has she been like this the whole time?' Rachel asked Natasha, trying not to laugh, as the photographer abandoned that idea and was wondering whether they could both fit in the chair together.

'Pretty much,' said Natasha. 'The only time I've seen her relax was when they took a shot of her in front of the floral mural in the drawing room, and I went over under cover of powdering her off and told her you couldn't really see her in the shot, because her dress and hair blended in with the wall.'

Rachel convulsed with laughter, her shoulders shaking, her head in her hands.

'That poor photographer,' she said.

'I know,' said Natasha, 'I've worked on shoots with animals that were easier to photograph than Tessa. I've tried all the tricks I use on sulky models and nothing's worked. I've given her a neck massage and everything, haven't I, Mattie?'

She nodded. 'And she's so beautiful, your sister,' she said. 'Why is she so uptight about having her picture taken?'

'No idea,' said Rachel. 'She's always been weird about it. We've hardly got any pictures of the three of us as kids, because she'd run away as soon as she saw a camera. Which was pretty sad, considering Natasha's dad is an amazing photographer.'

'Yeah,' said Mattie, nodding enthusiastically, 'Anthony Younger. I love his work.'

'Mattie's from Melbourne,' said Natasha.

'Aha, great. I thought I heard a bit of a familiar lilt,' said Rachel. 'G'day, Matt.'

'G'day, Rach,' said Mattie, grinning.

'I thought you said your "boss" was coming with you,' said Natasha.

'I've left him with Mum,' said Rachel, pulling a face. 'It feels a bit weird having him here. I want to get rid of him as soon as I can.'

Natasha just raised her eyebrows and said nothing. She wasn't getting involved in that one. Rachel was like a belligerent schoolgirl about work sometimes, it was always her against 'them' in an oddly immature way.

Rachel was so good at what she did, Natasha didn't understand why she didn't start her own agency. Rather than wasting her energy angsting about the 'boss', she should be the bloody boss. It was so unlike Rachel not to go for it, but maybe with the girls to consider, she just thought it was too risky. Damn shame. It was different for her, she only had herself to think about. Fortunately and unfortunately.

Rachel was looking over at the shoot again. The photographer had turned away from Tom and Tessa and was in deep discussion with the art director. This was the crucial shot for her product. That chair was so photogenic – she'd had an amazing response to the snap she'd taken of it on Instagram –

and she couldn't let the photographer give up on it. If they got this picture right it might end up on the cover of the magazine. Time to step in.

'I think I might go over and see if I can move things along a bit,' she said to Natasha.

'Want back-up?' asked Natasha, feeling guilty that she'd been so engrossed in conversation with Mattie, she hadn't been giving Tessa enough support.

'Yeah,' said Rachel, 'I think we need to do our sister act, chill her down a bit, make her laugh. Tea might be a good place to start actually ...'

'Mattie,' said Natasha, standing up and consciously putting her professional head on again, 'would you mind making Tessa some tea? There's Earl Grey in the cupboard above the kettle. She likes it weak, not much milk, no sugar.'

'Sure,' said Mattie and headed for the kitchen.

Rachel and Natasha locked eyes.

'Let's do this,' said Rachel.

Natasha nodded and the two of them headed over towards the group.

'Hey, Tessie,' said Rachel in a sing-song voice, like she'd just strolled in, 'how's it all going?'

'Hi, Rachel,' said Tessa, her face lighting up when she saw her two sisters walking towards her. She felt like the cavalry had arrived.

'Hi, Tom,' said Rachel, then she walked over to the photographer, putting out her hand. 'Hi, I'm Rachel Lambton, Tessa's sister. Just come to give her some moral support, hope I'm not interrupting. Do you mind if I watch?'

Rachel played for time, introducing herself to the whole crew, until she saw Mattie emerging with the tea. She took it from her and went over to Tessa, handing her the mug.

'Here you are,' she said.

'Oh, thanks, Rachel,' said Tessa. 'Just what I needed. This has been hell,' she whispered.

'Don't worry,' said Rachel, 'I was looking at the set-up just now and from where the photographer's standing it's clear he's really only focusing on Tom, and with your dark hair and the shadows from the trees, you just kind of blend into the background. I could hardly see you. I wasn't even sure you were in the picture.'

The look of relief on Tessa's face was so palpable, Rachel knew she had to act quickly.

'And I think this is the last shot they need you to be in, the rest are just of Tom,' she said, making it up as she went along, 'then we can go inside and have some lunch.'

With that, she practically hopped back to the photographer and spoke quietly to him, her back to Tessa.

'You've got a very short window of normal with her, while she drinks the tea,' she said. 'Then you'll be back to the traumatised rabbit face.'

He looked at her for a moment, glanced over at Tessa, then turned back to Rachel and nodded, smiling. 'Nice one,' he said.

'And don't give her any direct instructions, if you can avoid it,' added Rachel. 'Pretend you're a wildlife photographer and she's a nervous endangered lemur ...'

'Cool,' said the photographer, his camera raised, already shooting.

Happy with her mug of tea, Tessa didn't even notice it was happening, but Tom did, sitting on the edge of the chair, his now famous cheeky chimney-sweep grin on full-beam, putting his head from one side to the other, like the pro he had become.

Rachel took her place next to Natasha, behind the crew.

'You're a bloody genius, Rachel Lambton,' said Natasha, under her breath. 'I wish I had you on some of my fashion shoots.'

'I just want my chair on the cover of that magazine,' said Rachel.

Cranbrook, 5.47 p.m.

Going back into the house to get a shawl for her mother, as the first hint of evening chill settled on the garden, Rachel heard some very strange noises coming from the room which Tessa, rather pretentiously, Rachel thought, called 'the library'.

'Howzat!' a male voice called out, after a loud crash like a pile of deck chairs falling over.

She peeped round the door to see Simon, jacket off, shirt sleeves rolled up, high-fiving her middle nephew Archie, while Daisy skipped about in a victory dance.

'Way to go, Simbo,' Archie was saying. 'That was a full strike, making it four, two to us.'

'No way,' Finn butted in. 'Ari kicked two of them over ... so they don't count. That bowl is null.'

Equally fascinated and alarmed, Rachel quickly pulled back behind the door before any of them saw her and spied on the scene through the crack of the hinges.

'Friendly fire, Finn, my man,' Simon was saying, his hands spread out in an innocent gesture. 'They would have gone down with the others anyway, Ari just got there before I did ... but if you're not happy, I'll take my turn again. Not a problem.'

'OK,' said Finn, 'let's make it the best of five.'

After two cartwheels, which generously displayed her bright pink knickers to the room, Daisy was doing high kicks, clapping her hands underneath the raised leg.

'That's all right, that's OK, we're gonna beat you anyway ...' she sang.

Rachel turned round and leaned against the door, her eyes closed. She hadn't seen Simon since he'd gone off with Tom and the photographer for a tour of the salvage yard after the shoot, while she'd been chatting up the magazine's art director and covering the Lawn & Stone furniture with plastic sheets so it wouldn't get damaged before it was collected. She'd been rather hoping he might already have left.

But here he still was and hanging out with the kids, of all things. That was so bonkers – everyone in the office knew he couldn't be bothered with children – and potentially disastrous, considering her two were among them. Daisy was capable of anything.

It was nearly six now, on a Friday. The working week was officially over, didn't he know it was time to naff off? Surely he'd soon tire of the company of a super-attitudinal adolescent, two gawky younger boys, a very mouthy nine-year-old girl and a junior goodie-goodie? But with his triumphant shout on scoring another full strike, without Ari's accidental help this time, she wasn't so sure.

She wondered if she should just barge in and order the girls upstairs to change out of their school uniforms, breaking up the party, but when she turned back to peep through the door crack again he was helping Daisy get into the correct bowling crouch and she looked so happy she just couldn't do it. She'd have to find another tactic to send Simon – Simbo! – Rathbone on his merry way.

'Bravo, Daisy-Day! Ten men down …' she heard him cry out, after another loud crash of skittles, and she nipped across the hall and up the stairs, before anyone could see her.

Simon wasn't thinking about anything. His only concern was to win the game, irrespective of the fact that the combined age of his team was double that of the other one, as a result of his forty-seven years. In that extraordinary room, where painted wide-eyed animals appeared to peep out of the bookshelves, the only thing that mattered to him was knocking wooden skittles to the ground.

Sport had always affected him that way. Reducing him to bone, muscle, hand and eye, and the sheer determination to beat the other bastard. It was why he'd always loved it so much. When there was a game to win, whoever it was against, nothing else troubled his mind. He'd even forgotten about Rachel.

Coming back downstairs with her mother's shawl, a beautiful mirrored and embroidered Indian thing she'd had for years, Rachel was happy to find Tessa in the kitchen, making jugs of cordial.

'My boss is still here,' Rachel hissed at her. 'He's playing skittles with the kids, in your library.'

Tessa smiled. 'I can hear them,' she said, as another cheer rang out. 'Sounds like they're having a great time.'

'But I want him to *go*,' said Rachel.

'Why?' said Tessa. 'Mum's invited him to stay for dinner. She says I know him ... do I?'

'Mum's done what?' said Rachel, too appalled to answer Tessa's question.

'She's invited him to stay for dinner. It would have been rude not to.'

'Did he say yes?'

'I don't know,' said Tessa, getting irritated.

Couldn't Rachel ever relax? It's not like she'd had to shop for the dinner, with special catering for several picky children, get the table laid and cleaned up afterwards, or make endless jugs of drinks for people.

'Go and ask her,' she added. 'She's entertaining the magazine people. That's who I'm making all this for. They're finally finished.'

'Didn't she ask them to stay for dinner as well?' said Rachel.

'She did, actually,' said Tessa, now rolling her eyes to match her sister. 'I'm happy to say they declined, but she was right to do it, I can see that.'

Although I never would have, she thought. She wished they'd all go, the whole damn lot of them. Everyone. She loved seeing her sisters, but with so many other people there as well it was just too much. She had a headache already.

Rachel saw the strain on Tessa's face. She had the perfect house for it, but entertaining large numbers had never been her thing. Even when she had their seventy-four-year-old mother to do the food and everyone else to help, it seemed to be too much for her.

Rachel felt a flash of irritation. Tessa should hire proper caterers if she couldn't handle the pressure, it wasn't like they couldn't afford it and Tom could claim it as a tax deduction. 'TV's Tim Chiminey and his wife, Tessa, entertaining at their charming artistic home.'

But seeing Tessa's hand go up to her temple – she'd always suffered from migraines – sisterly affection won out. And she did owe her for having the Lawn & Stone furniture in the shots.

'Let me do that for you,' she said, putting out her hand to take the knife Tessa was using to cut orange slices. 'Go upstairs and have a breather, you've had a full-on day.'

'Really?' said Tessa, her face brightening, 'I am feeling a bit whacked and there's going to be at least twelve for dinner, so it would be great to have a bit of time out before that.'

'It's fine, I'll take over on the drinks and I'll send word up to you when it's time to eat.'

'Oh, thanks, Rach,' said Tessa, kissing her cheek and practically running from the room.

Twelve for dinner? Rachel did a mental tally and even including Branko, who'd brought the girls down on the train, she couldn't get past eleven. So twelve would mean Simon was staying. She'd have to suss that out and quickly.

Natasha, Branko and Mattie were sitting with their bare feet in the rain water that had gathered in one of the old copper tanks Tessa and Tom had dotted in various picturesque spots around the garden. The heat was going out of the day, but it was still very pleasant to paddle the water with their toes, jeans rolled up, sitting on cut-down oil drums, sipping their drinks and chatting.

It turned out Branko and Mattie went to a lot of the same bars and nightclubs.

'I can't believe I've never seen you before,' Mattie was saying.

Branko smiled mysteriously.

'I don't look so much like this when I go out,' he said.

'Ooh,' said Natasha. 'Do tell.'

'I don't tell, I show,' said Branko, tapping his phone.

He scrolled through some pictures and then handed the phone to Mattie, while looking closely at her reaction.

'You know this person?' he asked.

'No way!' said Mattie, slapping her thigh with the hand that wasn't holding the phone. 'That is fabulous. You look amazing. Check this out, Natasha.'

She handed Natasha the phone and after she'd tilted her head a few times so she could make the picture out in the still bright daylight, she could see that the person in it – a beautiful woman, in elaborate make-up, with a full beard – was actually Branko.

'Wow,' said Natasha, 'nice make-up. That's a great lip.'

They all burst out laughing.

'Thank you, Natasha,' said Branko, looking thrilled, but a little shy. 'I never feel I could tell you before, but I love your work ... I follow on Instagram.'

Mattie and Natasha laughed again.

'You too?' said Mattie. 'That was the first thing I told her ...'

'I get best ideas from there,' said Branko.

He put his hand out for the phone again, scrolling through the pictures. 'This one,' he said, handing it back to Natasha, 'you recognise?'

'I sure do,' agreed Natasha, looking pleased, 'it's my Roberto Cavalli show look, last season.'

Branko nodded. 'This I like,' he said.

'Wow,' said Mattie, leaning over to see. 'You've done that shading really well where the eye colour comes down onto the cheek. Nice work. Are you going to go pro? You can be my assistant when I'm Natasha's assistant.'

'No,' said Branko, shaking his head. 'Is just for me.'

'Why has Rachel never told me about this?' asked Natasha.

'She don't know,' said Branko.

'Doesn't she see you going out?'

'I don't change at house. She thinks I work in wine bar – I work in drag bar. I keep my things at friend's place. Is better.'

'Are you worried she'd mind?'

'Not Rachel,' said Branko, 'the children. They might say to father that Branko wear high-heel shoe, he would not like and that would be bad for Rachel.'

'You're right about that,' said Natasha, imagining Michael's reaction to a cross-dressing manny – he'd given Rachel a hard enough time about her even having a male au pair. 'That's very considerate of you. I'm absolutely certain Rachel wouldn't mind, but I respect your preference for privacy. I won't say anything to her.'

'Thank you,' said Branko, 'but I don't ask you to keep secret, because I show you. My choice. I have no shame, or problem, but sometimes is better to keep different parts of life separate.'

Natasha turned her head to look at him, quickly. It was like he was speaking her own thoughts. Was he making some kind of point? No, she decided. He was just talking about himself.

Mattie was looking serious, nodding at Branko. 'And could it spoil it all a bit if everyone knew?' she asked.

'I think yes,' said Branko. 'At home was impossible to be this way, I am used to two lives. Since childhood I was like this. I learned to keep that Branko just for me.'

'Can I see some more pictures?' asked Natasha.

'Look at all,' said Branko, passing her the phone.

She scrolled through, more impressed with every new look she saw. He wasn't dressed as a woman, or as a drag queen, but as a very beautiful, slender man in what is considered women's clothing, with very glamorous hairstyles and make-up. He didn't wear wigs, but styled his own long, thick black hair in all kinds of intricate up-dos. The beard somehow just added to the overall effect.

Natasha handed the phone to Mattie and looked closely at Branko's face. She reached out her hand and, holding his chin gently, turned his head from one side to the other. He had amazing bone structure.

'Have you ever thought of modelling?' she asked.

Branko laughed. 'You joke? In suit I look like undertaker.'

He pulled a gloomy face to illustrate his point.

'I meant womenswear,' said Natasha.

Branko's eyes widened.

'You mean like Andrej Pejic?' he asked. 'But he is blonde, very pretty – and he is now actual woman. I have heavy beard and shoulders of a man. I like dresses, but I am still a man.'

'I'm not sure what I mean, Branko,' said Natasha, 'but you're something special and I'd like to introduce you to some people I know.'

Branko threw his arms wide. 'This I love,' he said and the three of them clinked their glasses in a toast.

Branko downed his wine in one go and after catching Mattie's eye and grinning, Natasha did the same thing.

'Hic,' said Mattie, also draining her glass.

'Shall we have some more?' said Natasha. 'It is Friday.'

'I get it,' said Branko, standing up and heading back towards the house.

The two women sat in silence for a moment after he walked away, paddling the water with their toes and Natasha turned her face up towards the sun, relishing a rare moment of complete relaxation.

It was very unlike her to drink more than one glass of anything, she couldn't risk her mental faculties being dulled the next morning, not even at the weekend, and it felt really good to let up on her cast-iron self-discipline for once.

Her eyes snapped open when she felt drops of water splash on to her face. Mattie was smiling at her.

'Hey, sleepy,' she said. 'I don't want you to nod off and fall in.'

'I'm just really enjoying doing nothing,' said Natasha.

'Do you not allow yourself much downtime?' asked Mattie.

Natasha sighed. 'I guess not,' she said. 'Always got my eye on the next thing.'

'Well, there's a reason you're as successful as you are,' said Mattie. 'Slackers don't get to work for American *Vogue* and do the Cavalli show.'

'That's true,' said Natasha, 'but I do sometimes wonder if I shouldn't let myself have a bit more fun.'

Mattie didn't say anything, but looked at her steadily, a smile tilting her lips. It really was a beautiful mouth, thought Natasha, and she considered herself a connoisseur of them.

'It was really fun hanging out with you today,' she said quietly.

'Yeah,' said Mattie, 'it was. Loads of fun. We should do it some more.'

And not taking her eyes away from Natasha's, she reached over with her toes and stroked the top of her foot.

Rachel was counting on her fingers again. Five kids, three sisters, her mum, Tom and add another two for Branko and Mattie, who she'd been quite surprised to hear was also staying for dinner, that made the twelve Tessa had mentioned, but she hadn't known about Mattie. So if Simon stayed that would make it thirteen. That was the last straw. He wasn't meant to stay. He mustn't stay.

'What did Simon say about dinner?' she asked her mum casually.

She'd stupidly blurted out her horror at the idea to Tessa, but she was now safely upstairs having her lie-down and Rachel knew she must be more discreet this time. It was always easier to get your own way if people didn't know what you were up to.

'Sorry, Rachel, what did you say?' asked Joy, clearly having to make an effort to bring her consciousness back to the earth plane. She and Tessa were permanently astral travelling as far as Rachel could tell. Neither of them had a mortgage to worry about, which probably made it easier.

'I was just asking if Simon was staying for dinner,' said Rachel. 'Tessa mentioned you'd asked him.'

'Oh yes,' Joy replied, her face lighting up in a way which made Rachel's heart sink. 'He's so charming and I thought it would be good for him and Tessa to have a chat about her murals, but I haven't seen him for a while. Is he still here?'

Rachel nodded. 'He's playing skittles with the kids,' she said, partly for the sheer amusement of saying the words.

Joy smiled broadly. 'How lovely,' she said, 'I think he needs a bit more light-heartedness in his life.'

Great, thought Rachel. Joy had known Simon for about five minutes and was already full of bright ideas about how he needed to change his life. She'd be helping him to open his heart chakra next.

Damage limitation was getting more urgent by the moment and there was no point in reminding Joy or Tessa that this was a career issue for her, neither of them would get that. Joy's catering and yoga teaching had always been cash-in-hand stuff, not a proper career trajectory with planned goals. And Tessa's idea of work was painting another stoat on the library wall.

'So is it all work for Simon?' Joy asked, in an insistent tone Rachel was all too familiar with. There was a real risk of Simon becoming a 'project'.

'He is pretty focused on the business,' said Rachel, 'but he goes to the country every weekend, so I think he gets his downtime in a concentrated two-day burst. That's why I was wondering if he was staying for dinner tonight, because he's normally well on his way to Herefordshire by this time on a Friday.'

'Is that where his family are?' asked Joy.

'I've no idea,' said Rachel, now getting seriously bored with the subject. 'He keeps his personal life very private. His husband may be getting his dinner ready at this very moment, for all I know.'

'Oh, he's not gay,' said Joy, with utter confidence.

Rachel couldn't be bothered to argue. No one knew what the set-up was at Simon's country pad. Despite all their best attempts to find out through the old school network and heavy hints that they were weekending in the west Cotswolds themselves, none of the women in the office had come up with anything useful. One of them said she'd heard he visited his parents, but that sounded unlikely to Rachel because he never mentioned them and he didn't strike her as a mummy's boy.

'Well, I'm working out numbers, so the kids can start laying the table. I'll go and ask him what his plans are,' said Rachel, happy to see Tom coming back after seeing off the magazine crew. Good timing. He could sit and talk to Joy and she wouldn't be tempted to go into the house to persuade Simon to stay.

Simon was lining his eye up for the crucial shot of the game when he was suddenly distracted by a shape approaching on the other side of the French window. He knew it was something he liked, but it took a moment for him to realise it was Rachel, silhouetted against the low evening sun. The curve of her hips had become so familiar to him it was almost totemic.

The ball slipped from his hand and dribbled pathetically towards the skittles.

'Aw, Simbo,' said Archie. 'What are you doing, man? That was well lame.'

'Noooooooo!' wailed Daisy.

Finn, Ari and Hector were whooping with victorious joy, but Simon didn't notice any of it. He'd completely forgotten about the game and his feet were carrying him over to where he had seen that familiar figure.

'Ah!' said Rachel, acting surprised to find him there as she opened the glass door. 'There you are. I didn't know if you were still here.'

Simbo, she wanted to add.

'Oh,' he said, raking his hand through his hair and suddenly feeling half naked without his jacket. 'I was just, er, playing ...'

'Simbo lost us the game, Mummy,' said Daisy, appearing at his side and looking up at him accusingly. 'You totally nixed that last shot, Simbo. What happened?'

Shit, thought Rachel. This was no good – and a very good reminder of why she had to get him the hell out of there and fast.

'Come and have a drink, Simon,' she said loudly, making a death-threat face at Daisy behind his back. 'We're all sitting in the garden. It's still so lovely ...'

If it wouldn't have been grossly inappropriate, she would have grabbed his hand and dragged him out, but the best she could do was to start walking purposefully and hope he followed. He did. He could get his jacket later, he told himself. Right now the only thing that mattered was staying as close to Rachel as possible.

'I didn't know you liked bowling,' she was saying.

'Ah, well, I heard the pins going down when I was walking through the hall earlier and I couldn't resist having a go,' he said, 'and once I start playing a game, I tend to get rather involved.'

'Well, you're very honoured my oldest nephew gave you the time of day.'

'Finn?' said Simon. 'Good man, Finn. Quite a fine bowler.'

He really was the oddest mixture, thought Rachel for the second time that day, relieved as they turned the corner of the house and she could see Joy and Tom still sitting at the table, with Natasha, Mattie and Branko approaching from the opposite direction.

'Here we are,' said Rachel. 'Would you like some sangria, Simon? It's just red wine and lemonade, no brandy, but then, you're driving aren't you? Perhaps I could get you a soft drink ...'

She watched as her poison dart hit home. The relaxed expression left his face and was immediately replaced by the slightly tense look she was more familiar with. He glanced down to look at his watch, before realising he'd left it in the library with his jacket.

'It's about twenty past six,' said Rachel, trying not to let an edge creep into her voice. Time you were off, matey.

'Gosh, is it that late already?' he said. 'I better get going. Hopefully I'll miss the worst of the traffic going from here.'

Rachel wanted to punch the air. Yes!

'Oh, aren't you going to stay for dinner, Simon?' piped up Joy. 'I've made some lovely curries.'

Rachel dug her nails into her palms.

'I would have loved to,' said Simon, with genuine warmth and regret, 'but I have to get off. I'd completely lost track of the time.'

'Come down again,' said Tom. 'It was really interesting what you were saying earlier about us getting some separate press for Hunter Gatherer, I'd love to talk to you some more about that.'

'Perhaps the three of us could have lunch, to talk about it, in London,' suggested Rachel, accidentally putting too much stress on the last word and hoping no one had noticed. *London.* Not my sister's house, full of my family.

'Good plan,' said Simon. 'Let's make that happen. Well, thanks so much for the delicious food today, Joy. It was a pleasure to meet you.'

He leaned down to kiss her, and Joy couldn't resist the opportunity to put her hands on his shoulders and keep the contact for just that extra little moment.

'Such a shame you haven't caught up with Tessa,' she said.

'Perhaps she can join us for the lunch,' said Simon.

Not if I can bloody help it, thought Rachel. Business and family should be kept as separate as possible. This was a one-off aberration.

'Good idea,' said Tom. 'We set up the salvage business together, so she should definitely be there.'

Even if she does very little with it now, he thought. But maybe this could help change that.

'I'll show you out,' said Rachel to Simon, before someone suggested Joy needed to come to that lunch as well and Daisy.

With all thank yous and farewells finally made, Simon and Rachel walked back to the house together, entering via the library, so he could pick up his stuff. The kids were still in there, fooling about and just as Rachel was leading him through to the hall, a great wail went up.

She turned around to see Ari holding her head, her face doing a good impression of Munch's *The Scream*. Daisy was holding a skittle in both hands, seemingly frozen with guilt and fear.

'Daisy hit me with the skittle ...' Ari sobbed out, and Rachel dashed straight over to them, Simon forgotten.

He stood by the door for a moment wondering what to do. Should he wait to say goodbye to Rachel? It seemed rude just to walk away, but Daisy was now crying too and it seemed intrusive to stand and watch as Rachel tried to calm the girls down, pulling Ari into a hug, her other hand holding tight to Daisy's upper arm.

At least it got him over one problem, thought Simon, quietly closing the library door behind him. He'd been wondering whether it would be right for him to kiss Rachel goodbye, as he would have anyone else in this situation, which was now, by any standards, entirely social.

But he made a deliberate point of never socially kissing his staff, even though they were the kind of people who greeted virtual strangers with two cheek pecks, so it would have seemed odd to do it to Rachel this one time.

But he so wanted to. To get that close. To be able to smell her hair.

Pausing by the front door to check he had his sunglasses and car keys, he heard footsteps on the stairs behind him and turned to see a dark-haired woman coming down them. A really beautiful woman, who looked rather familiar. She had curves like Rachel, slightly fuller, but with that same differential between the waist and hips he found so alluring.

Her face was a little like Rachel's too, but it wasn't that which made her familiar, he was sure he already knew her from somewhere.

'Oh, hello,' he said, walking over with his hand extended. 'I was just leaving. You must be Tessa.'

'Yes,' she said, her green eyes widening as she looked at him. She reminded him of one of the animals peeping out from the library walls.

'I'm Simon Rathbone,' he said, as their hands clasped. 'Er, Rachel's boss.'

So you are, thought Tessa. You're Simon. That Simon.

And you're *that* Tessa, thought Simon, realisation crashing over him like surf as he suddenly remembered where he knew her from and dropped her hand, which he realised he had held rather longer than a normal handshake.

Tessa felt her cheeks growing hot. How many years ago had it been? A twenty-first party, a marquee in the garden, a house in the loveliest Devon countryside.

That field, down by the river, remembered Simon. Cornflowers and poppies. The sky growing dark above them. Stars coming out. He'd always wondered what had happened to her.

Why had he never made the connection between her and Rachel before? He'd known that astonishingly beautiful girl had been to art college and was called Tessa. He'd just never connected her with Tessa, the muralist, or Tessa, Rachel's sister.

Simon. That beautiful young man. A sportsman's body – and stamina. Her blush grew hotter remembering. Why had she never seen him again after that summer night?

Then she remembered she'd had to leave early the next morning to get a lift. How beautiful he'd looked sleeping and how hard it had been to close the door behind her. She hadn't left a note because she couldn't think of anything to say that was special enough. If she didn't hear from him first she was going to ask her friend where she could find him, but then very soon after – had it even been the following week? – she'd met Tom.

Simon swallowed. He'd woken late the next day, spent from making love all night, in the bed they'd shared in her guest room back at the house, to find her already gone. Not even a note.

All the way home in the car he'd planned how he was going to track her down through their mutual friend, but that was just before everything happened – was it even less than a week later? – and his life had changed forever, like a door slamming shut.

Tessa licked her lips nervously. Should she say something? Remind him they'd met before – and in the most heavenly of circumstances? But how did you say that? Don't you remember, when we were young, we shagged like crazed rabbits?

Simon knew he needed to say something. Either to acknowledge their previous encounter, or to fill the increasingly awkward silence that was hanging between them. But how did you say that to a grown woman, the hostess of the house where you had spent the afternoon, a wife and mother, the married sister of your employee? Lovely to see you again, you were the greatest fuck of my life.

'Well, great to, er, see you, Tessa,' he said. 'I'm afraid I've got to get off now.'

Oh my, that was an unfortunate choice of phrase in the circumstances.

'Ah,' said Tessa, at a loss for anything more coherent.

'I was talking to Tom earlier about helping to get some fresh press for Hunter Gatherer,' said Simon, thrashing around for something to ground the moment in reality.

He'd been about to mention the proposed lunch, but was struck by an image of sitting at a restaurant table with Tessa, her husband and Rachel. There was no way he could ever do that. It would be way too weird.

'That would be great,' said Tessa, intensely grateful for the lifeline. 'I do think the business gets a little bit neglected these days.'

She trailed off, realising there was a criticism of Tom inherent in that statement, which suddenly felt terribly disloyal and wrong.

'I'll look forward to hearing more about it from Tom,' she said firmly, emphasising his name for her own reassurance as much as anything.

'Great,' said Simon, nodding like a twitching twit. 'Well, see you later.'

What had he said now? He had to get out of there.

'Bye,' said Tessa weakly, as he headed outside.

She stood in the doorway, watching as he opened the door of a big black car. He had one hand on the steering wheel, his foot up on the door frame, ready to climb in, when he paused and turned back to look directly at her.

There was something so compelling in his expression. His brown eyes were looking intently at her, and they were filled with sadness. Tessa found herself stepping out of the front door and running over to the car. She didn't stop until she was right up to him, their bodies almost touching. She laid her hand gently on his.

'I remember you,' she said, gazing up into his handsome face.

'I could never forget you,' said Simon, turning his hand over to hold hers. He squeezed it tightly.

For a moment they stood just looking into each other's eyes and then without consciously thinking about it, Simon lowered his lips very slowly onto hers. She responded immediately, pushing her mouth against his, before he quickly pulled back, knowing that if he'd stayed there another instant, his tongue would have slid into her mouth.

She wished it had. It had taken all her self-control not to do it to him.

Simon looked down and, seeing Tessa's breasts rising and falling beneath her dress, remembered with complete clarity how they had looked when he had undressed her that summer night, so perfectly high and round, the pink nipples hardening under his fingers. He wanted to reach over and touch them again so much, he had to grip his fists by his side not to do it.

It was only the sudden thought that three babies had suckled there since – the boys he had just been playing skittles with, for fuck's sake – that brought him to his senses. They could look out of the library window and see them at any moment. So could Rachel.

What the hell am I doing? thought Tessa, stepping back a little, so she could no longer feel the warmth of his skin against hers.

'I'm so sorry,' said Simon. 'I shouldn't have done that, but the memory was just so strong, it took over.'

'No, I'm sorry,' said Tessa. 'I don't know what came over me either, it was just such a surprise to see you again.'

He smiled at her, that sad look back in his eyes. 'A very nice surprise,' he said. 'I can't believe I've never made the connection before.'

He didn't want to say 'with Rachel' but he knew she'd get it.

'I suppose Tessa and Simon aren't exactly unusual names,' said Tessa, the words hanging between them after she spoke. Tessa and Simon. Is that what it might have been? Have you heard the great news about Tessa and Simon? Let's ask Tessa and Simon over. That's where Tessa and Simon live.

'Well, I'd better get going,' he said, summoning all his resources to behave normally.

'Have a good trip,' said Tessa.

Simon got into the car, turned on the ignition and lowered the window. There was another frozen moment, gazing into each other's eyes, neither wanting to break the spell. In the end it was Simon who did it, buckling his seat belt, then turning back to Tessa again.

'It's good to see you again,' he said quietly.

Tessa just nodded, silently, tears suddenly filling her eyes. Then he released the handbrake and accelerated away, his arm out of the window in a final salute as he turned onto the road.

Tessa stayed in the same spot in the drive for a few moments after he'd gone, just watching the dust settle.

Cranbrook, 8.25 p.m.

Tom looked around the dining room, smiling. The table was crammed with people talking, laughing, drinking wine, relishing Joy's food and generally having a relaxed good time. It was what that room was made for – what the whole house was made for. He just wished it happened more often.

He glanced over at Tessa who was chatting with Joy and Rachel, and looking even more beautiful than usual. Perhaps it was Natasha's expert make-up, but Tom thought it was more to do with being surrounded by people she loved and felt entirely at ease with. And there were fewer and fewer of those.

They hardly ever entertained any more. Tessa just couldn't handle a lot of random – as she called them – people in her space. Even friends they'd known since they first moved to Cranbrook more than twenty years ago.

Tom worried about her. He knew that when he went away for work she often didn't leave the house for several days. Waitrose delivered and if the weather was fine the boys cycled to school and back again, so she didn't even need to do the school run any more.

So she could spend the entire day working on a group of tiny insects on a wall in a dark corner of the library, or grubbing about in the back of the salvage sheds. She'd always been happy in her own company, lost in her work, but this was getting unhealthy.

And now Finn had told him he wanted to be a weekly boarder at the grammar school all three boys attended. His house master had suggested it, quietly telling Tom he thought it would greatly reduce the aggravation between the emerging young man and his parents, and improve his behaviour in general if Finn spent four or five nights a week away from them. Then when he did go home, he'd appreciate it more.

Increasingly distressed by the tension between himself and his oldest son, Tom thought it was an inspired idea. But how would Tessa take it? Especially as Archie had got wind of the plan and thought he'd like to try this weekly boarding lark too. In two years' time Hector would be old enough to join them and then Tessa would be entirely alone all week with just her paints and imaginary creatures for company. That wasn't a good idea. Not at all.

Tuning back into their conversation, Tom heard Joy telling Rachel how much she'd liked her friend Simon.

'He's not my friend, Mum,' said Rachel. 'He's my boss. I work for him.'

'Can't you be friends with someone you work with?' asked Joy. 'I had a wonderful time in Brisbane doing catering with Pattie and we're still great friends. In fact she's coming over to stay with me later this year. I don't know why you have such a hostile attitude towards Simon, Rachel, you seem quite blocked about him.'

Tom was watching Tessa as Joy spoke and saw her becoming increasingly distracted by what was happening at the other end of the table, where Ari was sitting on Finn's knee, teaching him clapping games.

Tessa adored the way his young cousins still brought out the boy in Finn, his sweet and playful true nature. It was like having her adored boy back for a while whenever they visited and she wanted to make the most of it. She got up from her seat to go and join them.

She also wanted to get as far as possible from the subject her mother had just brought up with Rachel – Simon. That was still way too weird to deal with. She felt guilty for even letting the thought of him pass across her mind.

What if Rachel ever found out? He wouldn't tell her, surely, would he? What a hilarious coincidence – I shagged your sister years back, in a field, ha ha ha. Maybe she should have said something, asked him not to mention it. But somehow she didn't think he would. The look in his eyes had been so sincere. Not at all the triumphant gaze of a cocksman laying his eyes once more on a youthful conquest.

An image of Simon's face suddenly popped into Tessa's mind, so vivid and clear, a shiver passed over her. He had such pretty eyes for a man. It was the only word for them, a sort of golden brown, deep-set, and the way they crinkled up when he smiled was just so appealing. She pulled a heavy shutter down on that line of thinking and locked it.

Tom watched Tessa walk past the table, smiling to himself. She thought she was fat. Sure, she was carrying a little more weight than before she'd had three kids, but it just made her look sexier. Ripe.

Her deliciously round bottom moving beneath the soft fabric of her vintage dress made Tom feel immediately turned on. Some pleasant X-rated images of Tessa in the lovely underwear she always wore flashed through his mind. She was his wife, he was allowed to think dirty about her.

He was surrounded by attractive young women working in production on the TV show and the producer was a fine-looking alpha female who took very good care of herself, but while Tom enjoyed having them around and even indulged in a little bit of harmless verbal flirtation, none of them turned him on like Tessa still did.

A couple of the TV crew had made it quite clear they were up for it, but he'd never been tempted. He knew other guys in telly who took full advantage of all that was on offer, but his work life was so sweet Tom wasn't going to do anything to jeopardise it. Or, more importantly, his family.

Thinking about work made him turn his attention back towards his mother-in-law, who was still on the subject of Simon Rathbone.

'I do think it would be good if he could talk to Tessa about her mural work,' she was saying, and Tom saw Rachel cross her eyes with frustration, clearly wanting a break from talking about anything to do with work.

But it had given Tom an idea. He'd follow up that suggestion of Rathbone's about getting some dedicated press for Hunter Gatherer, separate from the 'Tim Chiminey' brand, then get Tessa to take it on as a project.

She was always hinting that he was neglecting 'their real business', as she called it, in favour of the telly stuff, so why not manoeuvre things so that it gradually became her responsibility?

They'd set it up together in the first place, so it wasn't like she didn't know how it all worked. It was a shame the way she'd drifted away from it when they'd had the kids and after a certain point, she just seemed to lose her confidence around it.

He knew she still loved the whole salvage thing, she was always poking around the yard looking at the stock and re-organising it to look prettier. Getting involved with it again would get her out of the house, mixing with people, and if Rathbone could also get her commissioned to do some murals, that would be great too. She needed an identity of her own again, not just as the Chenery boys' mum and Tim Chiminey's wife.

And it wouldn't do his image any harm to have a wife who was a well-known salvage dealer and/or muralist either. His agent, Barney, had explained to him how the leverage of a power couple was so much greater than the sum of its parts. Tessa certainly had the looks to carry it off, she just needed to get her professional sense of self back.

He'd set up that lunch with Rathbone and Rachel as soon as possible. Plan.

Rachel thought she would actually go mad and run screaming around the room like a banshee if her mother mentioned Simon one more time. Joy had glommed on to him as a project, the way she sometimes did with people, and it could drive you potty until she got over it.

'It's going to happen, Mum,' she said, hoping to achieve with mollification what she'd failed to do with irritation. 'Tom and Tessa are going to have lunch with me and Simon very soon, aren't you, Tom? We're going to get them some fresh press coverage for the salvage yard – which I do think is a great idea, Tom, by the way and not just because I thought of it – and I'll make sure the mural thing comes up, as well. OK?'

'Definitely,' said Tom, 'we all agree with you, Joy. Tessa needs to get out there again, using her talent. And there isn't really any more wall left for her to paint in this house, so she'd better move on to someone else's.'

Rachel put her arm around the back of her mother's chair and gave her brother-in-law's shoulder a friendly tweak. He glanced at her behind Joy's head and winked. As so often, his easy charm had done the trick.

'Right,' said Rachel. 'I think it's pudding time, don't you, Mum? You stay where you are – or move to another seat, if you feel like it. I'll get the kids to help me clear the plates and bring it in.'

'Ah yes,' said Joy, her gaze suddenly fixed on the end of the table, 'I think I would like to sit with Branko for a while.'

Clocking the look in her eye as she said it, Rachel mentally wished him luck. Joy would be cleansing his chakras before he'd finished his chocolate mousse.

Daisy was upstairs in the spare room, sitting cross-legged, playing with Polyvore on Natasha's iPad. Natasha and Mattie were lying on the floor on either side of her, making comments and suggestions.

'I just don't like that shoe for you,' Daisy was saying, changing Natasha's choice of a pointed flat to some dizzying heels.

'But it's all about the glamour flat this season,' Natasha said, laughing. 'And I'm wearing tight red leather trousers in this outfit already, I'll look pretty cheap in high heels with those.'

'Flat shoes are for losers,' said Daisy. 'As soon as I'm allowed to wear high heels I'm never going to wear flat shoes again. I'm going to burn them all on a big bonfire. When will I be allowed to wear them, do you think?'

'You'll have to ask your mum,' said Natasha.

Daisy pulled a face. She was still furious that Rachel had made her eat dinner upstairs on her own as punishment for hitting Ari over the head with a skittle. She'd refused to listen to her explanation of how annoying Ari was being about winning and Daisy had missed out on everything as usual. It so wasn't fair. Ari would always wear flat shoes. Ari was a flat shoe.

Natasha understood though. She'd sneaked up earlier to give Daisy her iPad to play with and as soon as she'd been able to escape from the dining room she'd come up again to hang out with her, bringing a big bowl of chocolate mousse and Mattie with her. Daisy thought Mattie was really really nice.

'I'm going to do an outfit for you now, Mattie,' she said. 'Where are you going?'

'I'm going out dancing,' she said.

'Where?'

'A really cool club.'

'In London?'

'No, in Rio.'

'Oooh,' said Daisy, 'that's in Brazil isn't it? Where the Olympics are going to be. They like the beach there.'

Mattie turned to Natasha and made an impressed face. Natasha smiled back at her, the proud auntie.

'Actually,' said Mattie, 'the club I'm going to is on the beach.'

'That is so cool,' said Daisy, her eyes opening wide as the possibilities sank in.

She quickly tapped the word 'bikinis' into the search box. Mattie and Natasha laughed out loud.

'Are you going to make me wear high heels with my bikini?' asked Mattie.

'Yeah,' said Daisy, as though it was the dumbest question she'd ever heard.

'I won't have much fun dancing on the sand in heels,' said Mattie.

'I'll make them wedges,' said Daisy, selecting a pair of vertiginous multi-coloured Christian Louboutins.

'I want a lot of gold chains,' said Mattie, 'around my waist and my ankles.'

'Nice,' said Daisy. 'And a big hat. You might get sunburnt.'

Mattie lay back on the floor and looked up at the ceiling. Tessa had painted the Milky Way across it, with the Southern Cross, in luminous paint, so it glowed.

'Amazing ceiling,' said Mattie.

'My clever sister,' said Natasha proudly. 'My dad is a big fan of sleeping outside under the stars like this, we've all done it with him. I don't remember the big outback road trip thing we did because I was too little, but he took me on some great camping trips when I moved back with him for a while. Have you ever slept in the desert?'

'No,' said Mattie. 'I'm more of a typical Aussie. I've never strayed further inland than a suburb where there's really good Lebanese food.'

Natasha laughed.

'There,' said Daisy. 'I've finished your look, Mattie. What do you think?'

Mattie rolled over onto her front and looked at the iPad.

'That's genius,' she said, 'I love my hat, I love my chains, I love my Chanel hula-hoop bag.'

'Yeah, I thought you could play with that if you got bored dancing,' said Daisy.

Mattie and Natasha burst out laughing again. Daisy beamed at them.

'So,' she said, 'I need someone else to dress. Who are you going to go to this club with?'

Mattie lay back down again and turned her head so she was looking straight at Natasha, who turned to look back at her.

'I'm going to the club with Natasha,' she said and, as she spoke, she reached behind Daisy's back and took hold of Natasha's hand, twining their fingers together.

Natasha looked at her steadily and smiled, very slowly. Then she squeezed Mattie's hand back.

Tuesday, 3 June

Outer Circle, Regent's Park, London NW1

Simon looked at his reflection in his shaving mirror and tried to give himself a good talking to. For the first time he could remember, he didn't feel like going into the office.

Even on the relatively rare occasions when he had a hangover, knuckling down to some concentrated work always seemed like the best way to get over it. But this Tuesday morning, going into the office was not an appealing prospect.

He'd been so relieved the day before that he'd had a visit scheduled to a client's new workshop just outside Oxford, on the way back from Herefordshire. With a long lunch and visits to some high-end antique dealers he knew nearby, Simon had managed to string it out until late afternoon, giving him an excuse to be away from the office all day, but there was no escaping it this morning.

The problem was Rachel. He was simply dreading seeing her. Having to look her in the eye and be normal, not shouting: 'I once shagged your sister like a wild animal and I want to do it again. Immediately. And very often after that. If not sooner.'

He was terrified that whatever he tried to say to her would turn into the word 'Tessa' as it came out of his mouth.

Tessa Tessa Tessa Tessa. It had been going round and round in his head, a one-word ear worm, ever since he'd driven away that Friday evening, leaving her standing in the driveway. Never had it been harder to keep his foot on the accelerator when all he'd wanted to do was jump on the brakes, turn round and go back to her.

He'd tried to control his imagination, but all the way to Herefordshire, and again on Monday's return journey, his brain kept replaying a scenario where he had gone back, pulled up outside the house and she'd immediately climbed into the car with him, without saying a word. Then he saw them driving off into the sunset, to a new life together.

He hadn't gone so far as to sketch out any dreary details of that new life – like where they'd live and what on, and what would happen about her children and the not inconsiderable issue of her husband. In his nostalgia-addled head it had just been enough that they were together.

And he'd had even less success in preventing himself fast-forwarding to what would happen next in that scenario. Before he could help himself, they were back in that beautiful meadow, a squashy bed of clover beneath the carpet of wild flowers ...

Ouch! He'd cut his chin. It didn't matter how many times Simon's brain replayed it, and even despite his best efforts to joke the power out of it, by mentally labelling it 'Summer lovin' had me a blast', the effect was immediate and, as he'd just discovered, potentially injurious.

'Bloody hell,' he muttered, as the bright red blood dripped onto his grey-and-white marble wash basin. What was happening to him? One chance meeting with a middle-aged woman he'd known years before and he was like a sex-obsessed fourteen-year-old infatuated with his French teacher.

It was hard to fathom, but seeing Tessa again, the woman who had made such a deep impression on the twenty-two-year-old Simon Rathbone, fresh out of Bristol university and hungry for experiences, seemed as transformative now as it had then.

The thing was, he was beginning to conclude, that while he'd had his pick of gap-year and uni girlfriends before meeting Tessa, plus various liaisons in his adult life, nothing else in his sexual history had come near that one night with her.

Of course the setting had been ludicrously romantic and they'd both been in their most perfect physical prime and a fresh state of youthful naivety, before the cynicism of experience could set in, so it wasn't surprising he remembered it infused with such a golden glow.

But beyond that he still felt in some fundamental way that although their time together had been so brief – not even twenty-four hours – there'd been a depth of connection he'd never had with anyone else, before or since.

What would have happened, he wondered, staring at himself in the mirror, the blood still dripping from his chin, if he had got in contact with her the following week, as he'd meant to, before everything changed so dramatically for him? Or if all that had never happened? From a start like that would they have inevitably ended up together, as a couple? Would different versions of those young chaps he'd played skittles with be his children?

Furious with himself for this uncharacteristic mental indulgence, he threw his razor into the sink with such force it bounced right out again and landed on the floor. Snap out of it, Rathbone, he told himself angrily, picking it up and washing it under the tap.

Glancing at the clock on the wall behind him he saw he was already running behind schedule and now he'd have to clean every trace of the blood away before it stained the marble, which would probably make him late for the office. Simon was never late. He always got in an hour before his staff.

Even earlier recently, as he'd had quite a lot of extra work to deal with on the boring financial side of things. With his clients' rather relaxed attitudes to paying their bills, it had always been a bit of a juggling act, but with a recent hike in the rent on the Sydney Street building he was beginning to feel as though he was doing it on a high wire, standing on one leg. All the more reason not to let one rather ludicrous chance meeting with an old flame put him off his game.

He stuck a bit of loo roll to the still-bleeding nick on his chin, picked up his phone and texted his PA saying he had an unexpected appointment first thing – entirely fictitious – and resumed shaving, after turning on Radio 4, loud.

Lots of depressing news about wars and the state of the economy might keep his mind off historic hanky panky at least until he had a face tidy enough to show the world.

An hour later, safely arrived at the office, Simon was actually glad that Rachel was her usual twenty minutes late. Being installed in his leather Charles Eames swivel chair behind the barrier of his shiny white desk, everything just as he liked it, made him feel a little bit protected.

But that was undone the moment Rachel appeared in his office doorway wearing that navy shirtdress. The one that always made him feel a bit funny in the head. Or rather lower than his head. To his great surprise it still had the same effect.

He knew he'd been well on the way to being completely infatuated with Rachel, but after that extraordinary encounter with Tessa, and the subsequent mania, he'd assumed all his feelings for her younger sister would be gone. Surely one obsession would push out the other?

But one look at her curvy shape and her lovely bright face, and he felt exactly the same twinge of longing Rachel always inspired in him. Now he was more confused than ever and, even behind his desk barrier, felt horribly exposed. Not only was he dealing with inappropriate thoughts about one of his staff, he had now added to it some kind of weird incestuous obsession with her sister.

He could only find it in himself to answer Rachel's perfectly valid and brief enquiry about a detail of the Lawn & Stone press trip, by pretending to be concentrating on something very important on his computer and being quite short with her. And he was intensely grateful that his curt reply ensured that she didn't actually come into his office, as he feared she would, but legged it off as soon as she had his reply.

Once she'd gone Simon leaned back in his chair, stretching his legs out, hands linked on top of his head, staring up at the ceiling and sighing loudly. There was only one way to deal with this escalating and increasingly creepy situation.

He would have to get himself properly laid. And soon.

Rachel got back to her desk still smarting from Simon's rudeness. Why did he have to do that? She knew he was busy, but was there really any need to act like she was intruding inappropriately by asking him a pressing question which pertained only to the greater success of his business?

She wondered why she tried so hard. Maybe she should just cruise along like the other women in the office, most of whom seemed to spend their entire time there making personal phone calls, shopping online, or checking Facebook to see if there were any less than fabulous snaps of themselves which needed taking down after a weekend of japes in Hampshire.

But of course, she was still on probation, so she had to keep trying. More than that, it was who she was. She simply loved work, lived for it, was constantly inspired by the challenge of it; the game of getting new business and keeping the clients they already had happy, delighted with the service they were getting.

Apart from fun times with her daughters, nothing in her life beat the thrill of securing a really great press, television or online mention for one of her brands.

Work and family were the two balancing platforms of her life, she thought, scrolling through her emails and filing them in the relevant client folders. But they only stayed balanced if they were kept separate. That was why she'd been so uncomfortable having her boss mixing socially with her extended clan the previous Friday.

Maybe it was odd, as her mother had said, but work was too important to Rachel to be able to ease off about any aspect of it just because she was in a family setting. The two things just didn't go together.

It had been fine for Simon, because it wasn't his family. He'd been infuriatingly relaxed and chummy down there – what a contrast to the grumpy bastard she'd just spoken to. He'd played skittles with the kids, for god's sake.

What points she'd score with her colleagues if she shared that nugget of gossip with them, but she wouldn't. Rachel didn't go to work to make friends. She went there to be the best. And if Simon couldn't appreciate how good she was, he could get stuffed.

She'd already started making a few tentative enquiries at other agencies, in case it didn't pan out with Rathbone's, but she really didn't want to go anywhere else. Rathbone & Associates was the best PR agency at the elite end of interiors, and that was where she belonged. But Mr Rathbone really did need to start showing that he knew how lucky he was to have her in a work context, as well as being all nicey-nicey with her family.

Putting his recent unpleasantness out of her mind, Rachel refreshed her email inbox again to see if a key editor had responded yet to her invitation to the Lawn & Stone Tangiers trip. There was nothing from her, but an email from Daisy and Ari's father made her just as happy in a different context.

After some passive-aggressive crap about how he'd had to rearrange all his plans for the entire month after she'd insisted on having the girls the previous weekend, he confirmed that he was 'willing to accommodate her' and have them the following one.

Rachel danced her feet under her desk to express her delight. The girls going to Michael's could mean a weekend of carefree bliss with Link. She grabbed her phone to text him and his reply came back almost immediately:

'Great. And I'm not in the shop so we can hang out on Saturday too. Come here Friday after closing and we can ride down together.'

Rachel's heart sank a little at the thought of the long bike ride, but then remembering the last time, when they'd taken Link's preferred route via Richmond Park and stopped briefly in a thicket of trees for a delicious interlude, she thought she could handle it.

There was just the issue of the flat front tyre that she was fairly sure was a puncture. She didn't have a clue what to do with it and she could hardly take it into Link to get him to fix it. That would be the same as admitting she never rode the thing.

She knew how often her friends who really did cycle to work got punctures on London's streets, often strewn with broken glass. Knowing how to mend a tyre was part of riding a bike in London. Rachel didn't even know how to pump the stupid things up properly.

She opened Google and tapped in a search for other bicycle shops within easy wheeling access of her house, but then had a better idea and texted Branko to ask if he knew how to fix the tyre. Two minutes later her phone pinged in reply.

Rachel looked down at it and grinned. He did.

Thursday, 5 June

Hôtel Costes, Paris

Natasha was lying in bed with Mattie. She looked down at her face and ran her forefinger gently over the contours of those beautiful lips. Mattie opened her mouth and gently bit Natasha's finger, smiling up at her.

'Ow,' said Natasha, 'I need that finger.'

'You certainly do,' said Mattie, giggling, and Natasha laughed too, pulling her hand away and running it slowly down Mattie's body.

'Mmmm,' said Mattie, turning over and stroking Natasha's breasts, making her whole body tingle with residual pleasure from what had gone on most of the night and seemed about to start up again.

Natasha had been so nervous waiting for Mattie the evening before in a tiny bistro on the Saint Michel canal, well away from the more fashionable restaurant where the rest of the crew were celebrating the end of the three-day Paris shoot.

She'd bowed out, claiming a busy schedule the next day, but as she waited, constantly checking her phone, she'd wondered if she'd been crazy making the arrangement. It wasn't like catching up for a quick coffee, after all ... Will you have dinner with me in Paris?

Perhaps she'd been under some kind of spell cast by Tessa's rather magical house, surrounded by the people she loved the most. Had it made her view Mattie through a false rosy glow, or would she still find her as attractive when she saw her again?

Passing the time until Mattie arrived – she'd just sent a text saying the Eurostar had arrived twenty minutes late – she flicked through the photos from the day they'd met. Mattie and Branko sitting in Tessa's garden with their feet in the water of the copper tank. Mattie in a group shot holding up their glasses at the dinner table. Mattie playing with Daisy and Ariadne. And one of Mattie by herself, looking straight into the camera. Natasha had felt almost giddy as she looked at it.

The heavy eyebrows and the dark blonde hair, side-parted and slicked over one eye. The full but finely sculpted lips, which were Natasha's weakness. She spent her days painting colour onto famous pouts, so she'd made a study of them and Mattie's were as luscious as any she'd seen.

From the moment she'd seen those beautiful lips, she'd longed to find out if they'd feel as good to kiss as they looked. And now, after that romantic dinner and the night together in her hotel suite, she knew they did.

She had just bent down to kiss them again when there was a knock on the door. They froze, looking at each other with wide eyes, Mattie's hands still on Natasha's breasts.

'Room service,' Natasha whispered.

'Shall I go and hide in the bathroom?' asked Mattie, pinching Natasha's nipples a bit harder.

Natasha thought for a moment – as well as she could, with what Mattie was doing. It was Paris, she told herself, no one would blink an eye at finding two women in bed together, but they were at the hotel where she always stayed for work. A hotel that was such a part of the fashion world it was practically a label in its own right. She was certain that the news of who had been in Natasha Younger's bed that morning would be around the industry in no time.

'Would you mind?' she asked, feeling horrible about it.

'I've done worse,' said Mattie, kissing her quickly, then hopping off the bed and heading for the bathroom. Natasha watched her go, as gorgeous from behind as she was from the front, and looked forward to resuming what had just started, but meanwhile there was the waiter to deal with.

'*Attendez-vous un instant*,' she called out towards the hotel room door. '*J'arrive …*'

Natasha smiled to herself at the appropriateness of the French double entendre, which was the same as the English one. I'm coming. I will be soon, she thought, getting out of bed and grabbing a bathrobe.

As soon as the waiter had gone – and it took a while as he wheeled the breakfast in on a trolley, which he then turned into a small round table, lifting up flaps on either side – Natasha called to Mattie that it was safe to come out.

'Oooh,' she said, her face lighting up, 'a hotel breakfast on one of those special tables. How glamorous.'

Natasha smiled. On trips like this, she normally got up running and grabbed a green tea when she got to the studio, and it was so lovely to have someone to share her luxurious hotel suite with.

'Do you want to eat at the table, or in bed?' she asked.

'At the table, duh,' said Mattie, heading back into the bathroom and coming back out wearing a robe the same as the one Natasha had on. 'We don't want any crumbs in the bed, do we?'

Natasha grinned at her and reached into the ice bucket for the bottle of champagne she'd ordered to arrive with their breakfast. She popped it open and poured them both a glass. They toasted each other and lifted the metal plate covers, exclaiming with delight at the eggs benedict they'd completely forgotten ordering the night before.

'I'm sorry about the bathroom thing just now,' said Natasha after they'd both had a few mouthfuls.

'Don't worry,' said Mattie, shrugging, 'that kind of crap sort of goes with the territory, doesn't it? I know we're in Paris and this is a very sophisticated hotel, I'm sure they see it all here, but sometimes it's easier not to confront things full on, isn't it? I can't always be bothered.'

Natasha didn't answer immediately, chewing her food and wondering what territory Mattie meant exactly. She was still mulling it over, when Mattie started speaking again.

'You should have seen the bother I used to get into before I came out to my parents,' she said, shaking her head and laughing. 'I had to hide naked under my first girlfriend's bed for over an hour one time, when her mum came in for a heart to heart with her and sat there yacking on. I thought she'd never go. It was so funny.

'And then when I was at art college, my folks thought the woman I was living with was my flatmate. It was such a relief when I finally told them. They were a bit surprised – I guess I'd done almost too good a job of keeping it from them – then they were cool. My mum says now she always "suspected". I don't know if that's true, but they're fine about it, that's all that matters.'

She paused for a moment, pulling her legs up onto the chair, and took a long sip from her champagne glass, looking right at Natasha.

'But it seems like you haven't come out to your family yet,' she said.

Natasha looked down at her plate for a moment. She'd known this conversation would probably have to happen at some point. She'd just hoped it might not be during this gorgeous Paris interlude.

'No, I haven't,' she said.

'Any particular reason?' asked Mattie. 'I mean, they are a seriously cool bunch of people. Your mum is amazing, your sister has a trans nanny, for god's sake ... they didn't seem like people who'd be upset.'

Natasha put her elbows on the table and rested her head on her fingers, rubbing her temples. Suddenly she didn't have much of an appetite any more.

'It's not coming out to my family that bothers me,' she said. 'It's the rest of the world.'

'How come?' said Mattie. 'Surely it's your family that's the hard one? The industry you and I work in could hardly be more gay friendly.'

'It's gay friendly to men,' said Natasha, sitting up straight again.

'I've never found it a problem,' said Mattie, frowning.

No, thought Natasha, at your level, it isn't. But when you're dealing with the highest elite of the modelling world, some of them from cultures where it's still illegal to be gay, it could be risky.

All it would take was one big name who didn't want to let a *lesbian* touch her face and her whole career could come crashing down, even if nothing was ever said publicly.

The camp gay man was an established feature of the high fashion scene, absolutely central to it, but there was still a weird double standard for gay women. She'd heard enough bitchy comments about 'ugly dykes' and 'miserable lezzers' to warn her well away.

It was getting better, but slowly, and Natasha wasn't interested in being some kind of sexual-politics trailblazer; she just wanted to carry on doing what she did, at the level she'd worked so hard to get herself up to. So, for the time being, she was in the same bind as those Hollywood leading-man heart-throbs who had to hide in beard-crammed closets, or lose it all.

But she didn't want to go into all that, not in the heavenly Paris bubble they were in – and that wasn't the only issue. There was another reason Natasha hadn't come out and maybe that was something she could talk to Mattie about. As well as finding her devastatingly attractive, she felt so comfortable with her, so she thought she could – and maybe she should.

'The thing is, Mattie,' she said, leaning over the table towards her, 'the whole coming-out scenario, saying "I'm gay, I'm a lesbian" and all that, defining yourself by your sexuality, I just don't feel entirely comfortable with it. I don't even know if I am "fully" gay.'

She did the inverted commas thing with her fingers.

'You were fully gay last night, sweetie,' said Mattie, raising her glass, before draining it.

Natasha did the same and re-filled both glasses.

'Last night I was a big old lesbian and I loved it,' she said, 'and I fully intend to be a big lesbian again in the very near future, but does that mean I have to formally and publicly identify myself under that label? Can't I just be a person who really likes having sex with people of her own gender, but has also had relationships with guys? Not for a long time, it's true, but I have enjoyed sex with men in the past, Mattie. Haven't you?'

Mattie looked at her with no expression. 'No,' she said.

Natasha felt the hint of a chill come between them and her heart sank. Why the hell had she risked this conversation with someone she liked as much as Mattie? And so early on? Why did it matter how gay she was? It felt like some kind of crazy percentage game – I'm 85 per cent lesbian, I'm 100 per cent – but she'd dug herself in this far, she might as well keep going to try and salvage it.

'Have you ever had sex with a man?' she asked.

'No,' said Mattie, shaking her head very slowly. 'That is a concept that has zero appeal to me. I have loads of men friends, but I've never met a man who triggered any sexual attraction in me whatsoever.'

'Do you mind that I have?' asked Natasha, gazing across her barely eaten breakfast at Mattie, trying not to let a catch of tears come into her voice. Why had she started this? she thought again.

Mattie looked back at her for a few more moments and then Natasha saw her expression soften.

'Look, Tashie,' she said, gently, 'it's not a concept I particularly want to linger on, because I don't really want to think about you ever having sex with anyone else other than me – male, female or anything in between, before now, or after. Just me. And a lot of it. OK?'

She stood up and went around to Natasha's side of the table, unlooping the belt of her bathrobe on the way and letting it fall to the ground. Then she untied Natasha's robe and after pulling it open climbed onto her lap, pressing her naked body against hers.

'And now I'm going to remind you how a real lesbian does that, OK?'

For a moment Natasha was too surprised – and happy – to speak. So she just smiled and surrendered to Mattie's kiss.

Cranbrook

Tessa woke up to find herself in an empty bed. That was unusual, because she always woke up first, at 7 a.m., conditioned by years of child rearing and school runs, then she'd get up and start breakfast for everybody.

Her brain not yet quite fully awake, she tried to remember if Tom had said anything about needing to get up early the night before ... Tom. It hit her like a punch to the stomach and she rolled over on her side, bringing her knees up towards her chest, trying to push the memory away. At the same time it sunk in that she wasn't in her own bed either. She was in one of the guest rooms on the top floor of the house.

The night before something had happened for the first time in all their years together. Tom had initiated sex and she'd pushed him away at the crucial moment.

She couldn't believe she'd done that to him. That was one area where they'd never had a problem. They seemed to have fairly matching appetites for it, but whenever she wasn't in the mood, he was always fine about it.

What had been so awful the night before was that she had changed her mind at the very last moment. He'd come into the bedroom and found her brushing her hair, sitting at her dressing table in her underwear. Things had progressed as normal, but once Tom had taken her over to the bed and was reaching down to stroke her into near ecstasy before climbing onto her, something in her head had snapped.

She'd been very turned on, she remembered, Tom had commented on it as his fingers touched her, but then she realised with horror it was because her brain had popped up an image of Simon's face. Simon's face as it had been – young, beautiful, and looking down at her, making love to her in that field.

She'd been so shocked by what her subconscious had done she nearly cried out. And not in the way Tom might have expected at that point. Then she had actually, physically, pushed him away, saying the word: 'No.'

'No. I can't. I'm sorry.'

She'd heard Tom swear – so unlike him, but it wasn't a situation they'd ever been in before – then she'd fled to the bathroom and locked herself in, sobbing with shame and self-hatred.

She'd knelt on the floor, her forehead on the cold edge of the bath, feeling so ashamed and frightened that somehow Tom could know what had been going on in her head. And fear that she would have to tell him what had happened to explain her behaviour.

After a few moments she'd heard a gentle tap at the door.

'Tessa,' said Tom's voice, sounding concerned and bewildered. 'Are you all right? What's going on? Can I come in?'

'I'm sorry,' she said. 'I'll be out in a minute.'

'OK, my Bunny,' he'd said, using his pet name for her. 'Let me know if you need me.'

Then, with great relief, she'd heard his footsteps leaving the room and as soon as the clatter of him going down the stairs had faded away, she'd left the bathroom, grabbed her dressing gown and run out of their bedroom and up the stairs to the top floor. Still not ready to see anyone, she'd locked herself into the bathroom up there, hoping Tom would go to bed without looking for her.

He did and she'd climbed into the cold spare bed, lying for hours unable to sleep for her tormented thoughts, which were a horrible mixture of guilt and some kind of weird longing for Simon – a man she'd had sex with once and hadn't seen for over twenty-five years. It was so crazy, Tessa had begun to wonder if she was slipping into some kind of menopausal madness. She genuinely didn't feel rational.

Seeing Simon again, after all that time, had somehow catapulted her back into remembering how it felt to be her younger self again. The days when big-name decorators had fought over her – and every man's head had turned to have a second look when she walked down a street.

What was so odd was that they weren't things she'd been the slightest bit aware of missing all these years. They'd disappeared from her life quite naturally as she'd become very happily tied up with starting the business and being a mother, but now she was reminded of them again, it had set off a strange yearning inside that made her feel very unsettled.

She'd believed she'd been her most happy in recent times, but now she felt oddly guilty for not appreciating those more glamorous days when she'd had them. Had she let it all go too easily?

In the early hours, as the birds were starting to sing, she'd finally managed to drift off, still worrying how she was going to face Tom in the morning and now, here she was, lying awake again in the unfamiliar bed, no closer to knowing how to handle this bizarre situation.

She pulled the covers over her head for a moment. Why oh why had Rachel brought that wretched man to her house? Then she pulled them down again just as fast, realising she had no idea what the time was – Tom might still be asleep, the boys would be late for school.

Jumping out of bed, she ran down the stairs in what seemed like a silent house and, sure enough, all the beds were empty and the clock on the table next to her pillow told her it was already twenty past ten. She stared at it in disbelief. She never slept in, but then it had probably been nearly five in the morning before she'd gone to sleep.

No wonder she felt so befuddled, and no wonder the house was so deathly quiet. They were all long gone. And she wasn't sure whether to be relieved or worried that Tom hadn't come to find her before he left.

Turning back towards the bedroom door, thinking a cup of tea would help clear her fuggy head, she noticed a small vase of wild flowers on her dressing table, with a note leaning against it, in Tom's writing.

> Tessa, my love. I left you to sleep because you seemed so upset last night. Hope it wasn't something I did. Please ring me as soon as you get up to tell me you are OK. I've just heard that the Scottish shoot has been brought forward so I'll stay up in town and go straight to the airport tomorrow. I'll be gone for the weekend, I'm afraid. I'll let you know more when I have the details. Take care and if something's wrong *tell me*, my precious little Bunny. T xxx

He'd underlined the words 'tell me' three times. It was a thing between them, how Tessa bottled things up and didn't talk about what was really worrying her. That was why Tom called her Bunny, because apart from a bit of chewing, rabbits didn't make any noise.

Tessa stood staring down at the note for a few seconds and then brought it up to her lips and kissed it, loving Tom more than ever in that moment, for being so kind and understanding.

Which then turned into another stab of terrible guilt, when she realised how glad she was she didn't have to see him for a few days.

London W1

Simon turned his head and smiled contentedly at the woman lying next to him. She smiled back.

'Good to see you haven't lost your touch,' she said. 'I was beginning to think I wasn't ever going to hear from you again.'

'Ah, well, you know how it is, Jane,' he said, 'I've been really busy at work recently. We've been pitching for some serious new business and it takes all my energy.'

Plus I'm spending my days with a woman I'm very attracted to who stimulates my brain as much as she does my gonads, which has stopped me giving you a second thought. Until another woman reared up out of my past and set my testicles on fire.

'All work and no play makes Simon a dull boy,' said Jane, reaching her hand beneath the covers and giving his cock a gentle squeeze.

He smiled at her again. She hadn't lost her touch either, he had to admit. Jane had always been an exocet missile in bed. She was great looking, too, with the small waist he so admired in a woman and great legs.

Rachel's curves were better though. And Tessa's, but he was trying desperately not to think about either of them. That was why he was in this hotel room with Jane.

'Have you got to be anywhere soon?' he asked her, feeling himself responding to her fingers. Not bad for his age, he thought. They'd already had at it twice.

She giggled.

'Why?' she asked, increasing her activity.

'Well, I might want to pitch for your business ...' he said, reaching for her.

Some time later Jane got out of the bed and headed to the shower. Simon sat up, leaning back against the pillows, feeling at one with himself for the first time in days. He'd let her go and then eat a room-service dinner, and watch some telly, before heading home. Might as well get the most out of the room he'd paid for.

He found the remote control and turned on the television, scrolling down until he found some cricket, quickly turning it off again when Jane came back into the room. Even in a set-up like this there were basic levels of respect.

She was applying lipstick at the mirror over the desk, when he noticed her looking at him in the reflection.

'I've got some exciting news, I haven't told you,' she said, turning her eyes back to her lipstick.

'Yes?' said Simon. 'Go on.'

She got a small bottle of scent out of her bag and sprayed herself liberally, with a couple of final spritzes to her hair.

'Just in case there's any residual aftershave up there,' she said, smiling at him.

'Is that your news?' said Simon.

'No,' said Jane, turning to face him, picking her handbag up off the chair. 'Andrew and I are getting married.'

'Congratulations,' said Simon, his mouth in auto-respond mode for such an announcement. 'Who's Andrew?'

Jane laughed.

'He's a guy I've been seeing for the last year or so. I never thought I'd get married again, but he took me to Positano to propose and I thought why not? He's very generous and I'm getting older, I might not get another good offer. Third time lucky and all that.'

'Well, that's marvellous. I hope you'll be very happy. When's the big day?'

'Mid-September. Do you want to come? We're getting married in Italy too, lots of people coming for a long weekend. You'd know loads of them. It's going to be a hoot.'

'You're very kind, but I've got a big work trip then, so I wouldn't be able to take any more time out of the office.'

'Suit yourself, party pooper.'

After pausing to push her feet into her high-heeled pumps, she came over to the bed and leaned down to kiss him, her handbag – a Birkin, he noticed, how obvious – looped over one arm.

'Bye, Simon, darling,' she said, sliding her tongue quickly into his mouth and out again. She was a naughty one.

'Have fun with your fiancé,' he said, smiling up at her and reaching round to squeeze her behind.

'Not quite as much fun as with you, but at least Andrew and I go out in public together. Normal behaviour, dinner in a restaurant, introducing to friends and family, commitment and all that.'

'I wouldn't know,' he said.

'No, you wouldn't, you're emotionally retarded, so it's fortunate you have other qualities. Don't leave it so long before you call me again, OK?'

Simon nodded, smiling encouragingly and said nothing. Sure, I'll call you again, he thought, as she walked towards the door, her tempting bottom wiggling as she went. Right after your next divorce. I might be a messed-up weirdo, who can't take on a proper emotional relationship, but I do have some sort of a moral compass and married women are definitely off the map.

Which reminded him of Tessa and why his freakishly rekindled passion for her had been so catastrophically wrong. Not only was she the sister of his employee, for whom he also had complicated feelings, she was a married woman and a mother of three. A total no-fly zone.

He'd have to contact one of his other lady friends. Or two. He mustn't let it go so long again, leaving the normal healthy physical appetites unattended the way he had. It just led to complications and muddled thinking.

Feeling as he did now, entirely satisfied by several hours of vigorous sex with a marvellous-looking and very enthusiastic woman, he couldn't quite understand how he'd allowed himself to get into such a state. He needed all his wits in order to concentrate on the business. Get back on the program, Rathbone. Buck up, don't fuck up.

He checked the menu and called down to order a steak, rare, took a beer out of the mini bar and then picked up the remote and turned the TV back on, leaning back against the pillows, absently scratching his chest. Contentment.

Scrolling through the channels for something more edifying than Northamptonshire versus Sri Lanka, he stopped when he heard some familiar title music, which he recognised as a show he liked, but couldn't immediately place.

It took a moment before he realised he was looking at the soot-smeared face of Tessa's husband. Immediately he felt his own cheeks turn hot, in something like a blush, and his stomach turned over, his equanimity destroyed in a flash.

Was there no escape?

Friday, 6 June

Heathrow Airport

Tom was sitting at the departure gate playing Candy Crush on his phone. They'd just announced that boarding was going to be delayed, although they hadn't said for how long, so there was no point going all the way back to the lounge in case it was only a few minutes.

He'd already signed a couple of autographs and was hoping that if he kept his head down and looked engrossed with something on his phone no one else would approach him.

It wasn't that he minded being accosted by total strangers, in fact he rather enjoyed meeting people who watched the show. Apart from the odd idiot – usually young blokes who'd had too much to drink and were showing off to girls – they were generally very nice and it was interesting to hear what they liked about it, so he could pass the feedback on to the producer.

And in all honesty, it still gave him a bit of a kick the way it seemed to thrill people to meet him, even if it was just for a moment. It didn't cost him anything and they went away all pink and beaming, with a celebrity selfie to show off to their friends.

It was just that particular morning he wanted a bit of time to himself to think, before he got immersed in the hectic business of filming the show. He was worried about Tessa.

He'd already been concerned about her becoming increasingly isolated, staying at home on her own too much, and now she'd had this strange freak-out. That had been so weird.

It wasn't the missing out on sex aspect that had bothered him – although he had wished she'd changed her mind at a slightly earlier stage – it was the hysterical outburst after that. It just wasn't the way their relationship had ever been. They weren't door-slamming, china-throwing, drama-queening people. And they certainly weren't separate-beds people.

Of course, he told himself, trying not to let it show that he'd noticed a woman was taking what she thought was a covert snap of him on her phone, the obvious reason for it was staring him in the face. It was Tessa's age.

She must be starting on the woman's change thing, which he remembered had made his own mother go rather peculiar when he was a teenager. The menopause. His poor Bunny. He hoped it wouldn't be too hard for her, especially as the timing couldn't be worse, with Finn and Archie about to start weekly boarding.

She'd been very brave when he'd discussed that with her, but he knew the reality of not having two of her babies in the house several days a week would be tough on her, however difficult Finn could be.

Combined with her general isolation and this new outbreak of womanly weirdness, it could all get very difficult. And he hadn't had a chance to talk to her yet about his upcoming trip to LA to discuss doing a US version of the show.

Perhaps he should speak to Joy about the menopause thing. She'd be bound to know some herbal tisane, or tincture Tessa could use to help her through it. Although he did hope his wife wouldn't start going about clutching a cluster of crystals.

Meanwhile, he'd just have to do what he could to bolster her confidence and reassure her that his feelings for her would never change, even if she did have the odd crying fit and didn't always feel like a bit of rumpy pumpy when he did.

Most importantly he needed to get her involved with life again, seeing people, doing stuff outside the house. Which reminded him of the idea he'd had after the magazine shoot: to get Rachel and that Simon bloke doing some PR for Hunter Gatherer and to have Tessa looking after it all, which she'd really have to if this US thing took off. His agent, Barney, was pretty confident it would.

That was just the boost his sensitive little Bunny needed, so as the announcement began, inviting business-class passengers to come forward to board the plane, he quickly sent Rachel a text, asking her to set up the lunch they'd discussed with her boss, him and Tessa the following week.

That should sort it, thought Tom, flashing his best TV-star grin at the flight attendant who was processing his boarding card at the gate. She smiled back at him, blushing and looking a bit flustered.

Tom chuckled quietly to himself as he walked down the tunnel to the plane. It did give him a kick doing that, he couldn't deny it – and why not? She'd have something to tell her friends and he enjoyed being able to bestow those little treats on people. It didn't cost him anything. Barney called it 'sowing ratings seeds', Tom preferred to think of it as sharing the love.

Either way, he thought happily, settling into his seat and doing the smile thing again with the young woman who had just come to hang up his jacket, now he could relax into being Tim Chiminey again for a few days.

Leave dreary old Tom Chenery and all his middle-aged anxieties behind for a while. Bring it on.

Sydney Street

Rachel got Tom's text during a full staff meeting, where Simon was outlining his vision for Rathbone & Associates 'going forward', which was just one of many irritating business-speak clichés he'd come out with so far in his spiel.

She wondered whether he'd been on some kind of motivational management course, he was so fired up about it all. He had a whiteboard and a PowerPoint on the go. If there'd been a sofa in the boardroom, Rachel thought he might have jumped up and down on it like Tom Cruise. It was giving her the pip.

Reading Tom's message, she groaned inwardly at the prospect of being forced to mix family and work again so soon after the shoot.

She now deeply regretted ever suggesting to Simon the idea of them doing PR for Hunter Gatherer. She'd been a bit too clever for herself and hadn't thought through the full implications of what she was saying before it was already out of her mouth.

She was running through them in her head, when Simon said something that made her start listening properly again. He was telling them about a bonus system he was introducing for staff members who brought new clients to the firm.

'If we bank real cash money from a new client you've brought in, you'll be rewarded in your very next pay packet, ten per cent of the first six months' fees,' said Simon. 'What's good for the firm is good for us all. Think of us as the John Lewis of PR – well, not exactly, I am still the sole owner ...'

That's better, thought Rachel, finding she was glad to have old bastard Simon back, rather than this weird new happy-clappy Simon. But the bonus thing was interesting.

She was already working on some prospective new clients and it would certainly make the Hunter Gatherer idea more appealing. The extra money would more than make up for the family/work irritation.

She'd accidentally opened a credit card statement that morning, before she'd realised what it was – she'd thought it was an invitation, or she never would have opened the thing – and had felt nauseous looking at it, realising it was going to be hard for her to make even the minimum payment that month.

And that was just one of her cards. She'd been doing some more of those alarming sums on the Tube that morning and had spent the rest of the journey wondering what she could put on eBay that weekend. So this new bonus thing couldn't have come along at a better time.

Re-reading Tom's text and wondering how much ten per cent of the first six months of Hunter Gatherer fees would be and how quickly she could get that first payment to land in the Rathbone & Associates account, she snapped back to attention when she heard Simon say her name. Everyone in the room was looking at her. Oops.

'Are you with us, Rachel?' Simon asked, one eyebrow arched. 'Or thinking about something more important?'

'I was thinking about some new business I might be bringing in,' she said, raising one of her own eyebrows to mirror his. 'I've just had a text from the prospective new client. He wants to have lunch with us next week.'

'That's great,' said Simon. 'Just what I'm talking about, but perhaps you can put your phone away now until after we've finished this meeting? Basic business manners and all that ...'

You utter fucker, thought Rachel, as a palpable frisson passed through the room. Oh, wouldn't that give them something to whisper about at one of the after-work drinks sessions she never went to. How Simon had told the new girl off in front of them all. Just when she'd been showing everyone up with her digital media contacts and getting a new client's product into *You* mag.

It was like working on *Gossip Girl* with that lot sometimes. They were genuinely nice and smiley and fun, all perfect manners according to the official courtesy codes of their class – Monday morning kicked off with a flurry of thank-you letter writing for most of them – but about as mature as a gaggle of teenage girls underneath.

Rachel made a show of turning off her phone and putting it face down on the table in front of her. Then she lifted her head, pasting on her most interested expression, as if she couldn't wait to hear what fascinating thing Simon was going to say next. Or Cruisey, as she was going to think of him from now on. The smooth bastard.

Back behind his desk, Simon felt bad about how he'd treated Rachel at the meeting. Of course, she shouldn't have been texting during his presentation, it was as rude as keeping your phone on the table at dinner, but he still shouldn't have shown her up in front of the rest of the staff like that.

Especially as he knew they already felt threatened by her. She was smarter than them, worked harder, had better contacts and exponentially better ideas, as proved by her success securing the Lawn & Stone business. And who knew? With all that concentrated female intuition, maybe they'd also figured out that the boss man had special – and grossly inappropriate – feelings for their new colleague.

And he knew that was exactly why he'd been so harsh towards her again. Despite his most enjoyable afternoon with Jane and that bonkers lust flashback for Tessa at the weekend, there was no question that he still felt exactly the same about Rachel as he had before.

Which wasn't just the physical thing. He did think she was gorgeous, but really it was her perky brain, so bright, so sassy, so always after the main chance – just like him, but without the hang-ups – which made him feel like a giddy schoolboy.

So, he thought, reviewing his recent behaviour, in one week he could vigorously shag one woman, be sexually obsessed with another and still feel emotionally strung out about a third.

Was he some kind of split personality psycho freak?

Saturday, 7 June

Ham, Richmond, Southwest London

Rachel woke early, the light of the morning sun on the river dappling over her face. For a moment she felt a sharp pang of sadness that it wasn't Ariadne waking her up, climbing into Mummy's bed, clutching her favourite teddy, as she did every morning, but then she turned her head to look at Link.

In the peace of sleep he looked even younger than his thirty-two years, one arm thrown behind his head, his smooth chest bare above the covers, slowly rising and falling, hardly a line on his face.

Rachel felt a flutter, remembering the night before. They'd cycled all the way down to Ham from Queen's Park, stopping at a pub by the river to eat, arriving at the houseboat still in the long June evening light.

Then sitting on the deck with a bottle of wine, Link quietly playing his guitar, Rachel just being, not thinking about anything, watching the sun starting to set.

And when it was properly dark they'd gone below to the cabin and slowly, exquisitely made love. It was never a furious passion with him, but steady and quiet in the loose-limbed way he did everything, with no end and no beginning, just rolling pleasure until they both fell into a deep satisfied sleep.

Used to the demanding early starts of young children, Rachel was immediately wide awake. She lay there for a while staring up at the wooden roof, enjoying the movement of the houseboat shifting gently on the water, until she started to feel restless.

Nine years of parenting had made her forget how to have a lie-in. She looked at Link again, as he turned his head and licked his lips in his sleep. Should she wake him with a below-the-waist hello? She'd done that before, but he was so deeply asleep it didn't seem right to disturb him.

Sitting up, she looked out of the window – or was it a porthole? It wasn't round, so she decided in this hybrid boat and house, it was a window. A swan was paddling along with five cygnets in a row behind her. It was a lovely sight, but it made her miss the girls again. Rachel wanted her cygnets swimming along in her wake.

But, she reminded herself, looking out at the refreshingly different river-level view, with a police boat chugging past and rowers skulling on the northern side, at least she wasn't waking up on Saturday morning on her own. She'd never got used to that. The first weekend Michael had the girls after the separation had nearly killed her. She'd ended up going down to spend the rest of it with her mum, for comfort.

It was about the only time she could remember being glad Joy was a joojie moojie weirdo. She'd held Rachel tight and let her bawl into her shoulder, never making any told-you-so remarks about the separation, although Rachel knew Joy thought she'd been hasty. Then she'd made Rachel lie down on some cushions on the floor with a blanket over her, and with the room lit by candles and scented with incense she'd taken her on some kind of guided meditation.

Rachel didn't remember much about it – in fact she was fairly sure she'd just fallen asleep – but when she came around

Joy told her she'd guided her through a past-life experience when Michael had been her controlling father and by letting go of that karma, she'd be able to come to terms with her journey with him in this lifetime and grow from it.

In short, a load of utter cock. She'd had Tashie in hysterics on the phone telling her about it the next day, but it had been a very restful deep sleep and Rachel had felt much calmer about everything when she'd woken up from it.

Then Joy had made them comforting bowls of dhal and rice, and they'd watched an old film curled up on the sofa together, Rachel eventually lying with her head on her mother's knee, which she knew was some kind of regression into being a child herself, in lieu of being with her own offspring, but she didn't care. Or need her mother to explain it to her as some other mystical nonsense. It was just wonderfully comforting to lie there with Joy stroking her hair.

After a trip to the flea market together the next morning and coffee and herbal tea in town, before getting the train back to London, it hadn't seemed too long until she was united with her poppets again. Which was especially satisfying when Daisy had told her the weekend with Dad had been 'as boring as going to the dentist'.

He'd taken them to the Science Museum. Daisy said it was full of mean boys who wouldn't let her get near anything with a button she could push and Ari had been aghast that the gift shop didn't seem to sell anything pink. Rachel had made a mental note to take them to Selfridges the following Saturday. That was the kind of museum her girls liked. Especially with a visit to the gelato bar.

So after that first miserable childless time as a separated mother she'd learned to plan ahead and pack every weekend without them with grown-up activities: visiting her mum,

Tessa, or friends with places out of town; having people to stay; and going on Easyjet minibreaks with single pals.

Those trips away were good for work too, because she got great ideas – and top Instagram shots – and had met up with bloggers she admired in Copenhagen, Oporto and Bruges. She'd also found some interesting possible clients for work, who wanted representation in London.

So that was all constructive – especially with this new-business bonus Simon had just announced. But the main thing was to make sure she never again woke up alone in her house on a Saturday morning.

Which was what had made meeting Link so amazing. On her weekends without the girls she was as free from responsibility as he was and they could spend thirty-six hours in a bubble, just the two of them.

He did have friends, of course, he'd get texts and calls while they were together, and sometimes he couldn't meet her because he already had plans for the weekend. But she'd never met any of his pals, or introduced him to hers.

It wasn't that kind of relationship – if that was even the right word for it. What was it then? A friendship? It wasn't quite friends with benefits, or 'fuck buddies', as some of her franker girlfriends called men they met up with from time to time for no-strings, good-times sex. She and Link had a lovely unpressured meeting of minds, combined with delightful meetings of other bits.

Other bits which Rachel realised were now stirring, when she felt Link's hand reach out and squeeze her thigh. She turned away from the window and smiled at him.

Tunbridge Wells

Joy and Muffin were lying on the bed together, enjoying the early morning sun streaming in through the open window. Muffin was stretched out, his back resting against Joy's legs, maximising all available sources of warmth. Joy was sitting up, propped by pillows, eyes closed, slowly stroking the blissed-out cat.

She was opening herself to the universe, trying to understand the source of the uneasy feeling she'd woken up with. It wasn't just the letters, although she'd had two more of them.

There'd been a second one from the solicitors the week before, which she'd shredded without opening it and then just a couple of days ago another had arrived, in a different envelope, addressed simply to Elsie Ainsworth. No Lambton on it, which was even more alarming. Elsie Ainsworth really was a dead name, where on earth had somebody got it from?

There was no logo or returning address on the envelope to give her any indication where it was from so she'd destroyed that one without reading it as well. She hadn't been able to get it out of her hands quickly enough. Seeing that long-discarded name neatly printed on the envelope, like it was perfectly normal, gave her the heebie-jeebies.

She'd meditated on the issue several times since and while all kinds of possibilities for receiving the letters had come into her head, some of them more persistent than others, she had always batted them straight out again.

However she looked at it, there was only one conclusion to make: there was nothing that could be in letters addressed to that name which it would benefit her equilibrium to know, so discarding them unread was the right thing to do. She was in no doubt about it. Things left in the past needed to stay there. For the good of all.

The unsettled feeling she had now was more to do with her girls. Things beyond any of their control were moving. Change was coming, she knew it. It didn't feel negative in itself, necessarily, but change was unsettling while it was in progress and it could make people behave impulsively. Make them do things they might regret later.

She had often wondered if it was the shock of puberty which had made Natasha make that sudden decision to move back to Brisbane with her father that time. And she was sure the changes brought on by motherhood had contributed to Tessa's self-isolation and Rachel's impetuous divorce.

Joy opened her eyes and looked down at the cat, who was now stretching all four of his legs out in an ecstasy of physical comfort.

'Secrets, Muffin', she said. He looked back at her with his golden eyes. Human trifles, they seemed to say. Go on, bore me. Joy found his indifference very calming.

'Something a bit dark at the heart of it,' she continued. 'Someone has a secret and it's eating them alive, without them realising it. I'm not sure if it's the secret itself, or the effort of keeping it. I've got to tread carefully, Mr Muff, to find out what this is all about, so it can't hurt my girls.'

The cat looked at her impassively for another moment and then got busy licking the fur on his chest. Joy smiled down at him. How she wished humans could live entirely in the moment the way cats did.

She closed her eyes again, breathing in, breathing out, letting go of outcomes, trying not to think about anything, until the anxiety about her daughters elbowed its way forcibly back into her consciousness. It was no good, she'd just have to give in and actively think it through.

'How can I best support my girls?' she said out loud. Having Muffin there gave her permission to do that, but she was really asking herself, or the Higher Power inside her, as she preferred to think of it. And as she spoke, she realised she already knew the answer.

'That's it, Mr Muff,' she said, stroking his head. 'I just need to be with them, then I will be able to protect them. I wonder how that will unfold, but it surely will. Brace yourself, puss. Change is coming for us, too.'

Then she closed her eyes and allowed herself to drift back to sleep, absolutely certain that now she understood how she could safeguard her daughters, the universe would make it happen.

Muffin curled up and went back to sleep too.

Monday, 9 June

Cranbrook

Tessa was sitting on the high stool by the phone in the kitchen, trying to think of excuses to get out of this ridiculous lunch Tom wanted her to have with him, Rachel and Simon the next day.

It was Monday morning, Tom was still in Scotland, the boys had gone to school and she had nothing else to think about. It was going round and round in her head, driving her potty.

She'd tried going for a walk through the yard with her phone, to see if there were any good Instagram shots to take in the morning sun. She'd tried working on the new mural, based on the Great Barrier Reef, she was doing in the guest bathroom, but she couldn't settle to it. Nothing had felt quite right in her world, since that shattering encounter with Simon.

Over a week later, the overwhelming feelings seeing him again had aroused had mostly abated, until she sometimes wondered if it had actually happened. But then out of nowhere, a vivid recollection of that moment out by the car would pop into her head, and the sense of utter desolation she'd felt when he'd driven off would come back in all its intensity. It had happened all right.

She'd hardly thought about him in all the years since that night in Devon, she'd been too busy with kids, the business and Tom – darling Tom – but in that instant it had felt as though she'd been waiting all her adult life for Simon to come back.

She wondered what strange game her heart was playing with her and knew that only time and distance would help her move on again. So the last thing she needed was to reignite her feelings, by seeing Simon again at a stupid lunch that she really didn't need to go to.

After grasping her head with her hands for a moment and shaking it, she picked up the phone and dialled Rachel's mobile.

'Hey, sis,' said Rachel, surprised to hear from Tessa. She wasn't a great one for the phone. 'What gives?'

'Hi, Rachel,' said Tessa, feeling a sense of dread at even raising the subject. 'I'm just ringing about the lunch Tom has arranged with you for tomorrow.'

'Oh yes,' said Rachel, 'about us doing some PR for Hunter Gatherer. Great idea, don't you think? Capitalise on the publicity the TV show is giving him to get some separate media for the salvage business. So people know how great Hunter Gatherer is in its own right, not just something that nice Tim Chiminey does in his spare time.'

'Yes ...' said Tessa, uncertainly.

She could see that what Rachel had said made perfect sense and it would help assuage her anxiety about how Tom was neglecting the business for that wretched TV show. He'd just told her he was going to America for something to do with it, for heaven's sake.

'And it's the perfect moment for your business too,' said Rachel. 'Distressed industrial is the biggest trend in interiors right now.'

'Yes, I do see what you mean,' said Tessa.

A bit of concentration on the core business was exactly what she'd wanted for ages; it was just the prospect of having to sit opposite Simon, and possibly see him on other occasions, and act as if she'd never met him before that she dreaded. She didn't know how she could possibly do it.

She was still wondering what to say next when Rachel started speaking again.

'To be completely straight with you, Tess,' she was saying, 'I did have some doubts at first, about mixing family and work, but I really do think some PR now would work brilliantly for your business – and there's another thing. If it comes off, I'll get a new-business bonus from Simon, because it was my idea and I really need the money right now. I had to tell you that, to be transparent, but it's not the only reason I think you should do it. I really believe it would be great for your brand. So the sweet thing is, we'll both benefit. Win win.'

Tessa closed her eyes, glad they weren't on Skype, so Rachel couldn't see her anguished expression. She knew her sister was struggling with money. She'd lent her some just the month before to pay off a credit card. Could she be so selfish as to deny Rachel a bonus she so badly needed, just because she was freaked out by seeing Simon again? No. She couldn't. Blast it.

'Oh, that's great, Rachel,' she said, trying to sound enthusiastic. 'I can see it's all good, but I just wondered, do you really need me at the lunch tomorrow? Surely you, Tom and ...' oh, she'd have to say his name, no, she just couldn't, 'er, your boss, could nut it all out without me. I haven't been involved with Hunter Gatherer properly for so long, I don't see what I'd add to the conversation.'

Rachel smiled fondly at the phone, glad her brother-in-law had already rung her with strict instructions not to let Tessa squirm out of going to the lunch, as he knew she'd try to do.

Because as well as the obvious benefit to the business, he'd told Rachel, he was planning to use the PR campaign as a way of getting Tessa actively involved with it again, and out of the house occasionally. And Rachel could see that her sister really needed that. It had been clear at the photo shoot that she had the self-esteem of a squashed slug. Natasha had commented on it too, shocked that Tessa could have let her hair get in such a state.

'Hmmm,' said Rachel, 'well, when Tom rang me to confirm the lunch he mentioned that he's going to be away a lot in the next few months – he said he's going over to the States to do some promotion for the show over there, which is pretty amazing – so I think it's vital you're on board with the PR campaign from the very start. You'll have to be on the spot to look after the media while he's away, so you're more important than him in this really.'

'Oh,' said Tessa, all hope of getting out of the dreaded lunch draining away. 'I see what you mean. OK, well, I'll see you tomorrow then …'

'Great,' said Rachel, 'and apart from all that stuff it will be so lovely to see you up here, you hardly ever come to London any more … and Tess, don't be anxious about this, I'll be doing it with you. I'll be running the account and the campaign and it will be fun, you and me doing it together. I think you'll enjoy it. I'm excited.'

'Well, yes, that does sound great,' said Tessa, feeling the first tiny twinge of optimism about the whole thing.

She said goodbye and paused for a moment, looking at herself in the mirror on the wall. Her awful grey roots had come back the moment she'd washed out Natasha's miracle cover-up powder and now they were even worse. She couldn't possibly go to the lunch looking like that.

She looked down the numbers on a piece of paper stuck to the fridge for a mum from the school who used to be a hairdresser in London and would do a quick root touch-up for Tessa in her kitchen, wondering, as she punched the number into the phone, who exactly she was doing it for.

Herself, so she wouldn't feel like a terrible provincial frump in the no doubt ultra-fashionable London restaurant Rachel was taking them to? Or was it really for Simon?

Tuesday, 10 June

Regent's Park

Simon looked at himself in the mirror in his dressing room. He held a tie up next to the collar of his immaculate white shirt, then took it away again, opened a drawer and pulled out a burgundy silk square with white polka dots. He stuffed it into the breast pocket of his jacket. Yes, that was better than the tie.

He stood for a moment, tweaking the points of the handkerchief to make it look less contrived, as if he had casually just thrust it in there, which he had, but it never looked that way when you did. Then he stopped and looked at himself face on. At the immaculate shave he'd just done and the hair he'd had trimmed the day before.

What the fuck are you doing, Rathbone? Why are you wearing the navy Brioni suit which makes you feel like Daniel Craig's much hotter younger brother? What – and who – is this preening for exactly?

Of course, he always wore one of his sharpest suits when he was gunning for new business. It was part of his arsenal, always being the best-dressed man in a room. Not in a dandy way, just quietly, subtly, killer well dressed. It was the same logic as the flashy car. Be better than everyone else. Female potential clients wanted to ravish him, male potential clients wanted some of his glamour to rub off on them, or to ravish him, or both.

But was that exactly the kind of rubbing off he was thinking about this morning? Or was his lower brain – the one neatly curled up in his Calvins – more concerned with pleasure than business?

Perhaps he should change ... they were going to Café Colbert, after all, not anywhere stuffy. He could wear a jeans-and-jacket combination, play it all down a bit. He looked at himself again, smoothing his dark blond hair over the sides of his head. Fuck it. This was how Simon Rathbone rolled.

And maybe if he was true to the man he had become, he wouldn't feel so controlled by the one who had rolled around in a field with a beautiful young woman all those years before.

Tessa hurried down Sloane Street, feeling very hot and desperately wishing she and Tom could have arrived at the restaurant together, but he was coming straight from the airport. She hoped she looked OK. A vintage floral dress might not be the norm for this particular part of London, but it was what she felt comfortable in, and it was a hot day for June and she wasn't going to put a bloody jacket on.

A woman strode past her wearing white jeans, cut short to reveal skinny brown ankles, with a floaty silk top, boat-necked and striped like a matelot jumper, big black sunglasses and a very expensive-looking handbag over one arm. Her other hand held her phone clamped to her ear, a chunky gold bangle on her wrist.

Tessa felt like something out of Beatrix Potter next to her and regretted bringing her old French basket into town. It was fine in the country and it had felt fine at the Royal Academy where she'd been to an exhibition before heading for the restaurant, but probably didn't count as a handbag in Chelsea.

She had a pair of kitten-heeled sandals in it, which she'd planned to change into near the restaurant, but in the gritty heat of the city her feet already felt swollen and sore in her ballerina pumps. If she took them off she'd never get them back on again. London and all the people in it would just have to take her as she was.

Rachel was already waiting at a table on the far left of the room when Tessa walked into the restaurant, which was a great relief, especially as Simon wasn't there. Perhaps he wasn't coming after all.

'Tessie!' said Rachel, standing up to greet her and giving her a big hug. 'Come and sit on the banquette next to me. We can look out at everyone and the chaps can lump it with their backs to the world. They should have got here on time if they wanted the good seats.'

Tessa smiled and slid in beside her, wondering whether it would be worse to sit next to Simon and risk touching him, or sit across and have to keep meeting his eyes. She was telling herself to get over it when a waiter appeared and put a glass of champagne down in front of her. She turned to Rachel to see her holding one in the air.

'Cheers, big sis,' said Rachel. 'Welcome to the wonderful world of Rathbone & Associates.'

Tessa picked up her glass. She didn't often drink at lunchtime, but it would be churlish not to join in with Rachel's well-intentioned enthusiasm and maybe a bit of Dutch courage was exactly what she needed to get through this torturous occasion.

'To Hunter Gatherer,' continued Rachel, 'becoming the best-known salvage merchant in the UK – then the world –

and to you, my fabulous, talented, gorgeous big sister, helping to steer it on its groovy way.'

Tessa clinked glasses with her.

'To Hunter Gatherer,' she said. That she could drink to at least. She certainly didn't feel fabulous or gorgeous.

'Where's, er, your boss?' she asked Rachel after they'd chatted for a bit about the kids. 'Isn't he joining us?'

Oops, mustn't let the hopeful tone come through too strongly.

'Slime-on?' said Rachel, in the derisory tone she reserved for figures of authority. 'He had some meeting out of the office this morning, he just texted me to say he'll be along shortly. Where's Tom?'

'On his way in from Heathrow. He's been in Scotland since Friday doing stuff for *Tim Chiminey*.'

Her voice, when she mentioned that, took on a contemptuous tone similar to Rachel's talking about her boss.

'You really hate that show, don't you?' said Rachel, quite surprised by the vehemence of it.

Tessa nodded. 'Yes,' she said. It felt good to say it.

'What in particular about it?' asked Rachel.

'What's not to hate?' said Tessa, feeling an unaccustomed anger rising to the surface. She looked at her champagne glass. It was empty. Oh well. 'I hate that everyone in Cranbrook treats me differently – mostly with resentment – because my husband is a "celebrity". I hate that women ring the business number day and night to try and speak to him. The only thing worse is when they turn up at the house ...'

'Eek!' said Rachel. 'Does that happen much?'

'Enough,' said Tessa. 'I hate all the nasty comments I get on Instagram and in emails to the business address, that's all ghastly, but beyond all that, I just hate how it's changing Tom, or should I say "Tim"? He loves it, Rach.'

'And here he is,' said Rachel, spotting her brother-in-law arriving, stopping for a moment, framed in the arch at the entrance to the dining room. If he wanted people to notice him, they had.

Rachel watched as he walked towards them. People staring. Nudging each other. Pointing. You could almost hear the whisper going around the room. 'Tim Chiminey ... on the telly ... that chimney bloke ... ooh! I love him ...' And this was a sophisticated spot in Sloane Square. She started to see Tessa's point. Also why it might be affecting Tom.

One woman stopped him, grabbing his arm as he passed, and took a selfie of them together, all her friends at the table giggling excitedly and then insisting on the same. One of them kissed him, full on the lips.

'See what I mean?' asked Tessa. 'Shall I go and challenge her to a duel? But look at his face, he loves it.'

Rachel could see she was right. Tom – dear old lovable junkyard Tom – was almost strutting as he continued over towards them. He looked quite ... well, smug. There was no other word for it.

'It won't last forever, Tess,' she said quietly, 'and then he'll have to come back to reality. Meanwhile, milk it for all you can for your wonderful business.'

'I will,' said Tessa, marvelling at what she'd just witnessed. It had been a while since she'd seen Tom out and about in London and she was appalled at his almost preening behaviour. It was far worse than she'd realised.

'Sorry I'm late, girls,' he said, leaning over to kiss them both. 'Got here as soon as I could.'

'Had a few fans to service, I see,' said Rachel.

Tom laughed, turning on his TV smile as the waiter came over.

'I see you've already had a cheeky *coupe*,' he said, pointing at Rachel's empty champagne glass. 'Let's have a bottle of Veuve. I'm in the mood to celebrate.'

'Great,' said Rachel.

Coupe? thought Tessa. *Coupe*? Chicken bloody coop.

'What are we celebrating?' she asked Tom, hoping her distress at his cringe-making behaviour wasn't too obvious.

'Having lunch with my beautiful wife and my lovely sister-in-law in London for a change, rather than some boring country pub in Kent. Taking Hunter Gatherer onto the next stage. And just finishing a few days' great shooting for the show.'

'I've already ordered two more glasses,' said Rachel, as another waiter arrived with them on a tray, 'so we'll drink those while we wait for the bottle. Here you are, Tom.'

She poured half the champagne from her flute into the empty wine glass at his place setting, then she raised hers in a toast.

'To the show,' she said, kicking Tessa gently under the table with her foot, while raising her glass and smiling at Tom.

'To Hunter Gatherer,' said Tessa.

'To my beautiful wife,' said Tom.

They were all sipping their champagne, when Simon walked into the restaurant. Rachel felt her eyebrows fly up. He was wearing a fabulous suit, with Gucci loafers and no socks, his hair was combed back, and he looked even smoother than usual. She could see one of his big cigars peeping out behind the polka-dot silk square in his breast pocket, the dickhead.

As he crossed the room towards them, people were checking him out too, as they had Tom, but not because they recognised him. He looked like a film star they couldn't quite put a name to.

'Simbo,' she called out, unable to resist, 'we're over here.'

'I see you, Raquel,' he said, lobbing it right back at her. God, she was cheeky.

But before he could think anything more about Rachel, there was Tessa. Looking up at him like a startled fawn. A startled fawn in a flowery dress very similar to the one she'd been wearing the night he first met her all those years ago. Had she done it on purpose?

For a moment Simon faltered, almost tripping over his own feet, then he took a deep breath, squared his shoulders and strode towards them, smiling his oiliest professional smile. However he felt on the inside, no one was going to know.

Simon Rathbone, love-struck fool, was stuffed firmly back into his box and Simon Rathbone, businessman, PR legend, *GQ* best-dressed list regular, Range Rover SDV8 driver, Chester Terrace apartment owner, alpha male, sat down at the table.

After greeting everyone, apologising for his lateness, shaking Tom's and Tessa's hands and nodding at Rachel, he picked up the glass of champagne she pushed towards him and drained it in one.

By the time they'd finished the second bottle of champagne Tom had committed to funding a fully fledged PR campaign for Hunter Gatherer. Rachel high-fived Tessa and whispered into her ear.

'Bonuses 'r' us!' she said and Tessa grinned at her, happy she'd been able to contribute to her younger sister getting the financial boost she so needed.

Not able to hear what she'd said, but sensing she was getting a bit above herself, Simon looked at his watch ostentatiously. Rachel didn't miss the hint and glanced down at her phone. It was ten past three. Late enough for any client lunch, even if the client was your own sister.

'Well, this has been great,' she said, snapping into professional mode, or as near to it as she could get after all the fizz, 'but if we're all clear what the plan is, I better get back to the office.'

She was hoping Simon would tell her to relax and stay. No such luck.

'I'll see you back there later,' he said.

He had to keep her in her place. He'd already let his guard down too much. For someone who didn't normally drink at lunchtime, he'd embraced it with enthusiasm and, far from being as awkward as he'd expected, the lunch had gone very smoothly, feeling more like a catch-up with friends than a business meeting.

And sitting diagonally across from Tessa, he'd been able to avoid looking at her directly too often, addressing most of his remarks to Tom, who was sitting next to him, or to Rachel when it was a pure work topic.

It had all gone as well as it could have in the circumstances and the really great thing was that Rathbone & Associates now had a very nice new prestige client, with a strong brand story he could really work with, committed to a twelve-month full-service contract. With the perfect account manager already in place to look after it. Top result.

After hugging her sister, Rachel left and immediately the atmosphere shifted. The pleasant buzz Simon had enjoyed from the champagne was starting to turn into a dull headache and with Rachel gone, the fun seemed to have evaporated. Simon wished he'd left with her. Especially when Tom announced he was off to the loo.

Suddenly Simon and Tessa were left sitting alone at the table together. He wondered if he should check the emails on his phone, any distraction, but before he could help himself, he found his eyes were seeking hers. She was already looking at him and their gazes locked.

'Hi,' he said quietly.

'Hi,' said Tessa, swallowing awkwardly.

What the hell do I say? thought Simon, then realised he didn't need to say anything. They were saying it to each other already with their eyes. Before he knew what he was doing his hand reached across the table and took hers.

She smiled weakly at him, squeezing his hand back, before pulling hers away quickly and putting it in her lap. What if someone saw? They all knew who Tom was in there and they might even recognise her. Tears filled her eyes, she couldn't help it. They were trapped from every angle.

'I can't quite believe I just got through that lunch,' said Simon.

'Me neither,' said Tessa. 'I tried to get out of coming today.'

'I'm sorry,' said Simon.

Tessa shook her head.

'Don't be,' she said. 'I wanted to see you. That's what I was really running away from.'

Her words hung in the air. She couldn't believe she'd said them. Without the champagne she never would have.

'I can't stop thinking about you,' said Simon.

Well, you, or your sister. One or the other.

'Same,' said Tessa.

But it doesn't mean I don't still love my husband, even though I couldn't make love to him the other night because all I could think about was your face.

'It's very confusing,' she said, 'I suppose it just took us off guard, being unexpectedly reminded of our youth, like that.'

Simon nodded, so relieved she'd thrown them both a lifeline. Talking about it in those mundane terms would take the mystery and magic out of it. Clever Tessa.

'Yes,' he said, '*recherché du temps perdu* and all that jazz. Yesterday when I was young ...'

When Tom came back to the table, shortly after, they were laughing like any two people who didn't know each other very well, but had things in common and had just enjoyed a fun and boozy lunch together, and Simon was able to get through the last little bit of it relatively normally.

He even brought up the idea of him agenting Tessa for mural work, which he could see went down very well with Tom. It wasn't until it came to making their farewells that the past tripped him up again. Literally.

Standing just outside the restaurant, Simon shook Tom's hand and was just leaning in to quickly peck Tessa on each cheek and back off right away, when two women passing spotted Tom and, in their excitement, grabbed him hard by the arms, squealing that they wanted their picture taken with him.

Their sudden lunge at Tom pushed him back into Simon, who lurched heavily towards Tessa. It all happened so fast, he had to grab her tightly to stop them both falling to the ground.

In that moment, her warm body tight against his, her breasts pressing against him, Simon found his head resting against her neck and, feeling the warmth of her skin, felt almost giddy. He heard himself let out a very quiet groan of animal desire.

Her mouth was next to his ear.

'Call me,' he heard her say.

'I will,' he said.

Wednesday, 11 June

Tunbridge Wells, 4.22 a.m.

Joy was lying on the floor of her kitchen waiting for the ambulance. It was very cold on the tiles and she was in a lot of pain, so she was grateful for the warmth of Muffin's little body curled up next to her.

'Here we go, Muffin my boy,' she said, reaching her hand down to stroke his back. The movement was a very bad idea and she cried out in pain. The injury seemed to be somewhere in her right hip, but moving any part of her body seemed to set it off.

She was just so grateful that she'd fallen close enough to the phone cord to be able to pull it down off the kitchen cabinet so she could call for help. Rachel was always telling her that she should have one of those personal alarm buttons hanging round her neck, but she'd always laughed it off, saying that her crystals were all the protection she needed. But of course, as it was the middle of the night when she'd come down to the kitchen to make a cup of camomile tea, she hadn't been wearing them.

She heard a vehicle pull up outside the house. At that time of the night – she looked over at the kitchen clock, taking care to move only her eyes, and saw it was nearly four-thirty – it was probably the ambulance. Thank goddess.

'Don't be alarmed, Muffy,' she said. 'Some noisy people are about to come in here and then they'll take me away, but don't worry, Tessa will come and get you very soon. You'll enjoy it at her house, there's a big garden with an orchard where you'll be able to hunt all day. It's just the change I told you was coming. Everything will be fine. For the good of all. So mote it be.'

She wondered again if she should ring Tessa now and tell her what had happened, but decided she had been right in her earlier decision that there was nothing to be gained by disturbing her at such an ungodly hour. Her oldest daughter was about to have a lot of stress dumped on her, she needed her sleep. The hospital would let her know. All in good time.

Let it unfold, she said to herself, closing her eyes and trying to relax, although it was difficult with the pain, on the cold, hard floor. Let it unfold.

'Mrs Younger,' she heard a voice call from upstairs on the street, 'can you hear me?'

'Yes,' she replied, surprised how weak her voice sounded. It was a frail old lady's voice. 'I'm downstairs in the kitchen ...'

'Can you answer the door?' asked the voice.

'No,' said Joy, 'I'm afraid I've fallen and I can't get up.'

She'd told the man on the 999 call that; she was surprised they were asking her such silly questions. If she could answer the door, she wouldn't have rung for a bloody ambulance. Calm, Joy, she told herself. It would help no one to be fractious. Breathe. But it hurt to breathe.

'My neighbour has a key,' she called out, 'the house to the left ... number 37.'

'OK, Mrs Younger, we'll try to wake your neighbour, but tell me first, can you breathe normally? Do you have any chest pains?'

'I can breathe, no chest pains, just my hip,' replied Joy, finding it quite exhausting to shout like that.

'Hold tight, we'll be as quick as we can,' said the voice, and Joy realised how much she wanted them to come and help her. She had started to shiver uncontrollably.

'It's just the shock, Muffin,' she said, more to comfort herself. 'If only I could get my Rescue Remedy down from the shelf there, I'd be fine.'

She pulled her arms up to hug herself for warmth and cried out in pain. A tear rolled down her cheek. She'd known change was coming, but this was a little harder than she'd bargained for.

Queen's Park, 5.46 a.m.

Rachel kept looking at her bedside clock to see if it was still too early to wake up the girls, who were both in bed with her. She'd been lying there sleepless for so long and desperately wanted a cuddle.

Ariadne had arrived first, waking Rachel just after two in the morning. Then Daisy had come in rubbing her eyes, saying that Rachel's light had woken her up and she'd got in too.

After that, with two girls splayed out in the starfish position, four little legs kicking like dreaming dogs, sleep had been impossible and she'd been lying there ever since, worrying how the hell she was going to balance out all the bills she had to pay that month.

Her salary and the child support Michael paid for the girls had both been banked when they were supposed to, doing no more than clearing the overdraft which had built up since her previous pay day. And she'd incurred extra bank charges for allowing her account to go well over her agreed limit the month before.

She didn't know how the bank worked that one out – you've got no money to pay us back, so we're going to fine you, so you'll owe us even more money you can't pay us back.

She'd already had to resort to buying food on her credit cards, but now she didn't know how she was going to stump up even the minimum required on them this month. Then they would hit her with penalty charges, too. It was like being pulled into quicksand of debt.

Rachel hated even saying the word in her head, but that was the truth of it. Debt. She had a mortgage, four maxed-out credit cards and a permanent overdraft. She was hopelessly in debt. All those weekends in Copenhagen and Bruges might have been great for her emotional wellbeing and work ideas, but they had been ruinous for her finances.

What had Simon said about the new bonus system? That he would pay bonuses in the next pay packet after the first money had been banked from the new client. It would be at least three months before they would even present a bill to Tom. She just hoped he'd pay it promptly.

Ariadne flailed around suddenly, raking her sharp little toenails down Rachel's shin and she couldn't stand it another moment. She got out of bed and headed downstairs.

At least she didn't need to worry about waking up Branko as well, she thought as she passed the door of his bedroom. He'd asked her for some time off and had left the day before, to visit friends in Paris. He'd said he wasn't sure how long he'd be away, a week or possibly two, which was a bit of a worry, but she could hardly refuse him, considering the very casual arrangement they had. And she was happy for him to have a holiday. Paris, how divine. Rachel wondered when she would ever be able to go anywhere gorgeous like that again.

She fired up her laptop on the kitchen table and, armed with a mug of tea, gathered together all the papers she'd let build up on one end of it – the Pile of Doom, as she thought of it – forced herself to open all the letters, and started filling out a spreadsheet of her debts.

When she'd finished Rachel sat and stared at it in disbelief. It was far worse than she'd realised. Catastrophic. How had she let herself get into this mess? And what the hell was she going to do about it?

After a few moments frozen by shock, Rachel laid her head on her folded arms and sobbed.

Who can I turn to for advice? she asked herself. That was almost the worst part of it, to feel so alone in this crisis. Tessa had already lent her some money, it had its own column on the spreadsheet. £3000. Not an inconsiderable amount.

What was she going to do next? Ask Natasha and get into even more debt with her family, which she had no prospect of paying back?

Joy wouldn't be able to help. She knew nothing about such worldly matters as interest rates – she'd never had a mortgage or a credit card, and she didn't have any savings, as far as Rachel knew – but what she did know, was how to get by on next to nothing.

She wasn't mean, she just knew how to be frugal. She said it was her upbringing, which had made her aware of the value of every penny, and after Rachel's dad had died so unexpectedly, it had been a very useful skill.

Joy still bought all her clothes in charity shops and her vegetarian diet, with rice, pulses, cooking oil etc. bought in bulk, cost very little. She used every herbal teabag twice and very rarely turned on her heating or even the hot water. And she moved around the house in the dark, never having more than one light on at a time. It drove Rachel potty when she went there. Joy's only indulgences were essential oils, crystals and joss sticks. And food for Muffin.

Why hadn't some of this super thrift rubbed off on Rachel? It wasn't like they'd been brought up to expect luxury. Tessa was more like Joy. She did allow herself lights and hot water, but even now Tom was raking it in from the TV show, she still wore the vintage dresses she'd had for years.

Rachel wondered how she'd allowed herself to become such a self-indulgent bourgeois urbanite who had to have prestige homewares and stay in boutique hotels? Was it because it just seemed normal in the professional world she inhabited, where everything was about the superficial?

Natasha certainly had to have all the trappings in her business too, far more so than Rachel actually, but she had the income for it, and all the freebies and discounts. Rachel's best Lanvin handbag had been passed on to her by Natasha.

And not only did Natasha make far more money than Rachel, she was also very clever with it. With endorsement deals on all her magazine credits – 'Make-up by Natasha Younger for OM Beauty' – she was a businesswoman as well as a creative genius, with quite a property portfolio in New York.

The crazy thing was Rachel knew she also had a good business brain, but it only seemed to kick in for other people. She'd never been able to understand how she could see so clearly the way to help her clients move their brands forward, but wasn't able to apply this clarity to her own financial affairs.

And it had all got a lot worse since she'd become a single mum. What would the girls' father, Michael, say if he knew what a vulnerable position she was in? What if she lost the house? Or went bankrupt, which, looking at the figures she'd just typed in, was a genuine possibility. He'd probably swoop in for custody. He'd let enough hints drop about that already.

Rachel suddenly found it hard to breathe. Her heart was pounding. Her mouth was dry. She felt faint. Was this what an anxiety attack felt like? She put her head between her knees and tried to take the slow breaths her mother prescribed for everything.

Thinking of Joy gave her another idea. She stood up and found an old bottle of Rescue Remedy in the back of a drawer. She put a few drops in a glass of water and started to feel better even before taking the first sip, because she was doing something active about her situation, not just sitting wallowing in it, even if it was just sipping some nasty-tasting alcohol infusion.

She leaned back against the kitchen counter and closed her eyes, feeling her pulse rate slow down. One thing she'd understood in this horrible lonely moment was that she desperately needed to talk to someone about her situation. Keeping her anxiety to herself like this was making it exponentially worse, she understood that, but that just took her back to where she'd started: who?

She couldn't tell any of her friends. It was too shame-making and she didn't want to be the subject of gossip, especially as so many of them worked in aspects of the interiors world and she really didn't want it to get around in that context. It had to be someone closer than that.

Joy? She'd just tell her to become a vegetarian, sit in the dark and trust the abundant universe. Natasha? It would be too humiliating to admit her failure to her much more successful younger sister.

Tessa? She was even less worldly than Joy. Tom? No. He and Tessa were clients now – a reminder of why she had been right to have misgivings about that family/business combination from the get-go, but it was too late now and she desperately needed that bonus, so she'd just have to deal with it.

Michael? No freaking way. Simon? He'd probably give the best advice of any of them, but there was no way she could let him know what a terrible mess she'd made of her financial affairs. He'd never trust her at work again.

She had to face it: she had no one. She felt tears pricking her eyes again, but then an idea struck her. Link. She could talk to Link about it. He didn't know any of her friends or family, he had no connection to the world of interior design and he was a very good listener. It was one of the things she liked about spending time with him.

And he must have some kind of financial nous, Rachel reasoned, because he owned his houseboat outright. He'd said something once about making a decision to accept compromises to own a place to live without being suffocated – that was the word he'd used – by a mortgage. It was spot on for how she felt looking at the figures on that spreadsheet. Suffocated. Smothered.

She'd call him later in the morning and see when they could meet up, not for sex, but to talk. Perhaps she'd invite him over to the house for the first time. It might be time to take their relationship onto the next stage. That was quite an exciting idea.

Noticing it was now 6.25 a.m., she switched on the kettle again. Time for another mug of tea she could drink sitting in bed with the girls, her very favourite part of the day.

But before she could even pour the boiling water onto the teabag, the phone rang. It was Tessa telling her that Joy was in hospital with a badly broken hip and might need surgery.

Tunbridge Wells, 6.40 a.m.

All the way to the hospital Tessa had to fight back tears, which wasn't very helpful while driving. The moment she'd had the call from the hospital she'd known it was all her fault. Karma for that terrible thing she'd done the day before. Asking Simon to call her! With Tom standing right next to them!

She'd felt the fullness of Simon's cock against her and she'd liked it. She'd had to consciously stop herself pushing her hips towards it. And she couldn't kid herself, she had deliberately pressed her breasts onto him.

What kind of a treacherous whore had she turned into? All those years of happy faithful marriage, she'd never so much as looked at another man, but bumping into a random one-night stand from beyond the mists of time seemed to have thrown all that out.

Now with those two deadly little words, she was risking everything for someone she'd hardly known twenty-five years ago, and the kind of person he seemed to be now – all London slickness, bespoke suits and big cigars – wasn't her style at all. He was the worst kind of urban smoothie, she was a country mouse, they had nothing in common. She couldn't imagine what he'd thought of her second-hand dress and scruffy basket.

And yet … in those quiet moments when they'd re-connected, none of that mattered. It seemed to strip them both back to the people they'd been when they were young. The connection was profoundly sexual, but somehow there was also an otherworldly innocence about it.

Tessa groaned, dropping her head momentarily down onto the steering wheel as she waited for the traffic to move forward at the big roundabout leading into Tunbridge Wells.

Whatever it was – some kind of late onset sex hormone surge? – it was putting everything she valued most in her life at risk and it had to stop.

She might not like the way Tom revelled in his fame, but she still deeply loved the man he really was. It was just a phase, this celebrity nonsense and, now she thought of it, he was probably having his own mid-life crisis. The male menopause.

It must have been strange for Tom when Finn had grown taller than him and started bringing girls home. Although he'd never said anything other than a few wry comments, that must have messed with his head a bit. No wonder he got off on the adulation of total strangers.

Which was hardly a terrible crime compared to what she'd done. She'd kissed another man, fully, knowingly, on the lips, nothing social about it. She'd pressed herself against him and enjoyed feeling his body in return and she'd talked to him about the connection between them. She'd pictured his face so vividly when Tom was trying to make love to her. She'd asked him to call her. It was infidelity in everything but the act.

And worst of all, the thing which had kept her awake for most of the previous night, was the fear that Simon might actually take her at her word and ring her. Because she didn't know what she might do if he did. After what had happened outside the restaurant, she didn't trust herself any more.

Tessa put her head down on the steering wheel again, pulling it up sharply when the person in the car behind her beeped their horn to let her know the traffic was moving.

A wake-up call is just what I need, she thought, accelerating off with a jerk and waving her hand up in front of her rear-view mirror in apology.

When Tessa arrived at the A&E department, Joy was just being wheeled back from X-ray.

'Mum!' she said, rushing over to the trolley and grabbing her hand. 'Whatever happened?'

'Your mum has had a nasty fall,' said the nurse who was helping the porter manoeuvre the trolley into a curtained bay. 'We're just waiting for the consultant to have a look at the X-rays and then we'll know if they're going to operate.'

Tessa could hardly take it in. Seeing her strong and vital mother, who still did her yoga stretches and sun salutes religiously every morning, looking so small and vulnerable in a wretched hospital gown, was a horrible shock.

'I'm so sorry, darling,' Joy was saying, grasping her hand. 'I couldn't sleep and I went downstairs to make some camomile tea and I missed a step in the dark and landed rather hard on the tiles.'

Tessa still couldn't speak. Operate?

'How did you get here?' she finally managed to croak. She felt as though she needed to put the weird jigsaw of the situation together, piece by piece.

'I was very lucky, because I could reach the phone cable to pull it down to the floor and then I called 999 for an ambulance.'

'Why didn't you ring me first?' asked Tessa, realising it was slightly irrational, as she said it. Lack of sleep, shock and guilt were all swirling around together and making her feel quite dizzy.

Joy squeezed her hand.

'I'll be all right, Tessa, my love,' she said. She waited for a moment, then, as the nurse and porter left the bay, she pulled Tessa closer. 'You didn't happen to bring any arnica with you, did you?' she asked quietly.

Tessa smiled, nodding conspiratorially and feeling better, back on more familiar ground with her mother. 'I always have some in my bag,' she said.

She poked around in her basket and after finding the small glass vial of homeopathic tablets rolling around in the bottom, she handed it to her mother.

Joy tipped one tiny pill onto her palm, put it in her mouth, and then handed the container back to Tessa.

'Remind me to take another one in fifteen minutes,' she said, 'and then twice more after that. If they do decide to operate on me, I'll need you to pop over to the homeopathic pharmacy to get a more powerful formulation for when I come round.'

Tessa nodded, perfectly understanding everything Joy was saying. She and her sisters had been raised on homeopathic and herbal medicines. The hospital felt like an alien planet to Tessa and she couldn't wait to get her mother out of there.

7.07 a.m. US Eastern Time Zone (12.07 p.m. GMT), West Village, New York

Natasha was heading back to her apartment after a particularly punishing Bikram yoga session when her phone beeped. Waiting on the corner for the lights to change, jogging on the spot, she pulled it out of her pocket and was surprised to see the text was from Rachel.

Her eyes grew big as she read: 'Mum has had an accident, broken hip. In surgery now. Please Skype me. I'm at office.'

The minute she got home Natasha rushed to her laptop and Skyped Rachel. Her face appeared immediately, looking pinched and tired.

'Hey, Tashie,' she said, 'great you could get back to me so quickly.'

'What the hell's happened?' asked Natasha, a break in her voice she hadn't realised would be there.

'She had a fall, going down to the kitchen at night.'

'With no bloody lights on,' Natasha interjected.

'Right,' said Rachel. 'She tripped going down the steps, landed hard on the tiled floor and she's broken her hip.'

'You said she's having surgery,' said Natasha, stricken at the idea of her mother lying in a hospital bed with antibiotic drips going into her.

'They say they've got to pin it or it won't heal correctly and she'll have problems walking,' said Rachel, looking as distressed as Natasha felt. 'Tessa's at the hospital. She's going to call me as soon as Mum comes out and then I'll call you. Will you be on your mobile?'

'Of course,' said Natasha, although she knew she'd have to turn it off during an important meeting that morning, possibly the most important work meeting she'd ever have. She couldn't cancel it, not even for this, but she'd check her phone the moment she came out. No need to go into that with Rachel. It would just sound worse than it really was.

'Are they going to give her antibiotics and crap like that?' she asked.

'Well, you know about those terrible hospital infections,' said Rachel. 'They're bound to. Tessa is taking in her remedies and we're just going to try and fend all that off as best we can. The main thing is to get her out of there as quickly as possible, so we can look after her ourselves.'

'Where will she go?'

'Tessa's. She's putting a bed in that room she calls the library. I've arranged a sleepover for the girls tonight, so I can go straight down and see Mum after work, but I'll have to come back after. I'd really like to stay down there to be on the spot, but Branko's taken some time off and Michael can't have the girls this week or next.'

Natasha hoped the sharp pang of guilt she felt didn't show on her face. She knew exactly where Branko was. In Paris. Doing appointments with Chanel, Dior, Lanvin ...

Ever since she'd contacted her friends at Storm model agency asking them to see him and they'd signed him on the spot, there'd been a lot of interest in him. He'd told her he wasn't going to hand his notice in to Rachel until he was sure the modelling was going to take off for him, but from the feedback Natasha was already getting she knew it would. She'd heard just the day before that Karl Lagerfeld was seriously considering him to open the Chanel couture show in a couple of weeks.

Natasha knew she seriously needed to explain all that to Rachel. Why the hell she'd interfered in – and wrecked – the excellent set-up her hard-pressed sister had with the manny her daughters adored ... but this was not the time.

'I'll come over as soon as possible,' said Natasha. 'I'll try to leave tonight.'

'That would be great,' said Rachel. 'Obviously I'll help as much as I can when she comes out, but I'm really pressured at work right now and with the girls ...'

'Don't sweat it,' said Natasha, still feeling awful about the childcare thing, but not able to stop herself thinking that she was possibly a little more pressured with her work.

She looked at the time on the laptop clock. There was just a little over an hour until she had to be at that meeting, which might change her life – and in a way which would enable her to help their mum out more, too. A lot more.

She needed to get going fast, looking amazing, and a glance in the nearest mirror reminded her it would take some work. Her face was as red as a baboon's bottom.

'I've got to go, Rachie,' she said. 'I should see you tomorrow, I'll text you when I know about flights – and let me know as soon as you hear about Mum.'

Jumping under the shower Natasha did a quick mental review of her work commitments. It was just coming into the madly busy time of year when people were rushing to get things finished before everyone disappeared out of New York for the summer, so going home would mean missing out on some seriously great editorial, but what could she do? Her mum was more important. No question.

But she also had some more of these crucial meetings the following week, which she really couldn't miss. So she'd zip over to see Joy now, come back to New York for the meetings, then head back to London again as soon as she possibly could for a longer stay, which would be more useful really as she'd be out of hospital then and Tessa would need the support.

And as she stepped on the scales for her daily weigh-in another idea occurred to Natasha, which made the prospect of a longer visit to the UK even more appealing. When she went over to help out with Joy, she could see Mattie again.

Sydney Street, 12.10 pm

Simon was staring at his computer screen, the email inbox crammed with the usual cluster of last-minute staff holiday requests for Wimbledon week, and wondering whether he should just put all the names into a hat.

It was the same every year and he did his best to be fair, although he knew there'd only be a sudden spate of 'tummy upsets' among those who didn't get official leave anyway.

Realising he was chewing his fingernails, he pulled his hand out of his mouth and slapped it hard with his other one. He couldn't start doing that again. He picked up a biro that was lying on the desk and chewed on that instead.

After a sleepless night, he'd done a hard session at the gym with a punching bag which had helped clear his head for a little while, but now he was in the office, all too aware of Rachel sitting upstairs, the anxiety had got hold of him again.

How the hell was he going to get over his weak moment with Tessa after that wretched boozy lunch? He never usually drank during the working day and this was a good reminder why not. He would never have agreed to call her if he hadn't been roasted on Veuve Clicquot – and he was sure she wouldn't have asked him to.

But while he could blame those silly indiscretions on the booze, it just went to show that no matter how much he and Tessa might want to deny it, they were still deeply attracted to each other and he couldn't just let the situation drift, as he might have with someone else, in the hope it would just peter out and go away, because he was going to have to speak to her and see her about the Hunter Gatherer business.

And even if he did delegate as much of the business side as possible to Rachel, there was still the inconvenient issue that she – the person who was also fast becoming his most valued employee – was Tessa's sister. Not even taking his feelings for Rachel into consideration.

He felt like yodelling with frustrated confusion.

Every way he looked at it, he was trapped and blocked. He had to tell Tessa he couldn't talk to her or see her for anything other than business, but how, even in simple logistic terms, was he ever going to have that conversation with her? He couldn't put it in an email, or a text.

He'd heard too many horror stories from foolish friends having affairs, being caught out through ill-timed use of those conduits. He and Tessa weren't having an affair, but something like that could make them look as though they were.

He didn't even feel comfortable at the prospect of phoning the house, in case Tom answered, or her mobile in case he was with her when she did. Tapping the biro frenetically against his front teeth, he realised he was also bouncing his knee up and down at high speed. All he needed was a cymbal under his arm and he could be a one-man band.

Perhaps he should use the work connection to contrive a trip down to the salvage yard, but really to see her and sort this ridiculous situation out? But then he'd have to get her alone somehow to broach the subject and, although he hated to admit it to himself, going on previous form, anything could happen in those circumstances.

It didn't matter what his rational mind told him, as soon as he saw Tessa he seemed to be reduced to a cerebellum on legs. Three legs.

Simon put his head down on his desk and groaned quietly. Just as Rachel walked into his office. Shit.

'Are you all right?' she asked.

'Of course,' he said, looking up at her from desk level and feeling like a total idiot, 'yes, no, I just dropped my pen on the floor.'

He waved the biro around in the air as proof.

'Is this a good moment?' asked Rachel.

'For what?' asked Simon, much more irritably than he meant to. Why couldn't he stop himself being snappy with her?

'I can come back another time,' said Rachel, wondering yet again why Simon was so bloody rude in the office, when she knew how charming he could be. He'd been great company at the lunch with Tessa and Tom the day before. It had been good to see him loosen up a bit with the drink.

'No, no, sit down,' he said, absentmindedly putting the biro back in his mouth. The clear plastic split in two with a loud crunch as his back teeth clamped down on it too hard.

'Ew,' said Rachel. 'Watch out, you'll get a mouthful of ink.'

'I know,' said Simon, picking bits of plastic out from between his teeth. 'Terrible habit, I must remember not to put random things in my mouth ...'

A smirk passed across Rachel's face, she couldn't help it. That would be a good line for the Arthur/Martha brigade to giggle about. She wouldn't tell them though. Simon might be a rude git at times, but she had more respect for him than that.

'So what gives?' he asked, dropping the bits of pen in his waste paper bin and sitting up straight. Sort yourself out, Rathbone, he told himself. This is the workplace. Business. The stuff that matters.

'I've got all the costs here for the first Lawn & Stone press trip with the editors,' said Rachel. 'I'd like you to have a look at them before I send them to the client. I've printed them out, so you can write comments straight onto them.'

'Great,' said Simon, reaching out to take the folder Rachel was proffering to him. 'I look forward to perusing them.'

Perusing? When did he ever use a word like that? What was happening to his brain?

'Goodo,' said Rachel, getting up from the chair. Simon's stomach turned over a little.

'And well done, for getting this together so quickly, Rachel,' he added, smiling at her.

She nodded in recognition and as he looked at her properly – her face, that was, his X-ray specs pervert eyes had already scanned the rest of her – Simon noticed that she was looking rather strained.

'Are you all right, Rachel?' he asked. 'You don't look quite yourself.'

Rachel was so surprised by the kindness in his voice, she felt tears spring into her eyes. Her hand flew up to her forehead to try and hide them, but then she gave in and sank back down into the chair.

'It's my mum,' she croaked out, tears escaping and spilling down her cheeks. 'She had a fall last night and she's in hospital. She's broken her hip and she's having surgery right now.'

'Oh no,' said Simon, 'that's awful. Poor Joy. But you must go, Rachel. Go straight down there, now. Don't worry about work, take the rest of the week off, that's much more important.'

Rachel stared at him in amazement. 'Really?' she said, wiping her wet cheeks.

'Of course,' said Simon, getting up from his chair and coming round to her side. Taking care not to bring his torso

too close to hers, he put his arm lightly round her shoulders
and gave her a freshly pressed white handkerchief, which he'd
just pulled out of his pocket. 'Take this and go.'

'That's so kind of you,' she said, dabbing the edges of
her eyes with his hankie and noting it had the letters 'SR'
embroidered on it. 'But I'll have to come back later, because
of the girls, their nanny is on holiday ... but it would be really
great if I could go to the hospital right away, to be there when
she comes round.'

'Go,' said Simon, 'and take off as much time as you need.'

'Thank you so much,' she said, smiling at him in a way that
made Simon move hastily back to his chair, safely on the other
side of the desk.

'Just tell me one thing before you go,' he said, taking
another biro out of his pot. 'Which hospital is she in?'

'The Royal Tunbridge Wells,' Rachel replied, surprised, as
he scribbled it down on his notepad.

'Please give her my very best regards for a speedy recovery,'
he said, 'I was very taken with your mother when I met her
that, er, time.'

'I will,' said Rachel. 'Thanks, Simon. You've been a brick.
See you tomorrow.'

She left his office, slightly amazed at this new compassionate
side of him, but still glad she'd resisted the temptation to tell
him her mother had felt much the same about him.

Simon might have his nice side, when he chose to show it,
but he was still the boss.

Friday, 20 June

Cranbrook

Rachel, Natasha and Tessa were all sitting round Joy's bed, drinking tea made with fresh mint leaves from the garden, the French windows wide open to let in the gorgeous sunny afternoon. Rachel had just arrived, much sooner than she'd been expected, because Simon had let her leave the office early again.

As soon as he'd heard Joy had come home from hospital on the Tuesday, he'd tried to get Rachel to take the whole week off, but she hadn't been able to take him up on it, because Branko was still away. Simon had also sent a bouquet of flowers to the hospital, with a very nice card, which Rachel had to admit was a very nice gesture. Joy had been thrilled and had already written him a note of copious thanks.

He'd been affectionately amused by her 'love and light' sign-off and had shown it to Rachel, who'd been slightly alarmed that he might suggest coming down to visit Joy himself, but so far he'd stayed just on the acceptably intrusive side of kindness. Generous time off was good, getting too personally involved in her family dramas was not.

Joy took a contented sip of tea and sent up a prayer of thanks that once again she was in Tessa's house, surrounded by her beloved daughters. She hadn't enjoyed what she'd had to go through to be in that situation, but it was worth it, to see them all up close and connected, as they needed to be.

And it was so wonderful to see Natasha for the second time in just over a week. She'd come over to visit Joy in hospital right after the accident, but she'd had to rush back to New York the next day for work, coming back again now Joy had been discharged, to stay longer and help Tessa out.

Despite having arrived on the red-eye only that morning, Natasha seemed to be in the best spirits of the three of them, which probably wasn't surprising considering what she was telling them.

'So, I finally had the big meeting with OM yesterday – you know the American cosmetics empire?' she was saying. 'And it's now all confirmed, signed and sealed, that they are going ahead with a whole range of make-up called "Younger by Natasha". How exciting is that? The name was my idea.'

They all congratulated her warmly and Natasha carried on talking, pink with excitement.

'The really amazing thing is that Ava Capel – she's the marketing genius who finds all the cult beauty ranges and gets OM to buy them and take them global, she's an absolute legend – heard I was planning to do my own line and came straight to me, saying they wanted to do it jointly with me from the outset.'

Joy lifted her mug to her face to take a drink, but really to hide her expression. Natasha looked so beatific with happiness, it made her feel quite teary.

'Normally,' she was saying, 'they wait until the small company has done all the hard work and the range is a success and then they swoop in, but for my range they're paying for all the R and D and everything.'

Seeing Tessa's and Joy's blank faces, she added: 'Research and development? Most start-up ranges don't even get past that stage, so it's a really really big deal.'

'That's fantastic,' said Rachel, 'are they going to go global with it right from the launch?'

'It's going to be exclusive to Barneys for the first six months,' said Natasha, 'because they want to position it firmly as a fashion forward high-end range, but then they're confident it will go straight into all the major upscale US department store chains and flight side, which is just amazing and they're planning the European launch one year on. I'd always planned to launch independently and do a slow grow, but to go right in with their economies of scale and that many doors is just amazing ... Then they mentioned stand-alones, so they're thinking in Mac terms right from the outset, it really is mega.'

'What do you mean by "doors" and "flight side"?' asked Tessa.

Natasha looked nonplussed for a moment, as if she couldn't understand how anyone would ask such a question.

'Doors means how many shops will stock the range,' answered Rachel, 'and flight side is another term for duty free isn't it, Tash?'

A particularly irritating bit of American retail jargon.

'Oh yes,' Natasha replied. 'Sorry about all the industry terms, but I've been thinking like this for months now, while we've been negotiating the deal, so it's all normal for me.'

'And presumably "stand-alones" are your own boutiques?' added Rachel. 'And "Mac", as in Mac the make-up brand?'

Natasha nodded enthusiastically and carried on, expanding on how she was going to make the range unique at 'point of sale' and 'tour the product', with 'customer face to face' and 'media local'.

Rachel groaned inwardly. Why not 'local media'? She'd like to see Natasha take on Simon in a marketing geek-speak clash of the titans.

To Joy's great relief – she hated talking about money more than almost anything – Natasha hadn't mentioned any specific figures, but it was clearly going to be a very lucrative deal. What a clever girl her youngest daughter was. Not that Joy understood half of what she was saying about it all, and at that moment she was more occupied with studying Rachel's reaction to the news.

A dark look had crossed Rachel's face when Natasha had first told them about it. Very fleeting, but clear to Joy who usually read her daughters' expressions like they were Reuters screens. It wasn't jealousy, that wasn't Rachel's style – or of the other two for that matter. Joy took comfort that she had raised her girls to be genuinely happy for other people's good fortune. Like her, they understood it wasn't a finite commodity.

But there was something about Natasha's wonderful news that had made Rachel, just for a moment, very uncomfortable in her skin. Joy immediately felt concerned for her, wondering what it could be.

Tessa's reaction was less complicated; her face broke into a beaming smile of happiness and pride in her baby sister, before quickly settling back into the distracted air that was her current permanent state. It was like a second shadow that followed her around. What could that be?

Rachel was on her feet now, hugging Natasha.

'Wow, Tashie,' she was saying, 'this is all so amazing. I'm so proud of you. Can we get free samples?'

Natasha laughed. 'You lot can have the full range – but only if you promise to show it to all your friends. I've still got to decide whether to give the UK launch exclusively to Liberty or Selfridges, what do you all think?'

Tessa looked like a frightened rabbit. She hated this-or-that, black-or-white questions, they sent her brain into overload.

'Selfridges,' said Rachel, without missing a beat. 'Bigger foot fall, more glamorous beauty hall ... and now I'm going to get us some proper drinks to celebrate this amazing news. Lucky I brought something special down with me. Must have had a premonition, eh, Mum?'

Rachel managed to keep her composure as she left the library and then practically ran to the kitchen and out through the door at the back of it, to where there was a big pantry with a second fridge in it.

She closed the larder door and leaned against it, trying to slow her breathing, feeling the same sense of panic that had overtaken her when she'd done the debt spreadsheet the week before.

Most of the time she managed to keep her financial anxiety under control, propping up the matchstick tower her life had turned into, moving bits of borrowed money from place to place, and assuring her various debtors that she would have an extra solid sum of money coming in sometime in the next three months.

Surely Simon would pay her the bonus by then? She felt fear nearly overwhelm her for a moment at the thought of what could happen if it took longer than that, but forced herself to shut the thought out.

Meanwhile, her really lovely 1960s Danish light fitting was finishing its eBay auction that Sunday night and bidding was already up to nearly £300 and likely to go higher, which would leave her a reasonable sum. She'd also put the Lanvin handbag on Vestiare and that should bring in a bit. Enough to pay for petrol, her commute to work and feed the girls for a couple of weeks at least.

For the first time ever, she realised she was genuinely glad they were with their dad that weekend, so she could save some money on groceries and they wouldn't be constantly pestering her for 99p iPad apps. Michael could buy them a few for once, the tightwad. And although she'd had to pay the train fare down to Tessa's, she'd save on power, water and food, staying there for a couple of days.

It was a lucky chance she'd had the bottle of champagne at home, left over from her birthday. She'd brought it down so she didn't have to shell out for a get-well present for Joy. Grabbing the bottle from the fridge, she picked a jar of olives and a bag of Kettle Chips off a shelf and headed back into the kitchen to put flutes on a tray and the snacks into bowls.

Then, finding a lipstick in her pocket, she slicked on a fresh coat, looking at herself in the mirror on the kitchen wall. After another deep breath, she set her shoulders and pasted on her happy face, before picking up the tray and heading back to the others.

The champagne turned the gathering into an instant party, greatly enhanced by the arrival home for the weekend of Finn and Archie, along with Hector. Joy saw how Tessa's face lit up when she saw them.

Maybe that was the cause of her distractedness, she thought. Tessa must miss the happy family chaos horribly now the older two were boarding at school four nights a week, especially as she'd lost the two of them at once. And it must be hard for Hector, too, suddenly being the only one at home during the week, after growing up always having two big brothers to knock about with.

No wonder the poppet spent so much time in there with her. In the few days she'd been there Hector had taken to doing his homework lying on the rug, next to the bed. He was lonely, poor lamb. Tom was away so much and Tessa might have been there in body, but her spirit seemed to be somewhere else entirely.

With Rachel directing proceedings, the drinks turned into dinner, the boys carrying a table over to the bed, so they could sit and eat there together with Joy. It was all very jolly, with the sense of occasion going up another notch when Tom arrived back from wherever he'd been – Tessa couldn't keep track – just as they were about to start eating.

'I can see you've been having a good time without me,' he said, picking up the champagne bottle and squinting down the neck. 'You've worked that one over good and proper ... you'll have to come and stay more often, Joy, but please don't feel you have to break something nasty first.'

'I know that, Tom,' said Joy, 'you've always made me feel completely welcome here, but the champagne was to celebrate Natasha's marvellous news – tell him, somebody.'

'Auntie Tash is a total legend,' said Finn, 'she's going to have her own way-cool big-time make-up range on sale in actual shops. I'll have a black eyeliner please, Auntie, and I'll be able to use my family discount as a total chick magnet.'

'Gosh, that's amazing, Natasha,' said Tom. 'Good for you. How exciting.'

Joy wondered if she was the only one who detected a slight note of irritation in his voice.

'Well, I better raid my secret stash of champers then,' continued Tom, 'because I've got something to celebrate too ... we've just inked the deal to do a first series of *Tim Chiminey* in the US. No pilot, they say they don't need to, because the

UK show is already rating really well there, so we're going straight to a ten-show series.'

He looked round at them all, grinning expectantly, but was met with a rather stunned silence. It was Archie who broke it.

'That's really cool, Dad,' he said, 'can I come with you? I can be the key grip, or the best boy.'

Laughter dispelled the tension and the others recovered themselves enough to offer Tom their congratulations, doing their best to sound genuinely pleased for him, while he tried not to let his hurt at their initial lukewarm response show. He was bewildered by it.

How come they were all so puffed up and excited about Natasha's deal, but so flat about his amazing news? Didn't they know how unusual it was for a show to go straight to network in the US? Barney said it was almost unheard of ...

Another awkward silence had fallen, before Tessa finally spoke.

'What does "inked" mean?' she asked.

Tessa and Tom were walking round the salvage yard together in the long summer light after dinner, something that had once been a daily ritual for them. It was a beautiful evening, the night before midsummer, and Tessa was very grateful for every moment that passed without Tom mentioning the TV show.

'That's a really nice bathroom suite,' he said, going over to have a closer look at a 1930s wash basin, loo and bath set in a glorious shade of sugar pink.

'Yes,' said Tessa, 'isn't it great? Came in yesterday. Coloured suites are going to take off again big time, I'm sure of it. I've asked the boys to look out for them particularly. We had a lovely 1950s powder blue one last week which went back out very quickly.'

'Excellent,' said Tom, delighted to hear she was taking an active interest in the business. 'Your instincts are always faultless about these things. What else do you think is going to be hot?'

Now that he was going to be away filming in the States for weeks at a time, Tom was really going to need Tessa to be properly hands on with the salvage yard again. Not just to get her out into the world a bit more, doing some PR stuff, but essential day-to-day management, overseeing the business.

As well as their long-term contacts in the demolition business, they had a good team of freelance dealers sourcing stuff for them, but the success of Hunter Gatherer had always derived from their personal input. Their taste, instincts and aesthetics. Good and reliable as Jack the manager was, Tom knew Hunter Gatherer would lose its special edge very quickly if they left it all up to him.

Tessa was still thinking how to answer his question about the next trend in salvage. She couldn't just give a glib response, it was too important, something she needed to think through.

'Well,' she replied eventually, 'copper's going to stay strong and I think brass will follow on from that. Any kind of metal as long as it's not chrome really … and raw wood more than shabby-chic flaked paint.'

Tom laughed.

'I hope you're keeping a note of these pronouncements,' he said, 'it's just the kind of thing that will be useful for Rachel and Simon. Have you heard from him since the lunch, by the way?'

Tessa turned away, crouching down and pretending to be looking closely at a crate of Delft tiles. Not trusting her face.

'No,' she said, replying slightly too fast. 'But Rachel has sent the contract through. I've printed it out for you to look at. I imagine it will all start happening, once we've signed that.'

'Ah, yes,' said Tom. 'That Simon's not one to give anything away unless he's sure he's going to be paid for it, don't you think?'

Tessa wondered how long she could carry on pretending to be interested in the tiles.

'That's rather what I gather from Rachel,' she said carefully. 'But the agency does have a matchless reputation for boosting design and interiors companies. That's why Rachel wanted to work there in the first place.'

When Tom didn't answer she looked over her shoulder to see him disappearing into the barn. Good. There was a lot of new stock in there, loads of fireplaces, overmantels and surrounds, which should keep him happily occupied for a while.

'Whoa!' she heard him exclaim, then his head popped out of the barn door. 'Have you seen this Carrera marble number?' he asked, his face bright with genuine excitement.

Tessa grinned, so happy to hear Tom sounding like his old self, not that phoney television stranger she didn't know, and walked over to the barn to join him.

Rachel and Natasha were in the kitchen, clearing up from dinner, when Rachel's phone pinged.

'What?' she said, as she read the text. 'I don't believe this! Bloody hell ...'

'What's happened?' asked Natasha, who was at the sink washing up saucepans.

She looked over her shoulder at her sister, who had sat down in one of the kitchen chairs, holding her phone on her lap and staring into the distance, a big frown between her eyebrows. She looked as though she'd been punched.

'It's Branko,' she said.

Natasha snapped her head away again, staring down at the soapy water and wishing there was a lot more for her to wash up. There was only a sieve left, dammit. She couldn't think what to say to answer Rachel. She had a horrible idea where this was going.

'You won't believe what he's done ...' said Rachel.

'Oh?' said Natasha, as casually as she could muster.

'He's in Paris, right? Having a break,' said Rachel. 'He said he might be gone for two weeks, which was fine. I don't have a problem with that, he's so great with the girls and works so hard in all his other jobs, he's earned it, but now he's texted saying he's staying another week "or long", which presumably means possibly longer. What am I going to do?'

Natasha put a few things back in the sink and started washing them again. Oh god, oh god.

'I could have been down here from the first bloody day Mum came out of hospital if he hadn't been away,' Rachel was saying, her voice rising in frustration. 'Simon said I could take the whole of this week off to help, but I couldn't take him up on it because Branko was in Paris and their dad couldn't have the girls. And now I'm buggered for another week. Michael's going to Dubai. I just can't believe it. Branko's always been so thoughtful and reliable.'

There was a catch in Rachel's voice at the end, almost as though she might be about to cry. Natasha dearly wished she could be beamed up to the Starship Enterprise. This was all her fault. Why the hell had she meddled in Branko's life? She was going to have to tell Rachel what she'd done.

The question was, should she do it now, while she was already upset, to get it over with, or tell her the next day, or even Sunday, so they could at least enjoy the weekend up until then ... and for Joy's sake? The last thing their mum needed right now was her daughters falling out when she was just recovering from surgery. She needed peace and calm and harmony for her cells to get on with their repairing.

Natasha decided to play for time.

'What are you going to say to him?' she asked, hoping Rachel's answer might give her an idea what she should say next.

'I honestly don't know,' said Rachel, sounding defeated. 'I can't yell and scream at him, because then he might not come back at all. God knows I've had enough other mothers trying to steal him from me, and I don't even want to tell him about Mum because it will just give him the guilts and it's not his fault that the timing is so catastrophic. There must be some reason he's staying longer – maybe he's met someone gorgeous? – and I don't want to spoil that for him. I really love Branko and he deserves good things. But I really need his support right now. What would you do?'

Natasha stood looking out of the window, hoping her stricken expression wasn't visible to Rachel in the reflection.

'Gosh ...' she started to say, her mind flailing around, then something wonderful happened.

Joy rang the little bell on her bedside table.

'It's Mum,' said Natasha, throwing the washing-up brush into the sink, 'I'll go and see what she wants.'

And she legged it out of the kitchen as fast as she could.

Saturday, 21 June

Cranbrook

Natasha was very relieved when she woke up late on Saturday morning to find that Rachel and Tessa had already gone out to do food shopping. She hoped they'd take a nice long time doing it, felt guilty for thinking that, but couldn't help herself. She was still in an agony of indecision about what she was going to tell Rachel.

Yoga. That was the answer. It would clear her mind. She was about to do some stretches in the bedroom when she remembered there was a fully qualified yoga teacher lying in bed, bored stiff, downstairs.

Joy was delighted when Natasha came in holding the yoga mat she never travelled without. She could also see a slightly strained look on her youngest daughter's face. The joy of the previous afternoon had gone. Something was bothering her and she needed to let it go.

'Oh, what a good idea,' said Joy. 'Would you like me to talk you through it? Is some nice simple Hatha OK? I think that's what you need, something balancing.'

Natasha nodded happily, spread her mat on the floor and lay down flat on her back.

'Very good,' said Joy. 'Close your eyes and breathe deeply and slowly ...'

Natasha melted into relaxation, Joy's low calming tones keeping her just the right side of sleep, until it was time to sit up. After that a series of fast sun salutations woke up her body and her brain, which seemed like a great result at first, but then, while she was trying to concentrate only on Joy's instructions – she'd forgotten what a great yoga teacher her mother was – her thoughts started to get louder.

Why the hell had she interfered with something which affected Rachel's life so fundamentally? She knew how hard it was for her being a single mum, trying to make a decent living when her ex gave her barely more than the minimum child support.

Natasha was well aware how much easier Rachel's life had been since Branko had come on the scene and she had another huge pang of guilt when she thought of how much her nieces loved their manny. He was brilliant with them.

Why had she done it? she asked herself, looking at her strong flat stomach arched up in a bridge pose.

'That's beautiful,' said Joy. 'Put your hands under your back and see if you can lift up a little more, but mind your knees, don't let them fall out to the side. Perfect, now hold that and breathe ...'

It was just that Natasha could see the potential Branko had for opportunities that would change his whole life. He only needed to be the hot thing for a couple of years and he could build up a very nice nest egg which would set him up with something lasting – property, his own business. Surely it would have been morally wrong not to help that happen for him?

Joy's voice brought her back into focus.

'Do you think you can do it without the wall?' she was asking. 'Half-moon pose ...'

'I think so,' said Natasha, getting into position, placing her hands on the ground in front of her, lifting one leg up straight behind her, then turning and raising her upper arm so she was balancing, on one hand and one foot, her body facing outwards. She fixed her eyes on the nose of some kind of weasel painted on the wall opposite and tried to stay in the moment, in her breathing, but still the thoughts came, poking at her.

Was she really thinking only of what was best for Branko, or was it actually some kind of power trip? Look! I can change your whole life, with just one wave of my mascara wand ...

Plus the prestige within her industry of being the one who had discovered the new modelling sensation and racking up invaluable favour debt with one of the most important international model agencies? Not to mention the credibility boost with the likes of Karl Lagerfeld.

So had she done it for Branko – or had she really done it for Natasha? The thought was so horrible, she collapsed out of the pose, falling onto her yoga mat, sobbing.

Ah, thought Joy, a release. I knew it was needed.

'Whatever's the matter, my darling?' she said, leaning over the bed as far as she could, which made her wince with pain. 'Come and tell me.'

Natasha's weeping had turned into proper gulping and wailing as the full shame at what she'd done to her overstretched sister washed over her. She could hear her mother talking, but couldn't hear what she was saying until the sobs died down a bit.

'I'm sorry I can't come down to you, my love,' Joy was saying, 'so get up on here and tell me what's wrong.'

Natasha lifted her head from what felt like the bottom of the sea and looked up at her mother's concerned face. She immediately got to her feet, walked round to the other side of the bed and climbed on very carefully beside her.

Joy wrapped her arms around her youngest daughter and kissed her head. 'Tell me what's going on, my love,' she said, in her so familiar voice with its slight northern bluntness still discernible, something Natasha found so comforting.

'I've made a terrible mistake,' she choked out.

'We all make mistakes,' said Joy, 'and admitting you've made one is a large part of putting it right. Tell me what's happened.'

Natasha looked up at her mother, her dark eyes full of tears. 'You know Rachel's nanny – manny – Branko?'

'Yes,' said Joy, cautiously.

'Well, when we were all here that weekend I got talking to him and ... the thing is ... he's really beautiful, he has amazing bone structure and I told him he could be a model.'

'Right ...' said Joy, waiting for the really bad thing, which she knew Natasha hadn't told her yet.

'And then,' Natasha's voice had gone so quiet, Joy had to strain to hear it, 'I introduced him to a model agent I know and now he's in Paris being fitted for all the couture shows ... and I never told Rachel about it, or asked her if she minded. I just went ahead and did it and last night he texted her saying he'll be away all next week as well and Rachel is devastated ... and she doesn't even know that he probably won't ever come back to work for her now. And it's all my fault.'

She started crying again and Joy made soothing noises, pulling her head onto her shoulder, and stroking her hair.

'There, there,' she said.

This wasn't what she'd been expecting at all. She'd thought Natasha was ready to tell her something deeper and more personal, perhaps about a married man – the situation Joy had long suspected was the reason for her youngest daughter not having a partner. The last thing she'd expected was something that affected one of her other girls. She'd just have to do her best to help smooth it over.

Natasha felt enormous relief at having confessed, and sobbed a bit more, but in more of a relieved, recovering way, than the painful racking of her first outpouring, so she was only hiccuping slightly when Rachel and Tessa walked into the room.

Tessa's face lit up when she saw the two of them on the bed together. It looked so right. Rachel felt a bit piqued. Why hadn't Joy ever asked her to lie on the bed for a cuddle?

'You two look cosy,' said Tessa. 'I'm going to make us some tea and we can all sit and drink it together.'

'I'll make it,' said Rachel, suddenly not wanting to be left alone with Natasha and her mum sharing their special moment.

She went out to the kitchen, putting away the food they'd just bought while she waited for the kettle to boil, glad to be busy. There were too many things she had to not think about. The money situation and the Branko nightmare vying for first place, each of them making the other more difficult to deal with.

Without Branko's help it would be hard to do her job properly, which wasn't great as she was still a little over a month away from the end of the trial period, and until she got that new-business bonus from Simon, she was too strapped to pay for any other kind of childcare.

The joy of the arrangement with Branko had been the simple barter set-up, with no money changing hands. It worked brilliantly for them both. Or it had until now.

Rachel went back into the library with the tray of mugs to find Tessa now also sitting on the bed, which wasn't quite as bad as when it had just been Natasha.

'Come and join us,' said Joy, 'I'm sure there's another corner we can squeeze you onto.'

'Oh, I'll be fine on this chair,' said Rachel, feeling too out of sorts to be so chummy-chummy.

Joy noticed and wondered if she already had an inkling what Natasha had done. Perhaps Branko had told her. Either way, the sooner she heard the truth the better. It was never good to let things like this roll on.

They sipped their tea and chatted about what they were planning to make for lunch and dinner until there was a natural pause in the conversation. Joy took a breath.

'Rachel,' she said in a tone of voice that made Rachel immediately sit up, 'Natasha has something she needs to tell you. Go on, Natasha.'

Rachel looked more closely at her younger sister and noticed her eyes were red. She'd been crying.

'I'm sorry, Rachel,' said Natasha, her voice wobbling as she spoke. 'It's about Branko ...'

Rachel stiffened. What was going on here?

'The reason he's in Paris is ... I introduced him to a model agent and they've signed him. That's why he's in Paris. He's doing fittings for the couture shows.'

'You did what?' said Rachel, bewildered. 'Branko? Modelling? Have you seen how skinny he is? I'm always telling him his waist is smaller than mine.'

As she said it, seeing the look on Natasha's face – what was it? some kind of weird awe? – she understood.

'Are you telling me he's going to be modelling women's clothes?' asked Rachel. As if that had any relevance to the bigger situation, she thought, even as she said it. Like what the hell am I supposed to do about childcare?

'He might be opening the Chanel couture,' said Natasha, her eyes wide.

Something in Rachel snapped. She stood up from the chair and threw her mug of tea onto the floor, where it shattered into pieces.

'Oh, *Chanel*,' she spat out, her voice vicious with sarcasm. 'Well, that's just fine then, isn't it, Natasha? As long as it's Chanel, it's perfectly all right that I've got no fucking childcare. I'd hate to inconvenience darling Karl Lagerfeld and little Choupette with my paltry needs. Well done you!'

Tessa looked terrified, her hands automatically flying up to her head at the sound of the mug crashing down. Natasha started to cry again, clinging onto her mother's shoulder.

Like the spoilt little brat she's always been, thought Rachel. Running to Mummy crying whenever she'd done something wrong. And Rachel having to be the big girl and understand that Natasha was only little and allowances had to be made for her. Well, not any more.

'Really, Natasha,' said Rachel in withering tones, 'that's simply marvellous you helping Branko out like that. Aren't you the lady bountiful? Dispensing your fashion blessings to the poor. Don't you worry, I'll be just fine trying to support my family on my paltry salary with no childcare – oh and we mustn't forget, we've got the school holidays starting in just over a month. Won't that be fun? I can take them to the office with me, my boss will simply love that. Not. Really, well done, Natasha. Top work.'

This was terrible. Joy didn't know what to say.

'Calm down, Rachel,' was the best she could do. 'I'm sure Natasha didn't mean to make things harder for you ... she just wanted to help Branko.'

Rachel turned to look at Joy, painful hot tears springing into her eyes. Was her mother really going to do that thing again? Make Natasha the injured party?

'I'm sorry, Mum,' she said. 'I'm sorry that Natasha has chosen the most difficult time to dump this shit on all of us, with your broken hip and everything, but you really cannot expect me to be fine about it.

'For some reason – maybe she'll get a kickback from the model agent, is that it, Natasha, a bit of extra money? Or maybe a few more free Chanel handbags? Whatever, for some reason of her own, she's mixed her fingers in my life and fucked it up royally. And my daughters' lives. They really love Branko and now they'll have to get used to someone else – if I can even find someone. Do you know how competitive it is in London for good nannies? You know what it's like being a single mother, Mum, I'd have thought you of all people would have a bit more sympathy for me in this situation.'

Rather than sitting with your arm around that snivelling overpaid underweight carbo-phobic fashion freak. She heard some more sniffing and looked over to see Tessa was crying as well. That was the last straw.

'Oh, do stop, all of you, please,' Tessa was saying, 'I can't stand it when you get shouty, Rachel.'

'Oh can't you?' said Rachel. 'Well you might get shouty if you had any idea what it's like trying to raise children on your own. Or even make a living for yourself. Can you remember what it even feels like to work? So you can stop crying. It's not about you, Tessa.'

The fact that being harsh to Tessa was like kicking a kitten just made Rachel want to do it more, but she forced herself to keep the rest of what she was thinking – tell it to your TV-star husband, go and paint another rodent on a floorboard – in her head.

There was the new Hunter Gatherer account to think of, so even apart from family ties, she had to tread a little carefully there. But looking round at their faces, all creased up in variations of hurt and guilt, Rachel's fury hardened. Felt bad, did they? Good.

'You know what?' she said. 'I've just about had it with all of you. So why don't you cosy up on mummy wummy's ickle wickle bed together and have a lovely time, while I go and find a way to make a bloody living and feed my children. Goodbye.'

Then she turned on her heel and stalked towards the door.

Tessa jumped off the bed to follow her, to beg her to stay so they could work it all out and make it better, but Joy called her back.

'Let her go,' she said. 'It will only make it worse if you try to talk to her now.'

'But we can't just let her leave ...' said Tessa, looking over at her mother and then back towards the door, which Rachel had just slammed.

'I think it's best,' said Joy, restraining herself from explaining that Rachel was far too much like her father to get over something like this immediately. She'd need a while to sit with it, before she'd be ready to talk to any of them.

Joy turned to look at Natasha who had said nothing. She had her hands clamped over her face. Joy gently pulled them away to see if she was crying again. She wasn't, but her cheeks were ashen.

'This is all my fault,' said Natasha. 'I'm so so sorry, Mum. You really didn't need this. Or you, Tessa. I'm so sorry.'

'I think it's Rachel who needs your apology more than me,' said Joy, with a very slight, but clearly discernible edge in her voice. 'I know you didn't deliberately set out to make things difficult for her, Natasha, but even though your intentions towards Branko were sincere, you did act thoughtlessly.

'The best thing you can do is sit with the knowledge of that, just as Rachel needs to sit with her anger and then when the time is right, you can apologise to her and really mean it, rather than just expecting to put things right immediately with the word sorry. It's not always enough just to say it, Natasha. It's not a magic charm.'

Natasha felt like she'd been slapped. Then she felt angry – she hated being told off like a five-year-old. Was she always going to be the baby in her mother's eyes? Why should she have to sit there and listen to that? She was a grown woman. A serious businesswoman. She'd apologised. What more did they expect? Rachel's reaction had been out of proportion. She swung her legs off the bed and stood up.

'I think I'll go for a walk in the garden,' she said. 'Need to clear my head after that.'

Still rankled, but not wanting to add to the upset, she squeezed her mother's arm gently, before heading off towards the French windows and out into the garden.

Joy closed her eyes and took some deep breaths. Had she spoiled Natasha hopelessly? Was this all her fault? She opened her eyes again suddenly – where was Tessa? Joy turned to see she was still standing in the middle of the room, frozen with indecision.

'Sweetheart,' said Joy. 'Let them both go. This is their fight. Natasha created this, she'll have to put it right and Rachel will have to find the compassion to forgive her. All we can do is love them both until they sort it out.'

'But shouldn't I go to Rachel, Mum?' said Tessa, looking so distressed, Joy cursed the knackered hip which stopped her rushing straight over to hug her. She reached out her hand instead. Tessa glanced back towards the door, then came over and took it in hers.

'Go to her, my beautiful gentle girl,' said Joy, 'I know you have to, but don't expect her to get over it any time soon. Drive her to the station, tell her how much we love her, that's all you can do now. It will pass, but it will take time.'

Tessa listened, biting her lip, then nodded and reached down to kiss Joy on the cheek. Joy patted her back and then both their heads turned quickly towards the door as they heard the loud thump of a heavy bag being thrown down the stairs.

Rachel was clearly ready to leave.

She rang Branko from the train. Unlike her pathetic, self-serving younger sister, she was a grown-up and knew it was better to get difficult conversations over with as soon as possible. He sounded relieved to hear from her.

'Natasha tell you then,' he said, when Rachel had congratulated him on his new career.

Yes, thought Rachel, but only after she'd got darling Mumsie on side first.

'I feel very bad, I want to tell you, but Natasha say I should wait and see if it would be real, rather than worry you and then nothing ... waste of worry.'

I bet she did.

'I'm thrilled for you,' said Rachel, almost even meaning it. No, she decided, she really did mean it. She was genuinely happy Branko was going to make some money and have a fun, glamorous time. He was a lovely man and he deserved the best. It was just the duplicitous, high-handed way her sister had made it happen that upset her.

'I can't wait to see your picture on the *Vogue* site,' she added, 'in fact, you'll probably be front-page news.'

'I tell my mother already in case,' said Branko. 'Better she know son wearing dress before seeing pictures.'

'Did she mind?' asked Rachel.

Branko laughed. 'No. She say I always like that ...'

Half an hour later, when Rachel was gazing out of the train window at the Kent countryside in all its midsummer splendour and wishing it could make her feel better, Branko texted her. He'd made some phone calls and found a friend who was interested in taking over his babysitting gig on the same terms. She was very nice, he said. Spanish. Called Pilar.

Rachel replied with a text of hearts, roses, champagne glasses, high heels and smiley emoticons and then rang the number he'd texted her. The young woman who answered seemed very pleasant and agreed to come round that evening for an interview. At least that was one bit of good news. Daisy could start learning Spanish.

Rachel's phone beeped and she looked down to see there'd been a call from Natasha's number while she'd been talking to Pilar, with a voice message. She pressed delete without listening to it. Right after she put the phone back in her bag, it pinged to announce a text. Also from Natasha. She trashed it without reading a word, turned off her phone and closed her eyes.

The beauty of the landscape was making the trials of her life almost harder to bear. The way she was feeling, a post-industrial wasteland would have been more appropriate, but she wasn't going to let all the crap take her down. No way.

Joy had always told her how like her father she was and you didn't get to be a minister in Harold Wilson's cabinet without being strong. Tough even.

Leaning her head back against the seat, Rachel pictured his face in the black-and-white newspaper pictures which had become stronger images of him for her than the few family photos she had, and felt a painful flare of sadness that he wasn't still around to help her through this.

'What would you do, Dad?' she asked him in her head.

She felt the tightness in the back of her throat which came before tears, but forced herself to sit up straight and set her shoulders. That's what her dad would have done. The one thing she could not surrender to right now was self-pity. The only way out of all her crappy situations was through action.

She thought for a moment and then tapped on her iPad to open a word processing document. One thing she could get onto right away was preparing a strategy plan for the Hunter Gatherer PR campaign, which she would present to Simon on Monday – along with a very calm and rational explanation of why it wouldn't be appropriate for her to manage the account.

She rehearsed in her head how she would explain it to him – casually, smilingly. 'It just doesn't feel entirely ethical, with the family connection ...'

By the time the train was pulling into Sevenoaks, she was chuckling to herself.

Tuesday, 24 June

Sydney Street

Simon sat in his office looking at his phone and feeling slightly sick. He felt like his teenage self trying to work up the courage to ring up some pretty girl he'd met. Except this was much worse.

He genuinely had to ring Tessa about the PR campaign, but he was terrified she might think he was ringing for the other reason. What if she had really meant it, when she'd asked him to call her in that mad moment outside the restaurant? What if it hadn't been an accident of champagne-fuelled folly?

She really didn't seem the type, but perhaps she was a player, like some of the married women he knew. How was he supposed to know? He could hardly ask Rachel, 'Is your sister a ho?' And even if it had been an aberration on her part, which seemed more likely, it was still ghastly because she would probably think that's why he was ringing – because in that momentary embrace, he'd said he would.

What a twerp he felt, but he had no choice, because the day before Rachel had presented him with a brilliant plan for the Hunter Gatherer campaign and then gone on to say that while she was happy to consult on it, she didn't feel comfortable to run the account herself, because of the family connection.

Simon had immediately protested, but her arguments were very persuasive and, while the thought of running that account himself filled him with dread, he had to admit she was right.

There was always a point in the PR process when the client started to question what they were paying for and it could get quite testy, until a really good bit of editorial came out. Even then, a lot of clients would think it was no less than they deserved and would have no idea how hard his company had worked to place it for them.

Simon could understand that Rachel would find that side of the job difficult to handle with her own sister and brother-in-law. And that meant he now had to ring Tessa. Aaaargggh.

He wished he could just ditch the whole thing, but he simply couldn't turn down any possible source of additional revenue and, maddeningly, he couldn't get any of his other staff to take on the account at this crucial first stage, because none of them had the basic understanding of who the client was and what they did, and he didn't have time to waste getting someone up to speed. Especially as the very specific nature of Hunter Gatherer would require much more finesse than a handmade rug company, bespoke kitchen installer or organic paint range.

He fully intended to pass the account on to one of the team as soon as possible, but for now the point of contact would have to be him. Fuck it.

He slapped his cheeks a few times to try and knock some sense into himself and then forced his forefinger to punch in Tessa's home number. She answered immediately and Simon nearly dropped the phone with surprise, because Rachel had told him that she often just let it ring. He had rather hoped to leave a very business-like message.

'Oh, Tessa!' he blurted out. Super twerp.

'Hello?' she replied, clearly not recognising his voice.

'It's, er, Simon. Simon Rathbone ...' he said, forcing a professional tone into his voice. He sounded like an easy-listening radio station DJ. *This is Simon Tosspot easing you towards midnight with some smooth tunes and lurve dedications.*

'Oh,' said Tessa, taken completely off guard. She'd assumed it would be Rachel who would ring to talk about the plans for promoting Hunter Gatherer and had been looking forward to it as an opportunity to talk to her after that awful scene. But instead it was him. *Him.*

Then a terrible thought struck her. In that moment of madness outside the restaurant she'd asked Simon to call her and now he was. Perhaps that's why he'd rung, nothing to do with the business, but because she'd said 'call me' like a tragic old slut, that day after the lunch. She shuddered at the memory.

'So,' said Simon. 'I, er, well, the thing is, we need to talk about the branding, so here I am.'

'Branding?' said Tessa, even more nonplussed. Something about branding cattle? They didn't have any cattle.

'Yes,' said Simon, feeling on slightly more familiar ground, 'to discuss plans for increasing Hunter Gatherer's profile.'

'Ah,' said Tessa, relieved it was about the PR thing, that kind of brand, but still horrified she was talking to the man who stirred up such confusing feelings in her. 'Yes. Right.'

She really wasn't making this any easier, thought Simon, although in some ways she was, because he was starting to feel a little irritated by her monosyllabic answers and irritation was much more helpful than befuddled lust. Irritation was a more familiar state, something he could work with.

So,' he said, in as brisk a tone as he could muster, 'Tom has asked me to get the campaign going so we've got something

solid to show him when he comes back from the States in –
when is that … a couple of weeks?'

Tessa picked up on the change of tone and was quite
surprised by it, but it did seem to snap her brain into gear at
last.

'Four weeks, actually,' she said. 'He's going to be away for
four weeks.'

Even as she said it, she couldn't believe her husband was
swanning off for that long and to Los Angeles of all places.
At first it was going to be two weeks, then it had become
four. A month. He'd made the smallest of suggestions that
she might like to come out for a 'set visit' – how she hated
those stupid TV phrases he bandied around now – but he'd
immediately qualified it, saying what a shame it would be so
difficult for her to leave Joy and with the school holidays fast
approaching …

To be fair to him, he had then offered to pay for home care
for Joy, someone who could also look after the boys, but Tessa
had known he was only doing the right thing, going through
the motions. He didn't really want her around while he was
making the new American version of *Tim Chiminey*, and he
knew she didn't want to be there either.

She was actually really glad Joy was going to be at the
house to keep her company while he was away … which gave
her an idea. She stood up straight and took a deep breath.

'Perhaps you need to come down to the yard and go round
it with me and the manager, Jack, so we can come up with a
plan together,' she said, surprised at her own forthrightness.
She felt like Rachel.

'That's a great idea,' said Simon, ready to throw an air
punch for the lifeline she'd thrown him – a necessary business
meeting, which also factored in the chance to talk to her about

the inappropriate stuff, as he knew they needed to do, with someone else nearby to stop anything disastrous developing. 'I'll have my PA email you and we'll set up a ...'

He just stopped himself saying 'date'. It was still a minefield, but if he could just get through this call without any more stupidity, he could begin to feel optimistic that this ridiculous situation might soon be behind them.

'... convenient time.'

Phew, made it.

'Great,' said Tessa. 'I'll talk to Jack right away, get him going on some ideas and we'll see you soon. Bye.'

She hung up the phone and stood for a moment, with her hand still on the receiver, quite amazed how she'd handled it in the end. She was particularly proud of the way she'd worked the word 'we' in, with regard to her and Jack. She didn't really know the yard manager all that well, she just let him get on with it while Tom was away, but with him and Joy around, it made her feel as though she would have a team on her side, to protect her against the bewildering effect Simon had on her.

Simon placed his phone back in its cradle and let out a deep sigh of relief. Mission accomplished without anything catastrophically embarrassing happening. He picked up a pen and crossed out the words 'Call Tessa' at the top of the to-do list he wrote by hand every morning to set up his priorities for the day. He always put the hardest thing first.

Then he pressed the intercom through to his PA and asked her to tell Rachel he would like to see her at her earliest convenience. Now he was feeling more confident he could handle the weird situation with her sister, it was time to put Rachel out of her misery.

He was going to tell her the trial period was over – a month before the official six months was up. He would confirm she had a permanent job at Rathbone & Associates and at a slightly higher rate of pay than he had originally discussed with her. He was going to make her a Senior Account Manager. She'd more than proved her worth and his genuine admiration for her great ideas and bankable contributions to the business made Simon certain he would be able to control his less professional feelings towards her.

Head before heart, he reminded himself. Banking before bonking.

Then he picked up his pen and added another item to the bottom of his to-do list: 'Call Jane'. She wasn't getting married for a few weeks yet; there was time for one more little get-together.

Wednesday, 25 June

Dalston, London E8

Natasha was having dinner with Mattie at a Turkish restaurant on Stoke Newington Road.

'Are you sure you're happy to eat here?' asked Mattie, clinking her beer bottle against Natasha's. 'There are loads of mega-trendy places around here now, but I love the food at this joint and I've been coming here for ages, before this whole area turned into uber hipsterville. I can't pretend I don't love living in the coolest part of London, but I don't always feel like being in a big scene when I go out for dinner.'

'I'd be happy anywhere with you across the table,' said Natasha, taking a swig from her beer. It tasted really good. She'd forgotten how great a cold beer could be on a summer night, it had been so long since she'd had one. Too much yeast, too much carbohydrate, too many chemicals. It felt good to let go of some of her rules for once. One of many ways Mattie was good for her.

'And I totally agree about the "scene" thing,' she added. 'I get so much of that with work, it's great to go somewhere low key.'

Mattie grinned at her and reached across the table for her hand. She gave it a quick squeeze and started to pull it away, but Natasha turned her hand over and grasped Mattie's, keeping it there, in hers, on top of the table.

Mattie smiled at her, a questioning look in her eye. Natasha winked at her. Another advantage of a cheap and cheerful local dive was no one to see legendary make-up diva Natasha Younger having a romantic dinner with a woman and then tell the whole industry about it.

'Did you ring your mum?' asked Mattie, after the food had arrived. 'Is she still progressing well?'

Natasha nodded, her mouth full of a delicious mix of lamb, yogurt, tomato sauce and pita bread.

'Yeah,' she said, swallowing and wiping her lips on the flimsy paper napkin. 'You weren't kidding, the food is great here. Mum's doing pretty well, thanks, she's very keen to be given the go-ahead to start physio. She's been exercising her legs in bed as much as she can, but she really wants to start moving properly.'

'Her years of yoga should help her get over it faster,' said Mattie.

'They're already pretty surprised at the hospital how quickly she's recovering, when she goes for her check-ups, but I'm worried this horrible upset with Rachel's going to set her back. So much of healing is about being in a calm environment, with a positive attitude and it's hard to hold on to that when your daughters aren't talking to each other – or, rather, when one of them isn't talking to the other two. It's really breaking Mum up.'

'Rachel still hasn't returned your calls?'

'Nope. I don't think she's actually blocked my number yet, although I wouldn't put it past her, but she's ignored voice messages to her home and office landlines and to her mobile.'

She ticked them off on her fingers. 'She hasn't responded to texts, emails, Tweets, Facebook posts or Instagram. I've tried

Skype and FaceTime, and I even commented on one of her Pinterest boards – and this morning I asked her to connect with me on LinkedIn.'

Mattie laughed. 'That is desperate,' she said and then sat silently for a few moments, chewing her food and clearly thinking it over.

'I am,' said Natasha. 'I already have a messed-up relationship with my father, I couldn't bear to fall out with one of my sisters as well. And I love Rachel so much. She's the only one of them who understands why work is so important to me. She feels the same way. From when I was tiny she was always a role model to me. She's so ballsy, she's never let anyone mess her around. And her kids, Mattie ... You've seen how I love them. I've got to make up with her.'

Natasha's voice cracked and she had to make a huge effort not to start sobbing into her dinner. The thought of a life without Rachel's jokes and her daughters' company was simply unbearable.

'Have you tried going to see her?' said Mattie, gently. 'While you're still in the same city, it seems a shame not to try. Once you go back to New York, it'll be much harder to connect, with the time difference and all that, and somehow it just feels different, even when you get a perfect connection. I always feel that when I call my parents in Melbourne. And, apart from all that, these things are always better sorted out face to face. You can't get the tone of voice when something's written down, especially in a text. They're the worst. I've known relationships that have fallen apart over a misinterpreted text.'

'I think you might be right,' said Natasha, feeling a small spark of optimism that she would be able to patch things up. 'Do you think I should just turn up at her house after work tomorrow?'

Mattie nodded. 'What have you got to lose? No one can say you didn't try to put things right if you've made that effort and I don't see how it could make things any worse than they already are. The point will come when it's Rachel's prerogative to accept your apology and then the buck will pass to her – and the moral high ground to you.'

It was Natasha's turn to sit and think for a few moments, but rather than pondering further on the problem with Rachel, she found herself thanking the universe, god, the goddess – whatever – for sending her someone who was as caring and sensitive, as she was beautiful and smart.

She half-stood in her seat and leaned across the table towards Mattie, putting her hands around her cheeks and kissing her full on the lips.

Thursday, 26 June

Sydney Street

The next morning Natasha was standing at the corner of the King's Road and Sydney Street, squinting at her phone to check the number of the Rathbone & Associates offices.

She looked up just as a tall man, in a beautifully cut suit, walked past her. He had a very good haircut, Natasha noticed with her professional eye, and when he turned around to glance back at her, she was a bit embarrassed that it might have looked as though she was checking him out. He looked familiar.

'Is it Natasha?' he asked, walking back towards her.

'Yes,' she said, realising who it was. Rachel's boss. She'd met him down at Tessa's that day. The day she'd met Mattie ... Everyone else had rather faded into insignificance after that.

'Simon Rathbone,' he was saying, his right hand extended.

'Natasha Younger,' she replied, shaking it. He had a good firm grip. So did she.

'What are you doing in this neck of the woods?' he asked. 'Coming to see Rachel?'

'Yes, I am actually,' said Natasha. 'I was just checking what number your building is.'

'Well, follow me,' he said. 'I'd be delighted to escort you. We're up nearer the top end.'

'Thanks,' said Natasha, amused by his rather charming old-school manners.

He was quite a package, she decided, now she could have a proper look at him. Lovely face, with a wide, generous mouth. He had the height, great shoulders – looked like a rower – the suit was clearly bespoke, the hair, a signet ring. She glanced down at his feet. Church's, she reckoned. Classic, but not stuffy. His suit was cut a little narrow, shorter on the leg, more the Italian style than Savile Row.

She wondered if she could ask him if it was Brioni, but non-fashion people didn't always understand questions like that. It could seem intrusive.

'How is your mother?' he was asking her. 'I was so sorry to hear about her accident.'

'Oh, she's doing pretty well,' said Natasha. 'Nice of you to ask. She's progressing much faster than the doctors expected. They're quite amazed by her actually. She's been doing yoga for over fifty years so she's in pretty great shape.'

'Really?' said Simon. 'Doesn't surprise me. Amazing woman your mother. I've only met her that one time, when I met you ...' he wouldn't go into where, better not start that up '... but I was so struck by her. Very handsome, too.'

As you all are. You three gorgeous girls. All so attractive in such different ways. This younger one was much taller than her sisters, had wonderful high cheekbones and, with her hair cut short on the sides, was rather androgynous. Striking looking. He'd have to make sure he didn't get a crush on her as well. The full hat trick. Wouldn't that be great? No, it wouldn't.

Handsome! What a classic. Mattie would love that.

'Are you over for long?' Simon was asking. 'You live in New York, don't you?'

What a lovely man, thought Natasha. Making conversation when he really didn't have to and with such ease. No wonder he was so successful in PR. But why was Rachel so weird about him? She always talked about him like he was the enemy.

'I'm going back tomorrow, actually,' she said. 'I hate leaving Mum, but I have a big work project on. I'll come over again as soon as I can.'

'You're a make-up artist, aren't you?' said Simon. 'Sorry, not being nosy, but Rachel's so proud of you, and the girls in the office are all terribly impressed.'

Rachel was proud of her? That was news. Natasha had to stop herself snorting with disbelief. He was probably just being nice.

'Oh, that's good to hear,' she said. 'When my make-up range launches over here, I'll have to send some samples to the office for them.'

Simon looked at her a little more keenly. Her own range. Impressive.

'Are you doing the range as an independent, or do you have a licensing deal?' he asked.

Natasha was equally impressed at his instant grasp of the options.

'It's a combination of the two,' she said, happy to talk to someone she didn't have to explain the basics to. 'I've got creative control and twenty per cent of the company and OM – you know, the big American company? – has the rest, but I've negotiated a clause so that I can never lose my name.'

Simon nodded, his eyebrows slightly raised.

'Very smart,' he said. 'I can see excellent business brains run in your family. I've just given Rachel a promotion, I'm so impressed with hers.'

'Oh, that's great,' said Natasha. Really great. He had no idea how great, because she might be less chippy towards me, if she's having a bit of success herself. More amenable to making up about the Branko thing and moving on.

'Here we are,' said Simon, stopping outside an elegant townhouse a few doors down from Fulham Road.

He walked up the steps and pressed the buzzer.

'Too bloody lazy to get my keys out,' he said, smiling at Natasha.

'Rathbone & Associates,' a well-bred voice answered.

'Rathbone,' Simon barked into the intercom, and when the lock released he pushed the door open and held it for Natasha.

'Welcome to my kingdom,' he said, showing her into a reception area, with a very attractive young woman sitting behind the desk, next to a large vase of flowers. 'Hi, Cressida. Natasha's just come in to see Rachel, I'll take her up.'

Natasha smiled at the receptionist and followed him up the stairs.

'She's on the third floor and no lift, I'm afraid,' he said, 'you know what London's like.'

One flight up, they passed a splendid high-ceilinged room on the street side with a big white desk and not much else in it, which Natasha assumed was his office – very sleek – and then continued up two more, ever narrower, flights of stairs to the top floor.

Natasha could see women in every office they passed. There didn't seem to be another man in the place. It really was his kingdom. Or his harem. He was like a potentate in there. All the staff sat up a little straighter when he walked past.

'Here we are,' he said, as they reached the top landing, and strode across it to the office at the back. 'Rachel's in the maid's room at the moment, but she'll be moving down to a better office, with her new exalted role … Rachel,' he said, 'I have a visitor for you. Found her wandering the streets.'

Natasha walked in to see Rachel grovelling around on the floor at the far side of her desk, her back to them, her bottom in the air. Her expression when she turned round and saw who was with Simon went from embarrassment at being found in such a position, to surprise and then fury, in what seemed like a millisecond.

'What on earth are you doing down there?' said Simon, starting to laugh. 'I'm going to leave you two to it. Lovely to see you, Natasha.'

Then he fled down the stairs to his office, mortified by the immediate reaction in his loins to seeing Rachel in that position. He sat behind his desk and put his head in his hands. Every time he thought he was over it, his urges under control, something like that happened.

Just thinking that brought the image of Rachel's glorious bottom, her skirt tightly pulled across it, back into his mind. Disaster. And now he'd confirmed the job, so he was stuck with her – and his inappropriate reactions to her.

Up on the third floor, Rachel didn't know which outrage to be more appalled about. That Simon had seen her crawling around on the floor like that – she'd been trying to fix the broadband, the cleaner seemed to have dislodged a cable – and just when he'd confirmed her as a Senior Account Manager. Or Natasha having the damned cheek to turn up in her office unannounced. How disrespectful was that, of her work? Typical.

'Hi, Rachel,' Natasha was saying, with some kind of patronising placatory expression on her face. It only hardened Rachel's heart more just to see it.

'What are you doing here?' she replied.

'I think we need to talk,' said Natasha.

'Oh, do you?' said Rachel. 'Well, I think I'm in my office, in the middle of my working day and I need to work – not talk to you. And I am, frankly, speechless.'

For a moment, she actually was. She was lost for words how angry and insulted she was that Natasha felt it was fine to barge into her office – and chumming up with her boss, making it even worse.

Natasha started to speak. She was going to apologise for arriving unannounced, then she was going to explain that she had to just turn up like that because she knew Rachel would never have agreed to see her. She also wanted to tell Rachel that she'd decided it was better to come to her office, than turn up at her house, because she didn't want the girls to witness any tension between their aunt and their mother.

But she didn't get a chance to say any of those things, because Rachel had walked away from her and was standing outside the door to her office with her arms folded and a face like granite.

'I'd like to see how you would react if I barged in, uninvited, on one of your precious photo sessions,' she said in a tight voice, 'so please do me the favour of leaving my work place, which I did not invite you into.'

'But we need to sort this out, Rachel,' said Natasha. 'For Mum ...'

Rachel was finding it so hard not to raise her voice, her words came out sounding cracked. She hoped Natasha didn't think she was fighting back tears, because she most certainly wasn't.

'You should have thought about Mum's wellbeing, before you wrecked my precariously balanced life, without giving a thought to anyone except yourself, Natasha. None of this is my fault and I'm not going to let you make it my fault, no matter how hard you play your mummy's-little-baby card. I will speak to you about it when I'm ready, not when it suits you and certainly not during my working day. Now – get out.'

She said the last two words with such vehemence she was sure they'd been heard by everybody on that floor of the building, but she couldn't hold it back any longer. Natasha had to leave.

'OK,' said Natasha, knowing she was beaten, 'I'm leaving, but I'm not going to give up, Rachel, I will make it up to you. We will get over this.'

'Just go,' said Rachel, feeling spent.

And after one last imploring look at her sister – who closed her eyes and shook her head – Natasha turned and headed down the stairs.

Simon looked up as she walked past the open door of his office. He started to get up from his chair, so he could show her out of the building, but just in time noticed she had tears streaming down her face and stayed where he was.

Whatever had gone on up there?

Thursday, 3 July

Cranbrook

Tessa was in the barn with Jack. Under the pretext of familiarising herself with the stock, she was trying to bond with him a bit, so she would feel more part of a team when Simon arrived – due in less than an hour, she realised with a sickening lurch – to discuss plans for promoting the salvage yard.

It wasn't going quite as well as she'd hoped, as Jack seemed to be much more interested in how many square metres of floorboards they had than the way the lovely old glaze on a ceramic doorknob had crazed over time.

He was perfectly nice, and very handy to have around the place when she needed anything heavy moved, but he was very much one of Tom's men's men, the unreconstructed blokes he had always enjoyed working with on building sites and renovations, although he equally relished the company of the campest interior decorators and the rogues from the near-criminal end of salvaging. Tom's ability to get on with all sorts had played a large part in his success. Tessa had always wished she was better at it.

'I'm not sure exactly what's in the back here,' Jack was saying, scratching his armpit. 'It was already pretty full up when I started here and with new stock constantly coming in at the front end, I've never had the time to get across it.'

'Ah,' said Tessa, opening a cardboard box Jack had just lifted down from the top of a cupboard for her and finding it full of lovely old brass coat hooks. 'I remember these. They were part of a big job lot we bought from British Rail, when it still was British Rail ... gosh, that must have been twenty years ago.'

She smiled to herself, examining one of the hooks more closely. It had taken on a rich dark patina that was really beautiful, after all those years sitting in the box. Turning it over in her hands, she could remember how excited she'd been doing the deal to secure a load of spare fixtures they'd had sitting in warehouses.

It had been her idea to get in touch with the main supply centres, the moment the privatisation of British Rail was announced in the papers, knowing it could lead to some spectacular finds. They'd made a lot of money from old station signs. 'Waiting Room' had been particularly popular, for some reason.

Tessa sighed. She'd forgotten how much she used to enjoy the game and chase of salvaging. How you had to think laterally and constantly keep ahead of the competition. That's why they'd called it Hunter Gatherer. You had to use all your animal instincts. The name had been her idea too.

Standing in the dark dusty shed she felt a sharp pang of regret, remembering how involved she'd once been with the business. She'd allowed it to slip away so gradually, her role decreasing further with the arrival of each child, when the plan had always been for her to combine motherhood with working for Hunter Gatherer. Which had seemed ideal, with it being right behind the house, but, somehow, she'd lost her focus.

Engrossed in the forgotten treasures, Tessa didn't hear the office phone ringing. Jack did and ran off to answer it, sticking his head around the door a couple of minutes later to tell her it had been her mum on the phone saying the 'PR bloke' had arrived.

Tessa froze, her right hand holding a brass door handle. Oh god.

'Right,' she said, dropping it as though it had suddenly become red hot in her hand. 'We'd better get over there.'

Stepping out of the barn into the bright daylight, Tessa noticed her hands were blackened from poking around in boxes which hadn't been opened for years and she asked Jack to wait for her while she popped into the staff loo to wash them. It was essential she arrived with him, as part of a professional team.

Trying to get the dirt out from under her fingernails, Tessa glanced up and caught sight of herself unexpectedly in the small mirror hanging on a nail over the sink. Without thinking about it, she realised she'd turned her head to the side and lifted her chin. She was appraising herself. Checking out how she would look to Simon.

Leaning forward, she put her forehead against the cool of the tiled wall and groaned quietly. Why wasn't she in control of herself in this situation yet?

She turned off the tap, dried her hands, and looked at her reflection more deliberately, smoothing her hair and wetting a corner of the towel to rub a smear of dirt from her forehead.

I'm a businesswoman, she told herself. Preparing for an important business meeting and I want to make the best impression, as any professional would. Then, wishing she had a lipstick in her pocket, she headed out to get it over with.

* * *

Simon was sitting at the kitchen table with Joy, a mug of tea and a plate of flapjacks in front of him. It was Archie's SpongeBob mug, Tessa noticed, the whole scene quite bizarre with Simon in his city suit, perfectly combed hair and shiny shoes. One of Hector's baby drawings of a dinosaur was stuck on to the wall just behind him, giving him a kind of halo of bright green felt tip.

He sprang to his feet when Jack and Tessa walked in, hearing himself say 'Aha!' like Winnie the Pooh coming across an unexpected Heffalump. Get a grip, Rathbone.

'Hello, Simon,' said Tessa, feeling her cheeks growing hot. Not blushing on top of everything else. Please no. She practically pushed Jack in front of her. 'This is Jack, who manages Hunter Gatherer for us ... Jack this is, er, Simon Rathbone & Associates.'

Not seeming to notice her muddled introduction, Simon was pumping Jack's hand and, seizing the initiative, Tessa reached over and took hold of Simon's hand when he let go of Jack's, shaking it very briefly before pulling away, greatly relieved she had solved the social kissing issue, which had been worrying her for days.

Simon felt a frisson through his whole body from the brief warm contact with Tessa's palm, then, just while he was registering how brilliantly she'd solved the nightmare of the kiss, which he'd been obsessing about on the drive down, their eyes met.

Fail.

It was all Tessa could do not to make a noise as she felt herself falling under the power of that oddly vulnerable gaze. Simon licked his lips and swallowed as he locked onto the green eyes looking up at him.

Joy saw it all.

Good heavens, she thought. What a connection there was between those two – and why had she never noticed it before? But then, when she thought about it, she realised she'd never actually seen Tessa and Simon together until now.

As she watched, they broke their gaze, and Simon turned to talk man blether to Jack, but Joy could see they were still bound to each other. It was as though their spirit selves were still gazing into each other's eyes, while their physical bodies went through the motions of appropriate social normality, like puppets.

What on earth was that all about? Whatever it was, it couldn't be right. Joy felt the equivalent of a warning siren go off in her head. Code Red, she thought, remembering the drills Tessa's father and his Cabinet colleagues had to learn at the height of the Cold War.

Manoeuvring herself carefully on her crutches, Joy got up from the table, saying that she needed to keep her hip moving, but really wanting to be able to observe from a slight distance.

The three of them started discussing the business, with Simon making notes, and on the pretext of wanting to get a piece of flapjack for herself, Joy hobbled over to the table, so she could have a look at his handwriting. Even in biro, it was a lovely hand. Bold, spikey and forward leaning. Creative, but very precise. Strong. Keen sense of himself, but then straight down tails on the Ys and Gs. Unfinished business.

Back by the cooker, standing on her good leg and propping herself against the kitchen counter, she started cutting the vegetables for lunch, putting her mind into neutral so it would tune in and out of their conversation. That way it would pick up what really mattered without her actively trying to figure it out. Let the subconscious do the work.

'So tell me more about the customers who come in,' Simon was asking Jack, whom he was finding rather unforthcoming. 'What age range are they? Do they come alone, with friends, or in couples? Or, at the weekends, is it a family outing? And what proportion of them would you say are trade, as opposed to private customers?'

'Well, I don't give them a census to fill in,' said Jack, looking pleased with himself, 'they're just people who need stuff. I sell it to them. I don't see why I'm supposed to know what star sign they are.'

Simon tried not to show his irritation. Tessa looked anxiously from one man to the other.

'No, quite,' said Simon, 'but it would be very useful to get a more detailed picture of the current customer base, so we can determine which kind of media would reach them most efficiently with the PR campaign and, more importantly, how we can broaden the range of customers. Then you can sell more stuff.'

Jack was looking blank. Maybe he was just stupid, thought Simon. He'd better not use too many long words.

Joy was wondering whether to bake some beetroots separately in tinfoil and then mix them in with the roast butternut and red onion at the end. She decided she would and as she was wondering if she would be able to bend down to get the foil out of the lower cupboard, she heard Tessa's voice chiming in.

'There's been a lot more women coming in since Tom's been on the television,' she said. 'They ring up all the time as well, don't they, Jack?'

'Yeah,' he said, 'I should tell them Tom's not here, but I'm available.'

He laughed loudly. Simon didn't. Tessa managed a weak smile.

'Interesting,' said Simon. 'The ones who come in – the fans – do they buy anything, or is it just celebrity tourism?'

'They buy small things,' said Jack. 'Knobs and knockers ...'

He smirked. Definitely stupid, thought Simon.

'And didn't you say lettering is very popular with them?' threw in Tessa, increasingly alarmed at the bolshie attitude Jack seemed to be taking towards Simon. She'd wanted him on her team, but not against Simon in this way.

'Yeah,' said Jack. 'The chicks like lettering.'

'Souvenirs then,' said Simon. 'There might be some interesting things we could do with that. Do you have any reference to the TV show around the place?'

'*God* no,' said Tessa, vehemently.

Now Simon and Jack both laughed. Joy looked over her shoulder at them. Tessa was blushing. Something she'd never done much. That wasn't a good sign, thought Joy, not at all. This would require very delicate investigation.

She gave up on the beetroot, she couldn't reach the foil, they'd have to do without it, then started to make her way over to the door which led into the main hall. She needed to lie down and she wanted to meditate on this situation.

'I'm just going to have a rest,' she told them, as she passed the table.

'You're not overdoing it, making lunch for us all, are you Mum?' asked Tessa.

'I've done what I can, Tessa, love, but I'll have to leave it now,' said Joy, putting her hand on her daughter's shoulder. She could feel the hot emotion pulsing beneath her skin. 'Can you put the butternut squash in the oven for me? And if you can be bothered, wrap the beetroots in foil and stick them in too. It will be ready about two, to give you time to get on with some work. Does that sound all right?'

'Perfect,' said Tessa.

'I'm so looking forward to eating your wonderful food again, Joy,' said Simon.

She smiled at him. She really liked the man, but she wasn't happy with the situation she was witnessing here. It couldn't possibly be good for Tessa, which was her main concern, but she didn't think it was at all what he needed either. He already had that horrible damage to his aura. He needed simplicity in his life, not more complication.

'That's very kind of you, Simon,' she said. 'I'm really only a sous chef at the moment, but I've got to do what I can or I'll go mad with this hip. I'll see you all a bit later.'

They stayed at the table a little longer, with Simon asking Jack what the bestselling items were currently and after being told 'dunno, different stuff ...' he started addressing his questions directly to Tessa, but that wasn't a great success either, because it meant he had to look at her – and also because it was clearly making her uncomfortable too.

'What do you think have been the most consistently strong trends in salvage over all the years the business has been going?' he'd asked, thinking it was quite a simple opener, but it seemed to throw her into a spin.

Tessa's mind had gone blank. She hadn't expected Simon to suddenly turn his attention on her like that, so she didn't have her guard up properly. She realised she'd been gazing at him passively, while he'd been talking to Jack, just enjoying the view.

'Well, you know, um, it's a long time since I've been really involved in the business properly,' she started, hearing how pathetic it must sound to both of them as the words came out of her mouth. If she knew nothing about it, what was she even doing sitting there? Why had Tom done this to her? Was it some kind of punishment? She just wanted to run away and do some painting and not have to analyse things and talk to people.

'Floorboards,' she said suddenly. That was the answer. Floorboards, it had suddenly dawned on her, when she'd stopped thinking about it.

'Yeah, that would be right actually,' said Jack, finally getting animated. 'That's pretty regular, people wanting old floorboards. We can't keep enough in stock, we've got about 1200 square metres at the moment, across different woods, but ...'

'And wash basins,' said Tessa, butting in before he started going on about floorboards again. 'The preferred styles change – matching coloured suites are coming back now – but people have always liked the wash basins. Old radiators were very popular for a while, but that's rather died off now. People have realised how much space they take up.'

Tessa felt better. She'd proved she wasn't completely out of the loop, she just needed to get her salvage head on properly again. Simon smiled at her, happy that she'd been able to recover herself. He'd seen the look of pure panic cross her face at his direct question and knew this was hard for her. Rachel had warned him that she'd lost all her confidence about the business and he didn't want to stress her out any more than necessary.

'Well,' he said, 'I think that's probably enough talking for now, why don't we get over there and have a good look at it all? I've only been round the yard quickly one time with Tom and it would be really good to see it from your point of view, Jack, you being the most closely involved day to day,' he added, making another effort to get the meathead on side.

They stood up and Tessa headed out of the back door, but Jack paused for a moment looking at Simon, a not entirely friendly smile on his face.

'Haven't you got anything to change into?' he said. 'It's not exactly clean in the sheds, you'll wreck your fancy suit.'

Simon looked down at himself, feeling pretty dumb. The city version of the country bumpkin. What had he been thinking, coming down to a working salvage yard dressed for lunch at The Ivy? He knew exactly what. He'd been thinking how good he felt in this suit. Comfortable and razor sharp at the same time. It was his lucky suit. His get lucky suit.

Tessa had stuck her head back into the kitchen.

'Something wrong?' she asked.

'I was just telling James Bond here, he's going to wreck his party clothes in the yard.'

Tessa's eyes immediately shot over to Simon. He felt naked, standing there in his stupid suit. Why the hell hadn't he put some old clothes on? It wasn't like he didn't know what to wear in the bloody country. He went there every flipping weekend.

'I'd lend him something,' said Jack, 'but my stuff would be too big for him.'

'Don't worry,' said Tessa, with an unusual decisiveness coming from the utter terribleness of the situation; Jack's appalling rudeness – and the impossibility of her standing there looking at Simon, so magnificent in his beautiful suit. It was very important she didn't do that for one more moment. 'I'll go and find something,' she said, practically running out of the door which led through to the laundry, where she was relieved to see one of Tom's old blue boiler suits hanging over the drying hoist. She grabbed it, snatched a wooden coat hanger off a hook on the back of the door and then headed over to the boot room to look for some suitable shoes. She picked up a pair of Tom's work boots and some old trainers of Finn's.

'This should do it,' she said, walking back into the kitchen and thrusting the boiler suit at Simon. 'What size are your feet?'

'Ten,' said Simon.

'I'm afraid it will have to be Finn's trainers then,' said Tessa, laughing as she handed them over, glad of the light relief. 'I'll run a Geiger counter over them first. You can change in the laundry out there and here's a hanger for your suit.'

'Thanks,' said Simon, feeling like the boy who had arrived at a new school in the wrong uniform, as he headed off towards the door Tessa had indicated.

She turned to Jack. 'You go ahead with Simon when he's ready and I'll see you over there in a minute, I've just remembered something I've got to do,' she said, not feeling the need to tell him it was lying face down on her bed for a while, in the hope of gathering herself for the next round of this torture.

'And Jack,' she added, putting a hand on his arm, 'can you please be a little more cooperative with him? I know it's not your thing, but this was all Tom's idea and we just have to get on with it, OK?'

He nodded, looking a bit sheepish, and Tessa headed out of the kitchen. As she passed the open door of the library, she glanced in and saw Joy sitting on the bed, her good leg bent up in the lotus position, the other one straight out, hands joined in prayer at her heart centre, her eyes shut. Tessa wondered for a moment what she was meditating on so deeply and then put it out of her mind as she concentrated on getting her own thoughts in order.

Despite a few minutes of precious solitude and splashing her face with cold water, it didn't get any easier for Tessa when she got out into the salvage yard with Simon.

It helped a little bit having Jack there – it stopped her immediately leaping at Simon and wrestling him to the ground – but it didn't help to make her less self-conscious about everything she did. She couldn't walk normally if she thought he was looking at her, she didn't seem to have proper control of her limbs, like a new-born foal.

Simon felt like a total prat in Tom's bloody boiler suit. It was a bit small, which didn't help. It was grabbing his bollocks and he'd had to leave it unbuttoned a lot lower than he would have preferred, and it was still stretched pretty tight across his chest.

Shame he wasn't wearing a medallion, he thought, catching sight of his pectorals down the open neck, as he looked at some roof tiles Jack was droning on about. Perhaps he should have left his shirt on underneath? But he felt enough of a berk as it was.

Bored with Jack's detailed explanations of how many tiles equalled one pallet – who cares, you moron? The important thing is what they *look* like and will people think that owning them might make their empty lives a little more complete? – he glanced across the yard to see Tessa bending over, looking at something on the ground, her dress riding up the back of her legs.

He looked away immediately. At least she didn't wear tight skirts, like Rachel, but what kind of deviant was he? Everywhere he looked, there seemed to be a woman's shapely backside facing him and making him think like a monkey. Oo oo ooo. A language Jack would probably understand.

It was stifling out in the yard, which wasn't helping. Simon could feel sweat running down his back, and swiped his hand across his forehead.

'Bit hot for you?' asked Jack.

'Yes, it's pretty warm out here,' said Simon.

'You want to try carrying marble fire hearths around in this,' said Jack, standing up to his full height and sticking out his chest.

Totally uncoordinated pumped-up rugger bugger, thought Simon. I could mince you in a fight, beefy boy.

'Keeps me fit, anyway,' added Jack, flexing one Arnie bicep and confirming him as a total bonehead in Simon's opinion.

'Oh, very good,' he said, as patronisingly as he could, suddenly feeling completely over the whole exercise.

While it was not to his taste, he could see that bits of knackered industrial kit could be very effective in the right interior. He got the appeal of old radiators, doors and wash basins. He was even interested in bricks, roof tiles and floorboards, but Mushbrain was now talking in great detail about guttering and that was a step too far. Guttering was of zero interest to anyone he would be able to reach through a sophisticated marketing campaign. Salvage was sexy. Builders' merchant was not.

'What have you found over there, Tessa?' he called out, walking away from Steroid Stan while he was in mid-flow. He was done even pretending to be listening.

'Oh,' said Tessa, looking up like a startled Bambi, 'it's these blue-and-white tiles. I keep looking at them, they're so pretty, but I'm not sure if they're genuine Delft, or something more ordinary.'

At the moment she looked up, Simon tripped on a bit of old metal – probably a bit of Meatloaf's bloody guttering.

'Shit,' he blurted out, just managing to right himself before he hit the deck.

Jack was laughing. Simon ignored it.

'Are you OK?' asked Tessa, noticing he still had his beautiful brogues on.

'I'm fine, but I've scratched one of my new shoes. Bloody idiot to wear them.'

'Well, I don't blame you for not fancying Finn's trainers.'

'Couldn't quite face it,' said Simon, smiling at her.

'I always wear steel toe caps,' Jack chipped in. 'Some of the stuff I carry could take your foot off if you dropped it.'

Simon and Tessa locked eyes, this time more in amusement than lust.

'Very sensible,' said Tessa, 'we wouldn't want a law suit.'

Simon sat down gingerly on a pile of bricks next to her and as he reached over to take a tile out of the crate, Tessa accidentally caught a glimpse down the front of the boiler suit of a taut chest and stomach, which looked remarkably like the ones she remembered from so many years before. She swayed slightly, crouching on her heels, and had to steady herself with her hand.

'I think they're probably genuine old Delft,' he said brushing the dust off the tile he was holding, a charming scene of a man with a spade. He picked up a few more. 'They all seem to be different, too, how lovely. Shall I take a few of them back up to town to show one of my antique-dealer pals?'

'That would be great,' said Tessa. 'It's been nagging at me, leaving them sitting around like this, that they might get sold off as a cheap lot, when they could be something rather special.'

'No, I wouldn't leave them out here.'

Where Norman the Moron might crush them beneath his mighty steel boots, he thought, as Jack lumbered across the yard and stood over them, hands on hips, blocking the sun.

'I was just going to show you the corrugated iron,' he said, a frown between his brows, clearly not happy with being abandoned during his guttering lecture.

'Ah,' said Simon, squinting up at him, 'it's just I don't think that the construction side of the yard is particularly relevant to what Tom and Tessa want me to do here. It's more the decorative side of things they want me to promote.'

Jack looked down at him, his eyes narrowed. Simon could practically hear the cogs turning.

'Can I go then?' asked Jack, addressing himself entirely to Tessa. 'I've got some phone calls I could be getting on with.'

'Oh, yes, that's fine,' said Tessa. 'Thanks for your time, Jack. You go and do whatever you need to do now.'

Yes, you do that, dearie, thought Simon, as Jack nodded in acknowledgement and walked off.

Simon restrained himself from expressing his relief. It wasn't good form to criticise somebody's staff to them, but when he glanced at Tessa, she smiled back at him, with a mischievous look in her eye, which reminded Simon for a moment of Rachel.

'I don't think Jack's so comfortable with the decorative side of things,' she said. 'He's very good with corrugated iron ...'

'And guttering,' said Simon.

'And he can carry very heavy things ...' said Tessa and she started to giggle, partly from the tension.

Simon was laughing too.

'He showed me his biceps,' he said, 'very impressive.'

'Oh, he didn't ...' said Tessa. 'I'm so sorry I inflicted him on you, I just thought he'd be able to tell you more about what's going on with the yard now, than I can. I haven't had that much to do with Jack, to be honest, and I didn't realise he was quite so ...'

'Guttering-y?' said Simon.

Tessa laughed again, nodding. 'Of course, we do need someone with that kind of expertise,' she added, thinking she should at least try to be a bit professional. 'A lot of people who come here are only looking for technical building materials, but I've never been very involved in that side of the business.'

That was more Tom's thing, she thought, but didn't want to say his name. It felt like a weird kind of betrayal saying it to Simon. It was bad enough seeing him in her husband's overalls. Especially the way he was bursting out of them, like Superman ripping off Clark Kent's suit.

'Well, now he's gone to do his thing, shall we get on with looking at the stuff I can successfully promote for you?' said Simon. 'I think you could really beef up the carry-away retail side here – you know, things people just take home rather than have delivered in a big truck. You might want to think about hiring someone else on site to work on that. Or you might like to do it yourself, Tessa. You'd be so good at it. Discuss that with Tom, because I'm sure we can work magic promoting the more decorative offer, but if it's Desperate Dan they have to deal with when they come in to buy, I don't think it will work out in sales.'

He'd mentioned Tom's name deliberately. Even despite the precarious seating and the heinous boiler suit, he felt so completely at ease with Tessa at that moment, sitting in the sunshine, a Delft tile still in his hand, he needed to remind them both of the situation they were in – but it didn't work. It didn't break the spell. He glanced over at her and saw that she'd turned her beautiful face up to the sun with her eyes closed. Savouring the day.

Is this what it would be like? Simon wondered, indulging himself just a little bit longer, in the companionable silence, with a woman he found almost overwhelmingly attractive, but also really liked. Someone he could communicate with in verbal shorthand. Who got his references and his jokes. Who got *him* ... Is this what a normal middle-aged relationship felt like, for those who were capable of having one? Comfortable, easy and nurturing. But, he reminded himself, it wasn't his middle-aged relationship. No more getting cosy, mister.

'Right,' he said, getting to his feet and stuffing both his hands quickly in the pockets of the boiler suit, when he realised he had been just about to put one of them out to help her up from the ground, 'how about you show me some of your finest beaten-up old crap?'

Tessa had felt so at ease with Simon, hanging out in the sunny yard, laughing about oafish Jack, she was beginning to allow herself to hope that she was finally getting on top of the weirdness. If she could be that relaxed with him now, with no one else around, maybe it would be all right working with him. And she so wanted it to be, because she was starting to feel really excited about being involved with the business again.

She was already having ideas about how she could re-style the yard, so the duller builders' merchant side of things would complement the more decorative stuff she loved, make a frame for it, rather than be off-putting. She could picture a winding path through the various areas – planks, doors, guttering, radiators all attractively ranked – making it a kind of journey of discovery. Rather than a big old mess of stuff, which it was currently.

Feeling more enthusiastic about the business than she had for years, she took Simon into the big barn which housed Tom's precious fireplaces, hearths and overmantels.

'Not sure about all this,' Simon was saying, running appreciative fingers over the carved roundels on a Regency marble fire surround. 'I mean, I love this surround, it's like the one in my office – and in my flat actually – but I'm not sure we should promote this side of the business so much, when it's already so well served by the TV show. That would just bring in more of the crazed fans.'

He was holding the front of the overalls together as he spoke. It was clearly too small for him, Tessa felt bad for suggesting it. Bloody Jack.

'Not that I think you should completely ignore that market,' Simon continued, walking along the line of fireplaces, 'there is clearly money to be made there, but it would have to be handled with subtlety, because it could very easily cheapen the Hunter Gatherer brand, which has a much longer life span, in my opinion, than the TV show.'

'I couldn't agree more,' said Tessa, thrilled that he understood that.

She knew Barney the Dinosaur was very keen on the idea of *Tim Chiminey* merchandising deals and was determined that Hunter Gatherer should not be in any way part of that. It was so good to know she didn't have to explain things like that to Simon. He got it.

'Come over here then,' said Tessa, walking towards the back of the barn, 'I want to show you the kind of stuff I think is being neglected.'

With every step they took towards the far end of the building, away from the sunlight streaming in through the open door, it got darker. Not familiar with the layout, Simon had to tread carefully until his eyes adjusted and by the time he reached the very back, Tessa was already stuck in, pulling things out of boxes to show him.

He did his best to admire the brass hooks, turned dark brown with neglect, pearlescent glass light fittings liberally dusted with the corpses of dead insects, and a large bundle of old roller towels, stiff with decades of accumulated dust, and tried to share her enthusiasm, while deeply hoping he wouldn't be expected to touch any of them.

Simon appreciated patina as much as the next highly visual sophisticate, he could coo over a flaking Italian fresco as excitedly as any overprivileged aesthete, but there was a point for him where attractive wear-and-tear went over into proper crumminess. This stuff was well beyond it.

He tried to picture the items she was showing him, not polished up like repro, but at least washed and dusted and placed in a more congenial environment than this filthy old shed. He felt like the still-living cousins of the dead daddy long legs were crawling over his head.

He pushed his hands back into the boiler suit pockets and then, realising it just pulled the gaping front of the hideous thing open further, took them out again and crossed his arms in front of his chest.

Tessa picked up on his discomfort. 'What do you think?' she asked tentatively, holding up a stuffed crow, wings outstretched, she'd just pulled out of a tea chest. It was part of the deceased estate of a taxidermist, the rest of it stacked up against the far wall.

Simon took a step back. Taxidermy, particularly birds, made him feel physically sick. He could practically see the fleas crawling over it.

'It doesn't matter what I think,' he said, carefully. 'I know how fashionable this kind of gear is at the moment and styled up the way you do it so beautifully in your own house, there's a huge market for it. I'm just not great with, um, seeing it in the wild.'

Tessa suddenly remembered Rachel once describing Simon's office to her – as an example of why he was a wanker. It was all white, she'd said, including the desk, which was huge and shiny and never had anything on it apart from a vase of white flowers, a pot of black biros and some exquisite bit of ancient Greek sculpture. Of course he'd hate this shed.

'Sorry,' she said, 'I forget that other people don't feel comfortable with ... this ...'

She gestured towards the stacks of old cardboard boxes, crates and pallets, with her free hand and then put the crow carefully back in the tea chest. She thought it was beautiful. She'd come back for it later and put it in the library.

'Let's go and sit in the garden, for a bit,' she said. 'There are some nice pieces out there we can look at and then it will be time for lunch.'

'Thanks,' said Simon, blinking furiously, then sneezing dramatically.

'Here we go,' he said, sneezing three more times in quick succession. 'I'm allergic to dust.'

Simon walked behind Tessa when they got out of the shed, hoping she wouldn't see him brushing his shoulders to remove any dead flies and other filth that might have landed on them. He'd never longed for a shower more.

She turned round to see him with his head down by his knees, frantically rubbing his scalp with his fingers. She burst out laughing.

'What are you doing?'

'I'm sorry,' said Simon, standing up quickly and running his hands over his head, knowing he probably looked like Krusty the Clown. On a windy day. 'I just can't help feeling I'm crawling with insects. I'm so sorry. I just hate stuffed birds.'

He shuddered involuntarily.

'I'm so sorry,' said Tessa, 'I had no idea you felt that way, or I never would have shown it to you.'

'No,' said Simon, 'the fault lies with me, I'm being very unprofessional. I'm fine now and isn't your garden lovely? I didn't get much of a look at it last time I was here.'

As soon as the words were out of his mouth he could have punched himself in the face. Just when things had been starting to feel a little bit normal – and he'd actually been oddly pleased to be revolted by her salvage junk, as it had put a little bit of much needed distance between them. Now that gap had closed over in an instant.

And it wasn't just him. He saw it on her face too, as soon as he said it, her expression changed and her eyes went down to her feet. Then they came up again and of course, he was still looking at her, frozen with the stupidity of what he'd just done and there they were, back where they'd started, gazing into each other's eyes in a dizzy wonder of attraction.

Simon sighed. They had to have that conversation. 'Is there somewhere we can go and sit?' he asked.

Tessa nodded and he followed her along a path, mown through a meadow of wild grasses and flowers, butterflies flitting about – sent by Central Casting, thought Simon – towards a stand of trees, which he could see, as they got closer, were all starting to bear fruit.

'It's an orchard,' he said out loud.

'Yes,' said Tessa, 'it's my favourite part of the garden.'

And the orchard is my very favourite part of my mother's garden, thought Simon, my sanctuary, but he kept that to himself. He had enough to deal with in the here and now, without opening that conversational portal. Oh really, where does your mother live? Do you see her often? Next question please …

They followed the path between the trees to a small clearing where there was a fringed swing seat, the cushions upholstered in faded yellow linen.

'Now that's my kind of salvage,' said Simon. 'What a lovely old thing.'

'I got it out of a skip,' said Tessa, laughing.

'Well, that's where you salvage scavengers have the edge on me. I miss out on these kinds of treasures, being a prissy clean freak. It doesn't look too dirty,' he said, inspecting the seats.

'It's not,' said Tessa, sitting down. 'Someone was gutting a lovely old house in Tunbridge Wells and I found this and a lot of other great things in the skip outside, all in perfect nick. People are just too lazy to sell stuff, so they chuck it out.'

'And clever magpies like you swoop down and pick it up,' said Simon, sitting down next to her and immediately wondering if he'd taken leave of his senses.

Sheltered beneath the floral fabric roof, the white fringe waving back and forth with the gentle movement of the swing, he turned to look at Tessa. She turned at the same moment and the two of them were locked there, inside the embrace of the seat, the sun shining on their legs, birds singing in the trees around them.

Tessa felt her stomach turn over. She'd felt so normal and at ease with him earlier, sitting in the yard, and then his obvious distaste for the things she so loved in the barn had finally made her feel the desperately needed separation had taken place. And now this.

Simon decided to stop thinking. He didn't have a sensible thought in his head, so he wasn't going to listen to any of them. He was just going to be. He reached over and took Tessa's hand. She didn't pull it away. And then they just sat there, rocking gently in the swing, in the sunshine, in the orchard. In the moment.

Tessa knew she should let go of Simon's hand, but she didn't want to. It felt so right sitting there with him. It was like the previous twenty-five years had never happened. This was the day after the night before. Instead of her slipping away while he slept, they'd woken up together, they'd come to the orchard and they were sitting in the swing. Twenty-something years old. The whole of their lives to come.

Neither of them knew how long they'd been sitting there, when they heard a bell clanging in the distance.

'That means Mum needs help with the lunch,' said Tessa.

'We'd better go in then,' said Simon.

They turned and looked at each other again. Simon tried to remember when he'd last felt so happy and when they stood up, it seemed perfectly natural to walk back along the path, towards the house, still hand in hand.

Just before they reached the edge of the orchard, Simon looked ahead and felt reality racing towards them. He stopped and turned to Tessa, who immediately faced him, reaching to find his other hand.

'We've got to leave the enchanted kingdom,' said Simon.

'I know,' said Tessa, smiling sadly at him.

Then he wrapped his arms around her and pulled her body against his, lifting her slightly off the ground. She felt the entire outline of him, pressing onto her, as though it were making an impression on her body, like a mould on clay.

She lifted her face and even with her eyes closed she knew his lips were coming towards hers. When they met, it was almost like an electric shock, the wave of desire that flooded through her and then they both immediately pulled away.

It had seemed so easy and simple sitting in the orchard, like that, just holding hands, but this one, fairly chaste, kiss immediately brought all the complications rushing back. They dropped each other's hands at the same moment.

'Let's go in,' said Tessa, 'Mum will be waiting for us.'

Joy certainly was waiting for them. At some cost to her physical comfort, she was standing on her crutches in the courtyard by the kitchen door, because she wanted to watch them come in together, to be sure she hadn't imagined the whole thing.

One look at the two of them, walking along, their cheeks flushed pink, but small frowns between their eyebrows, and her fears were confirmed. In fact she wondered if it wasn't already a lot worse than she'd first thought.

'Is Jack not with you?' she asked, just to fill the heavy silence.

'Oh, no, I think he's staying in the office,' said Tessa.

'Well, please come and give me a hand. The veggies are ready to come out of the oven, but I can't get down there to do it, although I did manage to get the rolls in. They'll be ready in about five minutes.'

'Sit down, Mum,' said Tessa, rushing in to help, quite glad to be busy, because it would stop her thinking. 'I think you're overdoing it.'

'What can I do?' asked Simon.

'Put these on the table, please,' said Tessa, passing him a handful of cutlery and three plates, then quickly pulling the roasted vegetables out of the oven and putting them on a large platter.

'There's parsley chopped to go on top of those,' Joy said, 'and I toasted some almonds.'

'Oh, Mum,' said Tessa, 'you shouldn't have done all that.'

'It's harder for me not to,' said Joy. 'But I will sit down now.'

She started lowering herself slowly onto a chair and Simon rushed to help, taking her crutches and propping them against the dresser.

'Anything else, Tessa?' he asked.

'No, I think we're all ready,' she replied, putting a bowl of salad and a cheese board on the table.

'Would you mind if I just go and change quickly before we eat?' asked Simon, but his words were cut off by the shrill ringing of a bell.

'That's the rolls ready,' said Joy, smiling brightly. 'Could you wait until after lunch, Simon? It would be such a shame not to eat them while they're warm.'

She wanted to get this over with and it wouldn't do any harm for him to be uncomfortable in that boiler suit. Tom's boiler suit.

Simon couldn't see how blazing hot rolls could get cold in the time it would take him to put his shirt and trousers on, but he nodded and smiled politely.

'Of course,' he said, 'but I will just wash my hands, if you don't mind.'

He headed out to the loo, while Tessa continued to fuss about, getting the salt and pepper, pouring a glass of water for each of them and putting a bowl of cherry tomatoes on the table. Joy left her to it. This was no time for chat.

'Well, this all looks lovely,' said Simon, coming back a few minutes later and leaning over the table to breathe in the delicious aroma from the hot bread. 'Mmm, they smell amazing. Did you really make them, Joy? With your hip and everything?'

'Yes,' said Joy, not bothering to explain they were a batch from some time ago, which had been in Tessa's freezer. She wanted them to squirm. The more uncomfortable they felt, the more truth they would spill out. This had to be sorted.

'This all looks splendid,' Simon was saying, valiantly trying to fill the vacuum, as Tessa served them all with the roasted vegetables and Joy passed round the salad. 'I've been dreaming about your food since the last time I was here.'

Joy just smiled at him, rather coolly, he thought, and said nothing. He didn't remember having to work so hard with her last time, then thought things might be looking up, when she reached over and patted his hand.

Tessa noticed how quiet her mother was and began to feel anxious. When she saw her fingertips lingering on top of Simon's hand her heart sank. Tessa had a very good idea what was coming. She wondered if she could escape, using the excuse of needing the loo herself and had just started to lift her bottom off the chair when Joy spoke.

'Stay where you are, Tessa,' she said.

Simon picked up on the tension and put his cutlery down, a large piece of roasted squash still speared on the fork.

'So,' said Joy, 'I don't mind which one of you tells me, but I would like to know what's going on between you two.'

Tessa closed her eyes as the worst-case scenario unfolded before her. Simon's mouth fell open in surprise, but he quickly recovered himself.

'Whatever do you mean?' he asked, remembering the key tactic. Always answer a tricky question with another question.

'Don't be slippery with me, Simon,' said Joy. 'I used to be married to a politician who ate the toughest radio presenters for breakfast. I know something's going on between you two and for everybody's sake – including your own – I would like to know what it is, so I can help you prevent any damage.'

'Muuum,' said Tessa, feeling and sounding about fourteen.

'You're a grown woman, Tessa,' said Joy. 'A mother and a wife. Please act like one. Whatever's going on, telling me will take a lot of the power out of it and you'll be able to control it more easily.'

Simon turned to Tessa and appealed to her for help with his eyes. She shrugged.

Simon tried another version of the question tactic.

'What sort of thing do you think it might be?' he asked, tentatively.

'That's what I want you to tell me,' said Joy. 'And no more questions as answers. Come on, one of you, it doesn't matter who. Start at the beginning.'

Simon looked at Tessa again. She closed her eyes and nodded. There was nothing else for it, he'd have to tell her.

'Twenty-five years ago,' he started, meeting Joy's gaze steadily with his own, 'I met the most beautiful girl I'd ever seen at a party in Devon. We danced together for hours and then we went out into the garden and found our way down to a meadow by a river and we made love there. Then we went back to the room she was staying in at the house and made love again. All night. It was the most beautiful experience of my entire life, but when I woke up the next day, the girl was gone and I had to leave too and ...'

He turned to glance at Tessa, who was looking at him with tears in her eyes.

'I meant to find out who she was, from the friend who had invited us both to the party so I could get in touch with her, but then ...'

He looked at Tessa again. How much to tell them?

'But then some other things happened very soon after and I was too distracted to follow it up, and then it seemed too late and I had to be content with accepting it as one perfect moment in my life, never to be revisited.'

He paused, sighed and picked up his glass of water. He took a long drink and after he put the glass down, he felt Tessa's hand come under the table and find his. He squeezed it tightly.

'Stop that, you two,' said Joy. 'I can see what you're doing.'

Simon glanced at her, surprised at her sharp tone, and let go of Tessa's hand.

'Go on, Simon,' said Joy, more gently.

'Then I came here that day – when was it, just over a month ago?' he turned to Tessa again. She nodded.

'I came here for the shoot, with Rachel – who works for me ...'

And please don't tell her any of this, I beg you, he thought, but it wasn't the time for that. He'd have to bring that up with Joy later. Just get this over with now.

'... and just as I was leaving, that day, Tessa came down the stairs and I recognised her as the girl from the meadow in Devon.'

Joy sighed and turned to Tessa. 'Is that how you remember it?' she asked.

Tessa nodded.

'And you never went looking for him either?'

'I met Tom the following week,' said Tessa in a whisper.

She turned to look at Simon and as their eyes met again, tears started rolling down her cheeks. Simon's hand immediately went to his pocket for his handkerchief, but it was in his suit trousers. He was still wearing that bloody awful boiler suit. Tessa's husband's boiler suit. Oh, this was too awful. Joy had made him keep it on deliberately, as a pointed reminder. Another man's property.

'So you re-met that day for the first time after all those years?' said Joy. 'That must have been quite overwhelming.'

'It was,' said Simon, relieved to hear something more like her usual kindness back in Joy's voice. 'Particularly for me as I haven't had much in the way of relationships since then – and particularly for Tessa, because she has.'

He looked straight into Joy's eyes and she smiled at him. He was a good man. She hadn't been wrong about that, but she still had to find out how far things had gone. She had to protect her daughter from ruining her own life and several others with it.

'So have you seen each other since that day here?' she asked, dreading what the reply might be.

'Only once,' said Tessa, wiping away her tears with a napkin. 'We had lunch with Rachel and Tom in London to talk about the business.'

'That must have been difficult,' said Joy.

'We drank a lot,' said Simon.

'That can make things worse,' said Joy.

Simon and Tessa glanced at each other.

'It nearly did,' said Simon, wishing he had a drink at that moment. 'You're very wise, Joy,' he added, leaning on the table, looking up at her, his chin in his hand.

'I'm just very old,' she said, thinking he looked about twenty, sitting like that. She could see how dashing he must have been as a youth.

'Mum picks up on a lot of things most people miss,' said Tessa. 'She's very intuitive.'

'I've noticed that,' said Simon. 'Is there anything else we can tell you, Joy? I know you have everyone's best interests at heart.'

'Thank you for understanding that, Simon,' she said. 'So just to get it straight, nothing has happened between you, apart from those two meetings and today – you haven't taken it any further?'

'I kissed Tessa in the garden just now,' said Simon, feeling he had nothing to lose. 'On the lips, but no tongues.'

Joy looked at him steadily, an amused look in her eyes.

'You're right to mention that,' she said, 'the tongues ... if there were no tongues, you haven't broken the seal.'

'The seal?' asked Simon.

'The seal of trust,' said Joy, as though it should be obvious. 'You've stayed just on the right side of it. Just. Oh, I'm so relieved. That makes all this so much easier to handle. Let's finish our lunch and then have tea in the sitting room. I need to lie down flat for a bit. I would suggest wine, Simon, but you've got to drive back.'

'Tea's fine,' said Simon, 'as long as I can have another of those flapjacks with it, but before I eat my lunch, I'm going to change back into my own clothes, if you don't mind now, Joy?'

She chuckled. She knew he'd rumbled her ruse and just liked him all the more for it.

By the time they were onto a second pot of tea, Simon felt like he was on some kind of high. More like they'd been drinking wine than Earl Grey, there was such an overwhelming sense of relief. He felt he could unclench his stomach for the first time since the shock of that sudden encounter with Tessa – and right after he had that thought, he told Joy and Tessa about it.

That was a dizzying revelation in itself. To talk about his feelings, openly and immediately with other people, without constantly checking himself. He felt quite giddy.

'I feel the same,' said Tessa, curled up on a sofa.

Joy was sitting with her legs stretched out on the sofa opposite. Simon was sprawled in an old club chair, the leather all cracked and falling to bits. He wondered what stinking skip Tessa had got it out of, but it was comfortable, he had to admit that.

'I've hardly felt I could breathe, since it happened,' Tessa was saying. 'I'm not used to keeping secrets. I had no idea it took up such a lot of energy. How do people have affairs and live like that?'

Simon said nothing. For a blink of a moment he was tempted to let go entirely. To tell them that he'd been living with secrets most of his adult life, but no. This venting with Joy and Tessa had been liberating and wonderful, but he feared that if he took it any further it would be spoiled. He wanted to keep this happy light feeling going as long as he could.

'I've often asked married friends who have affairs that very question,' he said. 'Who needs it?'

'Some people get a kick out of all that,' said Joy. 'It's the danger and risk they find exciting, as much as the person, but it's a very selfish pleasure. You two have done very well to resist.'

'I don't feel like I did entirely,' said Simon, 'because I confess I did allow my grubby male mind free rein to imagine certain things in great detail. Sorry, Tessa.'

She smiled and shook her head indulgently, feeling so happy that she hadn't even blushed. If he'd said that to her a few hours before, she would have foamed at the mouth with mutual desire.

Joy laughed. 'That just makes you a normal healthy man and I think it makes your self-control even more commendable. You wanted to do something very much and you didn't do it. What do you think gave you the strength to hold back?'

'All the same reasons as Tessa,' said Simon. 'Her children, her husband – her self-respect, my own. And I had another motive to keep me strong, which is that I value Rachel so highly on my staff.'

He let his words hang there. He had to bring Rachel up, so he could risk-manage that situation. Make them both vow never to tell her what had happened between him and Tessa, but that was it. He definitely wasn't going to open up about the added complication, even during this truth-fest. Your daughter/sister Rachel who I admire so much professionally and who also reduces me to a gibbering mess of testosterone lust jelly and adolescent crush.

He noticed Joy was looking at him very intently and hoped she wasn't about to have another of her spooky insights.

'It's very important Rachel doesn't ever find out about this, don't you both agree?' he added.

Tessa nodded.

'So none of us will tell anyone else about any of this, ever. I'm assuming that's agreed between us?' he said. 'Keep it safely behind that mystical seal of yours, eh, Joy?'

She didn't reply, just looked at him thoughtfully.

'Please tell us you agree to that, Mum,' said Tessa, sounding as anxious as Simon. It was one thing for the three of them to talk it out like this, but she was banking on that being the end of it. Cone of silence.

'Of course,' said Joy. 'I'm just considering how to manage the situation with regard to Rachel. I know how much her job means to her and we must be very careful for her sake.'

Because she's already dealing with Natasha's terrible selfish mistake. She doesn't need another sister's folly complicating her life as well.

'So I'm not sure you two should work together on this publicity drive for the salvage yard,' Joy continued. 'The less you see of each other the better. No risk of cosiness.'

Simon and Tessa both nodded their agreement.

'Couldn't Rachel do it for you?' Joy asked Simon. 'Wasn't that the original plan?'

'She's already told me she doesn't want to,' he said. 'She's uneasy about mixing work and family and, I must say, I think she's right.'

Joy smiled. Rachel was a canny girl.

'Is there anyone else on your staff you think would be right to do it?' asked Tessa, feeling secretly relieved on several levels.

She knew Simon didn't really like or understand the things she loved most about Hunter Gatherer and, as well as the personal complications, she'd been concerned whether it was going to work out with him running the campaign.

Simon sat and thought for a moment. Even apart from the weirdness with Tessa, he knew deep down he hadn't felt entirely comfortable with the whole scenario of Rathbone & Associates representing Hunter Gatherer from the outset. He'd just been bowled along by the prospect of getting some additional cash into his strained coffers, but while he understood how fashionable it was, how could he sell something he didn't even want to touch? Or inspire one of his other staff to do it?

'In all honesty, I really don't think there is anyone on my team apart from Rachel who could do it justice,' he said, 'and while it nearly kills me to turn away a nice chunk of business, I do think it might be better if I recommend another agency for you, Tessa. One which will fit much better with your set-up than mine.'

She smiled at him. So relieved he felt as she did and was being honest about it.

'Thanks Simon,' she said, 'I could see how you felt about my stuffed birds.'

'Stuffed is the word,' he said, grinning back. 'I'm a bit of a clean freak, in all honesty.'

'Definitely not right for Hunter Gatherer, then,' said Tessa. 'We only like things that are really properly befouled.'

They laughed and Joy smiled, happy they'd each come to the conclusion they couldn't work together on their own terms. Rachel had to be protected, she already had enough on.

The only person missing out now would be Simon, but he'd made the decision himself and seemed fine about it. Joy looked at him, sprawled in the chair, his long legs stretched out, gazing up at the ceiling.

He'd lost a lot of the tension he'd been carrying when he'd arrived that morning, but there was still that sense of unfinished business hanging around him. She had wondered if the giddy relief of confessing about Tessa might make him ready to talk about whatever that was, but it didn't seem like it. Maybe later.

'Well,' she said, 'if you two don't mind I think I'm going to go and have a little rest, before we start thinking about dinner. Will you stay, Simon?'

For a moment he was tempted to say yes. He felt so comfortable there with the two of them, just as he had the first time he'd visited Tessa's house, but better not to push his luck.

'Thanks so much for the offer,' he said, standing up, 'but I've got to get back to town, so I think I'll get going.'

Tessa got up from her sofa and Joy struggled to do the same. Seeing her difficulty, Simon rushed over to help, putting his hands under her arms with great gentleness and lifting her onto her feet in one sure move.

'Are you OK?' he asked her, putting his arm out to steady her as she found her balance on her good leg and then helping her onto her crutches.

'Thank you, Simon,' she replied, looking at him with one of her penetrating gazes. How easily and gracefully he'd done that. 'How kind you are.'

'I think you're the one who deserves the thanks,' he said, smiling, and while taking care not to push her over, he wrapped his strong arms round her in a warm hug.

'Thank you, Saint Joy,' he said, quietly in her ear, 'you're a marvel.'

He kissed her cheek and Joy lifted her hand and let it fall gently onto the side of his head for a moment. Not ready to spill it all out yet, she decided. But getting closer.

Friday, 4 July

Queen's Park

Rachel was standing in her kitchen waiting for the kettle to boil and looking at the new pile of letters that had arrived the day before, wondering if she could bear to open them. They weren't the dreaded brown envelopes of debtor tradition, companies pursuing you for money didn't seem to use those any more, it was all innocuous white ones these days, so it was hard to tell what you were in for before it was too late. It could give you the most horrible shock.

She'd learned not to open post when she got home from work because it guaranteed a sleepless night, and she'd promised herself the evening before that she'd get onto these first thing.

But now it didn't seem a good idea to do it before a busy working day either. It wouldn't do to arrive at the office feeling stressed out about her personal finances, when she needed to project confidence, success and positivity. Especially as she had some important meetings with three companies she was trying to get involved with the Lawn & Stone press trip.

She'd had a fiendishly cheeky idea to spread the costs across several complementary clients to everybody's benefit; the smaller outfits getting the kind of glamorous PR exposure they would never be able to afford on their own for a small fee, which, multiplied by three, would reduce the cost of the trip for the main client.

Lawn & Stone would also get some crucial referred cool cred by association with the more cutting-edge names, which would be very helpful in establishing them as a hip upscale brand, separate from the main mass-market company, which had zero design prestige.

Rachel was really looking forward to presenting her stroke of marketing genius to Simon as a done deal, once she'd signed a couple of them up.

She was also gagging to hear how he'd got on the day before, down at Tessa's house – or Hunter Gatherer HQ, as she tried to remember to think of it in the context. Even though she wasn't working on the account any more she still had a professional interest in it, with regard to the bonus she was going to get for bringing in the business.

She'd tried ringing Tessa a few times to get an update on Simon's visit but she hadn't heard back yet.

After sending Tessa a quick text – it would be great to know how it had gone before she saw Simon – Rachel picked up the envelopes and shuffled through them. There were a couple she recognised from the return addresses as credit card bills, the rest were more mysterious. Could be anything. Unlikely to be anything good. She tapped them against the palm of her left hand a few times, then noticed the time and threw them back on the table, running out of the kitchen and upstairs to see where the girls had got to. There was exactly five minutes until they had to leave.

It was times like this when she really missed Branko. The new au pair, Pilar, was very nice and the girls really liked her, super impressed that she was a real-life grown-up dancer –

missing the point that she wouldn't be their au pair if she was getting any work in her 'real' career – but she wasn't fully entwined in their family life the way Branko had been.

Although he often worked late in his various bar jobs, Branko had always got up in the morning to have breakfast with them. He said it reminded him of his own big family, back in Belgrade, to have a rowdy breakfast with kids, and he'd often already be up and making it before Rachel came downstairs.

French toast was his speciality and the girls still called it 'Branko *klebbe*', one of the many Serbian words which still littered their conversation, constantly reminding Rachel what had happened. She felt a little stab of renewed hurt at Natasha's betrayal every time.

Pilar's bedroom door was firmly closed as Rachel raced past, and she assumed she was still asleep, as it turned out was Daisy, who'd got straight back into bed after their wake-up call twenty minutes earlier. Ariadne was sitting on the floor, still in her pyjamas, engrossed with her doll's house.

Rachel wanted to scream, furious with herself more than anything, for not checking on them sooner, but managed to keep it together, issuing simple, firm commands and physically putting Ariadne into her clothes.

She got them to school just on time, still eating the Tunnock's tea cakes which had been the nearest thing she'd been able to grab to give them for breakfast. It wasn't ideal to have your six-year-old arrive in class with a luxuriant chocolate moustache, but in the circumstances, she was just happy they'd made it at all.

And then driving off on a relieved high, she was halfway into town in her car before she realised what she was doing. She hadn't paid the congestion charge and she didn't have anywhere to park when she got there. Horribly aware that parking rates would go up with every inch closer to Chelsea, Rachel started desperately looking for a car park.

She found one near the top of Edgware Road, parked and ran down to the Tube station, very happy it was on the District and Circle line, which would take her straight to South Ken. She might actually be on time for work.

Rachel didn't get to see Simon until after five that afternoon. Her meetings successfully accomplished by lunchtime, she was practically hopping from foot to foot with impatience to tell him her news – and hear his, about the trip down to Cranbrook, because Tessa still hadn't called her back – and kept finding excuses to walk past his office door, but it was always closed.

By the time he messaged her to ask if she'd like to pop down, most of the other staff had already gone. She tottered into his room carrying a large stack of magazines festooned with Post-it notes and dumped them on his desk.

Simon smiled when he saw her. She was so alive with enthusiasm. He'd had a day of tedious meetings with the landlord and the accountant, and then some of his less inspiring staff members, reporting on their dreary ideas for their dull clients. A shot of Rachel was just what he needed and she was looking particularly perky, with high colour in her cheeks.

'Good afternoon,' he said, as she sat down on the chair opposite him, bolt upright. 'Nice to see one of my staff is still in the office on Friday afternoon. I know you've been waiting to see me, sorry about that, what gives?'

'Well,' she said, reaching over to open several of the magazines at the marked pages and spreading them across his desk. He picked up the second-century Greek marble sculpture of a foot and put it on a shelf behind him. He didn't want it crashing to the floor with one of her more vigorous gestures. After a moment's thought, he moved the flowers, too.

'Are you familiar with this light?' she said, pointing at a wood-and-copper table lamp.

Simon nodded. 'Isn't it by that young bloke who just won the John Lewis award?' he said.

Rachel nodded, keenly. 'Exactly,' she said. 'And how about this rug?'

'I can't remember the name, but I remember seeing it at Decorex. I really liked the use of different textures on the dogs' heads. It was on a shared stand, wasn't it? The up-and-coming area ...'

'Yes,' said Rachel, 'the ones who've only been going two years or less, but Kit Kemp has just used their rugs right through her new hotel. They're going to be huge. And, finally – for now, anyway – this teapot?'

'Yes, that I do know. It's by my friend Richard Taplow's daughter, Mercy. She's the third generation of ceramicists in that family.'

'Bingo,' said Rachel, 'and all three of these exciting new brands would like to be part of the Lawn & Stone press trip. They will pay for their products to be shipped over to Tangier and will contribute something – not much, but something – to the travel costs for the journalists and me, ha ha. In return they will get exposure to the top-tier editors and bloggers we're taking and will most likely snag some choice bits of editorial, which is a brilliant opportunity for them at this stage before they have the budget to take on a PR company. And when their businesses have grown to that level, they'll already have a link to us. Kerching.'

The growing delight on Simon's face was like watching a moon rise.

'And Lawn & Stone will get the association with the cool award-winning young brands,' he said, clearly thinking it through as he spoke, 'which will help establish their place in the elite design market, as opposed to the trashy naffness of the parent brand ...'

'You got it, sunshine,' said Rachel, wiggling in her seat with excitement. 'Pretty good, huh?'

'Are these deals agreed?' asked Simon.

'Yep,' said Rachel.

'How much?'

Rachel smiled. It was so like Simon to bring it straight down to the money, but he did it with charm. He was never tacky about it.

'Just a grand each, but it will cover part of the air fares and enable us to give the editors proper limo transfers to and from Heathrow.'

'Have you told Arkwright Industries what you're up to?' said Simon. 'We don't want them thinking we're piggy-backing other clients on to their trip.'

'Yep. The old man loves to save money. That's how I sold it to him. I saved the brand-association aspect for the kids. What do you think?'

'I think you're a bloody marvel,' said Simon. He glanced at the clock. He could have one drink before he had to drive. 'Shall we have a glass of wine to celebrate? It is Friday, after all. I've got a nice bottle of white in the fridge.'

Rachel opened her mouth to say yes and then remembered her car. Dammit.

'I can't,' she said, 'I accidentally drove halfway to work this morning so I have to pick the car up on my way home.'

'Accidentally?' said Simon.

'Don't ask,' said Rachel, 'kid-wrangling stuff, but the good thing was I wasn't even late this morning.'

'Maybe you should drive every day.'

'Maybe you should get me a parking space.'

'Yeah, right, dream on. Shame about the drink, but this is brilliant work, Rachel. I'm thrilled, well done.'

'Can I have another pay rise?'

He laughed. 'Well, maybe not quite so soon after your last one, but if you carry on like this I'm sure you'll be promoted again fairly soon.'

'Well, at least I've got the bonus from the Hunter Gatherer business to look forward to,' said Rachel, seizing the opportunity to remind him of it. There wasn't likely to be a better moment, but she had to be careful not to let a note of desperation creep into her voice. 'When do you think I might get that?'

Simon's face immediately changed.

'Ah, yes,' he said, 'that's something I wanted to talk to you about.'

'How did it go yesterday?' she asked, still bright with enthusiasm. 'I've tried ringing Tessa, but she still hasn't got back to me and I'm dying to know how it went.'

Simon said nothing. Tessa was probably still letting everything which had happened the day before settle down in her head. He wished he'd had that luxury. Then perhaps this awkward issue might have occurred to him: that Rachel was expecting – and quite fairly – to get the new-business bonus for bringing in the Hunter Gatherer account. The bonus she now wouldn't be getting, because he'd pulled out of the deal for reasons he couldn't possibly explain to her, i.e. he'd temporarily been a weirdo pervert sex maniac sleaze bucket about her sister. Oh god.

'So did you and Tessa work out an action plan?' Rachel pushed on.

'Well, the thing is,' said Simon, shifting uncomfortably in his chair, 'Tessa and I had a good look at all the stock, with Jack, the manager ...'

'Why on earth did she get that Neanderthal involved?' asked Rachel, irritated. 'He's just a human forklift, he hasn't got a clue about any of the décor stuff.'

'I think Tessa felt he needed to be there, because he runs the business day to day.'

'Well, he shouldn't,' said Rachel. 'That's just Tom putting the nearest macho man in charge while he goes gadding off. That is exactly why Tessa needs to be running the thing.'

'I totally agree,' said Simon, 'and I told her that. I think she's ready for it too, she was very passionate about the stuff she showed me, they've got masses of stock in the barn that hasn't seen the light of day for years.'

Or a duster.

'So what's the plan?' asked Rachel. 'Are you going to make Tessa the face of the brand and leave Chimney Stack Jack and Tim Chiminey out of it? That's what I'd do. Get her styling pictures though, rather than personality-led pieces. She's terrible at having her photo taken, which is nuts considering what she looks like.'

'Well,' Simon said, turning Rachel's comment about Tessa's looks over in his mind and finding it hadn't sent him off on one of his perve-a-thons. That was a positive, anyway.

'You see ...' Damn, this was hard. 'Tessa showed me her old door knobs and stuffed birds and all that carry-on and I'm afraid I just don't relate to it, Rachel.'

She frowned. What on earth did he mean?

'I know the deep grunge end of vintage is red hot right now,' Simon continued, 'all that exposed brick, birds' nests and filthy old Chinese jackets on wire hangers about the place ... I know it's a moment, but I just don't love it and I can't represent something I don't love. It wouldn't ring true. I know myself and I know the clients I can work with and although I really respect Tessa's style – the house is amazing – it's not for me.'

'Are you saying you want me to take on the account after all?' asked Rachel.

'No. I'm saying Hunter Gatherer isn't right for Rathbone & Associates. It wouldn't work out well for either side.'

'You're going to turn away the business?' said Rachel, starting to feel quite nauseous.

'Yes. I know it's somewhat out of character, to put it mildly, but I think in this case it's the right thing to do. The brand just doesn't fit with the rest of our client roster, but don't worry, Tessa is fine about it.'

Rachel laughed bitterly.

'Oh, that's great then,' she said, 'as long as Tessa's fine about it.'

Now Simon felt really uncomfortable. Just when he thought he'd elegantly released himself from what could have been a very tricky situation, both personally and professionally, he now seemed to be stuck in the middle of some kind of sibling stand-off. The last thing he needed, frankly. He had quite enough of that crap in his own life.

'I'm sorry, Rachel, but she could see I didn't like it. Stuffed birds make me feel physically ill. So she totally understands it would be better for Hunter Gatherer to work with an agency which really loves what she does – who would you suggest, actually, have you got any ideas?'

'Are you kidding me?' said Rachel. 'Now you're asking me to suggest some other firm where someone else will get the kind of new-business bonus I thought was coming my way? Well, you can jolly well work that out for yourself, Simon Rathbone – and you can tell your new best friend Tessa that from me.'

She could have said a lot more but managed to stop herself. She was all too aware she'd just crossed a line with him anyway – exactly the kind of thing she'd known would happen with this toxic family/work combination. The only positive outcome she'd ever been able to see in this whole hideous scenario was the bonus and now she'd had all the hassle and upset, which had just made her be dangerously rude to her boss, without even that compensation.

How could Tessa have done this to her?

Simon blinked at Rachel's outburst. The 'new best friend' comment particularly hit home. Had Rachel seen what was going on between them when they had that lunch? Was that what this was really about? But surely she would have been odd with him right after, if that had been the case. He decided to wait and see what she said next. Always better to say nothing than to plunge in and make it worse.

Rachel closed her eyes for a moment to contain her anger. She might have had her job confirmed, but she still couldn't afford to blow it with Simon. Especially now she wasn't getting the £1000 she'd been relying on to start paying off her Barclaycard.

'I'm sorry, Simon,' she said, 'I shouldn't have been so outspoken. I'm just very disappointed about the bonus – I guess I'm just as money-minded as you are, in my own way.'

Just for different reasons, she thought. Like my children. She'd had an email from the school that morning telling her

Daisy would not be allowed to register for clarinet lessons for the next school year, until Rachel had paid the bills outstanding for the last two terms. That was just one tiny thing in the whole teetering mess that felt like it was about to crash down around her.

'Yes, I think that's why we work together so well, Rachel,' said Simon, seizing the common ground, with huge relief she wasn't angry for any reason other than the lost bonus.

He wondered for a moment whether he should offer her £500 as compensation. That might smooth things over, but the meeting he'd had with the landlord that morning had given him rather a lot to think about financially.

The lease on the building was nearly up and if he wanted to extend it, he was going to have to find nearly double the money, not just the rent rise he'd already had. He'd gone through all his options with the accountant that afternoon and it looked like he might have to lose a couple of staff members, at the very least.

And how could he make someone redundant when he'd just given another employee a little bit extra? That wouldn't look very good in an unfair dismissal case, but even apart from that kind of risk, the very thought of laying off staff made him feel ill.

Of course he could move the offices to cheaper premises, but in an industry that was all about image that could be disastrous. He could just imagine his rivals: 'Did you hear? Rathbone's had to downsize ... So funny ... Arrogant git.'

But it was more than that. Like his car and bespoke suits, the SW3 postcode on his letterhead was one of his business assets, part of the image of success which helped to keep him successful – or it had until now.

Still, he hated to see Rachel looking so deflated. She'd been like a little tornado of energy when she'd come tripping in with those magazines and now she looked as though it had all been beaten out of her. But he could hardly tell her his worries about the business.

He knew she wasn't a gossip, but he still couldn't risk it getting out to the staff and then, inevitably, to the entire design world. He'd just have to hope she'd bear up and he'd promote her again as soon as he possibly could.

'I tell you what, Rachel,' he said. 'Why don't I give you a lift up to your car? You'll get home sooner, to see those girls of yours.'

Rachel didn't reply immediately. Her first instinct was to tell him not to bother. A ten-minute lift hardly made up for a £1000 bonus, but then she thought, why not? The girls were going to their dad's that night, but at least it would mean she could see them for a few minutes before he picked them up.

Rachel was very quiet in the car, which made Simon feel even worse about what had happened. He began to wonder if he could pay her the compensatory bonus from his private bank account, so it didn't have to go through the company books. He'd think about it over the weekend.

Her phone pinged shortly after they set off and Simon heard her tut with irritation as she read the text. Then she slumped down even further in her seat. He'd never seen her so flat.

'Have you got something nice planned for the weekend?' he asked, sounding like his hairdresser.

'Well, I did have,' said Rachel. 'But the friend I was going to see tonight has just cancelled on me. She's met a new man and, of course, a last-minute invitation from him totally justifies her cancelling a long-term arrangement with me, because I'm just a worthless girlfriend.'

So I'll be home alone, she thought. The girls will be with Michael, I can't spend any more money on weekend trips and I can't even go down and see my mum, because she's staying with one of my bloody sisters, who both seem to be on a mission to destroy me at the moment.

'Oh, that's a bore,' said Simon, wishing he could suggest they had dinner together. What a golden opportunity, because it wouldn't be a date kind of thing, just two colleagues at a loose end on a Friday night. But no, he couldn't suggest something normal like that, because he had to go to the sodding country, didn't he?

After that, he did his best to make conversation with light remarks about things going on in their industry, but with Rachel's answers becoming increasingly monosyllabic he was relieved when they pulled up at the car park, which was a grotty-looking place.

'Shall I wait?' asked Simon.

'No,' said Rachel, 'I'll be fine. Thanks for the lift. Have a good weekend.'

'And you,' he said, wondering which of them was going to have a more miserable time.

Rachel gathered up her stuff and got out of the car. He looked up at the dismal concrete building. It really was grim.

'Are you sure you don't want me to come up with you, Rachel?' he said, out of the car window. 'This place is pretty seedy.'

Rachel paused. It was rather desolate and she would have liked a bit of company going up to the fourth floor. But at the same time, she just wanted to go home, see the girls before Michael picked them up and then get into bed and pull the covers over her head. She couldn't face another moment making polite chit chat.

'Thanks, Simon,' she said, 'but I'll be OK. You get on your way. I know you have a long drive on a Friday.'

'OK, see you Monday,' said Simon driving off, tooting his horn twice as he went.

Rachel watched him go, wondering who on earth he spent these mysterious weekends with. He never seemed to miss one, but he never talked about them. Whatever it was, it was likely to be more fun than the weekend that was ahead of her.

She fished the parking ticket out of her bag, pushed it into the machine and was horrified when she saw the amount she was expected to pay. Sixty pounds. How could it be £60 for one day's parking? She checked the time and saw that she had just gone over the eight-hour limit, which took the parking charge up from £40 – already a rip-off – to an unbelievable £60.

Why the hell hadn't she checked the prices before she'd parked? She'd just assumed it would be £20, maximum. She didn't have £60 to pay it. She had no credit on any of her cards, she didn't even take them out of the house with her any more, and there was nothing in her current account, only an overdraft already slightly over its limit.

The only money she had was the £360 left from selling that light on eBay and it had been a right palaver to turn that into cash, which she'd only been able to do thanks to one of the women in the office, who'd advanced it to her from what her husband gave her each week for 'groceries', in return for Rachel transferring the PayPal balance to her.

Rachel had felt slightly ill when she'd seen the fat wad of twenties in the woman's wallet. How could her life be so catastrophically different from the women she worked with?

But she'd been very grateful to get the cash and after using part of the precious bounty to fill the car with petrol, was keeping the rest at home, taking just £20 a day out with her and trying not to spend that. She'd stopped eating lunch, which helped. So she had that £20 note in her wallet and a bit of loose change, that was it, but if she left the car in there any longer it would just keep racking up higher and higher charges she couldn't pay. She had to get it out of there as soon as possible.

Who could she ring? She ran through her friends in her head, but it was Friday night, they'd all be at home cosy with their families, or out doing the things single people do on Friday nights. And what would she say to any of them? Oops, silly me, it seems I've mismanaged my money into a state of near bankruptcy, so I can hardly feed my family, so can you lend me £60 for a day's parking?

She put her hands over her face for a moment, hoping she wasn't going to have a panic attack. Could she ask Michael? No way, he'd just use it as ammunition when he dropped those little hints about suing her for custody of the girls and if he knew how bad her financial circumstances really were, he'd probably have a case.

She tried Link's phone, to hear a friendly voice as much as anything, but it just went to message. She'd sent him a text earlier in the week to see if he'd wanted to meet up that weekend and his reply had been non-committal. Which was fine. That was how loose and fluid things were between them, so she'd arranged to meet her treacherously unreliable girlfriend, on Friday, hoping she might see him on the Saturday.

Who else was there? No one. There wasn't anyone else, so she knew she had no choice but to get a bus home, pick up £60 of her precious cash and then take another bus back to the car park. Thank god it's Friday …

* * *

An hour and a half later, after she'd hung around at home a little to enjoy the girls' company, leaving just before Michael was due, Rachel was in her car at the exit of the car park.

She hit the indicator to turn left, north, back to Queen's Park, but in the few moments she was stuck there, waiting for cars to pass, she was hit by an impulse and switched the indicator to right. She hadn't heard from Link, but decided she'd just go down and see what he was doing. Anything was better than staying home alone, with just £300 between herself and destitution, terrifying unopened letters looming everywhere she looked.

The worst of the Friday traffic was over and she had a fairly clear run, her spirits lifting with every turn of the wheels away from home and all those responsibilities. She turned the radio up, opened the windows and for a moment, with the wind blowing her hair, almost believed it as she sang along. 'I'm happy ...'

Perhaps this was why Simon went away every weekend, maybe getting out of town to wherever it was – Herefordshire? – was his sanity de-compressor.

But as she passed a row of shops which told her she was getting closer to Link's place, she began to feel a little more nervous about just turning up there. Their liaison was blissfully free of structure, but it wasn't spontaneous. They always made plans. Sometimes at the last minute, but plans nevertheless. Of course, he very well might not be in, she reminded herself. She'd picked up that he had a pretty busy social life and she was aware that he may have other lady friends, as it were, although it wasn't something they'd ever discussed.

He knew she was divorced and she knew he'd had a fairly long-term relationship which had ended a few months before they met, but they'd never gone into the whole romantic history thing, or had a conversation about whether they saw other people. It didn't seem necessary. They were fine the way they were. No need to dissect it.

As she got close to the strip of riverbank where Link's houseboat was moored she remembered she was in the car. Well, she hadn't forgotten she was in it, but she hadn't considered the implications.

Link hated people who drove in London with a passion. It was the only subject that made him lose his laidback cool. And she hadn't been entirely ingenuous with him about her own car usage.

With this in mind she decided to park around the corner and walk to the houseboat, but then she considered how exposed she'd feel arriving on foot, if he already had someone there, or a group of friends. She'd feel a right lemon turning up then – Hi, I'm Rachel, Link's MILF – so she decided to cruise past at a safe distance in the car first and if it looked cool, she'd park around the corner and then walk back. If he asked where her bike was, she could say she'd got the train down.

But never having driven down there before she got a bit muddled about which was the turning to the houseboat dock and before she realised it, she was right alongside his place. Link was sitting on the deck and his head immediately turned towards her, surprised by the sound of a car, as everyone who lived down there seemed to be a committed urban cyclist. He stood up, frowning slightly. Oops.

'Rachel?' he said, moving along the boat to be nearer her. Shit. She killed the engine and got out. What else could she do?

'Hi, Link,' she said weakly.

He stood in the cockpit looking at her with his head on one side.

'I wasn't expecting you,' he said, seeming more puzzled than unfriendly.

'Ah, no, well, you see, I was just down your way and I thought ...'

Before she could finish, a beautiful young woman emerged from the cabin. She came up and stood next to Link, snaking her arm around his waist. She was wearing a sarong. Only a sarong. She had long tousled sun-bleached hair and her skin was the colour of a strong cup of tea.

'Oh, Rachel, this is Imke,' said Link, looking a tiny bit sheepish.

'Hi, Imke,' said Rachel, waving at her and feeling like an absolute idiot. She was still in her work clothes. A tailored skirt and a blouse, mid-heeled pumps. She felt like an air hostess. 'I was just passing and when I realised how close I was, I thought I'd just swing by and say hi.'

'Great,' said Imke, 'come and have a drink with us – or a coffee, as you are driving.'

It was obvious from her tone, and the very slight overemphasis on the word 'driving', that she despised city motorists as much as Link did. Rachel didn't miss the 'us' either.

All she wanted to do was to drive off at high speed – possibly with her middle finger raised out of the car window – but that would be an admission of the real reason she'd turned up. Booty call. More of a cuddle call, really, but equally tragic in the circumstances. So she took off her shoes, throwing them back into the car, and stepped aboard.

Link went down into the cabin to make her some coffee and Rachel did her best to chat happily to Imke. She was very nice actually. Dutch. Lived in Amsterdam. On a barge. Of course she lived on a fucking barge. Rachel felt so bourgeois sitting there in her office-girl clothes, her embarrassing polluting car in full view, knowing she lived in a boring brick house, no manner of a boat. A fully mortgaged middle-class ball-and-chain house.

Imke also let Rachel know, with champion-level subtlety and not unkindly, that she'd been seeing Link for several years. Rachel wondered how that had fitted in with his former long-term relationship, but decided she didn't care.

Link came up from below, holding Rachel's coffee and a glass of wine for Imke.

'You look hot, Rachel,' she said, taking the glass from him and letting her fingers linger over his. 'Why don't you get comfortable? I can lend you a sarong.'

'Oh, I'll be OK,' said Rachel. Doors to manual and cross check.

Link sat down with a glass of wine for himself and they passed a few minutes enjoying the evening sun, commenting on how big the cygnets had grown and how calm the river was. Rachel almost convinced herself she was having a nice time.

'So, Rachel,' said Imke, 'you are the woman Link met in the shop?'

'Yes,' Rachel replied, rather taken aback. She knew about her.

'He tells me about all his friends,' said Imke, putting an emphasis on the word 'friends', which made Rachel a little uncomfortable. 'It was true when he said how beautiful you are.'

'Really?' said Rachel. 'Are you sure you're not confusing me with someone else? But thanks anyway.'

What else had he told her?

'You have a great body for a woman who's had two children,' continued Imke.

This was getting creepy. Rachel glanced over at Link, expecting him to be cringing with embarrassment, but he was smiling at her in his normal way. He was clearly completely relaxed with this conversation.

'So do you have anything planned for this evening?' asked Imke.

That was normal, thank god.

'Er, no, not really. My kids are with their dad. I guess I'll be heading home soon, I was just nearby, for work, so I thought I'd call in.'

'You don't have to go,' said Imke. 'Why don't you stay with us?'

As she spoke she moved her body so the sarong fell to her lap, revealing breasts the same wonderful colour as her shoulders. Rachel was lost for words. She glanced at Link, looking for assistance, to find he was still smiling at her, with that characteristic playful look in his eye.

'Yeah, that would be great, Rachel,' he said, 'why don't you?'

As he spoke, Imke moved closer to Rachel and put her hand on her leg. Quite high on her leg and moving higher. Holy Jesus.

'Ha ha,' said Rachel, nervously, 'er, thanks, that would be great, but I'm pretty tired after work and I think I'll just be going ...'

She wanted to move Imke's hand, but it seemed rude. She wasn't appalled by the idea of a woman being sexually attracted to her, it just wasn't something she wanted to get involved with at that particular moment, with the man she'd been sleeping with for several months.

'I can relax you,' said Imke, moving closer.

'No, really,' said Rachel firmly, patting Imke's encroaching hand in a deliberately nanna, asexual way, and then moving away from her. 'I appreciate the offer. You're very lovely, Imke, and – well, Link already knows what I think about him – but I'm just not in the right place for this now.'

'You sure?' said Imke. 'A hot summer night, three beautiful people … what could be better?'

Having a normal relationship? thought Rachel. Someone to have a curry with on a Friday night, to talk about the news, watch a box set. She really didn't need to act out a porno film after a hard day's work and a major financial disappointment. She hadn't even had a shower.

'OK,' said Imke, 'maybe another time. I come over a lot, Link can tell you when.'

'Great,' said Rachel, 'thanks.'

No thanks.

What was the etiquette for this situation? Imke really seemed to be genuinely relaxed about it all. The Dutch must be like the Scandinavians, she thought. Pragmatic about pleasure. Rachel now knew she wasn't. The arrangement with Link had been so sweet. She'd loved the ease of it, but this had gone several steps too far into creepy free love.

'I think I'll be off, actually,' said Rachel, standing up. 'I just wanted to drop in to say hi. Bye, Link.'

He stood up and kissed her, right on the mouth, pushing in his tongue in the way which normally fired her up like a Formula One car. This time she had to stop herself shoving him away. She pulled back and it was all she could do not to wipe her mouth on the back of her hand.

'Bye, Imke,' she said, leaning around Link's broad shoulder, so she could see her. 'It was good to meet you.'

Not.

Imke wiggled her fingers at her, smiling.

'Text me,' said Link, as Rachel hopped onto dry land. It had never seemed so appealing. 'I'm here next weekend.'

'Great,' said Rachel.

I won't be.

She got into the car and didn't even bother to put her shoes on. She just wanted to get the hell out of there. Glancing in the rear-view mirror as she accelerated away, she caught a glimpse of them. Link's back to her, clearly busy snogging Imke. Yuck.

How odd. A man who had seemed the very embodiment of cool, carefree sexuality, now seemed almost sleazy. It was probably her problem. Imke was gorgeous, Rachel had nothing to do that night, maybe she should have stayed and had an adventure. What had made her suddenly go all prim?

She'd been happy to practically shag Link in his shop before, but something about that 'encounter' on the boat had just seemed too contrived. They'd seemed so relaxed about it, Rachel couldn't help feeling it was something they'd done many times before. Two sexual opportunists working as a pair. And they made her feel like some kind of sex accessory. The Rachel Rabbit.

It made her laugh for a moment, the idea of being a human sex toy and then it hit her. How tawdry. Her carefree times with Link, one of the very few things that had given her any simple pleasure in life recently – apart from the company of her gorgeous girls, when they weren't driving her bonkers – now seemed tacky and grim.

So what did she have, as she drove back to her empty house, on this gorgeous Friday evening? The gardens of the pubs along the river were packed with people having fun, enjoying rowdy Friday-night drinks with friends. Or a romantic tryst with a lover. A companionable time with a long-term partner. What did she have? Half a bottle of leftover white wine in the fridge if she was lucky and whatever crap she could find on TV, now she'd had to cancel Sky and Netflix.

As she sat at a red light, waiting to cross Kew Bridge, Rachel felt too desolate even to cry.

Sunday, 6 July

Cranbrook

Joy was lying in bed in the library, drinking a cup of hot water with lemon and chatting to Hector, Archie and Finn, who were very excited about an end-of-term production of *Cabaret* the school was putting on.

'It's really full on, Granny,' Archie was saying, his eyes wide. 'Some of the girls aren't wearing very much and the dances are quite, well, you know ...'

He stood up and imitated some splayed-leg, hip-thrusting moves. Finn guffawed.

'I'm only playing a waiter,' said Archie, pushing Hector onto the floor, so he could sit on the bed again, 'but I go to all the rehearsals anyway.'

'I'm helping with the lighting,' said Finn, 'and I go to all the rehearsals too.'

The two of them collapsed into laughter, Hector joining in as he battled Archie to get back on the bed, although Joy could tell he didn't really share his older brothers' interests in such areas yet.

Joy smiled at them, like three young bear cubs sitting on the end of her bed. How she adored spending these times with them and how deeply she felt for Tessa, knowing that the older two would be going back to school the next morning and wouldn't be home again until Friday night.

Never able to stay away from her boys for long when they were home, Tessa came in holding a clutch of envelopes.

'Your forwarded post is here, Mum,' she said. 'And this is weird – you've got a letter for someone called "Elsie Ainsworth Lambton". Who on earth is that? Did Dad have some kind of half-sister we don't know about?'

For a moment Joy was too appalled to answer, but then she recovered herself.

'Oh, it was a lodger I had briefly,' she said. 'It was just a coincidence that she had the same surname as your father. It's not an unusual name, I suppose. She was from the Northeast as well ...'

She trailed off. Never over-explain, that had been one of Robert's techniques and she was glad that the boys' play-fight had escalated, as it distracted their mother.

'Hey, you guys,' Tessa said, 'stop fooling around. You're going to hurt Granny carrying on like that, go and do some homework or something.'

The three of them loped off and Tessa stood by the bed, having another look at the letter.

'Funny, I don't remember her,' said Tessa, tapping it with her fingernail. 'I'm sure I would have remembered another Lambton, especially an Elsie. What a terrible name that is.'

'It was ages ago,' said Joy, hating to lie to her daughter, 'and she didn't stay very long. I get odd bits of mail for all sorts of people who've rented the house, or lodged with me, over the years. You can just throw it in the recycling.' Then she thought for a moment. 'Or just give it to me with the other stuff, Tess, love. I better have a look.'

To Joy's great relief, Hector's voice then came from the

kitchen, yelling, 'Mum! Finn is burning my book bag!' and Tessa threw all the letters onto the bed and rushed off to see what was going on.

With a creeping sense of foreboding, Joy picked up the envelope and was surprised to see this one wasn't from the solicitors. There was a Red Cross logo on it. For a happy moment she thought it might have been a simple appeal for donations, but then she remembered the name they'd addressed it to. The dead name again.

Suddenly she felt quite overwhelmed by ideas coming into her head that she really didn't want to have in there. She took some deep breaths and said a few oms, trailing off into a random hummed tune when the thoughts threatened to get the better of her. But she made herself keep trying to shut them out.

She couldn't be distracted by things from the past when all her daughters needed her to be strong for them now. Tessa was just getting over that strange situation with Simon, which could have gone so catastrophically wrong for her. Natasha and Rachel had fallen out so horribly and Rachel had lost her wonderful au pair.

Slumping back against her pillow, gazing out of the French windows at the end of the room into the green of the garden, the letter still in her hands, Joy realised it was Rachel she was most concerned about. She normally rang her mother regularly to see how she was getting on, but Joy hadn't heard from her for days.

She'd tried calling her that morning, but the home and mobile phones had both gone straight to message and she hadn't rung back even though Joy had asked her to. That was so unlike Rachel. She was always glued to her phone and constantly checking it, to the point where Joy found it irritating when they were together. Something was clearly up and it was more worrying that it was Rachel, rather than either of her other girls, who seemed to be in distress.

Her middle daughter was the feistiest of the three of them on the surface, but she didn't have the support of a husband, as Tessa did, or the stellar career and income to go with it, that Natasha enjoyed. But she did have the responsibility of her children and a mortgage. It was a lot to carry. Her sisters should be looking out for Rachel, not making her life more difficult.

Joy decided she would leave some more messages for her and if she didn't call back by Monday afternoon, she would ring Simon and ask him if he knew what was going on with her.

Feeling better for having made a plan about that, Joy felt more decisive about the upsetting letter. Moving carefully, so as not to jolt her hip, she got out of bed and took the letter over to the fireplace and, finding some matches on the mantelpiece, set light to it.

But as she watched it going up in flames, with a great sense of satisfaction, she realised she'd have to find some reason to explain the odd smell of smoke to Tessa.

Lies beget lies, she thought, secrets beget secrets.

Monday, 7 July

Manhattan, New York

Natasha couldn't remember when she'd been so happy. It was a bright summer morning in New York, and the oppressive humidity hadn't set in yet, just glorious sunshine, bare arms and legs, everyone a little bit more cheerful than usual.

She and Mattie had got back to Manhattan the afternoon before after spending a blissful Fourth of July long weekend together, just the two of them, out at Natasha's beach house on Long Island. The simple joy of spending that time hanging out, going for swims, watching movies, drinking wine, cooking dinner and making love with someone she felt so at ease with, felt like it had made up for years of destructive relationships.

They'd gone out early that morning to buy food to re-stock the apartment's fridge and were walking back towards the West Village, Mattie swinging the basket of organic vegetables they'd just bought at the farmers' market in Union Square.

'What else do we need for this veggie feast you're making me tonight?' asked Natasha.

'The best olive oil you can buy in Manhattan,' said Mattie.

Natasha turned to smile at her. To remind herself she was really there, by her side, and to check she still pleased her eye as much as she had the last time she'd looked at her, about ten seconds before. She did.

It was fascinating to Natasha that although she spent her days staring at the faces of the women who were officially the most beautiful in the world, she had never come across anyone she found as gorgeous as Mattie.

She was a good-looking woman by any standards, but it was the little flaws – the small horizontal crease that appeared above her top lip when she smiled, the scar on her cheek, her slightly heavy thighs – which made Natasha feel giddy. That and remembering how they'd spent the long hot night before. She felt a little flutter at the memory.

Without thinking she reached out to find Mattie's hand, squeezed it and didn't let go. It just felt right. Walking along side by side, not touching, just wasn't possible when you were as loved-up as she felt.

Mattie smiled at her and squeezed Natasha's hand back.

'So where shall we get the oil?' said Mattie.

'The best place would be Eataly,' said Natasha. 'It's in the other direction, up on Fifth, quite a few blocks from here, but it's so glorious out in this sunshine, I'd like a longer walk – and it's an amazing shop, I'd love to show it to you. We can always get a cab home.'

'Let's go then,' said Mattie.

They turned round, crossed back over 14th Street and headed up Fifth Avenue, not talking, just happy being together, the connection between them buzzing through their joined hands.

Natasha wondered if Mattie could imagine what a big deal it was for her to do that. She'd never risked a public display of affection with any of her lovers before. And it hadn't always been her choice.

An image of her last girlfriend popped into her head and

she relished all over again the relief that she could think of Anya now, without what had felt like a spear of pain being thrust through her. Mattie had freed her from that agony.

She hadn't told Mattie that Anya had texted her a couple of days before, saying she wanted to see her. 'I need you ...' it had said, and Natasha knew exactly the effect those words would have had on her if she hadn't met Mattie. She would have immediately arranged to see her, setting off yet again the toxic cycle that had tortured her for the past two years.

A few weeks of fevered phone calls, secret meetings, passionate trysts, then Anya telling her she could never see her again, warning her never to call, email or text her. Then just when Natasha was starting to feel she was getting over her, Anya would get back in touch. I *need* you. That was what she always said and Natasha could never resist her, then it would all begin again.

The soul-destroying dance of an affair with a married woman.

But this time Natasha felt no urge to respond. She'd deleted the text and the contact, then blocked her number. Over. Done. Never going back there, not when there was something so wonderful happening in her life now. Instead Natasha thought about the special present she had hidden in her underwear drawer. The ring the same as the one she always wore.

Lost in these happy thoughts, Natasha didn't see Blythe until they were halfway across the intersection, with the entrance to Eataly on the other side. She was coming out of the shop, juggling carrier bags and just as Natasha saw her, she looked up, straight at her.

Natasha immediately dropped Mattie's hand. Blythe had definitely spotted her – but had she noticed they were holding hands? Natasha smiled and waved at her.

'Mattie,' she said quickly and quietly, 'it's one of the people from OM. I'll introduce you, but I've told you the score.'

'I get it,' said Mattie, and Natasha wasn't sure if there was a slight edge in her voice or not, but at that particular moment she couldn't worry about it.

'Blythe, hi,' said Natasha, when they were next to her, channelling all the gushing insincerity of her industry as they air-kissed.

'Hey, Tashie,' said Blythe, 'great to see you. Are you buying food too?'

'Yes,' said Natasha, 'and I wanted to show Eataly to my friend Mattie here, she's over from London. Mattie, this is Blythe, who I'm working with on the range.'

Blythe and Mattie shook hands, grinning and 'hi-ing' enthusiastically at each other, in a way which made Natasha very happy because it showed the woman she loved understood exactly how these work relationships had to be conducted.

'Blythe is the director of marketing for OM and Mattie's a make-up artist too,' said Natasha, intensely grateful for the great cover story that gave her.

'Oh, really?' said Blythe with megawatt enthusiasm.

'Yes, I'm a big fan of your new radiant BB creams,' said Mattie, 'they've just come out in the UK. The texture is flawless.'

Natasha had to restrain herself from hugging her. That really wouldn't have helped.

'Oh, that's so great,' said Blythe, 'I'm so happy you like those, they've been really strong for us. I'll have to give Natasha some of our new products for you to take back to London, when she comes into the office later. We've used the same technology in a blush, it's really amazing.'

'That would be great,' said Mattie. 'I love being first with a new cult product.'

'So, I'll see you later at the office, Natasha, for our meeting,' said Blythe.

'Yeah, great,' said Natasha. 'I'm so excited about seeing the samples, I can't wait.'

'I'm saying nothing,' said Blythe, in a dramatic stage whisper, her large blue eyes open very wide, 'but I think you will be pleased ... very pleased.'

'Sounds great. See you later, then,' said Natasha.

'Sure,' said Blythe. 'Nice to meet you, Mattie.'

'And you,' said Mattie.

Blythe turned and headed down the street and Natasha practically ran into Eataly. She leaned back against the wall next to the door and closed her eyes for a moment, trying to calm her pulse.

Mattie laughed. 'Are you having a panic attack?' she asked.

'Slightly,' said Natasha, opening her eyes again and scanning the shop, in case there were any more of her key business associates in there. 'Do you think she saw us? You know, holding hands ...'

Mattie shrugged. 'I don't know, because I didn't notice her when you did. She was just one of a million people on a New York sidewalk.'

'I don't think she did,' said Natasha, frowning as she struggled to picture the exact expression on Blythe's face when she'd first seen her. She'd been very normal when they'd chatted, but when you were used to conducting business exchanges at such a level of fake excitement, it was hard to tell.

'How do you think she was with you?' she asked Mattie. 'Did she look at you funny?'

'I don't know,' said Mattie. 'I've never met her before, she just seemed like a typical beauty-company bimbo to me. So where's the olive oil in here, then?'

Natasha felt a flash of irritation. Blythe might be particularly gushy, but she certainly wasn't a bimbo. You didn't get to be marketing director at a company like OM unless you were very smart, and Blythe worked very closely with the big boss, Ava Capel. She'd already made a huge contribution to the development of the brand and Natasha didn't like her being talked about like that.

'Sorry, Mattie,' she said, 'but I have a meeting with Blythe and some of the other top people at OM this afternoon ... They're going to show me the proposed packaging for the first time.'

'All right,' said Mattie, holding her hands up in surrender, 'I understand how important all that is to you and it is a humungously big deal, I get it, but can we please move on? She seemed very happy to see you, she was nice to me, but we've got no way of knowing if she saw the grotesque horror of two women holding hands or not. She didn't look as though she needed trauma counselling, is that enough?'

'OK,' said Natasha, sighing. She was still smarting from Mattie's casual attitude to what had just happened. She didn't seem to understand how damaging it could be for her, which was quite hurtful, but still, she didn't want to spoil their time together. It had been such a magical morning up to that point.

'Right,' she said, standing up straight and making herself smile. 'Let's go and find us some amazing oil.'

Then she leaned in close to Mattie's ear and whispered: 'And when we get home, I might just rub it all over you ...'

Mattie giggled and they headed further into the shop.

Sydney Street, 12.30 p.m.

Simon was surprised to hear from his PA that there was a Joy Younger on the phone for him. He was pleased at the prospect of talking to her, but slightly alarmed that she might be calling to continue the Tessa conversation. That was something he really couldn't talk about in the office. In fact he didn't want to talk about it to anyone, ever again. Case closed.

'Hello, Joy,' he said. 'How lovely to hear from you this dull Monday lunchtime. To what do I owe this pleasure?'

Joy smiled. She found Simon's overly gallant manners endearing. She knew they were a front, a façade to hide behind, lest anyone should work out what he was really thinking or feeling, but over the years they had become part of who he was.

'Well, I'm sorry to bother you at work,' said Joy, 'but I'm ringing about Rachel.'

Simon sat up in his seat, alarmed. Had Joy intuited his inappropriate feelings about another of her daughters? Was she ringing to tell him to lay off her too?

'Yes?' he said cautiously.

'It's just that we haven't heard from her for a while and that's very unusual. She calls me most days – and I've left her lots of messages asking her to ring, but nothing. So I just wanted to ask whether she was in the office and whether she seems OK?'

Simon had a sinking feeling. He was fairly sure he knew why Rachel hadn't called Joy, but was it right to tell her? It seemed like a breach of Rachel's privacy to broadcast that she was furious because she wasn't getting some money she'd been expecting, because Joy had persuaded Tessa to take the business away from Rathbones. And, also, he didn't want Tessa to feel bad about it. Or Joy. This was tricky.

'I haven't actually seen Rachel today, Joy, and there are a few things I need to talk to her about. So why don't I pop up to her office and if I think there's anything for you to be concerned about, I'll ring you back. So if you hear nothing, no news is good news and she's probably just been busy.'

Which would give him more time to mull it over. At least, at a distance, Joy couldn't pull that stunt where she laid her hand on him in some form of psychic communion. He'd sussed that one out. He couldn't imagine what she got out of it, but there was no question the woman had an uncanny way of figuring out what was going on. He just hoped she couldn't do it over the phone.

'That sounds like a good plan,' said Joy. 'So in the nicest possible way, I hope not to hear from you.'

They ended the call and Simon ran up the stairs to the floor where Rachel's office was. Glancing into the rooms on the way up he saw all his staff were either out to lunch – hopefully luring in new clients, probably not – or chowing down at their desks. But when he got up to Rachel's office, she was tapping away furiously on her computer, not a sandwich or salad in sight, just a mug of tea.

'Hi, Rachel,' said Simon. He was about to ask her if she'd had a good weekend and just stopped himself, remembering how badly it had started. 'Did you get your car out OK?'

'Yep,' she said, not relishing the reminder of that misadventure and really hoping he wouldn't ask her about the rest of her weekend. An unwelcome sexual advance, which had wrecked one of the few good things in her life, followed by thirty-six hours under the duvet.

Rachel couldn't understand what he was doing up there. If he wanted to talk to her he normally sent her an email asking her to come down to Sir's office, or if he was feeling particularly pompous, he got his PA to call her. She certainly didn't think he'd come up just to ask about her car and she wished he would just get on with whatever he wanted to say and naff off again.

She had work to get on with, trying very hard to recruit some more new business she could actually get the bonuses for. She had some good prospects on the go and she didn't want to lose her thread.

Simon was still wondering what to do. Was it wrong to tell Rachel her mother had rung up, concerned about her? It seemed like he would be stepping over that line between work and family which she was so sensitive about.

Getting impatient, Rachel pressed print on the document she'd been working on and went over to the printer to wait for it. As she stood by the machine, with her back to him, Simon noticed that her skirt was hanging on her. It was slack around the waist and where it used to be so attractively filled with womanly shape at the back, it just hung loosely down.

It was funny it hadn't really registered before, but now he thought about it, she had been looking thinner. That day Natasha had come in and Rachel had been on the floor with her butt sticking out, while having his usual pervy eyeful he'd noticed there was less of her.

The document emerged and Rachel went back to her desk, getting busy with the stapler and looking up at him questioningly. Her face was quite gaunt, he realised, and there were dark shadows under her eyes. Joy was right to be concerned about her. She looked like she wasn't eating. Surely she wasn't doing that fasting thing several of his chubbier staff members were on? She didn't need to lose weight.

'What I came up for, Rachel,' he said, with more of his characteristic assuredness, 'is to ask whether you had time to have a spot of lunch with me today.'

She looked like she needed a good square meal and he was damn well going to make sure she had one.

Rachel hesitated. Her stomach rumbled. She'd eaten nothing since a bowl of plain macaroni with some nasty frozen spinach the night before. She was trying to feed herself eating only the food she had stored in her kitchen, leaving her precious cash in place to buy fresh stuff for the girls. She could go without lamb chops and salmon steaks and strawberries, but they couldn't.

Her first thought was to refuse him, because it would mean making conversation for an hour or so, and with what had passed between them on Friday it would be hard to keep it off the Hunter Gatherer debacle. Ugh, no thanks. She was going to say she had too much work, but then the thought of food got the better of her. Meat.

'That would be lovely,' she said, her mouth watering at the prospect.

'OK,' said Simon. 'I'm ready when you are, so come down to my office when you're good to go. I'll get a table at that little Italian I like around the corner.'

Lasagne. Tiramisu. Rachel felt her eyes start to prickle and pretended to be looking for something in her bottom drawer.

'Right,' she said, blinking hard a few times before coming up again. 'Lovely. I'll just finish this and I'll be down.'

Simon headed back to his office feeling quite light-hearted at the prospect of lunch with Rachel. She would be far better company than any of the people he wined and dined for work, but he was still wondering what his duty was with regard to her mother. Clearly something was up with her daughter, but was it really his responsibility to talk to her about it?

The delicious smells in the restaurant made Rachel feel quite giddy and it was a treat to be eating out in a nice place, even if it was with Simon. He hadn't seemed to have noticed that she didn't take clients or journalists out to lunch any more. She went to their offices, or met them for a quick coffee.

She played it to them as not wanting to infringe on their busy schedules, but really it was because, although pre-approved lunch expenses were reimbursed, she didn't have the credit to pay out for them in the first place.

Her colleagues would go swanning off to Chiltern Firehouse and the like with their clients, where they could get tables, because they went there in their own time as well. Rachel was increasingly hiding behind her lunch-is-for-wimps 'too busy' shield. And they'd stopped even asking her to join them for after-work drinks, because she always had an excuse to say no.

Looking round the room, nodding at a few antique dealers he knew, Simon's heart sank when he saw his friend Fergus. He was the dealer he'd dropped a few of Tessa's possibly Delft tiles off to the week before. He hadn't been in the shop at the time, so Simon had been waiting to hear his verdict. He just hadn't banked on it being when he was with Rachel. The last thing he needed her to be reminded of was his recent visit down to Hunter Gatherer.

But sure enough, just after they'd ordered – *tagliata* for Rachel, spaghetti vongole for Simon, just water to drink – Fergus came ambling over to their table.

'Rathbone,' he said, 'good to see you.'

Simon made the introductions and braced himself. Sure enough, he went straight into it.

'I've had a look at those tiles you dropped in,' said Fergus. 'They're very nice. Seventeenth-century Dutch, pretty good condition. How many would you say there were? I have a client who wants to use them as a skirting board, in the Flemish style, so she needs a lot.'

Simon tried to picture the crate to do a rough count, but then found himself with an all too clear image of himself and Tessa sitting next to it, the sun shining down, contentment in his heart. Thinking about her didn't flick the crazy switch any more, but it did remind him of how much weird secret history he now had with Rachel's family. What a mess.

'There are quite a lot,' he said. 'At least sixty, I'd say, and all in one piece.'

'I'd like to buy them,' said Fergus. 'Who has them? Anyone I know?'

'It's er, Rachel's sister, actually. Tessa Chenery of Hunter Gatherer salvage, down in Kent. Do you know who I mean?'

'No,' said Fergus.

They really do need a PR campaign, thought Rachel. This was exactly the kind of git they needed to know about them. For a moment she found herself wishing she could help Tessa. She knew exactly how to promote them to pompous arses like this Fergus, who'd think they were scooping a bargain, and to cool people who'd aspire to emulate Tessa's decorating style. It would be so easy to get Hunter Gatherer into *Country Life*, *Interiors* and *ELLE Decoration*. Possibly even *Grazia* and the *Telegraph*. And on all her key blogs.

But then she remembered all over again how her sister's flighty decision, helped along by Simon, not to go with

Rathbone & Associates after all had messed her up, short-changing her to the tune of £1000. Tessa hadn't even had the courtesy to discuss the decision to bail out with Rachel first, or to ask her whether she would consider running the account after all, if Simon didn't think he could do it. And she bloody well would have, to save the bonus.

So she had one astonishingly selfish sister, one unbelievably thoughtless one and a mother who just seemed to go along with whatever they did, regardless of how it impacted on her other child.

With all of that churning around in her mind, Rachel had stopped paying attention to what Simon and Fergus were saying and helped herself to another bit of deliciously crusty ciabatta out of the bread basket, dipping it in the saucer of viscous green olive oil.

She looked up again when she heard Fergus saying it was lovely to see her, or some such Chelsea smarm, and smiled back with equal insincerity. The bollocks.

'Well, that was a lucky chance,' said Simon, deciding now it had happened he would just have to brazen it out, pretend it was all business as usual. 'He would have driven a much harder bargain if we'd been in his shop, but he's had a couple of glasses of red. Loosened him up a bit. Your sister's going to make a nice little wodge of wonga out of those tiles. We'll just have to get them brought up here. Are you planning on going down to see them any time soon?'

'No,' said Rachel, delighted to see the waiter arriving with their food. If she was eating she couldn't speak and she didn't have anything nice to say at that moment. So, Tessa would be making extra 'wonga', thanks to Simon's little visit, but nothing for little sis. How lovely. This really was getting to be too much.

Simon didn't say anything else about the tiles. He'd always planned to get them couriered up to town anyway, it was just an opportunity to probe Rachel a bit. To see if the bonus disappointment was the reason she wasn't phoning her mum. Seeing the expression on her face as she tucked into her food, he was now certain it was and felt even worse about it.

'Now, Rachel,' he said, after they'd both enjoyed a few more mouthfuls, 'the reason I wanted to have lunch today was to apologise to you again for what happened with the new-business bonus you were expecting for Hunter Gatherer. It was jolly rough luck and not your fault it fell through and I feel really bad about it.'

Not as bad as I feel, thought Rachel.

She said nothing, just kept pushing the food in. She really did look half-starved. He never ate starters, but he wished he'd ordered one, so she would have felt free to. He'd have a pudding, which was something else he never ate, so she could.

'So, the thing is,' he continued, 'I would like to give you a compensatory bonus. It won't be as much – only £500 – but something.'

Rachel paused with her fork halfway to her mouth, then she put it back down on her plate. Five hundred smackers. That would be handy, especially if he could give it to her in cash, but she couldn't help it, she felt horribly patronised.

'It's very kind of you, Simon,' she heard herself saying, 'but I wouldn't feel comfortable accepting it. It would be very difficult if my colleagues found out I'd had a bonus and we hadn't actually got any new business ... and you know how things have a habit of getting out.'

And I don't need your charity, because I've got an uncomfortable feeling you might have sussed out quite how badly I need the money, from the way I reacted on Friday when I heard I wasn't getting it.

Rachel knew she was desperate, terrifyingly desperate, but she wasn't going to let anyone else know that. Especially not him.

'Oh, don't be daft, Rachel,' Simon was saying. 'Fair's fair, you did bring me the business ...' even if you did then complicate things by turning round and saying you wouldn't manage it for me after all '... so you do deserve some kind of reward for that. It was my decision not to take it on, in the end.'

'No, really,' said Rachel. 'I'm chasing up a lot of leads at the moment and I'm confident I'll soon reel some of them in. So when I do bring in new business which actually starts paying you, then I'll be happy to take the bonus I've earned.'

Simon was nonplussed. From her reaction on Friday he'd gathered she'd been relying on the money. When he'd been down at Tessa's she and Joy had spoken about how hard it was for Rachel, bringing up the girls and paying the mortgage on her own, even with the help she got from her ex-husband. Why was she being so silly about this?

For a moment he considered telling her about his own financial worries. He'd had an email from the accountant that morning advising him that he definitely did need to make at least two members of staff redundant, or move the office.

With the greatest reluctance, he'd decided on the redundancies and it would have been such a relief to be able to talk to someone about it apart from the accountant. Someone who would understand the nuances of the situation, with insight into who they could most easily manage without – and who could most easily manage without the job.

He had no intention of giving anyone sleepless nights over mortgage payments, if he could possibly help it, but it was still a horrible position to be in. He felt like an executioner.

Both of them were relieved to have a distraction when the waiter came over to ask them if they wanted pudding. Rachel ordered the tiramisu and felt like a child having a treat tucking into it, every creamy spoonful a joy. Why had she just turned down Simon's generous offer? she asked herself. Was she going nuts as well as broke?

Five hundred pounds would have kept her going with day-to-day expenses for a month, although paid into her bank account, it would just have disappeared into the black hole of her overdraft, so it was pointless anyway. It was cash she needed. The one useful thing she had done at the weekend was to make a list of other things around the house she could sell, and she'd already started putting them online.

But it had been generous of Simon to make the offer, she had to acknowledge that and, for a tiny moment, as she looked up at him spooning in his fruit salad, she was tempted to tell him about her situation.

He had such a good business head, he might be able to give her some useful advice and she remembered that softer side of him she'd seen, that strange day down at Tessa's, playing skittles with the kids.

He could be a total arsehole in the office – he had a reputation for it in their industry – and it had always suited her to keep the boss in a box marked 'The Enemy' wherever she'd worked, but she had to admit it, Simon did have a decent, kind side.

'Thanks for lunch, Simon,' she said, placing her spoon down next to her very thoroughly emptied bowl. 'It was really nice of you to ask me.'

He was glad to see that a good meal had made a difference. She looked much more like her old self, than the drawn, harried Rachel he'd seen lately. Then she smiled at him in a way that made him feel something like a flutter in his heart. He looked at her pretty face, as she settled back contentedly in her chair, and made a decision.

'You know, Rachel,' he said, suddenly, 'in the few months you've been at the company, you have become my most valued member of staff.'

It was time to be real about something. He was sick of filtering everything he said to her. Bone tired of it.

'In that short time I've really come to rely on you. Your energy and enthusiasm have lit up the whole office. And I think, in your own way, you actually care as much about the business as I do, which means a lot to me. It can be very lonely being the boss, you know.'

Rachel was completely taken aback. She'd never heard Simon talking in such a personal way before and he'd been so nice about her. It was almost too much.

'Thanks,' she said, blinking a couple of times, in case her eyes got any ideas about welling up. 'That means a lot to me. I do love my work, it means everything to me – apart from my girls, it's the most important thing in my life – and I love working for your company, it's the best in the business.'

'I'm glad we agree about that,' said Simon, laughing and sounding more like his usual arrogant self, but now she'd seen the softer side of him, it didn't piss her off so much. She could see it was partly ironic, or some kind of self-defence mechanism. He was a complicated man, there was no doubt about it, but over time he was beginning to feel a little bit more like a working friend than the big bad boss man.

'This has been great, Rachel,' he continued, 'I think we should start having lunch regularly and every time you bring in new business, we'll have champagne – and you'll get your bonus as well, of course.'

Meanwhile, he decided, signalling to the waiter for the bill, he was going to pay that money into her bank account anyway, from his private funds. Knowing how busy she was, he was fairly confident she wouldn't even notice, but he'd feel better knowing she had it.

After Simon had paid, stopped at three tables on the way out to speak to people he knew and waved at Fergus across the room, they headed back to the office. It was the first overcast day for what seemed like ages, with a distinct dampness in the air, and Rachel didn't feel nearly warm enough in the sleeveless top she was wearing, wishing she hadn't left her jacket in the office. She shivered and hugged her bag to her chest.

Simon noticed and his first instinct was to take off his jacket and drape it around her shoulders, but he stopped himself. He felt closer to her since his frank declaration, but that would be a step too far – she was still an employee rather than a friend – so he forced himself to let her get on with it.

Walking back along Fulham Road, Rachel stopped suddenly in front of a newsagent's, staring at the papers on the stand outside. Simon followed her gaze and saw that on the front of several of them was a striking photograph of a man with long black hair and an equally black beard – wearing a wedding dress.

'Chanel's bearded bride,' said the headline on the *Times*.

'Queen Conchita the Second,' was emblazoned across the *Mirror*.

Rachel reached out and picked up the *Times*. She read the caption and there it was: 'Serbian male model, Branko Stojanovic, in the Chanel couture show in Paris yesterday.'

Simon peered over her shoulder for a better look. It was a pretty surprising picture, but something about the bloke in the frock looked familiar.

'It's my manny, Branko,' said Rachel. 'My male nanny. The Serbian guy. He was at Tessa's place that time we went down for the photo shoot. Do you remember?'

'I thought he looked familiar,' said Simon. 'How come he's modelling for Chanel now?'

Rachel snorted. 'That's a long story,' she said and he saw her shoulders had slumped and she had that haggard look back.

'Would you like that paper?' he asked.

'Well, yes ...' she started, but he just took it from her hand and walked into the shop to pay for it.

When he came out she was holding the *Telegraph*, which also had a picture of Branko on the front, and looked quite ashen.

'Are you all right, Rachel?' he asked, and she couldn't hold it in any longer, tears started to pour down her cheeks.

Simon's hand immediately went for his pocket. He passed her his handkerchief and she tried to dry her eyes, but the tears just kept rolling down. All the hurt she had been holding back was finally coming out and she couldn't stop herself shivering.

This time Simon took his jacket straight off and draped it around her. While he did it he took a quick look at his watch. It was 2.25 p.m., he really should get back to the office.

Bugger that.

'Do you want to talk about it, Rachel?' he asked.

Rachel shook her head. No. No way. Then she looked up again and something about Simon's face made her reconsider.

There was a frown of gentle concern between his brows and, as she looked at him, he brought his face closer to hers.

'Are you sure?' he said quietly.

'Well,' said Rachel, 'if you've got time, it might do me good to tell someone ...'

'Come on,' he said, putting a protective arm around her, just below her shoulders. 'We'll go and have coffee and you can tell me what this is all about.'

As they walked back along the Fulham Road, away from the office, it felt natural to keep his arm there. He hadn't planned it as a move. His arm had instinctively shot out to comfort a creature in distress, as it would have to a frightened dog, or a spooked horse. And it had landed at just the right place, not too low on her waist, just lightly below shoulder level. It was a gesture of friendship, nothing inappropriate. But he couldn't pretend it wasn't nice to have her so close.

Rachel was a little surprised that his arm stayed there, as they walked along, but the warmth of another body close to hers was deeply comforting, as was Simon's jacket. The fabric of the lining was silky soft against her bare arms and it smelled lovely, of fine wool, expensive cologne and a more subtle scent underneath. Male musk.

When they arrived at a small old-school Italian café – not nearly trendy enough for any of his staff to frequent – Simon took his arm away to hold the door for her. She immediately missed it. How long was it since she'd walked down a street with a man like that?

She'd had plenty of delicious male contact from Link, but nothing as companionable as that arm had felt. It had always been nought to sixty in five seconds on the sex scale with him and Rachel was starting to understand just how much that wasn't enough.

Simon went to the counter to order and Rachel took a surreptitious deep sniff inside the jacket. She found the smell of it quite intoxicating. Simon always smelled nice, not overdone, just a light, fresh aroma that wafted subtly around the building with him, but combined with the fibres of the fabric and his man scent, it had some kind of atavistic effect on her.

She didn't ever remember feeling like this about Michael's jackets. He wore rather harsh aftershaves he bought at duty-free stores. Rachel thought Simon probably bought his in Jermyn Street.

While he was waiting at the counter he sent a quick text to his PA, saying he'd be back in an hour. No need to over-egg it with a fake explanation. The smiley proprietor offered to bring the coffees over to them, but Simon said he'd wait. He didn't want an interruption while he was talking to Rachel.

When he arrived back at the table, Rachel was looking a little better. More collected. As he sat down and pushed her coffee over to her, she picked up the lapel of his jacket and brought it up to his nose.

'Your jacket smells lovely,' she said. 'What is it? Something from Trumpers?'

Simon looked pleased.

'I get it from a little place in Milan,' he said. 'I stock up when I go over for the furniture fair.'

Of course you do, thought Rachel.

They sipped their drinks and holding the cup up to her chest in both her hands, Simon's healing jacket pulled close around her, Rachel felt properly warm again. Simon put his cup down on the saucer and leaned in a little across the table, resting his chin on his palm.

'So tell me what's been going on,' he said.

Rachel sighed loudly. Where to start? How far to go?

'Why did that picture of – what's his name? Branko? – upset you so much?' he pressed, when she didn't answer.

'OK,' said Rachel, sighing, then sitting up straighter. 'Remember when we were all down at Tessa's that day for the shoot?'

Simon nodded. He wasn't likely to forget it, but at least the memory didn't make him feel deranged any more.

'Well,' said Rachel. 'Branko brought the girls down for me, because we were all going to stay the weekend there and while I was off doing other things, he got chatting with my sister Natasha …'

Simon remembered Natasha fleeing his offices in tears and wondered if it was related to what Rachel was telling him.

'And she decided Branko would make an amazing model – of womenswear, as per the picture. So she was right, of course. No one gets to model for Chanel a couple of weeks after entering the business, unless they're pretty extraordinary, especially not a man with a beard. So fair enough, I'm happy for Branko, he's a lovely, lovely man and he deserves a better life than looking after my kids in return for a place to stay and then working all hours in bars.'

She took another sip of her coffee before continuing.

'But the thing was, Natasha didn't think it was necessary to tell me what she was doing and she gaily went off and introduced Branko to one of her model agent pals, who immediately signed him up – and no doubt paid Natasha a nice finder's fee.'

As she said that Rachel's voice had taken on a rather bitter tone that Simon had only heard once before, when he'd told her about giving up the Hunter Gatherer business. It didn't suit her.

'So then Branko asked me for some time off, to go to Paris for a break, but he was really there to do appointments with the big fashion houses and they all went mad for him. And so I was left without a nanny with no warning, just to satisfy Natasha's ego that she can create a modelling superstar overnight.'

Simon considered it all for a moment.

'I can see it must have been very difficult to be left without childcare like that,' he said, 'how are you managing?'

'Branko put me in touch with a friend of his, Pilar, so she's living with us now on the same terms. She's OK, but she's not like him, she only does the bare minimum, which is collecting the girls from school each day and staying in with them until I get home. The girls like her, but they really loved Branko, like a big brother, or an uncle. So Natasha wrecked all that without giving them, or me, a second thought. It was all about her, as it always is.'

'But don't you think Branko should have told you what was going on?' said Simon. 'It seems rather dishonest of him to say he was going to Paris for a holiday, when he was really having appointments about modelling.'

Rachel had mulled that over many times, the rights and wrongs of it going round in her head during the sleepless hours of early mornings.

'I understand that he didn't want to worry me at first,' she said, 'because he really didn't believe it would come to anything, it was all a bit of a lark, but then when it did take off, Natasha told him not to tell me.

'It was bad enough that she didn't involve me in the discussions at the outset – and I would have been happy for him, that's what's so insulting – but then, even after he knew he needed to tell me and wanted to, she just had to keep control of the situation in a way that suited her. I find that horrible. And there's more ...'

The colour was back in Rachel's cheeks and she had something more like her usual energy, but it was a darker, negative version of it.

'When she finally realised that she had to admit what was really going on,' she continued, 'she hid behind Mum to do it. She was literally lying on the bed with her. It was unbelievable. And my darling mum, much as I love her, seemed to put Natasha's feelings ahead of my real, actual needs, which is exactly what used to happen when we were kids. Natasha was the special baby and I always had to make allowances for her. Let her have the last of the ice cream. Give her my toy to play with. Tessa was that little bit older, so it didn't affect her so much and she was always away with the fairies anyway.'

She paused for a moment, draining her coffee and then laughed.

'Paging Dr Freud, eh?' she said. 'I can see that my middle-child hang-ups are part of it, but I still think I'm justified to be upset about Natasha's cavalier attitude to my life and my work, whereas we all have to take her work very seriously. She's done this big deal with OM – you know that huge American cosmetics company – and she's going to have her own make-up line ... boy, did we have to hear a lot about that.'

Simon held back. She didn't need to hear his opinion, she just needed to get it out. He could imagine how it must have been going round and round in her head, driving her crazy, thinking the same thoughts over and over again. He knew all too well what that felt like.

Rachel was looking more serious. She pursed her lips and looked straight at him.

'I sound like a jealous brat, don't I?' she said.

'No,' said Simon. 'You sound like someone who has been seriously hurt and put out, by a person you love, and I can see why you feel that way. You have children, Natasha doesn't and she didn't understand how much more serious that makes changes to your domestic set-up. Does Natasha have a partner?'

'No,' said Rachel, 'that's a bit of a funny thing about her. She had a few boyfriends when she was young, but never anything serious and as an adult she's never had what I would call a proper relationship. She's never lived with anyone. I think she's married to her work really ...'

'A bit like me,' said Simon.

'I suppose so,' said Rachel. 'I'd never thought of that before. Why don't you have a partner?'

'I've just never met the right woman,' said Simon. His stock response. He'd had it off pat for years, so this question could never trip him up. 'I have, how shall I put it, lady friends, I'm not a monk, but I've never met anyone I thought I could really share my life with and I'd rather stay solo than compromise. And I'm a bit of an OCD tidy freak, in case you haven't noticed. I wouldn't be easy to live with.'

Rachel laughed. So he was definitely straight. Unless he was lying, but she didn't think he was.

'Mum's convinced that Natasha is having – or had – a long affair with a married man,' said Rachel. 'She says she knows the signs of it being constantly on and off, the agony and the ecstasy thing. Mum thinks that's why Natasha is single. Apart from her mega career, she's been badly burned by that.'

Simon glanced at his watch again. 2.55 p.m. This was getting serious, but he still didn't want to break off. It felt too important for Rachel, and even apart from his personal concern for her, he didn't want his key member of staff to be an emotional mess, especially not with the Lawn & Stone press trip rushing towards them. She'd need to be on top form for that. So this was work really.

'Are you OK to stay a bit longer?' he asked her.

'It's more about whether you are, isn't it?'

'I'm good,' he said. 'I had noticed you weren't looking yourself, Rachel. I've been concerned about you. You've lost a lot of weight.'

Her head slumped down for a moment. It had felt good unloading all this stuff which had been making her feel so strung out and she really wished she could carry on and tell him all the rest of it, but she knew she couldn't. Not the money thing. That she'd been missing meals so she could feed her daughters. It would make her look like a bad businesswoman. Better to be an emotional nut job, than bad at handling a budget.

'I suppose, this has all been getting to me even more than I realised,' she said, 'and stress always puts me off my food.'

Simon remembered how heartily she'd enjoyed her lunch, but said nothing.

'And now there's this thing with Tessa, as well,' said Rachel.

Simon's head snapped up.

'What's that?' he said, as casually as he could muster.

'Just deciding to cancel the contract with us like that – once again, without consulting me, just like Natasha, although Tessa knew how it would affect me. I'd told her about the bonus, it only seemed right to be transparent about it, in the circumstances. It's like my sisters are ganging up to try to take me down.'

'But you know that was my decision as much as hers,' said Simon. 'You didn't want to run the account and without your input, I didn't think the agency was up to it.'

'She still should have discussed it with me, don't you think? Because I would have taken the account on after all, if you really didn't think you could, rather than let the company just throw it out.'

And me lose my bonus.

Awkward. Simon knew he should probably jump in now and suggest she did take it over after all and the whole thing would be back on. He'd get the business – which he needed – and she'd get the bonus, which she clearly needed, so it would be better for everyone. Except it wouldn't. Because it would inevitably lead to regular contact between him and Tessa and although things seemed to be OK now, he just couldn't risk that kicking off again. So he said nothing.

Rachel felt disappointed for a moment. She had hoped Simon would take the bait and suggest they start the contract up again, with her as the manager, but it seemed not and it was all tainted and weird now anyway. She just had to move on, accept the loss and damn well bring in some other new business as quickly as possible.

'So you're pissed off with both your sisters and your mum?' asked Simon.

'Pretty much,' said Rachel.

'Have you told your mother how you feel? She's such an amazing woman ...' he checked himself immediately, he had to be careful here. 'I saw her again when I went down to talk to Tessa about the business, we all had lunch together. She always seems to know what's going on with people. Wouldn't it be good to talk to her about it all?'

Rachel thought for a moment. 'You're probably right,' she said. 'It is really my sisters I'm angry with, not her, and I should tell Mum that. And she'd probably do her best to make it better.'

Simon smiled. He was sure Rachel would ring Joy now and he hadn't had to betray either of their confidences to make it happen. That was a good result and it might be a start to healing the rift with Natasha. From what Rachel had just told him, her younger sister had been very thoughtless, but she clearly knew it. He'd seen how distressed she was leaving the office that day. How complicated families could make things.

He focused his attention on Rachel again. She was smiling at him, quite shyly.

'Thanks, Simon,' she said. 'First a great lunch and now a counselling session. I think you might be in the wrong job, but joking aside, I do feel so much better for unloading.'

'You're very welcome,' he said. 'I've got to look after my star employee, so you can bring in that new business for both of us.'

For the briefest moment he wanted to tell her what was keeping him awake at night, but he stopped himself. It might be good for his equilibrium in the short term, but it wasn't good business practice. Morale would be destroyed if the staff knew what was going on and if it got around town, he'd lose his clients' confidence. That was the kind of downward spiral that could wreck a business, just what he was trying to avoid by not moving into crappy offices. He had to keep schtum.

'So, shall we go back to the office now?' he asked her. 'Are you feeling up to it?'

She nodded. 'I'm feeling better than I have for a while.'

They stood up and Rachel reluctantly unshrugged his jacket from her shoulders, breathing in one last lungful of its comforting smell, before handing it to him.

'You better have this back,' she said. 'It wouldn't do much for your image walking around the office in shirt sleeves.'

And it would look very odd to your colleagues for you to be wearing my jacket, thought Simon, slipping it back on. It was still warm from her skin, he could feel it even through his shirt. He felt that flutter in his heart again.

Glancing out of the café window, he saw the sky had turned a darker grey and the wind had got up. A bit of newspaper was being gusted along the street.

'Looks like it might rain,' he said, 'I'm going to put you in a taxi, or you'll get hypothermia.'

As they walked out of the café, he pulled a £20 note out of his wallet and handed it to her, raising his hand to hail an approaching cab.

'Thanks,' said Rachel, opening the taxi door, as Simon told the driver the address through the front window, 'but aren't you going to come with me?'

'I'll walk back,' he said. 'I want to look at something I saw in a shop window on our way past.'

And I can't arrive back at the office with you, because I know the collective female mind in there will immediately pick up the new closeness between us.

Rachel paused with one foot in the taxi. Then she stepped out again, went over to Simon and gave him a quick hug.

'Thank you, Simon,' she said, pulling away, but leaving one hand on his shoulder for a moment. 'You've been so kind. I'll see you back at the ranch, and I'll get a receipt for the taxi.'

Simon smiled and said nothing, stepping back onto the kerb and watching as the cab pulled off. He could still smell the scent of her hair.

Riding home on the Tube that night, Rachel still felt buoyed up by her lunch and coffee with Simon. His calm, quiet advice had really helped her to put it all into perspective and she was going to ring her mum as soon as she had a free moment after dinner.

With everything else going on in her life, she couldn't afford to be at war with her family as well. She needed their support. She might take a little longer to make it up with Natasha, but she wanted to smooth things over with Joy and Tessa as soon as possible. She felt really bad about ignoring all her mother's phone messages asking her to call.

She could see now she'd been unreasonable about the Hunter Gatherer thing, impulsively suggesting it, then backing off and then expecting to take it over again, when that suited her better. Tessa hadn't really done anything wrong. Rachel had just been ready to be hurt again, which was a bad frame of mind to be in.

She was putting the girls' dinner on the table and thinking to make the call to her mum the moment they'd finished, when the phone rang.

For a happy moment, she thought it might be her mum ringing her again, but when she pressed the button to answer the call, it was an unknown man's voice.

'Is this Rachel Lambton?' he asked.

Rachel was going to hang up straight away, thinking it was one of those call centres trying to get her to buy double glazing, or make an insurance claim for bogus whiplash. But something made her hesitate. There hadn't been that tell-tale pause before the person started speaking and his voice was quite harsh, not the overly familiar tone of the cold caller.

But he didn't sound like one of the people who rang her from the credit card companies or her mortgage lender, either. They always started out sounding very civil and she'd had to learn how to spot them, so she could put the phone down without admitting it was her they were speaking to.

'Who wants to know?' she asked cautiously, turning to the girls and miming a fork going up to the mouth, while she took the phone into the sitting room and closed the door.

'I work for BND Financial Services,' said the man, 'and I'm calling about the outstanding debt on your Vartora credit card.'

Rachel felt sick.

'What about it?' she asked, stupidly, playing for time.

'Our clients have instructed us to request an immediate payment from you. You are six months in arrears with a balance of over £7000 and we need a £700 payment from you today, or we will take further action.'

Seven hundred pounds? Where the hell was she supposed to get that from? She had put some of the stuff she was going to sell on various websites, but it would be a while before any of the money dribbled in.

'So, can I have your debit card number?' the man said.

'I don't have any money in my current account at the moment,' said Rachel, 'so that's not going to be much help.'

'How do you propose to make the payment then?' the man persisted.

Rachel didn't see what she had to lose. Any dignity she might have had was already gone.

'I've just put a lot of stuff on eBay and other sites,' she said, 'and I've got more ready to go. It should bring me in about that much, but not for a couple of weeks.'

'That's not acceptable,' said the man. 'We are under strict instructions from our clients to act now, because you haven't responded to any of their phone calls or letters. What assets do you have with a value of £700?'

Rachel's first reaction was to ask him: Are you kidding me? But then she had to remind herself: who was she to get hoity toity? She was horribly in debt, with several credit cards maxed out, in arrears on her mortgage, and it would be months before she'd actually see any kind of bonus, even once she'd secured the business from any of the companies she was working on.

She decided to try a different tactic.

'What will happen if I can't pay you immediately?' she asked.

'We'll come to your home and seize goods to the value of the debt owed to our client,' he said.

'The whole debt?' asked Rachel, feeling a chill pass over her.

'Yes,' said the man, 'it would usually be a car, or if that wasn't of sufficient value, we'd take electrical goods, antiques, jewellery, subject to valuation.'

'You'd just come and take them?' Rachel asked, incredulous.

'In July 2010, you signed a credit agreement with our client, agreeing to pay back what you borrow within the specified time frame. You haven't maintained your payments, so it is their legal right to seek compensation.'

'But what if I don't let you in?' she asked.

'Then you would be served with a court summons. You'd be liable for costs, as well as what you owe – and you have no chance of winning, so it could easily lead to bankruptcy.'

Rachel sat down heavily on the sofa. A £4000 sofa, she'd bought on that very credit card. It had seemed imperative at that moment, for her professional image and future prospects, that she had an elephant grey velvet sofa. But she'd be lucky to get £500 if she sold it now.

'So what's your plan? I need to know,' said the man, in a distinctly firmer voice.

Rachel felt tears prick her eyes.

'I have a diamond ring,' she said, a slight catch in her voice. Her engagement ring. Michael had suggested she should give it back to him when they got divorced, but she'd managed to hold on to it. She'd been planning to sell it to pay for the girls' university tuition fees when the time came.

'Have you had it valued recently?' he asked.

No, she hadn't, because she'd let the contents insurance lapse, when she couldn't pay the bill any more.

'The last time was two years ago and then I was told it had a replacement value of £15,000,' she said. 'But I'd probably only get £5000 if I sold it.'

'That will be acceptable as a first down payment,' said the man.

'But you said I only had to pay £700 now,' said Rachel.

'You owe our client £7000 and it's our duty to collect as much of it as we can. The ring will be a start and then we will pursue the other £2000. I'll just check I have the correct email address and I'll send you details of where to take the ring. But if you don't take it in tomorrow, we will come and get it from your house. Do you understand that?'

'Yes,' said Rachel, very quietly. His tone was now openly threatening and she was afraid. What if he came round when the girls were there? It was too awful to contemplate.

She confirmed that the email address he had for her was correct and he finally rang off. Rachel let the hand holding the phone fall down by her side and slumped back on the sofa, looking around her elegant charcoal drawing room, which had been featured on several prominent blogs.

She had some serious decisions to make. But first she was going to speak to her mother.

Tuesday, 8 July

Manhattan

As her cab pulled up outside the OM building on Fifth Avenue and the uniformed porter came over to open the door for her, Natasha felt excited to be going back into their offices again so soon. She was starting to feel part of the giant machine that was the global corporation.

The designs for her products that Blythe had shown her the day before were even better than she'd dared to hope, sophisticated and elegant with an urban edge, absolutely spot on for how she envisioned her brand.

To see the name 'Younger by Natasha' on the computer-generated images and mock-ups of shiny silver compacts, lipstick tubes and mascaras for the first time, had made her eyes well up with tears.

Blythe had put an arm around her shoulder and given her a squeeze.

'Starting to feel real, huh?' she'd said. 'It's going to be huge.'

So Natasha had been pleased when Blythe's PA had called that morning asking if she could pop over again in the afternoon to discuss the 'outline marketing strategy'. Last minute wasn't OM's usual style, but Natasha didn't hesitate before saying yes.

As it turned out it had meant leaving a job early, which was unheard of for her, but the meeting was with Blythe and her legendary boss, Ava Capel, so it was virtually a royal summons.

It had been a major coup when 'Miss Capel', as everyone in the company called her, had contacted Natasha as soon as she'd heard about her plans for a range on the beauty-industry grapevine. They'd lunched at the Four Seasons, and Natasha had been almost too surprised to speak when Ava – as she'd immediately insisted Natasha call her – had said she wanted to offer her a deal, for OM to fund the range from development through to launch.

Natasha had found all the contact she'd had with Ava since really inspiring. Her understanding of the international cosmetics market was so beyond that of anyone else she'd ever spoken to, it made Natasha feel as though she had been initiated into some kind of elite inner circle.

The meeting that afternoon was being held in Ava's office, a sanctum Natasha had only been privileged to visit once before. On the corner of the twenty-fourth floor, with picture windows looking right over Central Park, it was a pinnacle statement of New York success and despite all her years working with the most famous names in fashion and film – and holidaying and partying with them too – Natasha was impressed.

'Here she is,' said Ava, coming out from behind her desk to greet her. 'The next shining star of the beauty counter. Great to see you, Natasha. Take a seat. Would you like some green tea?'

Natasha said she would and Ava's PA poured the pale liquid into a tiny porcelain cup, from an antique Japanese teapot, and then offered her a plate of gloriously coloured macarons. Natasha chose a deep pink one and the impeccably groomed young woman put it on a plate for her, using silver tongs.

This ritual was repeated with Ava and Blythe, then they all ooh-ed and ah-ed and mmm-ed, taking tiny little bites from the macarons before putting them daintily back on their plates. Natasha knew none of the carbohydrate-laden treats would be touched again. It was all part of the dance.

The PA left the room and after pressing a button which made the windows darken, Ava opened a PowerPoint presentation, projected on the wall opposite her desk, showing an outline of what she called 'first ideas' for the advertising and promotion strategy.

The launch was still nine months away, but Natasha had already learned that OM left nothing to chance. Blythe had emailed her agent weeks before with the dates she would need to block out of Natasha's schedule the following year for personal appearances and television shows.

Her excitement growing, as she watched Ava's presentation, Natasha asked questions and made suggestions, then it was her turn to get out her iPad and show them some mood boards she'd put together for the print advertising campaign. She was very glad she'd already started working on them, before they'd formally asked her to.

'I love the feel of all that, Natasha,' said Ava. 'I think your ideas for print are fabulous, just as I would expect from you, and the next stage will be discussing them with our ad agency. I'll set up that meeting for us.'

She made a note on the pad on the desk in front of her and took a sip of her tea, before continuing.

'And now we need to think about your personality strategy, which is what I really asked you in here to talk over today.'

Steepling her fingers in front of her chest, she gazed off into the middle distance, clearly thinking it through as she spoke.

'The product is going to be amazing, no question about that, so the issue here is, what is the most effective way for us to put over to your customers the story of Natasha Younger, the person?

'Not just the famous make-up artist they've read so much about in print and online, who creates the amazing looks for fashion shows and magazine covers, we need them to feel they know the real woman behind the reputation and the fabulous products.'

She paused to drink some more tea before continuing, still staring into space, somewhere above Natasha's and Blythe's heads.

'We want them to understand just what it is about this make-up artist that makes all the supermodels love and trust her. The consumer needs to feel she knows you as they do, that you are her friend too, and that you're looking out for her just the way you do for Kate, Gisele, Alessandra, Karlie, etc. ...'

Natasha took a sip from her tiny tea cup to cover her excitement. She knew she was privy to something special here. The beauty branding guru in full creative flow. Crikey. She glanced over at Blythe who smiled and gave her an encouraging thumbs-up at hip level.

Ava turned her gaze to Natasha, looking at her very intently, as if she was trying to memorise her face. It was slightly unsettling.

'Obviously,' she continued, 'the media team will be pitching for major profiles and lifestyle pieces and we'd love to hear your ideas for that. Blythe and I were just saying before you got here that we'd love to offer your beach house to *Vogue* as a ten-page package for an early summer issue next year, how do you feel about that?'

'That would be great,' said Natasha, 'I just spent the long weekend out there and it was glorious. The garden is looking gorgeous and we could do some shots on the beach.'

'That sounds perfect,' said Ava. 'I've seen some really cute pictures of it you've put on your Instagram feed – actually could you bundle all that up on a private Pinterest board for us, so we can use them to prepare the pitch for *Vogue*?'

Natasha nodded.

'And talking about Instagram,' continued Ava, 'we love what you do on there, so keep that going and all the other social media, which you're also strong on. How many Twitter followers do you have now?'

Natasha picked up her phone and checked.

'138,789 right now,' she said, 'and I've got over 200,000 on Instagram.'

Ava beamed. 'That's terrific. We'll aim to double them both. Then there's online … We thought we could do webchats with a video link, so you can answer questions, while showing techniques live on a model.'

'That would be fantastic,' said Natasha.

'I'll ask my team to put some ideas together,' said Blythe, making notes into her phone. 'It would probably be best as a YouTube portal on the brand website.'

It was Natasha's turn to do a thumbs-up to her.

'And then,' Ava continued, 'we have to get across the street-style pics. We have good relationships with several of the key players and we can create opportunities for them to "run into you" wearing a casual look you've "thrown together".'

She laughed and Natasha joined in, feeling quite naive that she hadn't thought about how that all worked before, and making a mental note to go through her wardrobe forensically.

'We'll also need to work your major-league celebrity association angle,' Ava was saying. 'Your close working friendships with Gisele and other supers is a really strong story and it would be great to get some social pages shots of you with them and your designer friends. You're close to Tom Ford, aren't you?'

Natasha nodded.

'Great, we'd love pap shots of you with him, coming out of restaurants, that kind of thing. Who else would be good for that, do you think? Which actors are you closest to? We don't want it to be all fashion.'

Natasha hesitated. Her discretion with regard to her famous friends and associates was one of the bedrocks of her success, she wasn't going to start cynically using those connections to promote her own business, without asking them first. That would short-circuit everything. She'd have to think who might be glad of some exposure.

'I'll make some calls,' she said.

'Get back to us on that,' said Ava, 'meanwhile we can get the paparazzi strategy framework ready. From a certain point nearer the launch – can you work out the timing, Blythe? – we'll need access to your daily schedule, so we'll know where you will be when and with whom, and we can manage that.'

Natasha kept nodding and smiling, still excited, but starting to feel a little overwhelmed by the broad scope of their publicity plans. She'd expected press interviews, photo shoots, television, videos and in-store launches, but she hadn't realised she was going to be vaulted into the level of daily intrusion that people like her friends and neighbours Sarah Jessica Parker and Matthew Broderick lived with.

She knew the strain it put on them and even people who weren't at anything like their level of fame. Many was the neck rub she'd given to a young woman arriving at a shoot in bits after having one too many long lens aimed up her skirt as she got out of a car.

'And then, of course,' said Ava, smiling warmly at Natasha, 'the final piece of the magic will be those more personal lifestyle stories. In fact, Blythe and I were wondering whether you might like to do the beach house shoot with your girlfriend, as a couple story ...?'

Natasha heard Ava's words and then it felt as though the whole world had come to a standstill. Time stopped, everything had gone silent, she was frozen like a frame in a film. What the hell had just happened?

She turned to look at Blythe who was still smiling at her enthusiastically and then back at Ava, who also looked perfectly happy. So it's only me who's finding this weird, she thought. Holy shit.

'Blythe told me ...' Ava glanced quickly down at the pad on her desk, 'that Mattie is really beautiful and she's also a make-up artist, so that adds another great layer to the story.'

Natasha still couldn't speak. She looked over at Blythe again, who was nodding in agreement. Neither of them seemed to have noticed that Natasha had been struck dumb. Or possibly turned to salt.

'Yeah,' said Blythe, 'it was great running into you guys yesterday. You look so good together, I thought the pics would be amazing and I was even thinking, we could do some shots where you are doing each other's make-up, using the range, especially as you have such different colouring.'

'Oh, that would be great,' said Ava, 'what a fantastic idea. What do you think, Natasha?'

Natasha didn't think anything, except that she seemed to have been transported to a parallel universe.

'It's a dream story for us to place,' Ava continued, either not noticing Natasha's lack of response, or choosing to ignore it. 'I'm going to ring Anna myself to offer it and suggest the cover line, I've had a great idea for it. What do you think of this: "Lipstick Lesbians – Natasha Younger and her partner share their make-up secrets"?'

Blythe was clapping with delight.

'That is so great,' she said, 'don't you love it, Tash?'

No. She didn't love it. Not at all did she love the idea of her private sexual preferences being plastered on the cover of one of the most widely circulated magazines in the world.

And neither did she love the idea of Ava personally giving Anna Wintour the news that one of the magazine's most acclaimed make-up artists was a lesbian. Were they outing her by force? Is that what this was?

Ava was talking again, so Natasha made herself snap back to attention.

'Or how about this?' Ava was saying, gazing off into space again. 'Let me see ...'

She clicked her fingers and looked back at Natasha, smiling excitedly.

'Got it,' she said. 'What do you think of this? "Girls on film: make-up superstar Natasha Younger showcases her new range on her girlfriend". Or should it be "Girl on Girl" ...? Risqué, but fun.'

Blythe was laughing and clapping again and Natasha tried to paste something like a smile on her own face, as it began to sink in what was actually going on. They were outing her, but not in a mean and nasty way, it was more of a loving intervention.

They hadn't got her there to let her know they'd got wise to her secret love life and were disgusted – it was more like the opposite. They were telling her they knew she had a girlfriend and they were totally cool about it.

In fact they seemed genuinely enthusiastic at the prospect of marketing the range with her as an out-and-proud lesbian make-up artist. In their highly tuned commercial heads, they saw it as her Unique Selling Point.

And that was exactly what she didn't want. Not just because of her long-standing anxiety that being known as 'the lesbian make-up artist' could limit her career – she simply didn't want to be defined by her sexuality.

It wasn't that she was ashamed that she preferred to kiss women, she just didn't think it was the most interesting thing about her. It was how she was wired, as prosaic as preferring green tea to coffee, that's all there was to it. Straights didn't have to go public about their specific sexual preferences, so why should the details of her private life be public knowledge?

'Those are all brilliant ideas,' she said tentatively, knowing that the next words she spoke might be the most crucial of her entire career, 'but I hadn't really thought of the campaign being quite so personal.'

'Oh, come on, Tasha,' said Ava. 'You're one of the big players in the Instagram generation, this is how it works now, you know that – everyone's daily life is their currency. Edited, of course, for maximum fabulousness, but you can't expect to keep your professional and your personal lives separate any more. Your lifestyle is your image, and your image is your brand. Your name is going to be on those products – and you're going to have to own every part of yourself, Natasha, or it won't work.'

She looked at Natasha so intently as she said the last thing – 'own every part of yourself' – it was almost like it was echoing around the room. This was why this sudden meeting had been called.

Blythe clearly had seen Natasha holding hands with Mattie as they'd crossed the road to Eataly the morning before – but that wasn't the reason she'd hurried back to alert Ava. It was because she'd also seen Natasha drop Mattie's hand the moment she saw her. The issue wasn't that Blythe had figured out the true scenario, but that she'd seen Natasha trying to hide it.

Natasha looked over at her. She was still smiling, but it was gentler now, seeming to say: I hate to lay this on you, sister, but you need to wise up about this, get real with yourself.

So there was no point in even discussing how Natasha felt about it. They knew what they knew and they'd made it clear how they wanted to handle it. What was that business cliché? Not a problem – an opportunity.

An opportunity for them to flog her sexuality as a marketing concept to sell more product, but at what cost to her privacy and dignity?

Natasha felt a sudden flare of anger. She knew she should be relieved that her fear of losing the range if anyone found out she wasn't 100 per cent heterosexual wasn't happening, but this felt almost worse. She was being forced to come out as a flag-waving lesbian to keep it.

She knew she had to leave Ava's office fast, before she said something she'd regret. She needed to think long and hard about this, with a clear head, well away from Ava's penetrating gaze and Blythe's sympathetic one. She forced herself to meet Ava's eyes again and was relieved to see her warm expression had returned.

'So let's leave it there for now,' said Ava. 'You've got a lot to think about. A campaign at this level is a lot to take on. It's life changing and will require your full commitment.'

There she went, Natasha understood, reminding her again what the subtext was. Just in case you want to pull out now, while you still can. Because if you can't handle having your whole life on public display – you'd better tell us immediately, before we spend another moment or another dollar on you.

It was tough love, OM style, but at least Natasha knew where she stood. She forced herself to smile back.

'Thanks so much, Ava,' she said, 'it is a lot to take in, but it's incredibly exciting. I can't tell you what it means to me to be launching my range with you. I've probably learned more in this one meeting than I would have in years making endless mistakes, trying to do the brand on my own. I'm so grateful.'

Which wasn't a word of a lie, because she was sincerely glad she knew where she stood with them this early on in the process. All she had to do now was to figure out what the hell she was going to do about it.

Natasha left the OM building feeling dazed. Emerging onto the heat of Fifth Avenue, for a moment she stood rooted to the spot, not knowing which way to turn. Cabs were streaming past her, heading downtown towards home and Mattie. But she didn't feel ready to see Mattie yet. What was she going to say to her? Or anyone? What was she going to do about any of it?

The OM doorman came over to ask if she wanted him to hail her a taxi, and she thanked him, saying she was fine on foot, then walked up to the corner of 59th Street, waited for the lights to change and crossed over into Central Park. She needed space to think.

Her feet were walking, left, right, left, right, one after the other, but Natasha felt as though she were floating above her own body, she didn't feel connected to the ground at all. In just a few moments in that corner office her world had tilted on its axis and she was no longer quite sure where she belonged in it.

After leaving the main path and taking a few random turns she found an empty bench under some trees and sat down, leaning her head back, to stare up into the canopy of leaves. Trying to think. Trying to sort the jumbled ideas fighting for precedence in her head into some kind of rational order.

Listening to the rustling of the breeze in the branches, Natasha thought suddenly of her mother, feeling a stab of primal longing for her comforting arms. She'd like to sob onto her shoulder, to see her face which shone with love whenever she looked at her daughters.

What would Mum do in this situation? she asked herself. She'd grab her crystals, of course and then she'd probably meditate. Natasha didn't have any crystals with her, although she did have a couple back at the apartment, gifts from her mum, but the meditation she could do right there, without props.

She sat up straight and after shifting her handbag onto her lap and fastening her hands around it – she'd lived in New York too long to sit with her eyes closed in a public place with her bag unsecured – she started breathing slowly in and out, pausing at the end of each out breath, trying to release her mind of active thought.

Thanks, Mum, she thought, as she opened her eyes again ten minutes later, feeling much calmer. Thanks for raising me with all your yoga wisdom. Joy took all her new-age woo woo a bit far sometimes – Rachel was so funny about all that, she remembered with a pang, something else awful she had to sort out – but in times of crisis, Natasha always found it more reassuring than she'd ever admit to her cynical middle sister. And she knew Tessa felt the same as she did. She'd smile at Rachel's jokes, but without comment, and Natasha had long suspected she was as fey as their mum in her own way, but didn't want to talk about it.

Thinking about them Natasha had a sudden insight: were they a large part of the reason she didn't feel comfortable about the idea of publicly coming out as a gay woman?

Not because she was worried they would react badly – as Mattie had said, she didn't think you could meet three people less likely to judge her for her choice of partner – but out of shame for not having been honest with them about it all along?

That really might explain it, she thought, swivelling her head from side to side, trying to alleviate the neck tension that stress always gave her. On top of the guilt and regret she carried for going off to live with her dad that time, being gay had always felt like another way she'd made herself different from them.

Not that it was ever a choice. Her sexuality had been a realisation when she was fourteen and all her school friends were madly in love with boys and male pop stars and she'd realised she really wasn't, but that her heart did beat faster every time she looked at the strong legs of the lady PE teacher.

She might have spoken to her mum about it then, except very soon after it had all got messily tied up with her apparently impetuous decision to move back to Brisbane with her dad.

What had actually prompted the move was that she'd fallen in mad unrequited love with a girl at school. She'd been so terrified of her own feelings – and of being found out by her peers – that she'd used the excuse of wanting to live with her dad to run away to Australia, hoping that by getting away from the object of her passion, she'd get over it. She had, very quickly, but only because she'd fallen for another girl over there.

Natasha sighed deeply, closing her eyes again and feeling slightly nauseous as she always did remembering those confusing times. She hated even thinking about how she had hurt her mother – and her sisters – by doing that and how it had created a sense of separateness from them that had never quite left her.

Different father, living in a different country ... perhaps a different sexuality was just one difference too many. And now with this awful rift between her and Rachel, she felt more isolated from the family than ever.

The noise of skateboarders swishing past made her eyes snap open again and Natasha shook her head quickly a couple of times, to try and physically scatter those unhelpful thoughts. Dredging all that up now was not going to help, she had to concentrate on what was at stake here. Only the most important thing in her life: the make-up range she'd dreamed of starting since the beginning of her career.

But that wasn't all. There was the other most important thing in her life too, becoming more important every day. Mattie. Natasha could imagine all too clearly how she would react to this new situation – it was proof that what she'd been saying was right all along, that Natasha had been crazy to worry about coming out.

Mattie said it was a mental block – and that Natasha was 'mental' because she had a block about it. Even in her dismay, Natasha couldn't help smiling as she remembered the look on Mattie's face as she'd said that to her. But jokes apart, this same goddamn issue which had come up their very first morning after, in Paris, was still the one thing that caused tension between them.

And then, among the confusion, something she'd never understood about herself became clear to Natasha. This was why she'd put up with the complications of affairs with 'straight' women, culminating in the previous two years of torture with her married lover.

It may have been difficult, but at least those women hadn't demanded that Natasha come out. In fact, they'd begged her not to, in case it reflected back on them.

Then, even as that sunk in, something else came into her mind. She suddenly had a very clear memory of waking up that first morning of the Fourth of July weekend in her beach house, with Mattie at her side.

She remembered how happy she'd felt at the prospect of spending the whole holiday weekend together, just the two of them. No need to go to some forced Hamptons A-list barbecue, making sure she talked to all the right people, didn't drink too much, stayed well away from the carbs and was suitably thrilled by the fireworks.

The clandestine affairs with their stolen hours and secret kisses might have made her feel protected, but knowing she had three whole days when she'd be able to be entirely herself, with somebody who loved her for who she was, was worth so much more. Genuine togetherness. The thought of being without that now was unbearable.

There was no escaping it. She was going to have to tell Mattie what had just happened and find a way to talk it through with her, to come to a decision before Mattie went back to London in forty-eight hours.

She still didn't know exactly what she would say to her, how to explain all the complicated feelings, but she was already crystal clear about one thing. The two most important things in her life now were Mattie and 'Younger by Natasha'.

And if she wanted to hold on to both of them she was going to have to come out.

Thursday, 10 July

Cranbrook

Tessa and Tom were out in the barn opening boxes, looking for things to put along the 'story path' she'd designed to lead customers through the main yard to the barn without them quite realising it. She couldn't stop smiling, she was so happy he was there to help her, after arriving back from the big trip to the US the evening before, much earlier than planned.

'I knew the minute I walked into that man's office, which was on some kind of industrial estate, in the back of the LA beyond, the whole thing was a disaster,' he was saying, then having to pause while Jack did something very loud with a ring saw.

He was in the process of putting in some new – although actually old – windows to create a lighter and brighter curated retail area for pieces with instant appeal. Other stuff they were going to leave lying about in the still deliberately gloomy back end of the barn, looking as though it had been untouched for decades, for customers who actively preferred salvaging at the more basic level.

'How come?' asked Tessa, as soon as they could hear again. 'How did you know it was a disaster?'

'Everything in his office was brand new. It looked like he'd sent someone down to IKEA to buy a room set. Hideous.'

Tessa laughed. 'Did you ask him about it?'

'Yes,' said Tom. 'He said his decorator had done it and asked me if I'd like one of her cards. It was very shiny with a picture of her on it.'

'Blonde? Unnaturally white teeth?'

'Affirmative,' said Tom, 'and it just got sleazier from there. He kept referring to salvage as "second-hand junk". "So is there much cash in this second-hand junk of yours, Tim?" I'd love to see what he'd make of this.'

He held up one of the mangier-looking stuffed birds.

Tessa immediately thought of Simon and was hugely relieved to find it no longer affected her. Not even a pang. He was now a man she knew in her current life as a middle-aged married woman and a mother, not some kind of shamanic time traveller from their briefly shared youth.

One day she might even tell Tom about it, she thought. Especially if he stayed the way he'd been since he had unexpectedly arrived back the day before. She wasn't making any assumptions yet, but he seemed much more like his old self.

'So what was the final thing that made you decide to throw it in and come home?' she asked him.

Tom started laughing. 'When they sent me my call sheets for the filming and the first thing on my schedule was an appointment for Botox followed by one with a hair "colorist".'

He said it as per the American spelling. Col-or. Tessa laughed.

'That was it,' said Tom. 'I'd already been through an excruciating experience with the production designer who wanted to put me into this Red Adair–style red jumpsuit. Tight. I would have looked like a bull terrier coming down a ladder from the back – balls ahoy.'

Tessa was so amused by this prospect, she had to sit down on an upturned metal fire bucket to recover.

'But aren't you bound by some hideous legal contract?' she asked. 'We haven't got to pay them money to spring you from doing the US show, have we?'

'No, that all turned out rather well. I let the UK producers know how much the Yanks were planning to change the format and they were able to break off the whole deal as a breach of contract.'

'Did you get Barney the Dinosaur to do that?' asked Tessa.

A frown crossed Tom's face at the mention of his agent.

'He was a large part of the problem,' said Tom. 'He was so excited about breaking into the US "TV scene" he would happily have had me roasted on a spit in a Tudor-style inglenook live on air to stay in with what he thought was the network – although it turned out it never was the network he was dealing with. It was the tinpot production company, who wanted him to think they were big shots. The whole thing was monstrously tacky.'

'Gosh,' said Tessa. 'So where does that leave you with darling Barney?'

'I've dropped him,' said Tom. 'He was also trying to get me to sign away the rights to the Hunter Gatherer name for a line of "homewares" which were going to be manufactured – brand new – in China. "Tim Chiminey's Hunter Gatherer Salvage Style". Can you imagine?'

'All too well,' said Tessa. 'That has been the landscape of my nightmares for some time. But are you sure that's definitely not happening …'

'It's definitely not happening,' said Tom, putting his arms around her. 'I said no and without my signature he can't do the deal – and your signature, as a matter of fact. We own the name jointly. So that's not happening, but what is happening is that I'm going to spend a lot more time back in this yard, which I love, and with you, who I love even more. I'll still go off and fix the odd Regency fire surround for a desperate oligarch, but I'm taking some time off before I do any more TV.'

'Blimey,' said Tessa, 'I'm amazed. I thought you loved it so much ... the attention, the fans ...'

'It did turn my head for a bit, Tessa,' he said. 'I can't deny it. But we had dinners with various fifth-rank TV people while we were in LA and I realised what I could turn into. Fish face cosmetic surgery, hair weaves, aggressive dye jobs, a general air of desperation. No, thank you.'

Tessa wrapped her arms around him and squeezed tight, burying her face in his shoulder. She felt like she had the real Tom back. Not just back from the trip to Los Angeles, but from his strange sojourn in celebrity land. In that moment she realised quite how much she'd missed him.

Tom pulled away and lifted up her chin with his finger.

'You've got a big black smudge of dirt on your nose,' he said, smiling at her tenderly. 'It's very fetching, but what do you say, we go back to the house and clean you up?'

Tessa grinned at him and, grabbing his hand in a firm grip, headed towards the barn door.

Friday, 11 July

Cranbrook

Daisy spotted them first, her face squashed against the glass of the train door, as it pulled into Staplehurst station.

'There's Granny!' she yelled out. 'And Auntie Tessa! Look, Mum, they're both on the platform waiting for us. Brilliant, we'll get to go in Auntie Tessa's stinky car. You said we were getting a taxi.'

Busy gathering up their bags, Rachel didn't have a chance to look until the train had stopped, but sure enough, as the automatic doors slid open, there were two of the people she loved most in the world.

The girls leapt from the train like excited dogs, throwing themselves first at their grandmother – who was still walking with two sticks and had to brace herself – and then their aunt.

By the time Rachel disembarked, carrying everyone's things, her mother was waiting to greet her. Despite the sticks, Joy managed to enfold her in her arms and Rachel buried her head in her mother's shoulder and the familiar smell of lavender and rose geranium essential oils.

Then Tessa came over and put her arms around both of them, kissing the side of Rachel's head, and Daisy and Ariadne squirmed into the middle grabbing hold of anyone they could.

'Group hug! Group hug!' Daisy was shouting.

'I'm the ham! I'm the ham!' shrieked Ariadne, wriggling right into the middle.

'Can't you be cheese?' asked Joy. 'You know I don't eat meat. I don't want ham in my sandwich.'

'I'm the cheese! I'm the cheese!' continued Ariadne.

'I'm the chutney,' said Daisy. 'Granny, you can be the naan bread ... Nan bread, do you get it? *Nan* bread ...'

'Very good, Daisy,' said Joy, stepping back, so as not to be knocked over in the melee. 'You're a very witty girl. Your grandfather would be proud of you.'

'I'm the pita bread, Granny,' said Ariadne, putting her hand over her grandmother's where it was gripping a stick, as they headed off towards the station car park.

'Oh, well done, Ari,' said Joy, 'Grandpa would be very proud of you too.'

'But that's not even a pun,' said Daisy. 'Where's the wit in that?'

Joy leaned down towards her and, pulling the stick up towards her elbow, to free her hand, pretended to twist her ear.

'You're a wit nit,' she said, 'and you're both a couple of crumpets.'

Tessa was helping Rachel carry the bags.

'Thanks for coming to meet us, Tessie,' said Rachel.

'We've been so excited about seeing you all,' said Tessa, 'we couldn't stand waiting at the house any longer. It's been ages since we've heard from you ...'

'Nearly three weeks,' said Rachel. 'Very long by our normal standards. I'm really sorry, Tessa. I shouldn't have taken it out on you and Mum like that, especially with her still getting over that fall. It was Natasha I was angry with, but I couldn't help it, and I was a little bit angry with you, but that was just me bundling all my worries together.'

'I'm so sorry about that bonus,' said Tessa. 'I felt awful when I realised I'd stopped you getting it.'

'It's OK,' said Rachel. 'You'd already lent me £3000 – which I am going to pay you back, by the way – so I had no right to be cross with you about money. It was just with it coming right after the upset with Natasha, I was raw.'

'Are you still angry with her?' asked Tessa, stopping to adjust Daisy's and Ariadne's surprisingly heavy backpacks and because she wanted to hear Rachel's answer before they caught up with the others, who were making rather slow progress.

'No,' said Rachel, 'not like I was. I'm still bewildered why she did it, but I'm not angry any more, because I've just learned something very important the hard way.'

'What's that?' asked Tessa.

'Well,' said Rachel, putting her bags down too, 'I've discovered that if you push your family away out of anger, you're left in a very lonely isolated place to get over whatever made you feel hurt in the first place. Then that makes you feel abandoned as well as hurt, so then you start to feel bitter and go looking for reasons not to forgive them to justify your feelings ... and on it goes. A toxic downward spiral. It's made me understand how those terrible family feuds you hear about can happen.'

'Well, you're here now,' said Tessa, putting her arm round her younger sister and pulling her close. 'Definitely no feuds in this family. Now let's get us all back to the house for dinner.'

'And wine,' said Rachel.

'Definitely wine,' said Tessa, 'every kind of wine.'

* * *

Joy looked around the dinner table and sent up a prayer of thanks to have her beautiful family – very nearly all of them – reunited. Tom and Tessa were sitting so close together she was practically on his knee, their heads nearly touching, like a pair of lovebirds.

Joy believed head-to-head contact was as big a signifier of closeness between humans as it was in the animal kingdom and she could read the signals between them like a billboard. Nothing to worry about there any more.

Especially now Tom had seen through the illusory attraction of fame. He was a good man, she'd always known that and she was so glad Tessa hadn't gone any further down that dangerous path with Simon. Not that he wasn't a good man too, in his own way. Joy sincerely believed he was, just not for Tessa.

Turning her attention to Rachel, there was more to be concerned about. She was so thin it was quite alarming and had dark circles under her eyes, which Joy was certain indicated anxieties beyond the upset of falling out with her immediate family.

Even more worryingly, she'd lost her spark, that feisty appetite for life which always reminded Joy so much of her first husband. Although she was clearly happy and relieved to be reunited with her and Tessa, Rachel still looked quite defeated. Joy would have to find out what was going on there. And she hoped once she had, she might also be able to guide her to forgive Natasha. Then the circle would finally be complete again.

Or as near as it could be.

Saturday, 12 July

Cranbrook

Joy got her chance to talk to Rachel after lunch on Saturday. It was another lovely day and they'd eaten in the garden. After taking the last of the plates in to the kitchen, Rachel came back to Joy, still sitting at the table, so she wouldn't be left alone. Always going that little bit further than anyone else.

'Are you all right, Mum?' she asked, looking slightly perkier than when she'd arrived, after eighteen hours back with her extended family, but still drawn.

'Yes, darling,' said Joy, 'but perhaps you can help me take my walk. I'm supposed to walk for five minutes at least three times a day, but I need to have someone with me in case I fall again.'

'I'd love to,' said Rachel, enjoying the knowledge that she didn't have to make sure the girls would be looked after while she did it. In that house, there was always somebody around. 'Where shall we go?'

'Let's take a turn around the orchard,' said Joy. 'I'd like to see how the fruit is coming on this year.'

'OK,' said Rachel, picking her mum's sticks up from the ground and helping her to her feet.

Joy got her arms into the plastic cuffs and they set off slowly up the path mown through the meadow. Rachel looked around at the wild flowers with butterflies and bees flitting about among them and took a deep breath of the clean, chlorophyll-filtered air.

'I always forget how lovely it is here in summer,' she said. 'When you live in London and there are trees along the streets and Hyde Park and bits of grass in roundabouts and all that, you kid yourself you're still in touch with nature, but when you come down here and you're really *in* it, it makes you understand the difference. The bits of green in a city are like tropical fish in a tiny tank. This is the wide open ocean.'

Joy smiled, leaving her to drink it in. She could almost see the knots in her neck loosening. Her darling girl, she was wound like a tight spring.

'Are you OK, Mum?' asked Rachel, turning to look at her mother, who was taking a while to make it up the slight incline towards the orchard. 'Not too much for you?'

'As long as I take it slow and steady, I think mixed terrain is the best exercise for my hip, keeps it moving in all directions.'

'You should know, yoga guru,' said Rachel, smiling at her with something slightly more like her usual vivid life force, but the strain still clear across her face. 'Let me know when you've had enough.'

They walked on into the thicket of fruit trees, the sunshine dappled by the leaves, birds singing. Rachel paused and put her arms round a gnarled old apple tree, pressing her face against its trunk.

Joy laughed.

'Are you hugging that tree, Rachel Lambton?' she asked her.

'Yes,' said Rachel. 'I'm giving it a go. Come on, tree, give me your healing energy. Share your wisdom with me, oh mighty tree-ee. Am I doing it right, Mum?'

Joy tapped her on the bottom with one of her sticks.

'Cheeky,' she said, 'and you know – there is no right or wrong way, just however feels right for you.'

'It feels rather scratchy, if you really want to know,' said Rachel, turning her head so her other cheek was on the bark.

'Well, if you stop talking and just *be* for a few moments, you might get something out of it, letting go of intention and expectation …'

'I'm hugging a tree,' said Rachel, 'and I'm supposed to not think about why I'm doing it?'

Joy balanced her sticks against the neighbouring tree, a plum, then rested her body against it, wrapping her arms around the trunk, breathing out audibly through her nose.

'Ooooohhhhmmmm,' said Rachel.

'Stop it, Rachel,' said her mother, 'just quieten your inner and outer voices, especially the outer one, in your case, breathe and stop thinking. Just be. Try it for five breaths.'

After an initial urge to start giggling, or blow a raspberry, anything not to do what her mum advised, she finally surrendered to it.

When she opened her eyes again, she had no idea how long she'd been standing there. Joy was watching her, leaning back against her own tree. She smiled at Rachel.

'How do you feel?' she asked.

Rachel blinked.

'I feel rather good actually,' she said. 'Did I just go to sleep?'

'Not sleep,' said Joy, 'you went into a deep meditative state.'

'Blimey,' said Rachel, stepping away from the tree and rubbing her face. It felt lumpy where it had been pressed against the bark. 'I didn't think I could meditate. I always start thinking about not thinking and get so brain boggled I give up. Thanks, tree.'

She patted its trunk and then leaned forward and gave it a kiss.

'I'll never forget you,' she said. 'How was it for you?'

Joy shook her head, but she was smiling.

'Sorry, Mum. I hijacked your walk, do you want to go back now, or on a bit further?'

'Let's go on,' said Joy. 'I'm ready for a bit more exercise after my rest.'

They resumed their stroll, commenting on the fruit beginning to swell on the trees, until they came to the clearing with the fringed swing seat in it.

'Wow,' said Rachel, 'I haven't seen this one before. It's fab.'

'Tessa had it put out a few weeks ago. She said the shoot you did down here with the garden furniture gave her the idea.'

'Is it safe to sit on?' asked Rachel, giving the seat a gentle push. 'Most of her stuff is lethal.'

'I think it's OK, but perhaps you could try it first?' said Joy.

'Sure,' said Rachel, 'then we can both have broken hips.'

She sat down gingerly and moved the seat back and forth a couple of times. It didn't come crashing down.

'Seems good to me, let me help you.'

Rachel stood up again and braced the seat with her knee to keep it still, while helping her mother down on to it, then settled herself next to her. They sat in silence for a while, Rachel gently swinging the seat back and forth with one foot, just enjoying the peace among the trees.

Then Joy turned to look at Rachel.

'So tell me what's going on with you, Rachel,' she said, quietly.

Rachel turned her head quickly to look at her. She knew what a question like that from her mother really meant. Not just a general 'How are things with you?' chit chat, but 'What's going on that you're trying to hide?' She immediately turned her head away again. Was it not possible to keep anything private in her family?

'Come on, darling,' said Joy, putting her hand gently on Rachel's arm. 'I know something's very wrong and you'll feel so much better if you tell someone about it and nobody could care more than I do. You know I won't judge you, I just want to be able to support you. I've never seen you look so wrung out.'

'Is it that obvious?' said Rachel, turning to look at her mother.

'Yes,' said Joy, reaching out and tracing the black shadows under Rachel's eyes with her forefinger, then the two little lines that had appeared between her eyebrows over the past few months.

Rachel took a deep breath.

'I'm in debt,' she said. There, it was out. She'd told somebody.

'How badly in debt?' asked Joy.

'Very badly,' said Rachel. 'My salary barely pays off my overdraft each month and I can't even make the minimum payments for what I owe on credit cards – which adds up to £20,000 already and it keeps going up because I'm being charged late-payment fees and then I have to pay more and more interest on all of it, so it's getting worse at a constantly accelerating rate. It's like being on some kind of monstrous theme-park ride.'

Joy sat and took it in. Debt. A terrifying idea. No wonder Rachel looked so hunted.

'Can you pay your mortgage?' she asked.

Rachel shook her head.

'I'm in arrears with that as well,' she said. 'In the past couple of months, it's all I've been able to do to feed the girls.'

'Is that why you're so thin?' asked Joy.

She knew about that one. She'd been there herself. Not from debt, just from having hardly any income. Going without dinner herself, so the children could eat. Being a widowed single mum in the mid-1970s had been no joke.

Rachel nodded.

'Oh, darling,' said Joy, pulling Rachel towards her.

Rachel leaned stiffly against her mother. She thought telling someone would make her cry, but she just felt numb with the shame.

'I can see now why you didn't like hearing Natasha crowing about her success,' said Joy, wishing her youngest daughter could learn to be a little more sensitive about all that. Maybe she'd lived in New York too long.

'I don't resent Natasha her success,' said Rachel, sitting up straight and turning to look at Joy. 'I really don't. I'm happy for her, I'm proud of her, but it does make me feel like a failure, because I've got myself into the situation I'm in. It was me who overspent, I can't blame anyone else, but that was why I was so upset about what she did with Branko. It meant that on top of all my anxiety about money, I suddenly had childcare to worry about as well and the brilliant thing about the arrangement I had with him, was that it gave him what he needed and hardly cost me anything. Natasha didn't give any of that a moment's thought.'

'I can see that,' said Joy. 'She acted very thoughtlessly.'

'I'm thrilled for Branko though,' said Rachel, tears now beginning to well up. 'I really am. I would never have expected him to give up an opportunity like that. It was just the way Natasha didn't involve me in any of it, just went ahead and did it, as though I didn't matter, that was so hurtful, and then specifically telling him not to tell me ...'

Joy looked at Rachel closely.

'Did she really do that?'

'That's what Branko told me,' said Rachel. 'He'd wanted to talk to me about it, but Natasha asked him not to.'

'Well, that was high-handed of her,' said Joy. 'I can see why you were so upset. Did she try to contact you, to explain?'

'She came to the office,' said Rachel, 'but I just wasn't ready to talk to her then, it was too soon, so I sent her away and I've ignored her emails and texts and things ever since. With everything that's going on with the money – I've had bailiffs ringing up, Mum, I had to give them my engagement ring on Tuesday, or they were going to come to the house and take things – I just couldn't be dealing with that as well.'

'That's understandable,' said Joy, pulling Rachel's hand into her lap and patting it. 'When we have more than one problem the whole thing can bundle together and take on its own momentum, getting bigger and bigger like a snowball running down a mountain. The thing to do is to break it all down again, into separate bits and then try to approach them one at a time.'

'You're right,' said Rachel. 'And I think I am ready to talk to Natasha now, because I've made a decision what I've got to do about the money.'

'Really?' said Joy. 'And what is that?'

'I'm going to sell my house,' said Rachel. 'It came into my head while I was hugging that tree.'

'That's a big step,' said Joy. 'Where would you live?'

'The house has more than doubled in value since Michael and I bought it nine years ago. I can sell it, pay off the cards with the equity, and still buy a flat, possibly even without a mortgage. We don't need a big house and if I'm not wasting my energy worrying about debt, I can put all of it into work and make my own financial security.'

'I think you're very brave,' said Joy. 'It will be hard, but it does sound like it would get you out of a very difficult spot. Will you be able to keep the girls in the same school?'

Rachel thought for a moment.

'I don't know about any of that yet,' she said, 'I only just decided – well, my new tree friend decided for me. I will if I can, but if they do have to move it won't kill them. We changed school and country and didn't even go to school for one year ...'

Joy shook her head, sighing.

'I'm sorry, darling.'

'No, it's fine, Mum. It made me stronger, braver, not scared to go to new places and do new things. It made me who I am.'

Joy squeezed Rachel's hand, grateful for the absolution from something she sometimes still felt guilty about.

'And I'll tell you something else I'm going to do,' said Rachel. 'I'm going to Skype Natasha tonight.'

Rachel decided to try Natasha just before dinner. It would be early afternoon in New York and on a Saturday there was a chance she might be chilling out at home, or at her beach house. She sat on the bed in her room at Tessa's house, the iPad propped up on her knees and was pleased when Natasha responded immediately.

But then Rachel was so surprised at how her sister looked, she flinched.

'Tash?' she asked, squinting at the mess looking back at her.

It was Natasha, but not in a state Rachel had ever seen her in before. Her eyes were oddly bulging and red. Her mouth looked as though she'd been slapped, the lips all loose and puffy. Her hair was standing on end.

'Is that you, Tash?'

'Who is this?' said a voice, which sounded like Natasha's but an oddly strangulated version.

'It's your sister, Rachel,' she said tentatively.

'Rachel?' said Natasha, and started sobbing. 'I'm so sorry, I didn't mean to mess things up for you with Branko, I was so wrong ...'

'It's OK,' said Rachel, 'I was upset with you, but I'm over it. I mean, it was difficult, but anyway – I'm over it. That's why I'm Skyping you, but what the hell is going on with you, Tashie?'

Natasha's face disappeared. All Rachel could see was the top of her head, resting on her arms, and she could hear crying that was more like wailing.

'Tash!' said Rachel. 'Talk to me, what's happened?'

Natasha lifted up a face like a gargoyle, her cheeks sodden with tears. She was shaking her head.

'I can't tell you,' she said.

'Of course you can tell me,' said Rachel. 'Has somebody hurt you?'

Rachel was starting to feel really afraid. Had she been attacked? Natasha didn't answer, she was crying in that terrible way again.

'Do you need to call the police?' asked Rachel.

'No,' said Natasha, looking at Rachel properly for the first time, although her eyes didn't seem to be quite in focus. She shook her head. 'No. I did this to myself.'

I did it to myself by living a lie my whole adult life and building my whole precious career on it. So now I've lost the one person in the world who I feel totally myself with. Who loves me for who I really am. And who I could have spent the rest of my life with. Except now she's gone back to London and told me I'm a traitor to her, to myself and to my sexuality and she doesn't want me to contact her ever again. And I've thrown all that away because I didn't have the courage to be truthful about who I am.

She slumped back down onto the table and started crying again. The pain felt physical. She didn't know where to put it, where to be in her own body. Everything hurt.

'Look,' said Rachel, 'if I lived in New York, I would be coming over to your place right now – but I can't do that, so is there anyone there you can call? I don't think you should be on your own like this.'

Natasha looked up again.

'No,' she said, her expression darkening. 'There's no one I can call. I'm all alone on this one.'

'But you're not,' said Rachel, thinking how much better she'd felt since she finally rung Joy and even more so since their conversation this afternoon in the orchard. 'You're never alone, Natasha. You have us. All of us. Family. Now stay on the line, do NOT go anywhere – I'm going to get Mum.'

Natasha started to speak, a phrase which started with the word 'No ...' but Rachel cut her off.

'No, Natasha, you stay online,' she said, pointing her forefinger at the screen. 'I'm serious. If you're not still there when I get down to Mum, I will call the NYPD myself. OK?'

She jumped up from the bed, the iPad in her hand and ran down the stairs.

'Mum!' she called out. 'Where are you?'

She heard Joy's voice from the library and ran in there to find her lying on the bed with Muffin on her knee, reading a story to Daisy and Ariadne.

'I'm sorry, girls,' said Rachel, bursting in, 'but I need to talk to Granny. Please can you go and find Auntie Tessa for me and ask her to come here as quickly as possible? It's very important. I think she's over in the salvage yard ...'

After a moment's reluctance and then a gentle request from their grandmother to do as their mother asked, the girls ran out of the French windows in the direction of the yard. Rachel put the iPad against her stomach and spoke quietly to Joy.

'Mum,' she said, 'I've got Natasha on here and she's in a terrible state. I can't get her to tell me what's wrong.'

She climbed onto the bed next to Joy and handed her the iPad. Natasha's face wasn't visible any more, but they could see her chest and shoulders in a singlet. As they watched, Natasha's hand came down and landed on the tabletop, next to the computer, holding a glass. Then they saw her fill the glass from a bottle of vodka in her other hand and lift it up out of sight again.

Rachel and Joy looked at each other. Natasha hardly ever drank and now she seemed to be drinking neat vodka, at home on her own, on a Saturday afternoon.

'Natasha?' said Joy.

Natasha tilted the screen of her laptop forward so they could see her face again. Joy let out a shocked gasp when she saw her. Her hand went out and touched the screen of the iPad.

'What's happened, my love?' she asked.

Natasha closed her eyes, tears running down her cheeks. She wiped them off on her forearm, then opened her eyes, blinking as tears continued to roll out.

'Tell us what's wrong, Tashie,' said Rachel. 'Did someone hurt you?'

It was still the only thing she could think of that could have put her normally strong sister in this state.

'Me,' said Natasha, lifting the glass to her mouth and nearly draining it, then bringing it down hard on the tabletop. 'I hurt me.'

Joy and Rachel looked at each other again. Rachel hunched her shoulders and shook her head. She had no idea.

'Tell me what's happened, Natasha,' said Joy.

The Natasha-like person on the screen raked her hand through her hair, so it stood up even more and laughed bitterly.

'I've destroyed my own life,' she said, her voice slurring.

'Natasha,' said Joy, in a quiet, firm voice, 'I want you take the rest of that vodka and pour it down the sink. I don't want you to drink any more. Whatever's going on, it won't help.'

Natasha looked back at her and said nothing. Then they saw her pick up the bottle. Her arm went down again and there was a thud. It seemed she'd just dropped it onto the floor.

'OK?' she said. 'Vodka gone.'

Then she picked up the glass again and tipped it into her mouth, to drain the very last dregs from it.

Joy closed her eyes and took a breath. Rachel put her hand on her arm, seeing she was near tears and was very relieved when she saw Tessa coming in from the garden.

'What's going on?' she asked.

'Natasha's in a bad way,' said Rachel, pulling a face and gesturing with her hand for Tessa to come quickly over to the bed.

Tessa climbed up and peered at the screen.

'Tashie?' she said 'Is that you?'

Natasha hid her face in her hands.

'It's me,' she said.

'What's wrong?' asked Tessa.

Natasha lifted up her head and looked out at them and Rachel glanced at the mini screen to check that all three of them would be visible to her.

'We're all here for you, Tashie,' said Rachel, trying not to let the panic she was feeling show in her voice. Her sister was in a terrible state, drunk, at home, alone. 'Can you please tell us what's going on? What do you mean you've destroyed your own life? Has something bad happened with work?'

Natasha – or this strange new creature who looked like Natasha – snorted contemptuously.

'Something like that,' she said, 'or not. Depending how you look at it …'

Joy suddenly moved closer to the screen, as if something had just occurred to her.

'Natasha, my darling,' she said, 'is this something to do with a man?'

Natasha looked at her blankly for a moment and then she started laughing. It was an ugly sound. Not a laugh of humour, it was all bitterness.

'Come on, Tash,' said Rachel. 'Help us out a bit here, we only want to help you. You know we're on your side …'

'The thing is, Mum,' said Natasha, sounding a little bit more like herself at last. She closed her eyes for a moment, then breathed out and opened them again, looking at them all directly. 'It's not a man. It was never a man. Well, once or twice to try it, but I'm not into men. I like women. I'm a lesbian. I have sex with women. That's the problem.'

Joy, Rachel and Tessa sat and took in what she'd said. Rachel felt as though she could hear each of their brains working as they processed her statement and a lot of things fell into place. It all made perfect sense. Of course Natasha was gay. She couldn't believe they hadn't all worked it out years ago.

'It's not a problem for me, darling,' said Joy, sounding completely calm. 'I'm just sorry I've never picked up on it before, or you didn't think you could tell me. I hope you haven't suffered worrying about telling me – us?'

She turned to look at Rachel and Tessa. They were both looking surprised and smiling at the same time. Happy a mystery about their sister had been explained. Feeling stupid for not figuring it out themselves.

'That explains your butch haircut then,' said Rachel, hoping a joke might relax Natasha. 'And the girls will be thrilled to have a gay auntie … there's a girl at their school with two dads they're really jealous of.'

She looked back at the screen hoping to see normal Natasha back, now she'd finally told them what must have been eating her alive for years.

'Don't tell them,' said Natasha, harshly. 'Don't tell anyone. I've told you, but only because I could see you were about to call the cops. I'm not coming out, I'm just telling you, so you'll leave me alone.'

'What are you talking about?' said Rachel.

'Why do you want us to leave you alone?' asked Tessa. 'You know that's never going to happen.'

Joy sat up and brought the screen closer to her face.

'Natasha, my precious darling,' she said, 'I don't know what's going on with you, but something's very wrong. You can't come out to your family and then expect to go back into some kind of closet for the rest of the world. If something is keeping you from being open about your sexuality, there's something very wrong with your life. You need to come home and tell us about it, so we can help you fix it.'

Rachel and Tessa leaned in to see how Natasha reacted. As they watched, the hardness dropped away from her face. It was like watching dark storm clouds being blown away by a strong wind.

'Come over there?' she said. 'To England? London ...'

'Yes!' cried Joy, Rachel and Tessa in unison.

Natasha put both hands behind her neck and tilted her head from side to side, like an athlete limbering up. Then she sat up straight and looked out at them with something more like her normal expression. She pulled some tissues out of a box on the table and blew her nose loudly.

'You know, I think that's exactly what I need to do,' said Natasha.

'Great,' said Rachel.

'Come and stay here with us,' said Tessa.

Natasha nodded, smiling faintly. 'I will. Thank you. I'm going to book a ticket right now.'

'Tash,' said Rachel, leaning over to look at the screen more closely again, 'should you have some coffee, sober up a bit before you do anything?'

'It's OK,' said Natasha. 'I only had a few shots. I thought it would help, but it was horrible actually.'

Rachel smiled. 'That's good, although I am glad you only tried binge drinking with the lowest carb form of liquor. I'm glad you didn't let your standards slip ...'

Natasha smiled and then looked down for a moment, before meeting Rachel's eyes again.

'I'm sorry, Rachel,' she said. 'I'm really sorry I wrecked things for you. I've made a big mess of just about everything recently.'

'We've done all that,' said Rachel, 'forget it. It was a bore, but you're too important to me to keep holding on to that hurt. Like I said before, that's why I Skyped you, to tell you that.'

As she spoke, Tessa and Joy exchanged happy glances about what they were witnessing.

'Thanks, Rachel,' said Natasha, 'that means everything to me.'

'Now,' said Rachel, 'if you really are sober enough and the drunk thing was just a pose ...'

She paused to see what effect that jibe had. Natasha raised both her middle fingers at her, but she was smiling as she did it. Excellent.

'Get onto buying that air ticket so you can come and tell us what the hell is going on with you.'

'I will,' said Natasha. 'Thank you, my beautiful family. I'm going to do it right after we hang up.'

'Just let us know when you're arriving,' said Tessa. 'I'll meet you at the airport.'

'With me,' said Joy. 'We'll look after you.'

'I know,' said Natasha, still looking sad, but not completely destroyed any more. 'I know you'll look after me and I love you all. I'll be back in touch later.'

'One more thing, before you go,' said Rachel. 'I just want to confirm – you really don't want us to tell the kids, or anyone, what you just told us?'

Natasha put her hands up by her mouth, looking thoughtful.

'You know what?' she said. 'You can tell them. I've decided. I'm out. I'm going to tell the whole world.'

Joy, Rachel and Tessa cheered.

'We'll get the champers on ice,' said Rachel. 'And I'll download some k.d. lang ...'

'Fuck off,' said Natasha, but she was smiling.

'Hang on a minute,' Tessa interjected. 'If you're really ready to get this thing rolling there's someone right here you can tell now.'

Natasha licked her lips nervously.

'OK,' she said, 'I suppose I better get some practice in.'

'Finn,' Tessa called out through the door to the hall. 'Can you come in here a minute? Auntie Tashie wants to tell you something.'

'Sure,' said Finn, loping into the room, holding an enormous sandwich.

He came over to the bed, and Rachel handed him the iPad, which he took with the hand that wasn't holding the cheese-crammed doorstop.

'Hey, cool auntie,' said Finn, taking a bite of his snack. 'What gives?'

'I'm a lesbian,' said Natasha.

'Cool,' said Finn, still chewing. 'I'll introduce you to my friend Zoe, she's gay.'

He took another bite.

'That would be great,' said Natasha, 'but you better warn her, I've already got a girlfriend ... or at least I hope I have ...'

Rachel turned to Tessa and then Joy with wide eyes and an 'ooh!' face and did a happy arm dance.

'Coolio. Zoe's got a girlfriend too, you guys can hang out. See you later.'

Then, after handing the iPad back to his mum and cramming the last of the sandwich into his mouth, he headed out of the room again.

'Well, he didn't seem too bothered,' said Natasha, laughing, colour back in her cheeks. 'It'd be nice to think it would be that easy with everybody, but ... anyway, thanks, you three. It's weird and I'm quite freaked out, but I do feel much better for talking to you all. Thank you.'

Rachel, Tessa and Joy blew kisses at the screen.

'I'll let you know when my flight's due to get in,' said Natasha and, still waving at them, she clicked the call off.

Natasha closed her laptop and sat staring into space. Had she really just done that? Had she really just come out to her family? After all those years of keeping the truth locked inside, it had all happened so quickly, she'd made up her mind in an instant – but then neat vodka on an empty stomach could do that to you.

She almost felt like calling them straight back to check she had actually done it, but she didn't have to. Seconds later a text came through from Rachel.

'Hey, k.d.,' it said, 'great you are coming over. If you're going to spend some time in London while you're here, please please stay with me and the girls, we'd all love it xxx PS Can you get me Ellen DeGeneres's autograph?'

Typical Rachel. Straight in with the wisecracks, but there was her confirmation that, yes, she had just come out to her family. Blimey. She looked down at the text again and could see that as well as the silly tease, it was full of love and forgiveness. The invitation to stay was Rachel's way of confirming that. It meant a lot.

So she'd told her family – now who to tell next? Her agent? Her lawyer? Ava …? Well, there wasn't a lot to tell her. She already knew Natasha was gay, she'd made that blatantly clear. What she was looking for was Natasha's public commitment to it, so she'd have to ring her up and say something along the lines of 'Mattie and I just love your idea of putting pictures of us in *Vogue*, snogging over my lipsticks …'

She rolled the idea around in her head and tried to understand why she still didn't feel quite comfortable with it. She was out now, she'd made that decision – and she was about to call Mattie to tell her – but she still wanted to make the transition on her terms. There was something about the way Ava had handled that meeting which still felt a little like bullying.

Natasha stood up from the table and immediately had to steady herself. What had possessed her to drink neat vodka like that? Complete desolation and terror mostly, at the prospect of losing her brand and the woman she loved, unless she went public about her sexuality.

Looking down at the floor she saw that all the vodka had run out of the bottle and soaked into the rug. Bending carefully to avoid another dizzy spell, she picked up the bottle and took it out to the kitchen. On the way she caught sight of herself in a mirror in the hallway and nearly jumped with fright. She looked terrible. No wonder her family had freaked out when they saw her.

Grabbing a herbal energy drink out of the fridge, she glugged half of it down on the way to the bathroom, then continued to swig mouthfuls as she stripped off her clothes and stuffed them into the laundry basket. She needed to start afresh, everything clean and new.

She stepped into the shower and turned it on full, letting the water pour down over her head, washing away the dirty furtiveness of carrying such an immense secret around with her for so many years. Preparing for a fresh new start. With total honesty. The names of the people she had to tell going round and round in her head, as she lathered up the shampoo. Mattie. Agent. Lawyer. Ava ...

Mattie was the one she was excited about telling. She was absolutely certain all the hurt and rancour of that last awful day they'd had together would disappear the moment she told her she'd already come out to her family.

Her agent might need to sit with the news for a while, weighing up any negative implications there could be, but as a gay man himself, she couldn't see it being that much of a problem. And she had a strong suspicion he'd just laugh and say he'd always known.

She didn't know quite what she would say to her lawyer – probably just tell her what had happened in that last strange meeting with Ava, to put her in the picture and see if she had any comments to make about it.

But every time her thoughts came back to Ava she found herself getting stuck again. What was she going to say to her? Yes, Miss Capel, you were absolutely right, I am gay and I need to start being honest about it ... How had she put it? I am ready, finally, to own every part of myself.

That was true, she was, but not because Ava had told her she had to, in case the famous make-up artist's sexuality was disastrously revealed after the launch, putting the brand and OM's investment at risk.

She wasn't doing it for Ava or OM. She was doing it for Mattie. And herself. On her own terms.

Wednesday, 16 July

Sydney Street

Rachel had felt a little shy with Simon since they'd had that rather unexpected conversation in the café. She couldn't believe she'd opened up to him like that, and that he'd been so caring and thoughtful in response.

Now she needed to go and ask him for a favour and she felt awkward doing it, because he'd already been so kind to her. She didn't want him to think she was taking advantage. Which was funny, because previously, when she still thought of him as the enemy boss man, she wouldn't have thought twice about doing that. In fact, it would have amused her. She hadn't quite worked out their strange new semi-friend status yet, so she'd been slightly avoiding him ever since that day.

She was hanging around on the bottom step of the stairs outside his office wondering what to do – she'd started back up and come down again twice already – when he suddenly came round the corner.

'Rachel,' he said, stepping back in surprise. 'Whatever are you doing there? Are you lurking?'

'Yes,' she said. 'I need to come and talk to you, but I was just working out what to say ...'

Simon looked puzzled. He bloody well hoped she wasn't going to hand in her resignation or something terrible like that.

'Well, you'd better come into my office then,' he said, half tempted to suggest they go out to talk about it in that funny old coffee bar, but stopping himself just in time. He was a little concerned he'd gone a bit far that day already. Lending her his jacket had felt dangerously intimate. She'd looked so vulnerable and adorable in it.

Sitting down at his desk now, over a week later, he reminded himself to get back into professional mode. He'd hardly seen her since that strange, otherworldly afternoon and he wondered which of them had been avoiding the other more.

Rachel sat down opposite him and found her eyes immediately drawn to his jacket. It was the same one he'd lent her that day. She wished she could go and take a big sniff of it. She could smell his cologne faintly in the air of his office, but it wasn't the same as it had been bonded into the weave of the fabric by his body warmth. Mixed with his man smell.

She tore her eyes away from the fine navy blue wool and looked at his face. Get it together, girlfriend, she told herself.

'So, what did you want to talk to me about?' he said.

'It's really boring, Simon,' she said, 'it's a childcare thing and I know how all that irritates you.'

'Don't pre-judge,' he said. 'Spill.'

'Well,' said Rachel, 'I went down to my sister's at the weekend ...'

'Yes ...' he asked cautiously, still hoping she wasn't going to bring up the idea of doing Hunter Gatherer again, but she'd said it was something about childcare, so probably not.

'Actually,' said Rachel, unable to keep to the script she'd been rehearsing on the stairs, 'it's thanks to you I was down there, Simon. I can't thank you enough. It was what you said that finally got me to ring my mum and Tessa and then I went down with the girls and we had a wonderful time. And I made up with Natasha as well, so you're my new Kofi Annan.'

Simon chuckled. 'Well, I've been called a lot of things in my time, but it's very kind of you to give me that much credit. I'm sure I don't deserve it, but I'm delighted to hear you've sorted things out with your family. So what was the childcare thing you mentioned?'

'Well, when we got back from that lovely weekend away,' said Rachel, 'Pilar – remember, the au pair who took over from Branko, the bearded bride?'

Simon nodded. 'Not an image I would forget easily.'

'Quite. He looked amazing. Anyway, when we got back Pilar had left a note on the kitchen table to tell me she's got a gig dancing on a cruise ship and she had to leave immediately. So she's gone. No warning.'

'That's seriously crap,' said Simon.

'I know,' said Rachel, 'but when you only offer room and board, no wages, with no formal contract, you can't expect much loyalty. That's why Branko was such a marvel. He actually liked living with us.'

'So you've got no one to help you with the girls now?'

'Nope,' said Rachel, 'and the thing is, the last two nights I got mothers from school to have them until I got home and that was all cool, but today I don't have anyone. I've asked everyone I can think of and all their kids have archery and tennis and Chinese flute and bollocks like that, so what I need to ask you is – can I leave early?'

'Of course,' said Simon, without a moment's hesitation. 'What time?'

Rachel rushed to answer, before he could change his mind. She could hear herself gabbling but she didn't care. She had to nail this down.

'Well, they can stay on at school for an hour doing a club, so could we say, er, three? Then I would definitely be able to get there by four to collect them without panicking.'

'Fine,' said Simon. Just like that.

'Oh, thank you, Simbo ...'

Oops. It had slipped out before she realised, but he didn't seem to mind. He was smiling at her in that kind way again.

'I tell you what,' he continued, 'until you get a new nanny, you can leave at that time every day. It's fine with me.'

'Really?' she said.

'Yeah,' said Simon, 'you get more done here in a morning than your colleagues do in a week anyway – plus I know you work at home in the evenings as well, don't you? I've been reading your blog.'

Rachel nodded, feeling her cheeks grow a little warm.

'What do you think?' she said, knowing it was a needy question, but asking it anyway.

'I think it's great and I'd like you to do a house blog for Rathbone & Associates – writing about all the stuff we have going on, in a kind of company voice, if that makes sense, but so it has the personal charm of a blog, not like a corporate website. Does that appeal?'

'You bet it does,' said Rachel.

'Good. So how about we make that the special project you're working on for me at home – in case any of your co-workers start asking where you are?'

'Fantastic,' said Rachel. 'I'll start sketching it out tonight. We can do click-through to our clients' sites, so if they sell anything from a referral off our blog, we get a cut – and we can sell advertising on it as well, if we do it as a hosted WordPress site ...'

Simon smiled. There she went. Catching the idea and running with it. She'd already turned it into a revenue stream and she hadn't left his office yet. Such a dynamo. Like some kind of super-massive galactic entity, a constantly expanding ball of energy. She made him feel excited about his own business again.

Rachel headed out of Simon's office and he heard her feet running up the stairs at a fast lick. Sometimes he thought the two of them would get more done on their own, without all the hassle of a big staff distracting him from the core business of the company he'd set up on his own in his flat twenty years before. Every extra person he employed just seemed to bring another raft of time-wasting problems with them. And now there was the nightmare of the massive rent rise as well.

Simon turned around in his chair and looked out of his window onto Sydney Street. The day he'd moved into that building he'd felt like he'd finally made it. Achieved what he'd set out to do. He'd certainly proved himself by his own standards – even if it had never been enough for his disappointed father.

But now he was starting to wonder. He turned back again and considered the elegant proportions of the room. It was a very lovely office to have, but was it worth the sleepless nights it was causing him?

A piercing shriek of laughter from the hall outside snapped his attention back to the present. Putting his head on one side he listened carefully to find out what was making two of his staff so excited.

From what he could gather, they were both chartering yachts in Croatia that summer – and it seemed it might even be from the same charter company. Amazing! He just wished they could be that enthusiastic about what he was paying them to do.

Simon opened his top drawer and pulled out a cigar he'd been saving. It was time for a long walk, a slow smoke and a big think.

Cranbrook

Tessa, Tom and Joy were sitting at the kitchen table lingering after breakfast. Hector cycled to school every day now so, apart from making sure he left on time, the morning rush was a thing of the past. Tessa had missed it keenly at first, she'd felt pointless, but now Tom was back in body and in spirit, she'd learned to appreciate the luxury of a leisurely mid-week morning with him.

Tom and Joy were doing the easy crossword together, which had become their daily ritual. Tom said it helped to keep the brain nimble and Joy was turning out to be surprisingly good at them.

'Irish lake, five letters …?' said Tom.

'Lough,' said Joy.

'Isn't that four letters – L, O, C, H?' said Tom.

'That's the Scottish spelling,' said Joy. 'The Irish is L, O, U, G, H.'

'Really?' said Tom, reaching for his phone and tapping open the Google app. 'You're right. How annoying. OK, clever clogs, try this: Edmund something, seven letters, poet, starts with S …'

'Spenser,' said Joy, without hesitation. 'With a second S …'

Tessa zoned out, as they argued over the spelling and Joy said it was cheating for Tom to keep looking on his phone. Crosswords were not her thing and when she heard the clang of the letterbox closing she went out to the hall to collect the post, happy for the distraction.

Leafing through it on her way back to the kitchen –
mostly unsolicited catalogues she would put straight into the
recycling – Tessa saw there was another of those letters for
her mum's old lodger, Elsie, with the coincidental Lambton
surname.

'More post for your friend Elsie,' she said, dropping it onto
the table, as she noticed there was a Toast catalogue hidden
among the dross. That was worth a look.

Joy's head snapped up. After all the years of being Joy, it
took her by surprise that her childhood name still grabbed
her attention like that. She hoped Tessa hadn't noticed her
reaction.

'You made me jump,' she said, to cover up, reaching out for
the unwanted envelope and placing it out of sight on her lap.

Then seeing that Tessa was distracted looking through
something that had arrived for her, Joy left the table, headed
for the downstairs loo as fast as she could on her sticks, and
bolted the door behind her. Something she'd seen on the back
of this envelope had alerted her that this was one she needed
to look at more closely. In private.

Putting down the lid of the loo, she sat on it, closing her
eyes and trying to steady her breathing. Her heart was racing
so fast, she felt quite nauseous. She wasn't wearing any of her
crystals and wished she could go and get her rose quartz, but
she couldn't move from where she was.

Opening her eyes again, she turned the envelope over to
check the return address on the back and confirmed what
she'd thought when she'd first spotted the logo on the front.

This was the letter she had dreaded, but deep down
also desperately wanted to receive. It was from an agency
that helped adopted children to contact their birth parents.
Addressed to her, in the name she'd had when she'd given birth

to a son fifty-five years before, when she was just nineteen years old, his birth the reason her parents had cut her off.

She had to acknowledge to herself now, that from the moment she'd seen the first envelope addressed to her old name, a very small voice in the innermost part of herself had been telling her this was what it was about, but she'd refused to listen.

Now there was no escaping it. She recognised the logo on the envelope, because she'd seen it months before, chancing across an article about the agency in a newspaper she'd been leafing through in a café one morning, waiting for a friend to arrive.

For a very brief moment then she'd considered making a note of the agency's name and looking into it herself, but then her friend had turned up and she'd put it all out of her mind again, although it seemed her subconscious had retained the image of the logo.

So here was another secret coming to light, exactly as she'd expected. It had just never occurred to her it would be her own.

Joy took a deep breath and opened the envelope.

Thursday, 17 July

Sydney Street

Rachel had just put the phone down after confirming a breakfast meeting the following morning, with a bespoke curtain tie-back company she was very close to signing up for the agency, when it rang again.

'Rachel?' said Tessa's voice, sounding like she was down a well. 'Is that you?'

'Yes,' said Rachel. 'Where the hell are you?'

'I'm in the laundry,' said Tessa, whispering, 'I can't talk any louder …'

'What's going on?' asked Rachel.

'Natasha's here,' she said.

'Oh, that's great,' said Rachel, 'I didn't know we were expecting her today, did …'

Tessa cut her off.

'She didn't let us know, she just turned up half an hour ago in a taxi – all the way from Heathrow. She's in a bit of a state again, Rachel.'

'Again? But she's already told us the big secret.'

'That's all part of it,' said Tessa. 'Can you possibly come down? Mum and I are doing our best, but we need you,

Rachel. You understand all the business stuff and we keep saying the wrong things.'

'The business stuff?'

'They've cancelled her range, Rachel,' said Tessa. 'It's awful. She's in bits.'

'They've cancelled it because she's gay?' said Rachel. 'There are laws against that and I know she had some kind of big-shot lawyer negotiate the deal, so surely they couldn't pull that on her.'

'Well, it seems to be more complicated than that. They don't seem to mind her being gay, but she's had a big row with them over something else to do with it and they've cancelled the whole thing and she's in a terrible state. She's not really making a lot of sense and we need you, Rachel. You'll be able to get it out of her.'

'I'll be there as soon as I can,' said Rachel.

She sat back in her chair, her head spinning. Natasha had lost her deal? It was so dreadful, she couldn't process it. She had to get down there straight away – but what about the girls?

She knew she couldn't ask any of the mothers at the school. She'd noticed groups of them talking together would go quiet when she arrived at the school gate. She clearly already had a reputation as a user mum. And she couldn't ask Michael, because she knew he was away for business.

Her brain whirled as she threw things into her handbag, then closed down her computer. She'd have to come back up to town later, even if she could find someone to look after the girls, because she had that meeting with Passementerie de Paris in the morning, when she was fairly certain they were going to sign up. The contract documents were printed out already and she was glad she'd thought of it, grabbing them off her desk and putting them in her bag.

There was nothing for it, she'd just have to get the girls out of school again – they'd only been there an hour, she'd have to cite forgotten dental appointments – and take them with her, but first she'd have to ask Simon yet another favour. A whole day off. That was pushing it.

He wasn't in his office, but as she paused outside wondering what to do she caught the scent of his cologne on the air and followed it like a bloodhound. She found him downstairs, just opening the front door onto the street.

'Simon!' she called out. 'Can I have a quick word before you leave?'

'Sure,' he said, 'I was just going back to my car, I left something in it.'

'I'll walk with you,' she said.

'Is everything OK?' he asked, noticing she looked unusually flustered.

'Yes, no,' she said, 'this is so embarrassing, but I've got another family drama childcare nightmare going on.'

'Tell me,' he said.

Rachel stopped and turned to him.

'My sister Natasha …' my newly out lesbian sister, how much should she tell him? 'Natasha has come back from New York unexpectedly. Tessa just rang to tell me that she's turned up at her house in a taxi all the way from Heathrow in a terrible state, because – you know she was doing her own range with OM?'

Simon nodded.

'Well, it's been cancelled.'

Something about the way he was looking at her made her want to tell him the whole story. If she had more time, she'd suggest they went back to that café. She could imagine telling him everything in there and she'd love to know what he'd say in response.

'Shall we go and get coffee and talk about this?' said Simon.
Rachel smiled despite her anxiety.

'I'd love to, Simon, but I don't think I've got time now.'

'Just tell me what you need,' he said, 'and then we'll take it
from there.'

'I need the day off, so I can go down there and help
comfort Natasha – just today because I've got a breakfast
meeting with Passementerie de Paris tomorrow. I've got the
contract in my bag all ready for them to sign and I'm not
missing it, but I've got to go and collect the girls from school
first.'

'Hang on a minute,' said Simon, 'you're going to take the
girls down to Tessa's with you? Take them out of school?'

'Yes, like I told you yesterday, I have no au pair and there's
no one left for me to ask for after-school care favours, so I'll
just have to take them with me. There's nothing else for it.'

Simon thought for a moment, biting his lip.

'I'll look after them,' he said.

Rachel looked at him, blinking, assuming she'd heard him
wrong.

'What?' she asked, stupidly. She couldn't have heard that
right.

'I said, I'll collect the girls from school and stay with
them until you get back. Just text me the name and address
of their school – and the name of whoever I need to convince
I'm not a kidnapper – the time they need to be collected,
and I'll do it. And give me your house keys, so I can take
them home.'

'Are you serious?' said Rachel. 'Will you know what to do
with them?'

'No,' said Simon, 'but from what I've seen of Daisy, I'm
sure she'll tell me.'

'You are seriously going to collect my daughters from school? You know you'll have to leave work at three-fifteen latest, take them home, feed them etc.?'

'It can't be rocket science,' said Simon. 'I manage to do those things for myself.'

'Well, if you're sure, that would be wonderful – I don't know how I'll ever thank you. I'll ring the school to let them know a strange man in a sinister car is picking them up today, but I must admit I'm amazed.'

'I have a vested interest in keeping you happy at work,' said Simon. More than one, actually. 'And I don't want you to miss that meeting tomorrow either. That new business would be more welcome than you know.'

'Really?' said Rachel, looking at him with an eyebrow raised. 'When I'm over this crisis, you'll have to tell me more about that.'

'Yes,' said Simon, realising he did want to tell her. She was the only person in the world he wanted to tell. 'And that we will do in the café.'

Our café, he thought.

Our café, thought Rachel. Crikey. Then she realised she was standing on the corner of Sydney Street staring up at him like a gawping fish. She glanced at her watch.

'If I go now, I might make the eleven-fifteen ...' she groped in her bag. 'Here are my keys. I'll text you the school address stuff and ring them from the train.'

'OK,' he said, nodding with his kind face again.

Rachel touched his hand very lightly with hers.

'Thank you, Simbo,' she said quietly, and set off for South Kensington station at a run, feeling a funny little quiver in her stomach.

Cranbrook

Rachel caught the train with only seconds to spare, leaping into the back carriage just before the whistle blew, so when it pulled into Staplehurst, she had a long walk along the platform to the exit.

As she reached the door into the station building, she passed a woman looking a bit lost. Rachel turned round to ask her if she needed help and realised she knew her.

Rachel never forgot a face. It was a skill she'd worked hard at developing, because it was crucial for her job. She couldn't remember her name, but she knew she'd met her before.

'Hi,' she said, going up to the woman, who clearly recognised her, too. Then Rachel remembered who she was. It was the make-up artist from the Lawn & Stone shoot, the nice Aussie woman who Natasha had got on so well with …

Rachel could almost hear the clang as the penny dropped in her own head. Duh! She hated making stereotypical assumptions, but the two of them were like brunette and blonde versions of each other, the short hair, the tattoos, although Natasha was much taller and this woman had a more classically pretty face. She was like an adorable kitten with a short back and sides.

'I'm Rachel,' she continued, 'we met at my sister Tessa's house on that shoot for *You* mag.'

'Mattie,' she said, putting out her hand and shaking Rachel's. 'Good to see you again.'

'We were on the same train and didn't know, that's so annoying,' said Rachel. 'We could have chatted. Do you need a hand getting somewhere?'

'I'm actually going to Tessa's house, Rachel,' said Mattie. 'I'm going to see Natasha. I assume that's where you're going?'

Rachel nodded slowly. 'So you know what's happened?' she asked.

'Yes,' said Mattie.

'It's so shocking,' said Rachel. 'I'm bewildered, but let's get ourselves over there so we can find out more. I told them I'd get a taxi – or are they meeting you?'

'Natasha doesn't know I'm coming,' said Mattie, smiling shyly. 'I just came down on a hunch …'

Rachel thought for a moment. As there was clearly something else going on here apart from the outrage perpetrated by OM against her sister, it would be helpful to know what it was before she saw Natasha.

'Shall we have a quick coffee before we go to Tessa's?' she asked.

Mattie nodded, looking grateful.

They collected their drinks from the counter but the station café was so small, Rachel suggested they take them outside. She didn't need to say why, it was obvious – so they could talk more freely. The moment they were settled on a bench, she got straight into it.

'Natasha has told us she's gay, Mattie,' she said, 'and we all just wish she'd told us years ago. So many things make sense now.'

'I know,' said Mattie, 'I told her you'd all be cool about it. I knew how lovely you all were after meeting the whole family at the shoot, but she was just so scared because of her work. She thought she'd lose all her big clients – and now look what's happened? She was right.'

'But Tessa said it's not because she's come out,' said Rachel, 'it's some other reason. Do you know what happened?'

'It's complicated,' said Mattie. 'They didn't cancel it because she's gay, but because she won't be gay they want her to be gay.'

'OK ...' said Rachel, not feeling any wiser.

Mattie sighed deeply.

'They saw us together,' said Mattie. 'One of the executives from OM saw us holding hands on the street in New York and dobbed her in to the big boss and that was it, they called Natasha into the office the next day and ...'

'Just because they saw you holding hands?' said Rachel, incredulous.

'Well, it's more complicated than that, they carried on as though they had known she was gay all along and that was fine, they were totally cool with it, but then they wanted to use Natasha's sexuality – and our relationship – as a kind of novelty marketing thing. They wanted to do a big shoot at her Long Island house for *Vogue*, with us doing make-up on each other ... You know, her up close painting my lips, that kind of thing.'

'A bit of soft-focus girl-on-girl action?' asked Rachel.

Mattie smiled, clearly relieved Rachel got it without any more explanation being necessary.

'They even suggested "Girl on Girl" as a cover line,' she said.

Rachel laughed in appalled astonishment.

'Are you kidding me? Hot lesbo make-up session ... Lipstick lezzers get their gloss on ... Oh, that's just awful, no wonder Natasha's upset.'

Mattie laughed too. 'I'm so glad you understand,' she said.

'Well,' said Rachel, 'I've never seen Charlotte Tilbury or Bobbi Brown fellating a lipstick to advertise their make-up brands – or Tom Ford for that matter.'

'You totally get it,' said Mattie, but she sighed and looked regretful as she spoke. 'But unfortunately, I didn't.'

Rachel studied Mattie's face intently, but didn't say anything.

'When she came back and told me what they'd said at that meeting, and tried to talk all her confusion about it over with me, I wouldn't listen,' Mattie continued. 'All I could say was that if she wasn't prepared to come out and be totally at ease with it and everything involved in that then she couldn't really love me. I told her she was a weekend lesbian and then I stormed out telling her never to contact me again and went to stay with a friend until it was time for me to fly back to London. She had no idea where I was.'

Rachel reached over and squeezed Mattie's hand. She could see she was close to tears.

'And even when she rang me,' Mattie continued, 'and left a message telling me she'd come out to you guys and it was all great and she was going to tell her agent and lawyer next and she was really happy she'd done it, I still wouldn't speak to her. I just couldn't get over the fact that she hadn't been happy and relieved that the people at OM didn't mind her being gay. Still having doubts after that seemed like a betrayal.'

Rachel thought for a moment before she spoke. It was complicated. Very complicated.

'I think it was a normal reaction to a very weird situation to be shocked and hurt,' she said. 'And I think I can understand why you were disappointed in her initial reaction. You would've expected her to be thrilled that they didn't have a problem with it – and that clouded the other issues for you.'

Mattie nodded and smiled. 'Thanks, Rachel,' she said, 'I think you understand it better than I do.'

'Had you been together long?' asked Rachel.

'Since we met on that shoot down here,' said Mattie.

That made sense, thought Rachel. She remembered something Daisy had said about 'Natasha's new best friend Mattie'. Children always picked up on these things.

'So when did Natasha let you know she was coming here?' said Rachel.

'She didn't,' said Mattie. 'I rang her in New York yesterday, the moment I heard the news about her range being cancelled – things get around our industry pretty quickly. Then when she didn't get back to me, I rang her agent who told me she'd gone to London and I guessed she might have come down here. I thought it was worth a try.'

'Wow,' said Rachel. 'So you haven't actually spoken to her since you had the row after that awful meeting? You're really putting yourself on the line, I'm impressed, Mattie – and I've got your back. If Natasha isn't too pleased to see you at first, I'll be there for you, to help bring her round. Now, let's go and find a taxi.'

Mattie and Rachel needn't have worried. The expression on Natasha's face when the two of them walked into the library, where she was sitting on Joy's bed hunched over a mug of tea, turning from misery, to surprise, to joy was like watching time-lapse photography. Tentative at first, not quite sure she was seeing right and then the full realisation that Mattie really was there and smiling at her.

She sprang up from the bed and the two women locked together in an embrace.

'Oh Mattie,' Natasha sobbed, 'you're here. You came and found me ...'

'I'm sorry,' Mattie was saying at the same time, 'I'm so sorry I stormed out on you and ignored your calls. I was wrong.'

Catching a hard stare from Joy, who had climbed off the bed with remarkable speed for someone still recovering from hip surgery, Tessa and Rachel headed off to the kitchen with her on the pretext of making tea.

Keeping her voice down, Rachel filled them in about her and Mattie getting off the same train at Staplehurst, what Mattie had told her about their relationship, and why Natasha had the big falling out with OM. Joy was smiling happily to herself, holding tight to one of her crystals.

'Synchronicity,' she said, 'you two being on the same train. Very good news.'

'Mattie's very good news all around, as far as I can tell,' said Rachel. 'Fancy them meeting here, eh, Tessa? What an emotionally charged day that was. Natasha seeing the potential for Branko being the next Kate Moss and meeting Mattie all on the same afternoon.'

And Simon playing skittles so adorably with the girls, she thought.

Tessa made sure she didn't catch Joy's eye. Emotionally charged indeed.

Joy was still smiling, eyes closed, now holding three crystals. Off to Planet Neenar, thought Rachel.

'This house must be on some powerful ley lines, eh, Mum?' she said, winking at Tessa, who shook her head, smiling indulgently.

'Something like that, darling,' said Joy, her eyes still tight shut, praying hard that the positive energies in the house would help her welcome another family member into it.

'Are you going to stay over, Rachie?' asked Tessa.

'I can't,' she said, 'I've got to go back for the girls. Michael's away and now that Pilar's done a runner on me, it's a bit hard getting people to help out with childcare. I didn't tell you that, did I? The new nanny left the other day without any warning ... just a note on the kitchen table. Found it when I got back from here last Sunday. Heinous, but I don't want to talk about it in front of Natasha and make her feel bad about it. She's got enough to deal with.'

'That's very thoughtful of you, darling,' said Joy, her eyes open again. 'But that's terrible about the nanny leaving you in the lurch like that. What have you done about the girls today?'

Her mother was looking at her rather intently. She certainly wasn't going to tell them that Simon was the new Mary Poppins, it was just too weird. She still couldn't quite believe it herself.

'Oh, I was able to get someone to have them for a few hours ... it'll be fine, but I have to get back reasonably early. I've got an important meeting tomorrow morning.'

Joy was still looking a bit beady-eyed, so Rachel was relieved when Natasha and Mattie came into the kitchen, their arms round each other, looking very happy and a bit shy.

'You all met Mattie at the shoot, back in May,' said Natasha, 'but now I can introduce her to you properly as my ... well, my partner, I guess.'

'Hi, Mattie, Tashie's partner,' said Rachel, grinning and waving at her.

'Welcome back, Mattie,' said Tessa.

'Welcome to our family,' said Joy, standing up and walking over to them, putting an arm around each one and pulling them close to her. She kissed each of them tenderly on the top of their heads.

'Love and light,' she said.

Rachel nearly got the giggles. Joy carried on like a new-age pope sometimes, but it was all so well meant she didn't think Mattie would be too put off. In fact, she looked as though she liked it. That was good. She'd have to get used to all kinds of carry-on like that, if she was going to be hanging around with their tribe.

Over lunch, Natasha explained the legal details of her situation; how OM had a clause in the contract that meant they could cancel the deal at any time up to six months prior to the launch, with no redress, compensation or explanation.

Her lawyer had questioned it, but they'd refused to budge, and Natasha had decided to accept it, because it was that or no deal – and she'd been so certain they would never use it.

'That's probably the thing that's killing me the most now,' she said, holding Mattie's hand on her lap. 'If I'd been honest with my lawyer and my agent about all this from the outset they could have protected me better, but I thought I could just carry on living behind my lie as I have all these years ...'

'You don't think you could make yourself some kind of new test case for gay rights?' asked Rachel. 'A more subtle form of discrimination? Forcing you to exploit your sexuality against your wishes.'

'I don't know,' said Natasha. 'It's difficult because none of it was ever discussed in clear language. It's all in this weird double talk.'

She screwed up her face into a fake smile.

'"Well, if you don't feel you can give the brand identity your full support by doing the kind of personal publicity we feel is required in the current market, we aren't certain how we can take it forward with you."

'They never actually came out and said: you're a big dyke and we want to sell your range with you as a lezzer poster girl, because it's a new angle and it will make us look modern and cool. Or: we've got to be clear from the start that you're a deviant, or there will be a revolt if you get outed after the launch. They just talked all this bullshit and in the end I lost it and it was actually me who said, all right if you won't let me do it as I want to, cancel the contract then – and they did.'

Everyone tutted and exclaimed how outrageous it was, but after that had all died down Rachel spoke.

'Were you calling their bluff?' she asked.

Natasha looked back at her steadily. Rachel always got to the heart of it. 'Yes,' she said, sadly. 'I really didn't think they'd cancel, not after we'd got so far along with development and they'd announced it to the press and everything, but they did.'

'Do you regret it?' said Rachel.

Natasha turned and looked at Mattie and then back at Rachel. 'No,' she said. 'I don't. They were bullies. Well, one of them was. It was really just one of them and I realise now, I don't want to work with her. If I'm going to do a range – and I am still going to do one – it has to be on my terms.'

They all clapped and cheered and congratulated her on her positive attitude and then, after it had died down, it was Natasha who spoke again.

'And although we got a bit mixed up about it all for a moment back there, the person who's helped me understand all that is sitting right here. Thank you, Mattie ...'

She leaned forward and kissed her on the lips

* * *

A few hours later, Rachel was back on the train, smiling at the memory of Mattie and Natasha's reunion. She rang her house to check in with Simon and the girls, but there was no reply. At 6.30 p.m.? She rang Simon's mobile.

'Hi,' she said. 'Is that Mrs Doubtfire?'

'Hello, Rachel,' said Simon.

She could hear a lot of noise in the background.

'It's your mum, girls,' he said, 'do you want to speak to her?'

'No,' Rachel heard Daisy saying, 'tell her hi, we'll see her later.'

'Well, that's nice,' said Rachel, 'I'm away for one afternoon and they've already forgotten me.'

'They have rather large ice creams in front of them,' said Simon, 'demanding their full attention.'

'Where are you?' she asked him.

'Fortnum's.'

'Are you serious?'

'Well, I had to eat something as well.'

'They'll never be the same again, but thank you so much. I should be back by eight, latest. I'll see you then.'

Rachel hung up, smiling to herself at the thought of her two darlings in their summer school dresses, sitting opposite Simon in his beautiful suit in the Fortnum's Fountain restaurant. She hoped they were behaving, but he hadn't sounded stressed, so perhaps they were. Blimey.

It was a lovely image, but it made her feel unsettled. She didn't know where to file it in her head, so she got the Passementerie de Paris contract out of her bag and ran through it again.

She'd been immersed in that for a while when she realised the train had come to a standstill, with no station in sight. Then the driver's voice came over the loudspeaker announcing there was a signal failure between Tonbridge and Sevenoaks and the service would be delayed for 'an indeterminate period'.

Rachel texted Simon and wondered who it was, exactly, Joy prayed to when she needed help.

Queen's Park

It was after nine by the time Rachel got home. Simon's car was parked outside, so she knew they were there, but he wasn't in the kitchen. Then she heard the sound of the TV from the sitting room and found him, jacket and shoes off, stretched out on the sofa fast asleep. Looking down at his relaxed face, all the usual tension gone, Rachel felt she was seeing him for the first time. He really was a good-looking man.

Not wanting to disturb him – or have him wake up to find her staring at him like a weirdo – she went quietly upstairs. The girls' bedroom was empty, but peeping around the door into her own room she found them both in her bed, clutching teddies, looking angelic. There was a pile of sugar sachets emblazoned with the Fortnum & Mason logo sitting on the bedside table – either a present for her, or supplies for a midnight feast.

Rachel pulled the duvet up over them, ran her hand over each of their dear heads and headed downstairs again, wondering how to wake Simon up. That was an interesting etiquette teaser. How do you wake your boss when he's conked out on your sofa?

So she was greatly relieved to find him now sitting up, blinking. His hair was all messy and she had to stop herself smoothing it down, as she'd just done with her daughters.

'Ah, Rachel,' he said, 'you're back. Sorry, nodded off on your sofa there for a moment.'

'That's fine,' she said, 'I'm so sorry I'm late, the bloody train got delayed, we were just sitting there for over an hour.'

'Don't worry about it. I got your text.'

'Were the girls OK?'

'They were good fun,' said Simon.

'They went to bed all right?'

'Not bad. I had to push them rather on the teeth-cleaning front and I was forced to read several tedious stories about a mouse who likes ballet dancing, but it was fine.'

'I don't know how I can ever thank you,' said Rachel.

I could think of quite a few ways, thought Simon. Several of them not for discussion in polite society.

'How's Natasha?' he asked.

'She's OK,' said Rachel. 'Not bad considering. Very bruised and battered by the experience, but I think she'll be much happier in the long run, than she was before.'

'That sounds good,' he said, pushing on his shoes and then standing up, looking around for his jacket.

Rachel picked it up off the arm of the chair next to her and handed it to him, resisting the temptation to bury her face in it first.

'Thanks,' he said, shrugging it on and then reaching up to smooth down his hair. 'Do I look unkempt?'

Rachel laughed. 'A little. There's a mirror in the hall.'

'Bloody hell,' said Simon, standing in front of it and getting a comb out of his pocket. 'Einstein. You could have told me ...'

'I didn't want to be rude, when you've been so kind and helpful. Would you like some coffee, or a drink or something?' she added, walking through to the kitchen.

Simon joined her, looking more like his normal self, his hair combed back, his collar sitting perfectly inside his lapels, a glimpse of pristine white cuffs at the end of his jacket sleeves. He glanced at his watch.

'Thanks for the offer, but I'd better go,' he said. 'I'll see you in the morning.'

'OK,' said Rachel, leading the way out of the kitchen and back down the hall to the front door.

Simon joined her in the small vestibule by the door as she opened it, standing very close to her. She felt her mouth go a little dry. He was so close she could smell him, behind the cologne, his own unique smell. She looked up at him to find he was gazing down at her. Realising her lips had parted very slightly, she quickly closed them. Was she breathing heavily? She hoped he couldn't hear.

She was so close, he would only have to move his head a couple of inches and he could kiss her. Should he do it? She wasn't moving away.

'Well, I'll see you tomorrow then,' said Simon, forcing himself to break the moment.

'Yes,' said Rachel, very brightly, as though he'd said something very fascinating and important.

'Good luck with that meeting tomorrow ...'

'Aha, fingers crossed,' she said. Jolly fucking hockey sticks.

'I'll be off then,' he said, making himself put one foot out of the door.

'Simon,' said Rachel, suddenly, touching his arm.

He realised he was staring down at her hand resting on his sleeve. He just so wanted it to stay there.

'Thank you,' she said, 'for looking after the girls. Thank you so much.'

'It's nothing,' he said, 'really ... it was fun ...' and he managed to take a couple more steps away from her. It was like playing Giant's Footsteps, but in the opposite direction.

'I'll buy you a coffee to say thank you,' she said, as he finally made it to the gate.

He looked back at her and smiled broadly. A coffee. In their café. That would be good.

After he'd gone, Rachel gave up on trying to fit into her own bed with the two girls already so deeply asleep in it, arms and legs everywhere, and tried to make herself comfortable in Daisy's, under her map-of-the-world duvet cover.

She couldn't sleep. So much was rattling around in her brain from the day. Running into Mattie at the station. The shock of Natasha's latest news. Seeing the two of them so happy together. Simon volunteering to look after the girls. Simon taking the girls to Fortnum's. Simon asleep on her sofa. Simon …

What was going on? Had she lost her mind? He was her boss. And he could be a right bastard when he wanted to be, but when she thought about it – he hadn't been a bastard to her for quite a while now. Really, he'd been nothing but lovely and caring and nice. An image of his kind smile came into her head and she got that giddy feeling in her stomach again.

She couldn't kid herself any more. That moment by the door, she'd really thought he was going to kiss her. And she'd wanted him to. Terribly. She wanted Simon Rathbone to kiss her. She wanted to kiss Simon Rathbone. Rachel lay there letting this new idea circulate around her system. It was going to take some getting used to.

And there was another thing she couldn't work out about what had happened just now. She could tell he'd wanted to kiss her, just as much as she'd wanted him to – and she was fairly sure he knew she wanted him to. They weren't fumbling teenagers, they were grown-ups and you developed an understanding of those moments.

Of course it was complicated because they worked together and him being the boss and all that, but when urges were that strong, didn't two single healthy people tend to give in to them and sort it out after?

So why the hell hadn't he?

Friday, 18 July

Regent's Park

Simon was running around Regent's Park. Not just jogging, like the people he passed, but proper *Chariots of Fire* stuff. Running to make the blood pump fast through his heart and into his veins, so that a good lot of it would flow into his mixed-up brain and help him to understand what the hell was going on.

He knew he was in love with Rachel now. It had gone way beyond the lust he'd felt from the first time he'd laid eyes on her perfect waist/hip ratio. That was all still a marvellous part of the package, but now he was in love with the total woman.

The funny, energetic, bright personality; someone who made him laugh and thought exactly as he did about business, that it was a tremendous game, a puzzle to work out and to win, with money the prize, but not in a ghastly greedy way. The chase as important as the winning, probably more so.

All of that seemed so clear and simple, but then he kept coming up against a brick wall. He wanted to take Rachel in his arms, to kiss her and tell her how he felt – he even liked her children, that's how far in he was – but there were so many complications.

Right up front, there was his bizarre history with her sister. What was the etiquette for that scenario? Then there was the heavy baggage of his own family, but perhaps she was the person he could tell about all that? After all these years of holding it in, stuffing it down inside until sometimes he felt like it was suffocating him, he was feeling more and more like she was.

And then there was the other big issue, probably the biggest one: that he also wanted to work with her. To the point where he was considering offering her a partnership, where they would ditch the company in its current old-fashioned, over-leveraged, overstaffed format and start again as Rathbone & Lambton.

No account managers on staff. They could keep some members of his current team on retainers, bringing them in as freelancers when they had big projects on, which most of them would probably prefer. They could take Wimbledon week off without asking. So just him and Rachel and his PA. Certainly not a big expensive building in Sydney Street, just a small sleek space, probably in Soho. Possibly even Shoreditch.

His stomach turned over with excitement at the idea of sitting across from Rachel in an office all day. Work would be so much fun with her to throw ideas around with. Then he couldn't stop himself picturing the two of them sneaking out for a romantic working lunch, which might develop into ... Aaaargh. There he went again, starting out with his work head on, only to be taken over by another part of his anatomy rather lower down.

And he was beginning to think perhaps now it wasn't all one-sided. Nearly twelve hours later, the memory of that moment by her front door was still vivid. He'd been so close to kissing her, he didn't quite know how he'd been able to stop himself.

Ever since that afternoon in the little Italian café, he'd been wondering if her feelings for him were changing and when he was standing close to her now he could feel it. He knew when a woman wanted him to kiss her.

So which was it to be: the business brain – or the trouser brain? He had to decide and he didn't have forever to make up his mind; there was an official deadline, because he wasn't going to renew the lease on Sydney Street and it would be up in three months. That decision he had made. Rathbone & Associates as it was now, was going to change, it was just a matter of into what? And with whom?

He came to a halt by the park gate nearest his flat and walked up and down, cooling off, getting his breath back and stretching his muscles. Crouching down to ease his knees he felt the grass was dry beneath his fingertips and lay down on his back, pulling his legs up to his chest and swinging them from side to side to loosen his hips.

Then he just lay there for a while, staring up at the London summer sky, bright blue earlier, clouds now beginning to build up. As they slowly passed across his gaze, the answer to all the competing questions came to him: he would ring Joy and ask for her advice.

Back in his flat, showered and shaved, Simon sat at his glass desk wearing just a pair of loose cotton track pants. The sky was fully grey now and it was very muggy. After checking there was nothing crucial in the diary, he'd emailed his PA to postpone all his appointments to the following week and decided to work at home for the day. He could think more clearly how to restructure the business when he wasn't constantly being reminded of all the people he was possibly about to make redundant.

And that wasn't the only reason. He didn't want to see Rachel yet. He didn't trust himself. Not until his head was clearer.

Catching sight of his reflection in the nearby window, Simon sat up straight, pulling back his arms and flexing his shoulders, so his pectorals pushed out. You look like a man, Rathbone, he told himself. So bloody well start acting like one. He tapped contacts on his phone and scrolled down to find Tessa's number, crossing the fingers on his left hand, hoping she wouldn't answer.

It was Joy who picked up. Lucky.

'The Chenery residence,' she said.

Simon couldn't help laughing at her formality.

'Really?' he said. 'But I was hoping to speak to Mrs Younger ...'

'Hello, Simon,' she said.

'How did you know it was me?'

Because I've been expecting you to call, thought Joy. The final secret. 'I recognised your voice,' she said. 'How are you?'

'I'm very well, thanks. How are you? Is your hip still mending well? And how's Natasha?'

Joy paused for a moment.

'I'm very well, thank you, getting better all the time and I'm happy to say Natasha is pretty good, too. Did Rachel tell you she was over?'

'Yes,' said Simon. 'She told me the range had been cancelled unexpectedly ... Dreadful news.'

'Yes, it was a terrible shock for Natasha. I'm glad she's here.'

'Best place she could be,' said Simon. 'Anyway, well, I bet you're wondering why I've called out of the blue ... and the thing is, Joy, I would really like to talk to you about something. You've already done so much for me, I can never thank you enough for how you helped me with, er, that thing and I don't want to be a pest, but I think you're the only person who can help me with something else, if it's ...'

'How about Monday?' said Joy. 'I'm coming up to London to see somebody and I could meet up with you first. Noon would be good, somewhere near the British Museum.'

'How about the café at the London Review Bookshop?' said Simon. 'It's in Bury Place, just off Great Russell Street.'

'I'll find it, Simon,' said Joy. 'I'll look forward to seeing you.'

She hung up and Simon sat looking down at his phone for a moment. If he wasn't going to go ahead with this, he had until Monday to come up with another reason for asking to see Joy.

Sydney Street

Rachel was half-gutted, half-super-relieved when Simon didn't come into work on Friday. The breakfast meeting with Passementerie de Paris had gone brilliantly and they'd signed a one-year contract, so she was desperate to tell him the good news.

She'd also decided on her way in that she was definitely going to ask him to have that coffee with her. In their café. Partly because she wanted to tell him the whole story about Natasha, to get his take on the business side of it – but mainly to test her instincts, to see whether she'd imagined those unspoken feelings between them by her front door the night before.

She kept going backwards and forwards about it in her head. One moment she was convinced it had happened, the next she told herself to forget it, she'd just been in a heightened emotional state after the Natasha/Mattie moment.

But she wasn't imagining how much she missed his presence in the building. Every time she walked past his office, she slowed down, wanting to string out the moment of feeling connected to him. She found herself stroking the name 'Rathbone & Associates' on the pile of letterhead in her desk drawer.

She really had gone doolally.

It was a relief as the time finally wound round to three, when she could leave, collect the girls from school and try to forget this nonsense, for a couple of days at least. Michael was having the kids that weekend and for once she was happy she'd be staying home alone.

The estate agent had been to value her house and it was going on the market on Sunday – the key day, apparently – she needed to make sure it was perfect for viewings.

Deciding to go the long way to the Tube, so she could check out the Conran Shop windows, Rachel was looking longingly at the florist stand inside the entrance – and reminding herself she would have to make do with flowers from Lidl for the house showings – when her phone rang.

'Hi, Rachie,' said Natasha's voice, sounding very cheerful.

'Hi, Tashie,' said Rachel, feeling a surge of love for her little sister. How could they have fallen out like that?'

'Are you still at work? Can you talk?'

'I'm on my way home,' said Rachel, 'my boss is letting me leave early until I sort out my childcare ...'

Damn. She didn't mean that the way it must have sounded. 'Sorry, Tash, I didn't say that to get at you, it's just the new nanny has left.'

'I know,' said Natasha, 'that's partly why I'm ringing. Mum told me about that and I have a suggestion to make.'

'Go on, then,' said Rachel.

'Can Mattie and I come and stay with you for a while?' said Natasha. 'I want to spend some proper time in London, I need a break from New York after what's happened and the thing is Mattie shares a house with four other people, one bathroom, one loo ... I can't do it. And I thought, if we could stay with you, we'd be together, we'd be with you – and I could see my beautiful nieces every single day.'

Rachel heard a catch in her voice as she said it, which made her own eyes fill with tears. 'I can't think of anything I'd like more,' she said.

'And we'll get them from school every day and look after them until you get home, so you won't have to leave work early,' said Natasha, sounding excited.

Rachel laughed. 'Well, there's only three more days of school before they break up for the holidays, but that would be a help.'

'Even better then,' said Natasha, 'we'll look after them in the holidays. Well, I'll do it on my own, when Mattie goes to work. I'm taking some time off, Rachel. A few weeks, before the shows all kick in again. I need to get my head clear.'

'That would be amazing,' said Rachel. 'Just having you around for a while will be wonderful. You two can have the nanny's room, with its own bathroom. When are you going to come up?'

'This evening?' said Natasha.

'Perfect,' said Rachel. 'I'll see you there.'

And after she rang off, it was all she could do not to skip up Pelham Street to the station.

Monday, 21 July

Bury Place, London WC1

Simon got to the café fifteen minutes early and moved tables three times before he found one that felt bearable. The woman behind the counter was giving him funny looks. He felt like pulling a face at her. What he had to say to Joy was so torturously personal, he really didn't want anyone listening in. He wished he'd suggested somewhere bigger, with dark corners. What if she told him to back off from Rachel? That he'd done enough damage with her oldest daughter and he could forget sniffing around the middle one as well?

For a moment he decided to call the whole thing off, it had been a mad idea, but then he remembered she was a woman in her mid-seventies and even if she had a mobile phone, he didn't know the number. He couldn't just stand her up.

He was still working on ideas for other reasons he could pretend he'd wanted to speak to her when Joy walked in, supporting herself on one stick. A glance at his phone showed him it was twelve noon on the dot and he felt a bell should start tolling.

He stood up.

'Joy, lovely to see you,' he said, pulling out a chair and kissing her on both cheeks, 'do sit down, let me get you something, the cakes are very good here.'

'I'd like some mint tea, please,' said Joy, looking rather amused, 'and if you are having some cake, get an extra fork for me.'

The lady behind the counter was smiling at him now. See? he felt like saying, I was just choosing the best table for my slightly disabled elderly friend. My possible future mother-in-law ... Ohgodohgodohgod.

After he got back to the table he kept busy unloading teapots and cups from the tray, fussing with teaspoons, milk jugs, the slice of coffee and walnut cake which was making him feel nauseous ... anything to put off the moment when Joy asked him what he wanted to talk to her about.

She said nothing, just sat with her hands folded in her lap as he farted about like an idiot with the tea strainers, rabbiting on, asking her about her hip and how the journey up had been and how beautiful he imagined the countryside must be looking ...

When sugar and milk had been offered – milk in mint tea? very good, Simon – the spare cake fork proffered and there was really nothing else he could say or do to fill the enormous vacuum of the unspoken between them, he gave in and took a sip of his tea.

'So how long have you been in love with Rachel?' asked Joy.

Simon nearly spat his tea back into the cup, but just managed to swallow it as he let out a mighty bark of laughter.

'How the hell did you know?'

Joy smiled. 'I just had a little inkling,' she said.

Back when you were very concerned that she never found out about you and Tessa, but it wasn't the time to remind him of that. Yet.

'So I'm right?'

'Yes,' said Simon, 'a hundred times yes. I think I've been a little bit in love with her from the first moment I saw her, but as I've got to know her better and to respect her attitude to work and the way she copes with bringing up the girls on her own and just having her around in the office ... it's just grown and grown.'

It felt so good to say it out loud, he wanted to run round the room kissing everyone in it.

'I'm delighted to hear it,' said Joy. 'I think you and Rachel would be wonderful together.'

'But ...?' said Simon.

'Well, I'm assuming the "but" is the reason you wanted to talk to me,' said Joy, 'because otherwise there's nothing stopping you. You're both single, so what is the "but", Simon?'

'Buts, plural,' he said. 'There's more than one. Well, the first one you know about – the thing with Tessa. That's odd by any standard and I feel I would have to tell Rachel about it first, because when I'm with her, all I want to do is kiss her. My whole body is screaming at me to do it and I'm beginning to think she might want me to, but then my head kicks in remembering the Tessa weirdness and I can't let myself. Like last Thursday night, after I looked after the girls ...'

Joy reached over and put her hand on his. 'You looked after the girls?' she said.

Simon nodded. 'She had to go down to see Natasha, and there was no one else she could ask.'

'You're a good man, Simon Rathbone,' said Joy, squeezing his hand. 'A very good man. Do you understand that?'

Simon's eyes dropped down for a moment. If Joy didn't know he was the last man on earth to let it show, she thought he might be close to tears.

'I do my best, Joy,' he said, almost whispering.

She kept her hand on his, turning it over and holding it in both of hers.

'Tell me what it is, Simon,' she said, 'the sadness you carry around, the secret you have locked away. I know it's another thing that's holding you back from Rachel, so you might as well tell me.'

Simon's head came up and he looked straight into her eyes.

'It's my family,' he said, his voice quite croaky. Not because he was about to blub, but because his vocal cords didn't know how to get out the words to tell anyone about this stuff.

'What about your family?' asked Joy, very gently, as though she were talking to a frightened toddler.

'I killed my brother,' said Simon, his gaze not leaving hers, 'and my other brother is as good as dead, but isn't. It might be better if he was. I broke my father's heart.'

Joy didn't let her eyes move from his.

'What do you mean you killed your brother?' she asked in the same low voice as before.

'Car crash. Dark country lane. One brother dead, the other brain damaged. I was driving.'

'Was it your fault?' asked Joy.

'Not really,' said Simon. 'No. The bloke who crashed into us was drunk. Very drunk. He went to prison. I didn't go to official prison, but I've been in a prison of my own ever since.'

'A prison of guilt?' said Joy.

Simon nodded his head.

'Even though you know it wasn't your fault?'

'Well, it's more a prison of my parents' resentment. They both blame me – my mother less so, but still a bit. It's not rational, I know that, but it doesn't make it any easier to live with.'

Joy said nothing, just carried on holding his hand in hers and stroking the top of it. Some of the tension had left him, since he'd told her, but there was still a lot there.

'Do you see them often?'

'Every weekend,' said Simon. 'That's where I go. Half my staff think I've got a husband in the Cotswolds, but I'm really in Herefordshire helping my parents look after my brother who's forty-five years old and can't feed himself.'

'How old was he when the accident happened?' asked Joy, finding it hard to get the words out herself.

'Twenty,' said Simon. 'I was twenty-two and the brother who died was twenty-four. He'd just finished at Sandhurst.'

They sat for a moment, the cruelty of the lives destroyed so young just hanging in the air between them. Two lives destroyed in one moment, thought Simon. Three lives wrecked so young, thought Joy. And him another middle child, like Rachel.

'Does your younger brother live at home with them?' asked Joy tentatively.

'Oh yes,' said Simon, 'they've always refused to let him be in a care home. The two main reception rooms of the house have been converted for him. They have carers all week, but at the weekend I go and help.'

'Because you want to?' asked Joy.

'Mostly,' said Simon. 'He's still my brother, the only brother I have now. The three of us were really close – like your girls – now there's just me and him. He hasn't been able to speak since the accident, but he stills knows me and I still love him. I can't just abandon him.'

'You said your brother was "mostly" the reason you go. What's the rest of it?'

'My mother. My father's not an easy man. He has very particular standards for life and people and I just don't measure up to them. My brothers were both in the army, as he used to be, and he can't understand why I didn't join the "family firm" as well. He loathed me studying art history at university and despises what I do, even though my income helps pay for the carers. Actually, I think he resents me even more for that. He's never actually said it, but I know he wishes it was me who died.'

Joy said nothing, in case he had anything else to get out. She wanted to tell him she thought he was being very harsh on himself – and his father – and that he was projecting all his self-loathing back on to himself, and filtering everything his father said and did through that belief system, in a perpetuating negative cycle of guilt and shame, but she knew when to keep her trap shut. Maybe one day she'd find a way to suggest those ideas to him, but she knew this wasn't it.

When she was sure he had nothing else to say about his father, she spoke.

'But your mother doesn't blame you so much?' she said.

'No,' said Simon, 'my mum is lovely. She's always pleased to see me. She's lost two of her boys and she has to live with my grumpy dad all week, so I think the least I can do is go and see her at the weekends, to try to bring some nice things into her life.'

'Not many people wouldn't make that sacrifice, Simon,' said Joy.

'Most people don't find themselves in this kind of situation,' said Simon. 'They don't know how they'd react.'

'But why do you keep it so secret? It's nothing to be ashamed of. I think it's wonderful what you do. You should be proud of it.'

'I just find it easier to deal with keeping it in a separate compartment from the rest of my life,' said Simon. 'I don't want to have to talk to people about it, answer sympathetic questions, explain it. And one of the reasons I've never married, or even had a proper serious girlfriend, is that I haven't met anyone who I trusted enough to tell them about it. Until Rachel. I know I could tell her and she wouldn't judge me, but at the same time, I don't want to burden her with my sob story and have her feel sorry for me.'

'Rachel has never told me how she feels about you,' said Joy. 'Or given any indication that there might be more between you than the work relationship – but that's normal for her, it doesn't mean anything. But this I can tell you, if she does return your feelings, this won't put her off, it will just make her like you more.'

'Really?' said Simon. 'Isn't it all a bit Mr Rochester? The angry dad and the crippled brother in the attic?'

Joy shook her head, smiling.

'No. You've seen what a close family we are – your loyalty to yours will really touch her. As it has me. I've known you were a good man since I first met you and this is more proof. So, does that get rid of that "but"?'

'Yes, I think it does. Thank you, Joy. But what about the Tessa issue? Do I have to tell Rachel about that before I can kiss her? I soooo want to ...'

He wriggled around in his seat like a schoolboy desperate to go outside to play.

Joy laughed. 'Kiss her then, you silly! Kiss her first and tell her about Tessa later. I don't think she'll mind if you tell her it was something that happened twenty-five years ago. You don't need to go into that odd re-connection thing that happened. I've thought about that long and hard, and I've decided it was a weird blip. A combination of you projecting your feelings for Rachel back onto Tessa and Tessa feeling very alienated from Tom, while he was in his TV thing, all mixed up with the poignancy of nostalgia – remembering youth in middle age and all that. It was a kind of perfect storm of emotions and I don't think it would be dishonest not to go into the full details of it with Rachel.'

'Do I need to tell Tessa I want to kiss Rachel?' asked Simon.

Joy shook her head, resisting a strong urge to chuck his cheeks.

'Absolutely not,' she said. 'You and Tessa have laid your past to rest, leave it there. Let me know when the time is right and I'll tell Tessa for you. I think she'll be delighted. She knows how lovely you are in the present tense, as a friend, and I know she'd like to see Rachel with a good man, as much as I would.'

'Wow,' said Simon, settling back in his chair and feeling more relaxed than he had for years. He stuffed a large forkful of coffee and walnut cake into his mouth and chewed it with gusto.

'That's all great,' he said, after he'd swallowed and was going in for some more, 'but there is still one more "but" ...'

'Go on,' said Joy, refilling her tea cup.

'As well as having a mahoosive soppy crush on Rachel, I also love working with her. She's brilliant at what we do. She's the only person I've ever worked with who thinks exactly as I do about business, and I'm worried that if we started having a romantic thing ...'

He paused and allowed himself a moment's pure pleasure at the idea of it.

'... it would be awkward to work with her as well. To be completely honest with you, Joy, I've decided to downsize my company into something more streamlined and modern, and an ideal scenario would be a simple business partnership between me and Rachel. Just the two of us.'

'But that's perfect,' said Joy. 'Rachel lives for her work – and her kids – but apart from them, she defines herself by work, so to combine it with a relationship would be her ideal scenario.'

Simon looked at her, wide-eyed. It was his perfect scenario too. Why had he never thought of that?

Joy put her hand over his again. The tension was gone. Finally, he'd released it. Then she looked at him across the café table, wishing she could see his aura again, as she had that time at Tessa's – she was sure it would be whole, that nasty black dent gone – but there was nothing.

It wasn't something you could force, she should have known better than to try, but while she might not be able to turn on such otherworldly insights to order, Joy could plainly see Simon's handsome face glowing with relief at having unburdened himself, and excitement at what lay ahead.

She put her hand up to his shoulder and pulled him towards her.

'Come here, you dear thing,' she said and kissed him warmly on the cheek. 'And now go. You have important things to do. Go and do them with my blessing.'

Simon beamed at her and after pulling out a £20 note, which he put on the table, tucking it under the edge of his saucer, he got up.

'Thank you, Joy,' he said, 'for everything.'

Then after checking she was OK to get on to wherever she was going next, with her stick, he hugged her and practically ran out of the café.

Joy sat at the table smiling to herself. She probably looked like a nutter, but she couldn't help herself, his hurry to get off – no doubt to his office and Rachel – was so adorable. She hoped to hear from him soon to say she could let Tessa know the good news. The sooner the better.

She ordered some more hot water for her mint tea and sat for a moment just enjoying the contentment of imagining Rachel and Simon together. It was so right and the girls would love it. He was just the man her spirited middle daughter needed.

There would be occasional fireworks, Joy could picture that, but only in a work context, and the other side of their relationship would help them get over it very quickly. The combined work and domestic life would suit them, just as it did Tessa and Tom. They'd be a dynamic combination in every regard. Simon would keep Rachel tested, and she'd never be bored with him. What a happy outcome.

There was so much to be grateful for, thought Joy. Tessa and Tom reunited in every part of their lives. Natasha and Mattie so happy together and helping Rachel out with the kids. And now this new partnership on its way, Rachel and Simon bound together in love and work, which she was also happy to think would help get Rachel out of her financial crisis. All was good with her family.

Namaste.

But now she had to find the courage to get up from this chair and walk around the corner and into the British Museum to meet that other member of it.

The one she had abandoned so long ago, as a tiny baby, and had never tried to contact since, for fear of unsettling what she hoped was the wonderful life he was having without her. She'd only ever wanted what was best for him and, in 1959, life with a nineteen-year-old single mother was definitely not a desirable upbringing.

For fear of going mad with grief and longing, over all those long years, especially once she'd had more children and knew just how strong the bonds became, she'd found a way not to allow herself to think about him consciously, in the front of her brain.

It was one of the things that had made her become so committed to meditation. At times when she thought she just couldn't stand the pain of wondering about him another moment, she'd learned how to take herself to a place of calm and get her anguished thoughts back in a manageable order.

But even when she'd mastered that skill, he'd always been there, deep down in her heart. His birthday had never gone unacknowledged by her, even if it was only to light a candle privately and say a prayer for him, wherever he was.

Once the law was changed and it had become possible for the birth parents of adopted children to try to make contact with them, once they were adults, she had wondered many times whether she dared to do it.

But the craving for contact was always outweighed by a dread fear of the outcome. What if he rejected her? What if he was hurt and angry with her for giving him up, like an unwanted gift? Then she would have to live with the knowledge of that, as well as the memory of his tiny perfect face. She didn't have the courage to risk it.

Over and over again, for fifty-five years, Joy had reminded herself to leave the past where it was. Nothing good could come of disturbing it, she'd told herself, only the risk of further pain. Living in the moment had become an essential survival mechanism for her, which was why she'd been so disturbed by those mysterious letters, addressed to her historic name, which could only have been something to do with the past.

Her first thought had been that they were to notify her of his death. If that was the reason for them, she didn't want to know. It wasn't until she'd recognised the contact agency's logo on the envelope of the last one that she'd dared to open it and read the contents. Her son wanted to contact her.

Joy sat staring down at her tea cup, marvelling at the turns of fate which had led her to be sitting in that café, conveniently close to the British Museum where she was about to go and be reunited with her adult son.

If her friend hadn't been late to meet her at the café and if she hadn't flicked through the newspaper and seen the article about the people-finding agency, she would have destroyed that letter unread, as she had all the others.

She sent up a prayer of thanks that she'd been given this opportunity – and another asking for it to be blessed.

It took all Simon's self-control not to shout at the taxi driver to hurry up. It was already twenty to two and Rachel would have to leave at three to collect the girls. The conversation he needed to have with her couldn't be rushed and he really wanted to have it in that café. Their café. It just felt right.

He stared out of the window as they drove along Oxford Street, not seeing anything, one leg crossed over the other knee, his foot jiggling frantically. But if they were going to go to the café, they'd have to walk there from the office wasting valuable time and what would he talk to her about until they got there? He thought making another moment's self-monitored polite conversation with Rachel might actually kill him.

Maybe he should text her and ask her to meet him at the café? That might be better. He got his phone out and tried to find the right words, but couldn't even get past the opener.

'Hey, Rachel ...'

'Hi, Rachel ...'

'Rachel ...'

'Howdy ...'

'Got time for a quick coffee ...?'

'Fancy a coffee ...?'

'I have some things I need to discuss with you ...'

Delete, delete, delete, they all sounded wrong. He was still trying to get the tone of it right when the taxi stopped, they were already in Sydney Street. Bloody hell.

He paid the driver and walked up the steps of the building to the door. He was about to press the buzzer, then he stopped. What was he going to do? Walk into her office and say something as stupid as those texts? Howdy pardner! Fancy a lil' ol' coffee?

Looking down at his phone he had a better idea and opened his favourites list. He tapped her name and lifted the phone to his ear. She answered immediately.

'Simon?' she said.

'Yes,' he said, 'I'm, er, would you ... look, can you just come downstairs and out of the building please? I'll explain when I see you.'

'OK,' she said, sounding surprised and rang off.

Rachel looked down at her phone. Come out of the building? Whatever did he mean? Oh well, at least she'd get to see him. It seemed like so long since last Thursday night and he hadn't been into the office yet today either. What on earth was going on with him?

She glanced at her handbag, wondering if she should comb her hair quickly and put some lipstick on, but decided to forget about it. She was too curious to find out what he was up to.

Rachel opened the front door onto Sydney Street to see Simon pacing up and down on the pavement. He turned and looked at her, a big smile on his face. She walked down the steps slowly, looking at him.

'You rang, sir?' she said.

Simon put out his hand and took hers, pulling her to him, then he wrapped his arms around her and after looking down at her face for one more moment, just to be sure she didn't have a horrified expression on it, he finally put his lips on hers. Rachel forgot everything.

Neither of them knew how long they stayed there, locked in that first kiss. Finally they pulled apart and looked at each other, both grinning.

'I thought you'd never do it,' said Rachel.

'It's nearly killed me not to,' he said.

'Can you do it again then, just to be sure?' said Rachel – and he did.

As they separated that time, something made Simon look up and he saw three of his sillier staff members leaning out of a first-floor window watching them.

'Enjoying the show, girls?' he called up to them.

'We sure are,' said one of them. 'It's about bloody time. We've all known you two were mad about each other for ages.'

Simon and Rachel looked at each other, incredulous.

'Did you know?' said Simon.

'Not until very recently,' said Rachel.

'Go back to your desks,' he called up to the women, who now seemed to have been joined by the entire staff. 'There's nothing more to see here. In fact, go home, all of you. I'm declaring today a national holiday.'

There was a loud whoop, followed by a crash as the window closed.

'I wish we could go somewhere private and talk about all this,' he said, raising his hand to Rachel's face, running his knuckle very gently down the line of her jaw and then tucking a stray strand of hair behind her ear. She turned her head and kissed his hand, then reached up and grasped it with her own, pressing it into her neck.

'But I know you've got to go and pick up the girls soon,' he continued. 'I could take you there actually.'

'I don't have to go anywhere,' said Rachel, pressing herself against him and pulling his arms back around her. 'I've got some very good childcare set up now. We've got all the time in the world.'

Wednesday, 24 December

Cranbrook

Simon was standing at the top of a ladder trying to attach a filthy old doll, with a skew-whiff tinsel halo, to the top of a very tall Christmas tree, with a piece of string. Daisy and Ariadne were giving him directions.

'She still looks drunk,' said Daisy.

'She's falling down,' said Ariadne. 'Make her straighter. She's going to fall off.'

'I think I'm going to fall off,' said Simon. 'It's not very easy from this angle. I can't get close enough to do it properly and the branches keep going up my nose. Can you ask your mother to cut the bottom three feet of branches off this flipping tree?'

'Mummy's busy,' said Daisy.

Simon looked over to where Rachel, Natasha and Tessa were all intently absorbed taking pictures of him trying to attach the Christmas angel to the tree, while the two girls eagerly looked up at him.

'Am I going to look very quaint on Instagram?' he called over to them. 'Perhaps you'd like me to put on a Santa suit? I'm sure Tessa's got a filthy old vintage one in a shed somewhere ... and perhaps you'd like to dress the girls up as angels, too, just to make it a little more hokey.'

'Stop being such an old humbug,' said Rachel, coming over to the tree. 'Get down from there and I'll do it. I've been putting that fairy up for years.'

'Oh, it's a fairy now, is it?' said Simon, climbing down to ground level, handing the doll to Rachel and looking at his hands with distaste. 'I thought it was an angel. Whatever it is, it needs a bath. It's putrid.'

Rachel giggled and put her arms around him.

'Ebenezer OCD,' she said, 'if I didn't know how much you are enjoying this really, I'd think you were a miserable old git.'

'Ah, that's better,' he said, pulling her closer and nuzzling her ear, 'I can wipe my hands on your dress.'

Joy arrived at the drawing room door, pushing Simon's brother in his wheelchair, his head and limbs supported, various tubes and bags accommodated on special holders.

'I thought Rob would like to see the tree,' she said. 'Oh, you haven't got the fairy on top, yet ...'

'That's because I'm useless,' said Simon, smiling at her and blinking a few times to push back what felt dangerously like tears coming into his eyes. Tears of gratitude for being there. With the woman he loved, her children, her family – and also his own family.

He could hear his father's laugh coming from the kitchen. A sound he had once thought he'd never hear again, but since he'd taken Rachel home to meet them and then, a few weekends later, gone back with the girls as well, a lot had changed.

Not just the tonic of children's laughter in that desolate house again, but he'd seen his parents' delight and relief that he'd finally done something for himself after all those years. That had been a revelation and now Simon understood that one of the reasons his father had been so angry with him was that he'd thought he was wasting the life he still had, when his brothers' had been so cruelly taken away.

'Your father and Tom are having great larks stuffing the turkey,' said Joy. 'It seems to involve drinking a lot of port, which is all fine by me, as my best Christmas present this year will be not having to touch the poor thing.'

Simon laughed and leaned down to make eye contact with his brother.

'Come on, Rob,' he said. 'I'll push you nearer the fire, so you can stay warm while you watch Joy, Rachel and the girls make a much better job of decorating the tree than I could.'

The small change of expression in his brother's eyes told Simon that Rob had understood him, and was amused.

Finn and Mattie came into the room and Tessa shrieked when she saw that her oldest son now had a wide streak of bright blue hair at the front of his messy black mop.

Natasha turned to see what had made Tessa squeal and immediately brought her phone up to take a picture.

'Make sure you get my good side, Auntie Tash,' said Finn, doing a twirl. 'What do you think?'

'It looks awesome,' said Natasha, moving back a little to get Mattie in the frame as well.

'Do you like it, Mum?' asked Finn.

'I, er, it's such a surprise,' said Tessa. 'Did you do it, Mattie?'

Mattie looked at Finn.

'You little rat,' she said. 'You didn't ask her, did you? And you promised me you had.'

Finn brought his hand up to his mouth and made a fake shocked face.

'Oh, no, it just slipped my mind, Mattie,' he said, 'I was going to ask her but then something distracted me.'

'I'm really sorry, Tessa,' said Mattie. 'He told me he had your permission to do this – I never would have done it without checking it was OK with you first.'

Tessa shook her head, laughing.

'Don't worry, Mattie,' she said, 'we're used to Finn's little ways.'

She came over and studied her son's face, pushing the lock of blue hair over a little to reveal his right eye.

'I actually think it really suits him. Brings out the blue of his eyes. Sorry, Finn, I'm sure you're disappointed, but I don't hate it.'

'Don't worry, Finn, mate,' said Simon, coming over, 'my father will hate it for everyone.'

Natasha had moved back a little further still taking pictures, now getting Daisy and Ariadne into the composition, Rachel up the ladder fixing the fairy to the top of the tree. She let the hand holding the phone drop down and looked at the scene with her eyes narrowed for a moment, then she reached over and put her hand on Simon's arm.

'Can you do me a favour, Simon?' she said. 'I've had an idea. Keep everyone here for me.'

She left the room and a few moments later, Tom and Simon's father came in.

'Natasha's given us orders to be present and correct in here, that's right isn't it, Harry?' said Tom, and Harry Rathbone agreed.

Simon observed the scene, still in a state of wonder that it was possible. The old man looked perfectly relaxed and only laughed and said 'Good Lord!' when Finn came over to ask him what he thought of his hair.

'And she says you've got to stay up there, Rachel, OK?' added Tom.

'Yessir,' she replied, saluting rather too enthusiastically and quickly grabbing the top of the ladder, when she nearly lost her balance.

'Whatever do you think she's up to?' Joy asked Mattie, as the two of them headed over towards the fire to sit with Rob.

'Tell me if you're getting too warm,' said Mattie, then quickly corrected herself, leaning in so she could see his face and he could see hers. 'Are you too warm, Rob?'

He blinked twice. No.

'That's good,' said Mattie and sat down on the floor, her back against the corner of the armchair Joy was in.

The next to arrive was Simon's mother, Kathleen, accompanied by a small, fair woman and a younger, taller one. They were each holding vases containing very large arrangements of red-berried holly and variegated ivy, decorated with various gaudy glass baubles.

'Oh, wow, those are amazing,' said Tessa, rushing forward to help them. 'Thank you so much. Let's put them down over here for now and then we can decide where they'll look best in a moment. Natasha wants us all to stay in here for some reason.'

'This is beginning to feel like the end of an Agatha Christie play,' said Simon, getting up from a chair near the fire so his mother could sit down, and going over to Rachel, who was still up the ladder. 'Inspector Poirot is going to arrive in a minute and tell us who done it.'

'If I don't get down from this ladder soon, I'll be the body,' said Rachel. 'I'm getting cramp standing up here, I could fall off at any moment.'

'You've done a lovely job on the fairy, though, darling. What do you think Daisy-Daze, has Mummy got the fairy on straight?'

'Straight enough,' said Daisy. 'She's always a bit wonky.'

'Like you?' said Simon, tickling the side of her neck. 'You're very wonky.'

From her vantage point up the ladder Rachel had a perfect view of her mother's face when the next group of people entered the room. Hector and Archie, looking very pink-cheeked, walked in with a tall dark-haired man, holding a pair of secateurs. Joy smiled radiantly as soon as she saw him.

It was her re-found son, Daniel. Tessa, Natasha and Rachel's half-brother, a new uncle for her girls and Tessa's boys – and a brother-in-law for Tom, and Mattie, who had married Natasha the month before.

'We've been helping Uncle Dan get the holly,' said Archie, 'I'm covered in scratches, completely slashed. Look, Mum.'

He held out his hands proudly to Tessa, to show her.

'Hello all,' said Dan. 'I hope we haven't been holding things up. Natasha said our presence was required in here immediately.'

'None of us have a clue what she's up to,' said Joy. 'Come and get warm by the fire and look at these beautiful flower arrangements Kathleen and your clever wife and daughter have done.'

Dan sat on the arm of the chair Joy was sitting in and they smiled at each other, both still a little shy, just five months on from their reunion. Rachel watched them from her lofty position, then turned her gaze to Simon and Daisy, who were now having a full play-fight on the floor, with Ariadne rushing over to join in, and felt what she realised was a pang of pure happiness.

It was a feeling so rare and special it took her a moment to recognise it for what it was and when she did, it took some self-control to stay up the stupid ladder and not fling herself off it to join in with them.

After a few more minutes, during which Rachel tried to start a chorus of 'Why are we waiting?', Natasha finally arrived back in the doorway and looked round the room quickly, doing a head count. Yes, they were all there, although it was hard to see Simon for little girls jumping up and down on him.

'Sorry to keep you waiting, people,' she said. 'I just had to go and do something. Great, Rachel, you're still up there and girls, if you can stop killing Simon for a moment, then you three can stand at the bottom of the ladder there ... Yes, that's perfect.'

She paused, looking round the room again, then asked Kathleen if she and Harry would take Rob and move over to stand next to Simon and the girls. She moved Dan to the other arm of Joy's armchair, with his wife, Jane, and daughter, Naomi, standing next to him. Then with Tessa, Tom and their boys, arranged between the fireplace and the Christmas tree, she went over to the door and looked out into the hall.

'Dad,' she yelled out. 'Tony! They're ready – are you?'

'I'm coming, darls,' a man's voice replied. 'Just making sure everything's working.'

Natasha came back into the room, followed shortly after by a tall man with a shock of thick white hair, heavy dark eyebrows, and high cheekbones just like his daughter's.

'What do you think?' she asked him, leading him over to the far side of the room where there was a writing desk.

Tony held up his camera and surveyed the scene.

'Pretty good, I reckon,' he said, passing the camera to Natasha. 'Have a look. I think I'd move the group by the ladder over into the frame a little.'

Natasha looked through the viewfinder.

'Spot on,' she said. 'Simon, Daisy and Ari, can you just move over to the left a little bit? Yes, that's better.'

She had another squint through the camera and handed it back to Tony. He looked again and smiled at her, nodding.

'I'll go and stand by Mattie,' she said. 'When it's ready, you come over and join us, OK?'

'Beaut,' he said and turned round, balancing the camera on the upper level of the desk, then leaning over to fiddle with it.

'Not long now, folks,' said Natasha, grinning at everyone as she took her place with her arm tight around Mattie, who was standing between Tessa's group and Joy.

'Can't happen a moment too soon for me,' said Rachel. 'The air is getting rather thin up here ...'

'Right,' said Tony, turning round and bounding over to Natasha and Mattie with a few strides of his long legs. 'Smile everyone!'

'Say, cheese!' cried Natasha, as her father stood behind her and Mattie and wrapped his arms around them.

'Cheese!' yelled everyone in response, laughing, except Daisy who said 'stilton!' and 'feta!', while the camera whirred and flashed a few times. When it stopped Natasha raced over to it, followed by Tony with his leggy gait. He picked up the camera and the two of them looked down at the screen.

'Can I get down from this flipping ladder now, Natasha?' said Rachel. 'My legs are going numb.'

'Yes, you can,' said Natasha, grinning at Tony and giving him a kiss on the cheek.

The picture was great. Everyone was in the frame, most of them looking at the camera, all smiling. Finn doing the traditional rabbit-ear fingers behind his father's head, Archie giving Hector a wedgie, Daisy pulling a goofy face. Mattie, Natasha and Tony beaming at each other. Tessa leaning her head on Tom's shoulder.

Simon with a hand resting on a shoulder of each little girl, looking up at Rachel on the ladder, who was smiling down at him. Joy looking beatific, holding her son's hand, her other arm around her new granddaughter.

All secrets shared.